Hit Reply

ROCKI ST. CLAIRE

New York London Toronto Sydney

An *Original* Publication of POCKET BOOKS

DOWNTOWN PRESS, published by Pocket Books
1230 Avenue of the Americas
New York, NY 10020

Library of Congress Cataloging-in-Publication Data
St. Claire, Roxanne.
Hit Reply/Rocki St. Claire
p. cm.
ISBN 0-7434-8624-2 (alk. paper)
1. Electronic mail messages—Fiction. 2. Friendship—Fiction. I. Title.

PS3619.T233H58 2004
813'.6—dc22

2004055278

First Downtown Press trade paperback edition December 2004

10 9 8 7 6 5 4 3 2 1

Designed by Jaime Putorti

Manufactured in the United States of America

For information regarding special discounts for bulk purchases, please contact Simon & Schuster Special Sales at 1-800-456-6798 or business@simonandschuster.com

When it comes to girlfriends, I am blessed in both quantity and quality. In the following pages, you'll find a piece of every female friend who has ever shared a bottle of wine, a confidence, a heartbreak, or a secret with me. But, in particular, three of these women influenced and inspired *Hit Reply.* So this book is dedicated to them. . . .

To Camille, the one friend who laughs at me more than I do. If not you, then who?

To Chris, the woman who has held my hand longer and more often than any other. You fought the big fight, my friend, and won.

To my sister, Debbie, the person who taught me to "think" and then encouraged me to turn my bedtime stories into real books. You broke the Napoleonic Code, wagged the Monkee's tale, and traced lady luck till you finally struck . . . Bonanza. I write because of you.

I love you all.

Hit Reply

TO: foreveramber@quicklink.com <amber fleece>
FROM: ClassReunion.com
SUBJ: Confirm membership
DATE: Thursday 7/29 8:45 PM

Welcome to ClassReunion.com, your connection to the past! We have received your electronic payment and membership survey response and are pleased to inform you that you are now included with your high school graduating class on the most popular classmate finder site on the internet. Your listing will read:

- Amber Fleece
- 28 years old
- Residing in Boston, Massachusetts
- Employed as Director of Traffic, Millennia Marketing
- Marital status: Single
- Email: foreveramber@quicklink.com

Have fun finding old friends and rekindling old flames. If you have questions, visit the site and press “help” for email assistance.

TO: wonderwoman@usol.com <stephanie hilliard>
FROM: foreveramber@quicklink.com <amber fleece>
SUBJ: I did it!!
DATE: Thursday 7/29 9:02 PM

Hey Stevie! Just got my confirmation from ClassReunion—I did it! I joined. Took three glasses of wine and an effing degree in engineering to master that electronic payment business—all for the privilege of sending one lousy email. It’ll take me three more glasses of wine and forty-nine drafts, or it *will* be lousy. ☺ I only have one shot at Gray McDermott. I gotta make him remember the glorious experience of relieving me of my virginity on prom night ten years ago. *That* really pissed off my date! Write. Soon.

Love.

Amber

PS. How’s the afterlife, my domestic princess? Haven’t heard from you for a few days. IM me if you get online tonight.

foreveramber@quicklink.com: wonderwoman@usol.com is sending you an Instant Message on Thursday 7/29 at 10:18 PM:

wonderwoman: Amber, are you still composing your email? Finally got the kids down. Are you there?

foreveramber: I am here. Merlot is nearly gone. But so is my brain and my nerve and my ability to type.

wonderwoman: Maybe you should let me preview your message to him—I'm sure it will be wonderful, but sometimes a second set of eyes can help. Like when you first started at the agency and couldn't, well, you know, write. ☺

foreveramber: She-devil. I could write. I just couldn't write as well as Madame Vice President Stevie Wonderwoman Walker. Hilliard. Whatever the hell name you use now. Are you still hyphenating?

wonderwoman: Oh, sure. No doubt it will carry a ton of weight when I apply for the coveted Kindergarten Room Mom position. BTW, you know what today is, don't you?

foreveramber: July 29 here. Whoo-wee! You are going to be 35 tomorrow. Happy Birthday Eve, Steverino. You are still gorgeous and women of all ages hate you.

wonderwoman: Thank you. It's easy for you to say that since you spent your last birthday at a Boston nightclub drinking raspberry flirtinis. I will spend the evening reading *The Little Red Hen makes a Pizza* and watching *My Lover, My Stalker* on Lifetime.

foreveramber: Brent still out of town?

wonderwoman: Till Saturday. Don't go there. So, what are you going to say to the one that got away?

foreveramber: Here's what I have so far: *Hey stud, I've thought about you every day for the last ten years and I hope you're not married and still gorgeous, funny, and built to last for hours.* Think he'll respond?

wonderwoman: That oughta get him to hit reply. With his . . . never mind.

foreveramber: And darla, his nevermind is something to revere, let me tell you. Speaking of gorgeous and built, remember you told me about a copywriter by the name of Tom Markoff who used to work at the agency before I got there? Well, guess who waltzed back into Millennia Marketing last week and landed his oh-so-fine tush in the office of Senior Vice President and Creative Director? <big evil grin>

foreveramber: Hey . . . Stevie? You still there? What's taking so long?

wonderwoman: I'm here. I thought I heard the Prince of Wails.

foreveramber: Your pants are so on fire. I recall a conversation back when I was your slave . . . er, administrative assistant. BTW, I finally hired my own—and who do I pick when I have my choice of Wellesley grads in leather miniskirts? A 45-year-old who looked suspiciously confused when I mentioned search engines.

wonderwoman: Why pick her?

foreveramber: She's sweet and eager and she worried about my cough in the interview. I know, I know. Freud would have a field day.

wonderwoman: Did I say anything? Go back to Tom. What conversation back when?

foreveramber: When you referred to Tom Markoff as the one man who turned you into liquid from the waist down.

wonderwoman: Mmmm. A total pool. But there was this one little problem named Mary Grace, mother of his child, woman in his bed, co-owner of his last name.

foreveramber: Mary Grace? Sounds like a minister's wife.

wonderwoman: Tom Markoff is no minister.

foreveramber: He's a hottie. Very Richard Gere–ish with a bit of a George Clooney thing going on. Even has a few silvers among the black hair . . . that hangs just a tad over the collar. *Tres bien, merci.* You two would make a stunning set.

wonderwoman: Hell*o*? Reality check, please. Remember the hyphenated last name? Kindergarten class mom? I couldn't last five minutes in the same room with that man.

foreveramber: Oh really??? So it was more than longing gazes across the conference room table, hmmmm?

wonderwoman: I can't believe he came back to Millennia. I'll never forget it when he quit.

foreveramber: You didn't answer, ww. Must inform you that at his first staff meeting, he not-so-casually asked if anyone stayed in touch with you.

foreveramber: Stevie? Are you there?

wonderwoman: The Prince is wailing for real this time. Gotta go. Email me the letter to Gray before you send it, okay? Don't blow your chance at the reunion of your dreams. Bye.

foreveramber: Oh, I don't give a dog bone anyway. He's probably fat, ugly, and doesn't look anything like Brad Pitt anymore. BTW, Stevie, you don't mind that I gave Tom Markoff your email addy do you?

foreveramber: Hey–Stevie Wonderwoman? You there? You there? Ruh roh.

TO: grayscale@connectone.com <gray mcdermott>
FROM: foreveramber@quicklink.com <amber fleece>
SUBJ: tripping down memory lane
DATE: Friday 7/30 2:00 AM

Hi Gray McDermott . . . remember me? Amber Fleece from Lincoln High? I saw your name on the ClassReunion.com list and couldn't resist saying hello. Hope you are well. I notice you live in Dallas. I'm still in Boston, running the Traffic Department of an ad agency. I live alone in Brookline, but still get out to the burbs to see my dad on the weekends. I hear rumblings of a ten-year class reunion next summer. Any chance you'd grace the old halls of LHS with your presence? Drop me a note and let me know how you're doing.

Best,
Amber Fleece

TO: wonderwoman@usol.com <stephanie hilliard>
FROM: foreveramber@quicklink.com <amber fleece>
SUBJ: Oops—I sent it to him first
DATE: Friday 7/30 8:00 AM

Happy Birthday, Steverella! The merlot weakened my resolve (amazing how it does that) and my finger hit . . . send. Trust me, it was pure drivel. As I re-read in the light of day, it sounded kind of *corporate* if you know what I mean. I wanted to be so effing funny but instead I sent an endless array of prepositional phrases that you would have hated. Sorry, but no one is funny after six glasses of wine and I knew that when I poured 'em and drank 'em. Did manage to squeeze in the "live alone" bit, though. Listen . . . is that Tom Petty singing? "The waiting is the hardest part."

Love.
Amber

TO: wonderwoman@usol.com <stephanie hilliard>
FROM: tmarkoff@millenniamarketing.com <tom markoff>
SUBJ: Feeling some wonder-lust. . . .
DATE: Friday 7/30 11:00 AM

Hey there Stephanie Walker. Guess where I am? Wandering the corridors of MM and it makes me ~wonder~ instead of wander . . . whatever happened to my friend Stephanie? The beautiful blonde with soul in her blue eyes and heart in her smile? I heard you got married and moved to ORLANDO? What's up with that? I might not have returned to the "new" Millennia as the conquering Creative Director if I knew you'd blown this popstand already. Ah, well, the ugliness of the past forgotten, it seems, at least by the His Majesty GW—I made him beg for me. The loveliness of the past, however, is remembered every time I walk by the video closet where someone else begged so long ago. Write if the spirit or anything else moves you.

Tom

PS. Happy birthday.

TO: afleece@millenniamarketing.com <amber fleece>
FROM: wonderwoman@usol.com <stephanie hilliard>
SUBJ: How you will die
DATE: Friday 7/30 2:00 PM

Amber, you sneaky, double-crossing, no good little witch. Sorry to attack you at work, but thanks for the perfect 35th birthday present. Just what I needed. A flash from my past to remind me of all the stuff that's missing from my life. Why did you give Tom

Markoff my email??? I'm married. He's married. He hasn't forgotten anything, either, I can tell you that. Oh fuck. My whole body went numb when I saw his name. I'll write back to him tonight. I better learn from your lesson and stop at two glasses before I hit reply. Oh fuck. I think I'll pack up the stroller and hit Saks to punish Brent for being gone on my birthday. Oh fuck fuck fuck fuck. I could kill you.

xoxox,

Stevie

TO: wonderwoman@usol.com <stephanie hilliard>
FROM: jdesmond@millenniamarketing.com <julie desmond>
SUBJ: RE: How you will die
DATE: Friday 7/30 2:04 PM

Hello. I am Julie Desmond, administrative assistant to Amber Fleece. Ms. Fleece is out of the office most of the day and asked me to review her email in anticipation of a time-sensitive message from a client. Unfortunately, I'm fairly new and didn't recognize all of the email addresses and opened yours in error. I will forward it to Ms. Fleece and sincerely apologize for the inconvenience.

Best wishes—and, by the way, Happy Birthday—35 is a really nice age—enjoy!

Julie

TO: tmarkoff@millenniamarketing.com <tom markoff>
FROM: wonderwoman@usol.com <stephanie hilliard>
SUBJ: Great to hear from you
DATE: Friday 7/30 9:10 PM

What a nice surprise! It's been so many years. I heard you were living in New York for a while. MM will thrive under your creative direction, Tom. I'm glad you and GW could get by your differences—he's not a bad guy to work for. Look how he's built MM from nothing to the biggest shop in Boston. Yes, I left the agency two years ago . . . I had my second baby and my husband accepted a promotion with his company, based in Orlando. So, I'm living the good life—taking care of my two children (a girl, Lily, 5 and a boy, Satan—just kidding—his name is Declan and he just turned 2). Things are great down here. Amazing weather and

ARE YOU SURE YOU WANT TO DELETE?
MAIL DELETED

TO: tmarkoff@millenniamarketing.com <tom markoff>
FROM: wonderwoman@usol.com <stephanie hilliard>
SUBJ: Right back at ya
DATE: Friday 7/30 9:13 PM

Look who's back in Boston! New York too easy for you, huh? I heard you broke into MM and strong-armed GW into a sweet deal that includes a corner office. Revenge is grand, isn't it? Good for you. It's true—I've climbed off the career ladder and landed in paradise with two beautiful, perfect, amazing children—Lily,

5, and Declan, 2. My husband, Brent, is the Executive VP of Operations for Grand Regent Hotels; we moved to the Orlando corporate headquarters right after our son was born. You might remember Brent. He was head of finance for Grand Regent when the hotel chain was a Millennia client. We built a lovely home in a nice development called Azure Lakes and I've been busy with some volunteer work, although the kids are pretty much full time. Hope you

ARE YOU SURE YOU WANT TO DELETE?
MAIL DELETED

TO: tmarkoff@millenniamarketing.com <tom markoff>
FROM: wonderwoman@usol.com <stephanie hilliard>
SUBJ: wonder-lust no more
DATE: Friday 7/30 10:00 PM

Well, hell, Markoff. Just when I thought it was safe to go online. Thanks for the note. I'm fine. Married, mothering, and delighted to never have to write a client conference report ever again. Stay out of that video closet, pal. It's a dark and dangerous place.

Stephanie

wonderwoman@usol.com: foreveramber@quicklink.com is sending you an Instant Message on Monday 8/2 at 11:11 PM

foreveramber: I know it's past 11, but please tell me you are still up, Stevie.

wonderwoman: I'm here.

foreveramber: Get any good birthday presents?

wonderwoman: Very beautiful pink diamond watch from Brent when he finally got home. Oh—and sensible underwear from my mother.

foreveramber: God love that woman.

wonderwoman: She sent some for Lily, too. Hers were cuter—they had butt ruffles.

foreveramber: Nice. Can we talk about me for a minute???

wonderwoman: What was I thinking?

foreveramber: Think about this: 68 hours and 14 minutes (well, really only 11 hours and 10 minutes) have passed since the sending of email to Gray. Nothing. Not a word. Noth. Ing.

wonderwoman: Maybe he's traveling and not checking email.

foreveramber: He strikes me as the kind of guy who would have a Sidekick to keep in constant satellite communications with the cyber-world.

wonderwoman: He *strikes* you? You haven't laid eyes on the man since you graduated from high school ten years ago. Wasn't he a musician of some kind? Give him a few more days. He'll respond.

foreveramber: I've always been too pushy with him.

wonderwoman: You don't even know if he's married, single, or gay.

foreveramber: Rule out the last one, babycakes. I had him.

wonderwoman: Yes, I heard. The prom. What happened that night?

foreveramber: He crashed the after-party and I had enough Tequila Sunrises (blech) to admit that I'd been lusting after him since ninth grade. Who could resist a drunk virgin in a homemade Vera Wang knockoff?

wonderwoman: No mortal man. Then what?

foreveramber: Ridiculously amazing mind-and-body-and-soul-connecting sex for three months. Then I went to U Mass and he went to follow his dreams, which, evidently, didn't include coming back to Massachusetts and marrying me. Never heard from again, as far as I know. But I've never forgotten him, Steve. And when someone invades your heart like that, it's . . . kismet. Fate. Destiny. Chemistry. Ever had it?

wonderwoman: Yes.

foreveramber: With Brent?

wonderwoman: By the way, I'm not speaking to you.

foreveramber: Yikes. Sorry about my new admin seeing that email about Tom Markoff. Julie's very sweet, don't worry.

wonderwoman: *Why* did you give him my email?

foreveramber: He wanted it. Did you write back yet?

wonderwoman: Yes. After a few pathetic tries. Why don't you google Gray?

foreveramber: I did. Nothing came up. But he is on Class-Reunion, so I know he's alive. Or in jail.

wonderwoman: Or married. Oh, that's redundant.

foreveramber: Stevie!? What's going on? Is Brent back for a while?

wonderwoman: He left again for San Diego for two days. That's the hotel biz.

foreveramber: Am I sniffing discontent in wonderland?

wonderwoman: I guess they would call it the seven-year itch, right?

foreveramber: Depends. What's itching?

wonderwoman: I am. Maybe Brent is. Hard to say since he's never around to scratch or be scratched.

foreveramber: Huge job, darla. He's in line for the CEO's job! You're a made woman. But you gotta put up with the travel. He loves you. He always has.

wonderwoman: Made? Made into what? I've done all the shopping and decorating I can do. Now what? Junior League? Good God–I sound like a suburban cliché. How did this happen?

foreveramber: You're still adjusting to the new life, new city. Wait till Lily starts kindergarten. You'll take over the school. Run the marketing. Do they have marketing in schools?

wonderwoman: PTA fundraising. Same difference.

foreveramber@quicklink.com: grayscale@connectone.com is sending you an Instant Message on Monday 8/2 at 11:39 PM:

grayscale: amber fleece? am i dreaming?

foreveramber: OH MY GOD. . . .

wonderwoman: What?

foreveramber: HE just IM'd me in a different session. OH. MY. GOD. BYE!!!

foreveramber: You're not dreaming. I'm real and living in your computer.

grayscale: kewl. one of my favorite boston chicks.

foreveramber: One of?

grayscale: amazing how many people this classreunion thing unearthed.

foreveramber: Sort of like worms. So what are you doing?

grayscale: living, working, playing music

foreveramber: Still? Playing bass? In a band? For real?

grayscale: why are you surprised? i told you that's what i wanted to do.

foreveramber: Is that what you do for a living?

grayscale: it's what i do to live. to make money, i paint.

foreveramber: Paint? I had no idea you were an artist.

grayscale: houses. i paint houses. and walls. garage doors and shit like that.

foreveramber: Oh. You have your own business?

grayscale: sometimes and sometimes i work for other people. sounds like you've embraced the business world with both arms.

foreveramber: Yeah, I work. I like it. It's fulfilling. I sound like an idiot, don't I?

grayscale: hardly. so, not married, huh?

foreveramber: Nope. You?

grayscale: not technically.

foreveramber: There's a Gray McDermott meaningless answer if I ever heard one. Either you are or you aren't, sugar. Which is it?

grayscale: n't. living with someone, though.

foreveramber: Just like a rock star.

grayscale: it's a little more complicated than that. can i email you?

foreveramber: I think that was the general idea of my original correspondence.

grayscale: there's an amber fleece smartass answer if i ever heard one. i'll be in touch.

foreveramber: Ten more years?

grayscale: not a chance. why do you think i joined this class-reunion thing? to hook up with tiffany sorensen?

foreveramber: They didn't call her *stiff*any for nothing.

grayscale: she didn't have that effect on me.

foreveramber: No? Then you're the only guy in our class who can make that claim.

grayscale: i had my eye on someone else.

foreveramber: Will you tell me about her?

grayscale: no. you will. bye, toots.

foreveramber: Bye.

TO: foreveramber@quicklink.com <amber fleece>
FROM: jdesmond@millenniamarketing.com <julie desmond>
SUBJ: Good Morning!
DATE: Tuesday 8/3 7:15 AM

Good morning, Ms. Fleece. I remember you check your personal email at home in the morning, so before you leave for the First Boston Bank photo shoot, here's a quick report:

- The photo shoot starts at 9:00 AM (**sharp,** according to Ms. Reinhardt's memo) at the Faneuil Hall site.
- The models have been confirmed this morning (I called them at home) and the photographer is already setting up. I have his cell phone if you can't find him when you get there.
- The conference report you dictated late last night is finished, proofed, and sent to everyone on the Alphaone Wi-Fi account.
- All open Traffic Jobs have been logged for the day and deadline notifications have gone to the Account Teams.
- Bud Fleece left a message on your voicemail—he wants

you to call him or email him regarding a blind date.

- Donald from the video store called to let you know your copy of *Troy* has come in, but they won't let you rent it until you return (and pay the late fee on) the following: *The Mexican, Legends of the Fall, Thelma and Louise* and *Meet Joe Black.* Would you like me to take care of that for you?

Julie

TO: jdesmond@millenniamarketing.com <julie desmond>
FROM: foreveramber@quicklink.com <amber fleece>
SUBJ: You Rock
DATE: Tuesday 8/3 7:17 AM

Thank you. Thank you. Thank you. PLEASE don't call me Ms. Fleece ☺. I'll never answer. I'm almost ready to leave for the shoot—still doing hair art. I will NOT be late. When Reinhardt issues an edict, we march. Oh—Bud Fleece is my dad and the blind date is Sam the Barber's son. Eeesh. Daddy never quits trying. Can you please call Blockbuster and tell Don to give me an effing break! The Brad Pitt Fest is nowhere near over. And can you google "grayscale" and "painting in Dallas" and see what you come up with? (In case you've never googled, just type in the words and it will give you a list of places that name has appeared on the internet. Try googling an old boyfriend sometime—you won't believe what you can find!!) YOU ARE THE BEST!

Love.
Amber

TO: wonderwoman@usol.com <stephanie hilliard>
FROM: tmarkoff@millenniamarketing.com <tom markoff>
SUBJ: still wondering
DATE: Tuesday 8/3 4:30 PM

This place is the pits without you. If I had known you morphed into June Cleaver, I would have asked for an extra twenty grand a year. Oh, yeah, I remember Brent Hilliard. How'd you ever hook up with that fast-track geek? Just kidding, Stephanie. Glad you're happy. It warms my . . . heart. But it would be a helluva lot warmer if you'd waltz in here with that real short red skirt (still have it?) and tell me you need a print ad written overnight. Ring any bells? Come on, babe. Let some British woman wipe your kids' noses and come back to work. I nailed the World Wide Airlines account. I remember how much you wanted that one way back when. You could handle that blowhard of a client. The account exec GW gave me is a bitch.

Wanna consult?

T

TO: tmarkoff@millenniamarketing.com <tom markoff>
FROM: wonderwoman@usol.com <stephanie hilliard>
SUBJ: you're wondering aimlessly
DATE: Tuesday 8/3 5:30 PM

Was that a job offer, Markoff? Sorry. The red skirt's retired and so am I. In fact, tomorrow I'm off to Disney World for the day. Then we're taking the Grand Regent jet to Puerto Rico for the opening of a new resort this weekend. So, as you can see, I'm booked. Good luck with WWA. That's a great account even with the blowhard client contact. And that's no AE breathing down your neck; that's VP Adele Reinhardt. You vill not cross her. But don't worry about der Fraulein. She can bust 'em with the best of 'em, but yours are brass. You can handle her.

xoxo

Stephanie

TO: jrush@spartbluesox.com <john rush>
FROM: jdesmond@millenniamarketing.com <julie desmond>
SUBJ: 25 Years Later
DATE: Tuesday 8/3 4:30 PM

Dear John,

The most amazing thing happened today. I googled your name just for fun. And there was information about a former pitcher for the Cincinnati Reds named John Rush. Could it be my old friend, Johnny "the Wild Thing" Rush? If you are the same John Rush, perhaps you remember me. Julie Yost from Pittsburgh. We met when the Reds were playing the Pirates. Point Park? Mt. Washington? Do I have the right John Rush? I'm looking for the one famous for his knuckle ball and slightly wild pitches. If so, drop me a note sometime. I am a divorced mother of a grown (20-year-old) son, live in Boston, and work at an ad agency called Millennia Marketing. Just wanted to say hello.

Take care,

Julie

TO: foreveramber@quicklink.com <amber fleece>
FROM: beantownbud@bostonbeerdistribution.com <bud fleece>
SUBJ: Blind Date
DATE: Wednesday 8/4 3:15 PM

Hi honey. Sorry I missed your call last night. The truth is, I wasn't calling about Sammy's boy. I was the one who had a blind date. Her name is Alice Ellis (for real!) and she's a nice lady. She's George Borowski's sister who just moved here from New York. I'm thinking of inviting her to the cookout on Labor Day. I just wanted to tell you ahead of time.

Love,
Dad

TO: foreveramber@quicklink.com <amber fleece>
FROM: grayscale@connectone.com <gray mcdermott>
SUBJ: still smiling
DATE: Thursday 8/5 3:00 AM

hey toots, just got in from a gig in east bumfuck, texas. been thinking about you and can't wipe the stupid ass grin off my face. really good to hear from you after all these years. the best thing about that hellhole called lincoln high was hooking up with you. i wrote a song about that summer, know that? it was called "when she cried." you inspired me—whaddya know? songwriting is still the best medicine in the world. sold three tunes in the last two years. a halfway decent band out of Nashville recorded "cried" and it did ok, the other two didn't amount to much yet. believe it or not the painting biz ain't bad. it pays the rent. which I share with a woman named dixie and her son mickey. he's a really great kid—nine years old and full of himself, so he needs a little straightening up. reminds me of someone i used to know about twenty years ago—ha ha. anyway, I was thinking about you at the gig tonight—glad you found me. did i say that already?

don't be a stranger.

gray

TO: wonderwoman@usol.com <stephanie hilliard>
FROM: afleece@millenniamarketing.com <amber fleece>
SUBJ: FORWARDING MESSAGE—Read attached first
DATE: Friday 8/6 11:15 AM

Oh God, Steve. Did you read that? He's illiterate. He's ee cummings with a paint brush and a bass guitar. Not to mention a live-in named DIXIE. Nashville?! Does that mean he writes COUNTRY music??? I had such high hopes for him. I know he didn't go to college when I did, but he was so *smart* and funny. He had such *po*. Now he's just . . . a loser. And I am just as much of a loser for being so disappointed. What did I want? For him to be a successful music exec (Rock and Roll or at least Jazz or something unrelated to Dolly Parton, thank you very much) waiting to boogie me back into his life for a big fat happy-ever-after?

Well. Yes.

But, no. He's living with a woman who probably sleeps under the rebel flag, raising her brat, and painting garages "and shit" — that's a quote. Not exactly what I had in mind. Was thinking more along the lines of rich CEO husband, big house on lake, 2.5 children. You know . . . YOUR FUCKING LIFE. Gotta go.

Love.

Too Blue to be Amber. And way too blue to be at this job today.

PS. The Creative Director looks particularly good today. Very hot in a pair of worn jeans—bulging and ever so slightly worn in *all* the right places. Great brown eyes and a sinful cleft in his chin. You have excellent taste. Are you ever going to tell me what happened with him? I heard he came *stag* to Adele the Nazi's little party last weekend. No minister's wife in sight. Hmmmm.

PPS. My dad had a *date*. Gross.

TO: afleece@millenniamarketing.com <amber fleece>
FROM: wonderwoman@usol.com <stephanie hilliard>
SUBJ: Gray's message
DATE: Friday 8/6 3:27 PM

Amber! Where did you get illiterate out of that message? So, he's shift-key challenged? He *wrote* to you, didn't he? And he was thinking about you. He evidently loves this nine-year-old boy enough to worry about "straightening him up" . . . and he didn't say he was "happy" or "in love" with Dixie (who can't be held accountable for what her mother named her) and he WROTE a SONG about you. Country is very big now, you know. (When did you cry, BTW?) You're selling him short.

Don't envy my life. Brent had to go to Puerto Rico alone because of some kind of hotel worker uprising there. So, instead of lounging by the pool and getting massages, I went kindergarten clothes shopping with a future member of Shoppers Anonymous who demanded no less than five pairs of Skechers. (Brent says the shoe gene is dominant.) The real highlight of the mall trip was when Satan escaped stroller jail and ran up the down escalator, undeterred by beads of snot flying from his infected nasal passages, and the little booger, pun intended, made it *halfway* up to handbags. It was like a Woody Allen movie, only I was not looking cool and Mia Farrow-ish, as you would say. All I got in the way of assistance was *that disdainful gaze* (you know the one) from the bitches at the Borghese counter. God help me. I just put him to bed . . . with only a tad more Baby NyQuil than the recommended amount. Stella McCartney is in her room holding her own private fashion show. And Mommy? Oh, she is eyeing that bottle of '02 Kendall-Jackson and wondering if 3:30 qualifies as cocktail hour down here in the vast cultural wasteland of the theme parks.

xoxox

Steve

PS. *Nothing* happened with Mr. Bulging Jeans.

PPS. Bud had a DATE? Cool.

TO: wonderwoman@usol.com <stephanie hilliard>
FROM: afleece@millenniamarketing.com <amber fleece>
SUBJ: Gray's message
DATE: Friday 8/6 4:18 PM

Okay, maybe you're right. He gets another chance. But he's out of the running for Prince Perfect because I like men who are stable, high earners, and not living with anyone with a name that rhymes with Trixie. (A pox on the Princesses at Borghese. Did you tell them you *managed* their effing ad campaign for a year???)

Love.

Amber

TO: jdesmond@millenniamarketing.com <julie desmond>
FROM: wildthing@usol.com <john rush>
SUBJ: John Rush Here
DATE: Sunday 8/15 5:46 PM

Wow. Really great to hear from you, Julie. I bet you thought I didn't remember you because it took so long to write back. Sorry. My team was on the road for a few weeks and I don't get emails from the home office. Better to use this wildthing email address to get to me. I sure do remember you, lady. I remember seeing you in the bleachers—blue shorts, white ruffles, curly blond hair, and a smile that could have lit a night game. I love this internet stuff—great to find people who would have otherwise been long lost.

I live in Spartanburg, South Carolina, and work as the pitching coach of a Triple A farm team here. I had to quit playing about eight years ago, just tore one too many tendons in my elbow. I'm divorced, too. In fact, I was married two times since I last saw you—have a kid from each one to prove it. The kids are the best part, believe me. I still live and breathe baseball, still throw a shitty knuckleball, and remember the taste of—oh hell, what was it? Strawberry lipstick. I can't believe you wrote after how we left things.

Stay in touch, okay?

Johnny

wonderwoman@usol.com: tmarkoff@millenniamarketing.com is sending you an Instant Message on Tuesday 8/17 at 10:17 PM

tmarkoff: Any chance you're on the computer, wonder girl?

wonderwoman: Hey.

tmarkoff: Are you relaxing by candlelight, sipping wine, and writing me an email?

wonderwoman: No.

tmarkoff: I was just about to send you a note and I decided to try this for more instant gratification.

wonderwoman: You always liked that.

tmarkoff: Not instant, Stephanie. Never instant. It's quiet at MM tonight.

wonderwoman: What are you doing there so late?

tmarkoff: Had to finish a complete overhaul of a WWA print ad that was a mess. I re-did it. It works now.

wonderwoman: I see you're still mired in humility.

tmarkoff: You told me you liked arrogant men.

wonderwoman: I must have been drunk.

tmarkoff: In New Orleans? Possibly. Probably.

wonderwoman: It was Chicago.

tmarkoff: We hit a few cities together, babe. You remember them all?

wonderwoman: Yes.

tmarkoff: So, what are you doing on the computer at 10 at night? I thought you'd be parading in front of Brent in a sheer negligee, trying for baby number three.

wonderwoman. You thought wrong. I'm emailing and reading newspapers from around the country.

tmarkoff: Oh, yes. The newspaper junkie. I remember that. So where's hubby?

wonderwoman: New York.

tmarkoff: What are you wearing?

wonderwoman: Go away, Tom. Get off my computer screen.

tmarkoff: I really need a consultant on the WWA account. Are you sure you want to give it all up to be wondermom, Stephanie?

wonderwoman: Get lost, Markoff.

tmarkoff: I will, when you answer the question.

wonderwoman: Why are you doing this?

tmarkoff: Doing what?

wonderwoman: Annoying me.

tmarkoff: 'Cause I'm sooooo good at it.

wonderwoman: No arguments from me. Good night.

tmarkoff: Come on, Stephanie. I'm just playing with ya, babe. From a thousand miles away. That's safe.

wonderwoman: Good night.

tmarkoff: Stephanie?

wonderwoman: What?

tmarkoff: Aren't you going to answer my question?

wonderwoman: Short yellow tee shirt and lace underpants. Good night.

tmarkoff: Wrong question. Great answer, though. Night, Stephanie.

TO: foreveramber@quicklink.com <amber fleece>
FROM: grayscale@ connectone.com <gray mcdermott>
SUBJ: songwriting
DATE: Saturday 8/21 9:43 PM

---

hey, amber waves of grain. i'm working on a pretty tune about a girl with mahogany hair. mahogany doesn't rhyme with anything. does yours still have that little bitta red in it? is it still long? still got all those curls?

are you happy, toots?

gray

TO: grayscale@connectone.com <gray mcdermott>
FROM: foreveramber@quicklink.com <amber fleece>
SUBJ: RE: songwriting
DATE: Saturday 8/21 10:38 PM

Monogamy. That rhymes with mahogany.

Yes, still have curls and the red comes and goes depending on my mood. It's kind of long, but worn back a lot in a half-assed attempt to go for the professional look at work. RE: happy. Sure I am. Have a very cool apartment, have lots of friends, and my dad is still out in Framingham, so I see him a lot. I like my job because I get to boss people around and tell them that if they miss their deadline, they're toast. Power. It's a heady thing. I don't make beaucoup bucks, but I manage to decorate myself in decent threads and paid off my '96 Mazda. I got into Pilates and even tried my hand at some kickboxing. So don't get on my bad side, buddy, I can kick your ass.

Are you ever coming home to Lincoln, Mass., to see your family?? Christmas or something? It'd be fun to see if you're still a decent-looking guy. ☺

Amber

TO: foreveramber@quicklink.com <amber fleece>
FROM: grayscale@connectone.com <gray mcdermott>
SUBJ: songwriting
DATE: Sunday 8/22 2:48 AM

it's damn near three am but i almost finished the song. it was scary-easy. you know why? i closed my eyes and heard your laugh. it sounded like the melody i wanted. then i remembered your smile, a little crooked but really quick and easy, and that made my heart beat to the rhythm. one deep breath of your scent and all i could think of was the time i annihilated you up at walden pond. so then i had the lyrics. it's called "back into you." i'm going to sell it to alan jackson or george strait and make a million dollars.

wanna help me spend it?

gray

ps. i don't go anywhere near what other people call family.

foreveramber@quicklink.com: wonderwoman@usol.com is sending you an Instant Message on Sunday 8/22 at 8:44 PM

wonderwoman: Are you there, Amber? I just read Gray's email that you forwarded this afternoon. Wowzer.

foreveramber: I'm here. No shit, wowzer. Who knew he was a freakin' ROMANTIC? About me? I swear I've read it 245 times.

wonderwoman: I would have, too, if someone sent that to me. Good heavens, the man is *sensual*.

foreveramber: What the hell do I write back?

wonderwoman: How about: Please send more.☺ So, what happened at Walden Pond?

foreveramber: Ground-breaking, tree-shaking, wave-making physical unions of the most intimate kind. Stevie! He's living with someone! He's a painter. He lives in Dallas. He's a wannabe songwriter. A <u>country</u> songwriter.

wonderwoman: He's a goddamn poet. Just have a little play-time with him on the computer. Be an inspiration to him. Get a cut on the million dollars he's going to make writing love songs about pond sex. Were you in the water, or on the grassy hill, or in that little hideaway at the far end?

foreveramber: All of the above. Can't believe I'm an inspiration to anyone or anything right now. Work's killing me—everyone wants something constantly. Dad called. He's dating (or something I don't even want to think about) this woman named ALICE ELLIS. Can you believe that? Even your boyfriend Tom pissed me off today. I'm just so damn tired.

wonderwoman: That's because you're up all night re-reading emails. He's *not* and never was my boyfriend. What did he do?

foreveramber: Demanded a miracle from a printer.

wonderwoman: Did he get it?

foreveramber: Natch. I bet that man gets *anything* he wants. Every woman at MM is panting over him. Except me, of course. I'm panting over a housepainter.

wonderwoman: He has that effect on females. He's left me alone for a week, thank God.

foreveramber: Things any better at home?

wonderwoman: Brent was home for a few days.

foreveramber: And???

wonderwoman: His job is killing him, too. Very stressful.

foreveramber: No chance of you guys taking a vacation in the near future?

wonderwoman: Going to a hotel is hardly a vacation for him. I'm just trying to make it as good as possible for him at home.

foreveramber: I'm sure everything will be fine.

wonderwoman: I'm not.

foreveramber: What's up?

wonderwoman: It's not pretty.

foreveramber: Come on. Spill.

wonderwoman: I think he's . . . oh forget it. It's nothing. It just really sucks.

foreveramber: TELL ME.

wonderwoman: I found something. Something kind of incriminating.

foreveramber: Ruh roh. What was it?

wonderwoman: A card. From somebody named Heather.

foreveramber: I hate that name. What did it say?

wonderwoman: She thanked him for taking care of something–not sure what. She said, "Don't forget, Brent. Your family lasts long after any job. They should be the most important part of your life."

foreveramber: Why does that sound like he's cheating?? It sounds fine.

wonderwoman: There was more.

foreveramber: What?

wonderwoman: She said he should "forget what happened" that they had been "caught up in the moment" and then she went all noble with the take care of your family part. I don't need some little slut doling out marital advice to my husband.

foreveramber: Did you ask him about it?

wonderwoman: I don't want him to know I looked in his briefcase. I was just trying to find his calendar so I could figure out when he'd be in town and we could actually go out to dinner.

foreveramber: Was it a lovey card? Funny?

wonderwoman: Just stationery with the letter H on the front.

foreveramber: Harlot. Who is she, do you know?

wonderwoman: I think she's the Director of Sales for Grand Regent's Resort Division.

foreveramber: So how has he been toward you?

wonderwoman: Ambivalent. He's *not* interested in me . . . if you know what I mean.

foreveramber: It's just a bad time for him. You might be jumping to conclusions. He has to prove himself in a new job. And you have to adjust to living there and not working. Give it time, Stevie. Marriage ebbs and flows.

wonderwoman: Big fat ebbing going on here.

foreveramber: I'm sorry, darla. Hang in there. Keep me posted. I better go and compose a note to the composer. Bye.

TO: wildthing@usol.com <john rush>
FROM: juliedes@connectone.com <julie desmond>
SUBJ: Hi again!
DATE: Sunday 8/22 11:00 PM

Hi, John. My son just helped me install software on a brand new home computer because he moved out about six months ago and took his. So, if I don't hear back from you, I'll know my first email on my new computer didn't work. Or that you'd rather I didn't write. Sorry to hear you've had a couple of divorces. It's the worst thing in the world, that's for sure. Mine was long overdue (oh, maybe 21 years . . . I was married for 22 years!). But, like you said, the kids are the best part. Willie moved out last winter, and now he's in college full time. That was sort of my wake-up call to get a life. I started at the ad agency about a month ago. It feels a little funny to be 45 years old and "just starting work"—my boss is a little spitfire named Amber Fleece who's in her twenties!! But she's so bright and funny and also endearingly disorganized. So, I'm struggling a bit with the spreadsheets, but I also get to use some of the mothering skills I developed over the past two decades. ☺

I'm glad you wrote back to me. Tell me what it's like in the minor leagues—anything like *Bull Durham?* ☺ Funny, that movie always reminded me of you. I can't believe you haven't forgotten the park bench incident either. Maybe someday you'll tell me what was going on in your head that day.

Take care,
Julie

TO: grayscale@connectone.com <gray mcdermott>
FROM: foreveramber@quicklink.com <amber fleece>
SUBJ: breathing again
DATE: Monday 8/22 11:00 PM

Needed 24 hours to catch my breath after that last email, Gray. Glad to be an inspiration to you. I'd love to tell you I inhaled *your* memory and ran the Traffic Department with legendary management finesse today, but that would be a lie. I screwed up just about everything I touched because my mind (and other parts) were melted by your lovely sentiments. You always had that power over me. Before you wield any more of it, want to give me a clue as to the state of your co-habitation with the woman who "shares the rent" with you? Call me old-fashioned, but . . . you know . . . it rhymes with mahogany.

Thanks.

Amber

TO: wonderwoman@usol.com <stephanie hilliard>
FROM: tmarkoff@millenniamarketing.com <tom markoff>
SUBJ: WWA Consulting Position
DATE: Wednesday 8/25 10:23 AM
CC: areinhardt@millenniamarketing.com <adele reinhardt> jbecker@millenniamarketing.com <jerry becker>

Hello, Stephanie.

Hope this finds you well. As we have discussed, the World Wide Airlines account is now one of the biggest clients of Millennia Marketing, demanding all of our resources and then some. The account team is seeking qualified consultants to augment our staff for special projects. Your background in travel-related advertising and consumer product announcements is ideal for such consulting. I understand your current situation requires you to remain at home. However, we have a specific need for a consultant to interview airline and aviation industry experts regarding a major new initiative for WWA. The findings (along with focus groups and other standard research techniques) will form the foundation of our creative advertising campaign. The entire project can be completed in a few weeks and meetings can be accomplished via conference calls at your convenience. We are willing to meet market-competitive contractor fees and would like to offer you the opportunity to conduct the research and present the findings to the account team. Please let me know if you are interested and when we can arrange for you to be briefed on the specifics.

Best regards,
Tom Markoff

TO: wonderwoman@usol.com <stephanie hilliard>
FROM: tmarkoff@millenniamarketing.com <tom markoff>
SUBJ: WWA Consulting Position
DATE: Wednesday 8/25 10:29 AM

That was a legit offer, Steph. I need a go-getter, a genius, a marketing machine on this one. I need you. I'll throw in "babysitter fees" to sweeten the deal.

Lemme know.
T

TO: wonderwoman@usol <stephanie hilliard>
FROM: afleece@millenniamarketing.com <amber fleece>
SUBJ: Fee for . . . service?
DATE: Wednesday 8/25 12:03 PM

My my my . . . that didn't take long. BTW, he's budgeted twice our normal consulting fee. Wish you could have heard Adele Reinhart pointedly ask: "Precisely what services does she provide for $150 an hour?" You *did* know your ol' buddy "Eva Braun" is on the account, right? I know you guys smoothed things over when you left, but do you have any idea how fast she moved into your office and slapped her Jimmy Choos on your old desk? Good thing you have me to run cover for you. I'll take a cut of the outrageous fee. Write.

Love.

Amber

TO:	afleece@millenniamarketing.com <amber fleece>
FROM:	wonderwoman@usol.com <stephanie hilliard>
SUBJ:	Trouble with a capital T for Tom
DATE:	Wednesday 8/25 2:20 PM

I doubt I'll do it. I knew der Fraulein was on the account—that's why he wants me. He recognizes a shark when he's staring one in the fake blue contacts. I also know exactly what new travel program he's talking about (been sneaking peeks at the trades online) and I would love the project. But . . . it's doubtful. Brent's in town—I may run the idea by him tonight. Kindergarten starts in five days.

xoxox

Steve

TO: wonderwoman@usol.com <stephanie hilliard>
FROM: afleece@millenniamarketing.com <amber fleece>
SUBJ: The Trouble with Tommy Boy
DATE: Wednesday 8/25 4:25 PM

Just thought you should know that Tommy Boy presented you as a "leading candidate" for the consulting position to the client this afternoon. I just saw the conference report. Like I said, what the man wants . . . the man gits.

Love.

Amber

TO: foreveramber@quicklink.com <amber fleece>
FROM: wonderwoman@usol.com <stephanie hilliard>
SUBJ: Wed night
DATE: Wednesday 8/25 10:20 PM

Brent just went to bed—after the closest thing to a fight we've had in a long time. Oh, Amber, I just don't know what I'm going to do. I didn't even mention the consulting job to him—I did mention Heather, though. Only because HE brought her name up out of the blue about four times. Each time my chest got tighter and the lump in my throat got bigger. Then, I just sort of let him have it. I expected him to laugh it off, tease me about being jealous or something. But instead, he got so defensive about it. That was the scariest thing. Then I got a little hotter, as you can imagine, and asked him point-blank why he never wants to have sex anymore. I expected, "I'm tired," in response. But that's not what I got.

Evidently, I'm not that *interesting* to him these days. That's not exactly what he said, but he made a joke about how all I talk about is the new mall and what the other mothers said at Petting Zoo. Well, fuck me. Or don't, as the case may be. WE AGREED that this was the best thing for the kids. WE AGREED to no nannies, no day-care, no working mother. WE AGREED that this was the right way to live. And now, I'm not fucking INTERESTING anymore.

Wait a sec.

Okay. I'm back . . . Had to pour another glass of wine.

wonderwoman@usol.com: tmark@quicklink.com is sending you an Instant Message on Wednesday 8/25 at 10:34 PM:

tmark: Hey wonder girl–you waiting for me?

Oh fuck fuck fuck, Amb. You are NOT going to believe what is on my computer screen. tmark sending me an IM. I gotta get rid of him. See ya—

xoxox

Stevie

tmark: I know you're online . . . I have the technology.

wonderwoman: A scary thought.

tmark: Get my email?

wonderwoman: Got it.

tmark: And?

wonderwoman: No thanks.

tmark: You're kidding, right? The budget is huge–trust me. And you'll love this project, Stephanie. It's right up your alley.

wonderwoman: My "alley" has taken a detour.

tmark: And wouldn't I love to go there. <lascivious grin> Seriously, Steph, don't you want to do something else with your time—in addition to being the world's greatest mom, of course.

wonderwoman: You have no idea what kind of mother I am.

tmark: I know what kind of woman you are. I remember the fire in your eyes on the job, your focus . . . your presence. When you walked into a room, everything else faded into black and white. I'm sure you are no different as a parent than you were as a professional. Stunningly competent.

wonderwoman: Wow. I'm speechless.

tmark: A first. Listen, this is a very cool project. It's a whole new approach to air travel. They are revolutionizing the flying experience.

wonderwoman: Can the PR, Markoff. I have other responsibilities.

tmark: Steph, we're talking 10, maybe 20 hours a week.

wonderwoman: I can't travel.

tmark: No travel.

wonderwoman: Really? No trips to Boston? Chicago? *New Orleans*???

tmark: That wasn't why I asked you, Stephanie. I really love your work. Anyway, you were a perfect lady in every one of those cities. It killed me, but you were.

wonderwoman: Sure. The image of propriety. Until the day you resigned at MM.

tmark: Some forces of nature are too powerful to stop.

wonderwoman: I'll never know why I could hold you off in hotel lobbies around the country, then ten minutes in a video storage closet and . . . bam.

tmark: Not bam. Almost bam.

wonderwoman: Bam for me.

tmark: Yeah, well. You owe me.

wonderwoman: That does it. No consulting. No way. Forget it. Good night.

tmark: I'm KIDDING, Steph. You don't owe me anything. I'm going to send you a consulting contract, okay? Look at the hours, the money, the work. Think about it and call me next week. Can you call me next week? Are you busy?

wonderwoman: My daughter starts kindergarten next week.

tmark: Perfect! You'll have the time.

wonderwoman: Declan's two. He's still at home with me.

tmark: Babysitter. Naps. Work in the evening. This is the NEW millennium, doll. This is how it's done these days. All over the world.

wonderwoman: I don't know, Tom. I have to think about it.

tmark: Don't think too hard. Go with your gut.

wonderwoman: I'll think about it.

tmark: We'll have fun.

wonderwoman: That's what I'm afraid of.

tmark: Don't be afraid.

wonderwoman: Bye Tom.

tmark: Call me.

TO: foreveramber@quicklink.com <amber fleece>
FROM: grayscale@connectone.com <gray mcdermott>
SUBJ: my rap sheet
DATE: Wednesday 8/25 11:30 PM

---

hi toots. how's the fast lane? sorry it's been so long . . . life got in the way. you asked about my whole deal—co-habitation status, i believe you called it. fair enough. here's the story. i met dixie at a gig about five years ago. really good kid, sweet, and as southern as her name. she was raising mickey alone—pretty tough for a 22-year-old girl. i was only a year older chronologically, but felt a lot older emotionally, and i connected with the little guy right away. anyway, we moved in together. we've been living together since then but in the last coupla years, mickey is what keeps us together. we both have had other relationships and have talked about how to break this off, but we haven't figured it out yet. she has some other issues. she never had a chance to be a teenager, you know? when i don't have a gig and i'm around to watch mickey, she sort of takes off to be with her girlfriends. i understand that and i really like the kid a lot—he's a funny little dude. so, we're like roommates now, me and dix. lately I've been thinking about moving on. problem is, i don't know what would happen to mick. i want to be sure dix has her act together before i take off and let her raise him alone. i had dogshit for parents—i don't want to inflict it on this guy. told you it was a little complicated.

anyway, i've been shopping "back into you" around to agents, too. had a few nibbles. will keep you posted.

gray

TO: foreveramber@quicklink.com <amber fleece>
FROM: wonderwoman@usol.com <stephanie hilliard>
SUBJ: God help me
DATE: Thursday 8/26 12:15 AM

That man. That *man*. Sheez, Amber. He almost talked me into it. But it was just my frame of mind—weakened by the fight with Brent and my sudden need to be *interesting* again. Tom told me I was "stunningly competent." You want to know how that felt? Amazing. Incredible. Delicious. Like a warm blanket on a cold night after being told by my very own husband that I am dull as dirt. No, Brent didn't say that exactly. To be fair, he wasn't mean. That was the horrible part. He had a gentle voice, a "this is serious, Steve, so pay attention" voice. Like he was warning me or something. I'm so scared. This is my *marriage.* My babies need a mother *and* a father—I don't want to subject them to a life of shared custody. Oh, God! How did I get to shared custody? We're just having a rocky time. I have to think. I have to figure this out. I can always figure everything out, right? That's what I do best. That's what you always tell me.

Gotta check the kids.

xoxox

S

TO: foreveramber@quicklink.com <amber fleece>
FROM: wonderwoman@usol.com <stephanie hilliard>
SUBJ: Thinking about it
DATE: Thursday 8/26 1:27 AM

You know what? I've just been sitting here thinking. I ought to take the consulting position. I believe Tom when he says I won't have to travel. I can handle his cyber-teasing. It actually makes me feel . . . "pretty" again. I can work in the mornings while Lily's in school, and I'll get a sitter for Declan, who will be right here with me. That's not deserting my children if I'm in the same house, right? I mean if there's blood or tears, I can just come out of my office and dry 'em up. This might be just the thing. You know, maybe Brent would perk up a little if I have my head around something other than baking cupcakes to celebrate our first tinkle in the potty. (He did, BTW. Yah! I mean Declan, not Brent.)

I could get into this assignment, too. World Wide Airlines. $150 an hour. Research the project, write up some findings and recommendations. No travel. Some flirting required. Complete by Thanksgiving. Be interesting again. It's actually the perfect solution. I'm going to make Tom wait a few days, though. I don't want him to think I'm too easy. Heh heh. You're a doll, know that? Thanks.

xoxox

Stevie

TO: wonderwoman@usol.com <stephanie hilliard>
FROM: afleece@millenniamarketing.com <amber fleece>
SUBJ: you're welcome
DATE: Friday 8/27 9:44 AM

Glad to be of assistance the other night. Love that I don't have to bother to be present to make an impact. Didn't write back because I was mulling over ee cummings's latest missive. They are *roommates* he says. And that works for him?!? It's like he's too lazy to find a woman/wife who is right for him, so he'll just stay with ol' Dix. I hate lazy men. Like using the effing shift key. How hard is that???? I can't believe I thought I was in love with him. I can't believe I've compared every other man to him for ten years. Oh well. Onward and upward. The weekend is upon us and . . . drum roll, please. I have a D.A.T.E. That's right, ladies and gentlemen, a date—and not Sam the Barber's Son.

Met him in the elevator in my building—he was visiting his

aunt. I like aunt visiting. It's so *responsible*. ☺ His name's Chet Caldsomething. Chet. Nice, huh? He's an INVESTMENT BANKER, hello. Kinda cute, too—not BRAD EFFING LAZY PITT cute. But not bad at all. Brown hair, brown eyes, with the preppie Izod thing happening. Saw him jump in a Beemer. So, I gave him my number (*before* I saw the Beemer, I'm not *that* superficial) and he called last night and we're going out to dinner. Whoo-wee. Real Saturday night date!

BTW, it's Friday here (it's Friday everywhere, I know) and the jeans are on display in the creative department. Tommy Boy looks sooooo fine, wearing that sexy lopsided grin that says he knows he's gettin' what he is wantin' and he is wantin' a consultant from O-town. But he couldn't possibly know that yet, right? That would mean you were *easy*. Ha ha ha ha. (Come on, did you sleep with him??? Fess up, chickie. I want to know.) I'll write Sunday and tell you what my last name is going to be.

Love.

Amber Caldsomething

TO: juliedes@connectone.com <julie desmond>
FROM: wildthing@usol.com <john rush>
SUBJ: Saturday
DATE: Saturday 8/28 6:30 PM

Hey, Strawberry, how ya doing? I was on the road for a long, long time, but I'm back. No games for a few days, then some playoffs—if we're lucky and can keep a very iffy hitting streak alive. Then I get a few months free, thank God. During the winter I do a lot of fly-fishing. I have a cabin up in the mountains and I go up there all the time. Then it's back to Spring Training. Sometimes I wonder what life would be like on a schedule that didn't involve baseball. I'm sure that's why I struck out twice with marriage—I'm married to the damn diamond. It gets in your blood, you know. The strategy. The plays. The pitches.

But, hell. That's not what I wanted to write to you about. I've been thinking about your last email. Picturing you—that pretty, pretty girl sitting so close to the bullpen at Three Rivers Stadium. I don't know if you've changed . . . but I have. The hardest part of getting older for me was losing my—elbow. HAH! You thought I was going to say hair! I've still got it (mostly), but the elbow is gonzo. Anyway, I've been thinking about the last time I saw you and the look on your face when I said I'd be right back. You know something, Julie, I'm really ashamed of that. I really handled that shitty. I was only 22, but I shoulda known better. And you know what? All the girls during my years in the majors—and, I'm sorry, there were just a lot of girls who wanted more than an autographed baseball—all those girls just disappeared from my mind over the years. But not Julie from Pittsburgh. The girl with the strawberry lips. The girl who said no. See? Your mother was right. Remember you told me that? You wrote it on a cocktail napkin in some bar in Pittsburgh. It said, "My mother says don't sleep with boys." Well, damn. Mothers are right, after all.

Sorry for the long email. Just had to get that off my chest. Hope you're having a good weekend.

Johnny

wonderwoman@usol.com: foreveramber@quicklink.com is sending you an Instant Message on Sunday 8/29 at 7:59 PM:

foreveramber: Any chance you're online?

wonderwoman: Hi there! How did the big date go last night???

foreveramber: Not bad, not bad at all.

wonderwoman: Details, please. All the gories.

foreveramber: Nothing gory. Modest chaste kissing.

wonderwoman: Do you like him?

foreveramber: Weelllll . . . yeah.

wonderwoman: Are we talking Mr. Right here?

foreveramber: Mr. Extremely Right. Politically speaking.

wonderwoman: Oh? A conservative?

foreveramber: I'm afraid so. He seemed *amused* by me. But . . .

wonderwoman: What? He can't kiss? He has bad breath? He eats with his left hand? WHAT is wrong with *this* one???

foreveramber: His jokes. They're REALLY bad. And he *did* go to effing Harvard, thank you very much. Don't they teach them anything at that school? Don't they tell them women HATE men who try to QUIP and CAN'T?

wonderwoman: Evidently not. So does he get another chance? Maybe it was an off night—and you tend to be sort of . . . critical.

foreveramber: I know, I know. But the benefit of the doubt is being generously doled out and I've agreed to another date. In fact, he asked me to go to a special Pops concert at Symphony Hall next week. With his parents.

wonderwoman: Holy Matrimony, Batman! His parents???

foreveramber: He has a slightly desperate feel to him . . . but who am I to criticize desperation? I live in that state.

wonderwoman: Guess what tomorrow is?

foreveramber: It's Monday here.

wonderwoman: First day of kindergarten!

foreveramber: WOW! Is she nervous? Excited? Having separation anxiety?

wonderwoman: *She* isn't. Mommy's a mess, though.

foreveramber: LOL! But you'll have your new consulting job, darla.

wonderwoman: Yep. I'm going to call Tom tomorrow. After the K'garten farewell scene. What time does he usually get in?

foreveramber: He's in when I get there at 8:30.

wonderwoman: You never got in the office at 8:30 in your life.

foreveramber: That's when I worked for you. Now that I'm out of admin hell, I'm a regular power junkie.

wonderwoman: Heard from the garage painter lately?

foreveramber: Not for a few days.

wonderwoman: Thinking about him?

foreveramber: Natch. Do you think I could stand to listen to country music?

wonderwoman: Only for true love.

foreveramber: I mean if, like, Garth Brooks starts singing "Back Into You," I'd have to listen to it, wouldn't I?

wonderwoman: Boots and spurs can't be too far off.

foreveramber: Yep, only that boy could make me want to be home, home on the range. I gotta go to bed. I'm exhausted. I can't shake this cold and am loaded up on decongestant.

wonderwoman: I'll email you after I talk to Tom. Guess we'll be working together again, huh?

foreveramber: Oh yeah! BTW . . . what did Brent say about the consulting gig?

wonderwoman: I didn't tell him.

foreveramber: ?!? Why not?

wonderwoman: He never liked Tom Markoff. (Imagine that.) I thought I'd just go ahead and do it. You know, get myself all *interesting* again and then spring it on him.

foreveramber: Well, that's a strategy. Bye!

wonderwoman: Bye! Feel better.

TO: afleece@millenniamarketing.com <amber fleece>
FROM: caldingerc@troyhillinvest.com <chet caldinger>
SUBJ: Great time had by all
DATE: Monday 8/30 8:45 AM

Just wanted to say that I didn't care that the Red Sox got blown out yesterday. Had too much fun with you on Saturday. My face still hurts from laughing. Don't make me chuckle in the middle of the first movement next weekend! (Laughing during movements can be dangerous <bg>)

Chester

TO: wonderwoman@usol.com <stephanie hilliard>
FROM: afleece@millenniamarketing.com <amber fleece>
SUBJ: ATTACHED message from alleged Harvard graduate
DATE: Monday 8/30 9:00 AM

See what I mean? Eeesh.

TO: wonderwoman@usol.com <stephanie hilliard>
FROM: tmarkoff@millenniamarketing.com <tom markoff>
SUBJ: Welcome aboard
DATE: Monday 8/30 1:00 PM

Great to hear your pretty laugh again today, Stephanie. I'm really glad you're taking the project. I promise you'll enjoy it. Sounds like you had quite a morning. I had no idea you were such a softie—it's just kindergarten. Wait till you do what I just did—

drove Casey to Amherst and said so long, buddy. Here's a credit card, a cell phone and everything I could teach you in 18 years. They didn't provide the "crying room" for parents that your school had (love the mini-Kleenex freebies with the date and school on them—the promo guys at Kimberly-Clark are geniuses). But I did have a little trouble with my contacts when I left the dorm.

Some WWA files are attached and more are on their way from the Traffic Department. Adele Reinhardt said she'd be sending you some background info on the program and she'll schedule our first conference call with the account team. She wasn't here when I left MM in the last millennium—is there a history with you two? Too much Lady Clairol in one room?

Just kidding.

I happen to know you're natural.

Tom

TO: wonderwoman@usol.com <stephanie hilliard>
FROM: afleece@millenniamarketing.com <amber fleece>
SUBJ: Chet
DATE: Monday 8/30 1:45 PM

Hey Steverella. Just googled my new boyfriend. Wow. Looks like he comes from a long line of overachievers. His grandfather started a business that his father runs. Looks like blue collar turned blue blood. So he won't totally hurl when he finds out my dad is a beer distributor named Bud. And he's definitely on the fast track at the investment firm where he works 'cause his name has been in the papers like thirty times in the last year. So what's a stupid joke or two next to a lifetime of security and ambition?

Which was not the point of this email. Congrats, darla, you're employed again. You'll be getting some mail from Julie Desmond, my assistant—who, BTW, gave me a blank look when I mentioned your name as the consultant Tom Markoff had hired for the WWA account. Either she's a total pro to the bone or she's completely forgotten the "he's married I'm married oh fuck fuck fuck" email. Anyway, she's going to send you a pack of client conference reports so you can catch up, and she'll include some artwork for the most recent campaign. (Tom's handiwork—verrryyy clever.) Eva Braun (I should be careful with interoffice email, huh?) will schedule the account conference call. Don't even think about being late. (As if you've ever been late for anything in your life. That was really a note to self.) Finance and Administration will send you some formal paperwork to sign.

That's the Traffic Report for this lovely Monday. I have not written back to Gray; I'm sure he's sleeping or painting or strumming on his bass. I do really owe him an email. But I'm thinking that first I'll drop Chet a note and say I had fun, too, and if he can just keep his mouth shut when stupid things want to come out of it, there could be a future for us.

Love.

Amber

TO: caldingerc@troyhillinvest.com <chet caldinger>
FROM: afleece@millenniamarketing.com <amber fleece>
SUBJ: RE: Great time had by all
DATE: Monday 8/30 2:00 PM

Hi Chet. I had a great time, too. I hope your face hurts from laughing and not because you caught my cold. I should be all healthy by the weekend—looking forward to the Symphony and meeting your parents.

Best.

Amber

TO: grayscale@connectone.com <gray mcdermott>
FROM: afleece@millenniamarketing.com <amber fleece>
SUBJ: Weekend update
DATE: Monday 8/30 4:00 PM

Hey Gray. Interesting insight into your living situation. Sounds like you have a lot of thinking to do. I would have written back sooner, but I had a lot going on this weekend. I guess I should tell you a little more about my life, huh? In addition to my job, I have a new boyfriend, Chet. He's an investment banker.

ARE YOU SURE YOU WANT TO DELETE?

MAIL DELETED

TO: grayscale@connectone.com <gray mcdermott>
FROM: afleece@millenniamarketing.com <amber fleece>
SUBJ: catching up
DATE: Monday 8/30 4:10 PM

Hey Gray. Thanks for catching me up on the details of your life. You sure have a lot going on there. As I do. So, drop me a line when you figure out where you're going to be living and with whom and let me know how things go with the song. If I don't write, it's just 'cause I'm so busy with work and my new boyfriend and all.

ARE YOU SURE YOU WANT TO DELETE?
MAIL DELETED.

TO: grayscale@connectone.com <gray mcdermott>
FROM: afleece@millenniamarketing.com <amber fleece>
SUBJ: your life
DATE: Monday 8/30 4:15 PM

I'll be around tonight if you want to IM me. We can talk about your life. And mine.

Amber

TO: wonderwoman@usol.com <stephanie hilliard>
FROM: areinhardt@millenniamarketing.com <adele reinhardt>
SUBJ: From Adele!
DATE: Monday 8/30 7:20 PM

Well, hello old friend! Such a delight to hear you are going to be working for me on the WWA account. I was thrilled when Tom mentioned your name among the list of consulting candidates after we learned Dale Freidman wasn't available. It's better this way. I used Dale on my last research project and he's fast and responsible—but no FUN! Your background in research and planning is just what we need on this account. The attached files should help you, but feel free to email or call ANYTIME you get stuck. My assistant is Dwayne Gallagher and he knows *everything and everyone* in case I'm out of the office—which I usually am!

I hope you're enjoying the dreamy life of a stay-at-home

mom. Amber Fleece in Traffic showed everyone the pictures of your little darlings and your house looked soooo nice! But, I just knew you couldn't stay on the Mommy Track forever—not our little Stevie Wonderwoman. And not when that persuasive Mr. Markoff comes knocking at your door. ;-) We've opened a MM email account for you to be sure we look completely professional in front of the client. For account-related activities, please use our server under your name shilliard@millenniamarketing.com. I've gone ahead and used your married name since the client doesn't know who Stephanie Walker is/was anymore.

The first account meeting is scheduled for this Wednesday, September 1, at 4:00 PM. I'll be out all day on a new biz pitch and meeting with El Presidente. Who, by the way, was thrilled to hear you were back with us when I told him. GW was always such a fan of yours! Hope you'll have everything read and digested by Wednesday. Just call the main number and you'll get connected to the conference room.

Adele

TO: wildthing@usol.com <john rush>
FROM: juliedes@connectone.com <julie desmond>
SUBJ: Mothers Are Right
DATE: Monday 8/29 8:45 PM

Hi John. It warms this mother's heart to know that Mothers Are Right. I hope my kid listened to me. My whole life, it seems, has been about doing the right thing. And somehow, a lot of it wasn't right after all. When I sat on that bench waiting for you, I kept telling myself . . . he'll be right back. He stopped to talk to one of the other players. He understands that I won't go up to his room like he wants me to. And it got later and later. The park got quieter. The shadow of your hotel across the water grew longer. And I sat there long after I knew you weren't coming back.

Then you know what I did? I went home and called Ray Desmond and told him, yes, finally, I would go out with him. And when I wore a white wedding gown a year later, I deserved to. I don't know what difference it would have made in my life to lose my virginity to a tall, good-looking professional baseball player I saw three times a summer for two years. Maybe I wouldn't have married Ray. But Will would never have happened, then. And I try to think about that, and not the years I lost. Anyway, I'm finally "out in the world" but still trying to do the right thing. I'm not looking back—well, not for too long. I'm glad the girl from Pittsburgh made an impression on you.

Take care,

Julie

TO: foreveramber@connectone.com <amber fleece>
FROM: wonderwoman@usol.com <stephanie hilliard>
SUBJ: Eva Braun Strikes
DATE: Monday 8/30 10:15 PM

Damn that woman. She scheduled the first account team meeting at the precise moment that hell breaks loose in my house. The Witching Hour. Too early for dinner, too late for a sitter. I just remembered why I hate her. All her phony exclamation points! Where are you? I tried IMing to no avail.

xoxox

TO: foreveramber@quicklink.com <amber fleece>
FROM: caldingerc@troyhillinvest.com <chet caldinger>
SUBJ: Late night
DATE: Monday 8/30 10:30 PM

Hi Amber. Still at the office trying to finish up the paperwork on an M&A project that should close tomorrow. Got your email. I even sent an IM on the off chance I could find you online, but you're not answering. Want to squeeze in a lunch later this week? I can brief you on the 'rents in advance of the Symphony.

Chet

foreveramber@quicklink.com: grayscale@connectone.com is sending you an Instant Message at 10:43 PM on Monday 8/30

grayscale: hey toots here i am. you there?

foreveramber: C'est moi.

grayscale: you said to im you, so here goes.

foreveramber: What are you doing tonight?

grayscale: just sent the rugrat to bed. dix is out. popped a brew. talkin' to you. it's nice.

foreveramber: Okay. I'll have wine with you.

grayscale: so how was your day, honey?

foreveramber: Fine. Busy.

grayscale: you like your job, i can tell.

foreveramber: It's perfect for me. I get paid to meddle in other people's business. What did you do today?

grayscale: painted a warehouse, then picked mickey up at school and took him to soccer practice.

foreveramber: You're a soccer mom!

grayscale: nope. i'm the coach.

foreveramber: I don't know why, but that's kind of sweet.

grayscale: i work their little asses off and make them do exactly what i say.

foreveramber: That's kind of what I do at work. Didn't realize we have so much in common.

grayscale: you know what else i did today?

foreveramber: What?

grayscale: i returned a call from an agent in nashville who wants to play "back into you" for a coupla artists. he wouldn't say who, but he's a pretty big shot with some mega names on his roster.

foreveramber: Wonderful! How long does something like that take?

grayscale: depends on who likes it and when they're recording. if somebody's in a big hurry, just a few weeks. if not, it can take months, even a year to record it. i feel really good about this one.

foreveramber: That's great.

grayscale: you inspired me.

foreveramber: How did I do that?

grayscale: by finding me. by caring enough to make me a priority. just like you inspired me to get the hell out of boston and try the crapshoot that is songwriting. did you know that?

foreveramber: You would have gone anyway.

grayscale: maybe. but when you looked at me, i saw the stars in your eyes. that gave me something i never had in my whole life.

foreveramber: what's that?

grayscale: confidence. you were the first person who ever believed in me.

* * *

grayscale: you still there, toots?

foreveramber: Just thinking.

grayscale: about what?

foreveramber: You. Us. About getting and giving each other confidence.

grayscale: i've been thinking about you constantly, baby.

foreveramber: And what do you think about?

grayscale: honey, you don't wanna know.

foreveramber: Try me.

grayscale: i think about the time we drove out past worcester and saw those horses.

foreveramber: Oh my God. Horse sex. I'll never forget that.

grayscale: remember how powerful it was? the noises they made? you were so scared. it was such a turn-on to see nature in action, animals doing what animals do. it was art.

foreveramber: As I recall . . . life imitated art shortly thereafter.

grayscale: that wasn't animals doing what animals do.

foreveramber: 'Cause animals don't usually do it in the backseat of an Accord.

grayscale: and they don't feel the way i felt when you came like thunder all over me.

foreveramber: Online blushing here.

grayscale: i knew you were satisfied 'cause you couldn't even make a joke. success!

foreveramber: A joke? Just the opposite, as I recall.

grayscale: yep. that's "when she cried."

foreveramber: I can't believe we're IMing about it.

grayscale: we're connected right now. just a satellite link apart. keyboard to keyboard. i can touch you.

foreveramber: Not exactly.

grayscale: with a satellite flash and a sea of dark blue . . . i'm lost in cyberspace and back into you.

foreveramber: Is that the new song?

grayscale: a line of it.

foreveramber: Can I "hear" the rest?

grayscale: on the radio. c'mere. closer. kiss me goodnight.

foreveramber: Ha Ha. Kiss, kiss.

grayscale: mmmmm. you taste good, kid.

foreveramber: More blushing.

grayscale: don't blush. close your eyes.

foreveramber: I don't know about this, Gray.

grayscale: just use your imagination.

foreveramber: It's in overload now.

grayscale: then imagine our kiss and how it feels. warm and sweet.

foreveramber: I think I better go to bed. Good night, Gray. It was fun talking to you. And other stuff.☺

grayscale: sweet dreams, angel.

TO: wonderwoman@usol.com <stephanie hilliard>
FROM: afleece@millenniamarketing.com <amber fleece>
SUBJ: digital getdown
DATE: Tuesday 8/31 9:45 AM

Sorry I didn't write back to you last night. I was online. With Gray. Oh God, Stevie, I got cyber-kissed. It was the weirdest thing. One minute, I'm just having run of the mill IM banter with a guy I haven't seen in a decade and the next thing I know he's giving me tongue across the miles. And the most bizarre part was . . . this is so embarrassing. I was . . . you know . . . sort of hot. A bunch of words on a screen and I'm getting damp down south. How pitiful is that?

Apologies for not responding to the message about the late afternoon meeting on Wednesday. But this morning I was in line at Starbucks with Dwayne Gallagher, the Nazi's admin, and mentioned the new biz pitch that she had and how it will delay the WWA meeting until the ungodly hour of 4:00. Ahem. No pitch. Dwayne Gossipmonger, God love him, told me the **meeting is not a client meeting at all,** but a manicure and pedicure. Followed by lunch and account status review with GW. A long-enough lunch to make the WWA account team meeting at 4:00 the first thing on her calendar. So there.

Love.

Amber. The online kisser.

TO: afleece@millenniamarketing.com <amber fleece>
FROM: wonderwoman@usol.com <stephanie hilliard>
SUBJ: manicures
DATE: Tuesday 8/31 10:15 AM

Do you think it costs more to manicure claws? Thanks for the heads up and keen investigative work. I'm spending today interviewing some sitters and reading the files. Will check my new MM email—in my married name—"since the client won't know who I am anymore." <eye roll>

xoxo

S

TO: wonderwoman@usol.com <stephanie hilliard>
FROM: hilliardb@grandregenthotels.com <brent hilliard>
SUBJ: Where are you?
DATE: Tuesday 8/31 7:30 PM

Hi Steve—tried to call a couple of times today and the line is busy—no voicemail. What's going on? Are you okay? How'd Lily do at school today? I'm going to a dinner meeting, but I'll have my cell and PDA on. Let me know if everything's all right.

Love ya,

B

TO: hilliardb@grandregenthotels.com <brent hilliard>
FROM: wonderwoman@usol.com <stephanie hilliard>
SUBJ: I'm here
DATE: Tuesday 8/31 8:28 PM

Sorry—had a phone problem all day and used the phone line for my computer. No voicemail when that happens. I don't want to call you in the middle of your dinner, though. Lily did fine today—better than yesterday. No tears (for either of us) and she made a friend. I think I'll be at the school a lot with the PTA and some other things, so I've hired Rosa's cousin (Maria) to watch Declan in the mornings. He's much better—the infection is completely gone. He really needed the antibiotics—I know you hate when they take them. Hope the presentation went well. I'll be up late—call me when you get in.

xoxox

S

wonderwoman@usol.com: tmark@quicklink.com is sending you an Instant Message on Tuesday 8/31 at 9:43 PM:

tmark: I see your little icon in the corner, Stephanie. Are you working?

wonderwoman: Hey. Just doing a little research.

tmark: All caught up on WWA and ready for tomorrow?

wonderwoman: You checking on me, Markoff?

tmark: Just making sure you're okay.

wonderwoman: I'm fine.

tmark: So true. All alone again?

wonderwoman: Except for my sleeping children.

tmark: Where's your spouse?

wonderwoman: Where's yours?

tmark: Watching TV upstairs.

wonderwoman: Go talk to her instead of me.

tmark: We're not talking.

wonderwoman: Ooh. Sorry. What's going on?

tmark: We never really talk. We talked through the kids and now they're both gone.

wonderwoman: That doesn't sound good.

tmark: It's not. Don't sweat it. What do you think of the WWA concept?

wonderwoman: I like the idea. Very out there for an airline—but such great advertising potential. It's time for comfort . . . luxury for the masses. That sort of thing. I've lined up interviews with a few industry experts and airline trade press reporters (who agreed to an embargo of the info, don't worry). I know exactly who to contact to develop the strategy and key messages.

tmark: You've got it all going on, Steph.

wonderwoman: Well, isn't that what you wanted to know?

tmark: Among other things.

wonderwoman: Don't ask.

tmark: Come on. . . .

wonderwoman: ☺ Okay, okay. It's pink and long and cotton and covers everything. Don't start flirting with me now.

tmark: When, then?

wonderwoman: Did you take Casey to Amherst all alone?

tmark: No. Why?

wonderwoman: You said "I"—you always say "I" when you talk about personal/family things. Isn't there a "we"?

tmark: Yes. There's a "we" but I don't want to make you uncomfortable.

wonderwoman: Why would I be uncomfortable? I talk about Brent. My HUSBAND. You have a wife. There's no subterfuge here.

tmark: I know.

wonderwoman: Well?

tmark: WWA is having a marketing staff meeting in Denver next month.

wonderwoman: Oh, here we go. I knew this was going to happen. I'm not going to Denver with you, Tom.

tmark: I don't want you to. Adele Reinhardt suggested you go.

wonderwoman: I sincerely doubt Eva Braun wants me in front of her client.

tmark: Now that's funny. Is that what you call her?

wonderwoman: Amber does. I just call her der Fraulein.

tmark: Amber? That's right. You two are buddies.

wonderwoman: Very much so. I hired her as my admin about five years ago, when I was pregnant with Lily. We're very, very good friends.

tmark: She's a piece of work.

wonderwoman: Don't be fooled by the one-liners and big hair. She's brilliant. Tom, you don't want a project update and I don't feel like chatting about colleagues. Why are you IMing me?

tmark: I want to warn you, but you evidently don't need it.

wonderwoman: About what?

tmark: Watch your back with Eva Braun.

wonderwoman: No news there.

tmark: She's very tight with GW.

wonderwoman: Gabriel Wycoming is the ruler of all he surveys. That would appeal to her need to climb to the top.

tmark: I think they're doing more laying down than climbing.

wonderwoman: REALLY?!? It would explain the four-hour lunch. However, I'm doubtful. Amber's never noticed anything.

tmark: Amber's not on the MM Board. I am. I see the dynamics.

wonderwoman: What do you see?

tmark: The usual telltale signs. Hair twirling. Eye contact. GW's woody.

wonderwoman: You liar.

tmark: Why would I lie about that?

wonderwoman: At work?

tmark: You are so precious. Yes, at work. I had one in every meeting I've ever been in with you—and it always lasted for about an hour afterwards.

wonderwoman: I didn't know that.

tmark: Bullshit. You knew it and loved it.

wonderwoman: I'm not a tease, Tom.

tmark: I know. That's what's so sexy about you.

wonderwoman: I did sort of suspect it that one time we

were pitching that start-up computer company in North Carolina.

tmark: Well, you were leaning on the conference table, with some really excellent cleavage on display.

wonderwoman: I shouldn't have worn that blouse.

tmark: We got the account.

wonderwoman: That's not why, you bastard.

tmark: No. My copy sang on that pitch.

wonderwoman: Hah! What an ego.

tmark: I loved that top, by the way. You look great in cobalt. It makes your eyes the color of the Aegean Sea.

wonderwoman: I've never been to Greece.

tmark: Neither have I. But I've been lost in your eyes before. And I remember all your clothes. You have terrific taste.

wonderwoman: A world-class shopper.

tmark: My other favorite was that black dress you had on the day I quit.

wonderwoman: I was in mourning.

tmark: You knew I was going to quit?

wonderwoman: No. I knew we had to do layoffs that day and I wore it on purpose. In solidarity with the seventeen people who shouldn't have lost their jobs.

tmark: You wore black, but I quit.

wonderwoman: You're noble. I needed the job. Anyway, you didn't have to quit.

tmark: I didn't quit for nobility or solidarity or anything so heroic. I quit because I had to.

wonderwoman: Why?

tmark: Because . . . I had a 12-year-old-daughter and an 8-year-old son.

wonderwoman: Why did you have to quit?

tmark: I had to keep my marriage together.

wonderwoman: Why would working at MM ruin your marriage?

tmark: Don't be coy, gorgeous. You know damn well I was head over heels with someone at work.

wonderwoman: Oh.

tmark: That took a long time for two little letters.

wonderwoman: I didn't know.

tmark: I told you.

wonderwoman: But we were . . . you know . . . in the closet. I thought you were just in the throes of passion.

tmark: I was in the throes of your underwear, as I recall.

wonderwoman: Stop.

tmark: Why?

wonderwoman: It's over. It's history.

tmark: I wanted you so much, Stephanie. I could have taken you right there on the VHS racks.

wonderwoman: I want to go now.

tmark: Okay. Talk to you tomorrow at 4.

wonderwoman: Great. Good night.

tmark: Stephanie?

wonderwoman: Yes?

tmark: Don't worry. You didn't do anything wrong.

wonderwoman: I did. But I won't. Good night.

tmark: Night, Steph.

TO: wonderwoman@usol.com <stephanie hilliard>
FROM: hilliardb@grandregenthotels.com <brent hilliard>
SUBJ: Too late to call
DATE: Wednesday 9/01 12:45 AM

Steve, I got your email, but dinner went really late and I don't want to wake you. Glad Dec is better. Kiss Lily for me tomorrow. I'll be home for sure Friday afternoon. Call you tomorrow from the airport—leaving here in the morning and going to Minneapolis. If you can't get me, call Cheryl at the HQ, she has all my numbers.

Love ya,
Brent

TO: shilliard@millenniamarketing.com <stephanie hilliard>
FROM: jdesmond@millennniamarketing.com <julie desmond>
SUBJ: Amber
DATE: Wednesday 9/01 11:30 AM

Hello, Stephanie. I want to be sure you received the package of conference reports I sent yesterday. I also wanted to inform you that Amber has called in sick today. She might try to conference herself into the WWA account meeting this afternoon, but I'm trying to get her a doctor's appointment. If you need anything from the Traffic Department prior to the meeting, please let me know.

Julie Desmond

TO: jdesmond@millenniamarketing.com <julie desmond>
FROM: shilliard@millenniamarketing.com <stephanie hilliard>
SUBJ: RE: Amber
DATE: Wednesday 9/01 12:15 PM

Thanks for your note, Julie. She must be pretty sick—she's not answering her phone. It's okay if she misses the meeting; I'll let her know what decisions are made. Good luck getting Amber to a doctor—she HATES them.

Stevie

TO: foreveramber@quicklink.com <amber fleece>
FROM: wonderwoman@usol.com <stephanie hilliard>
SUBJ: How the mighty have fallen
DATE: Wednesday 9/01 9:06 PM

Well, you missed it. You missed the whole fucking mess that I've made of my professional "work at home consulting" debut. But, you'll hear about it tomorrow, when you get in. Oh yes. I will be cube fodder for days. Did you hear? Little Stevie Wonderwoman got derailed on the Mommy Track. Oh fuck fuck fuck. But why wait for the conference report? In the interest of equality, I'll give you my version first.

Eva Braun opened with her usual fake greetings, then goose-stepped right into the agenda. She failed to mention the "new biz" pitch or her lengthy afternoon meeting with G-dub (Tom thinks they're playing bury the bone, BTW). She continually positioned me as "the research consultant" like I never ran a freaking advertising account in my life. But that's all right, I tell myself. I'm getting paid $150 an hour to be more *interesting* to my husband. I got my shit together. Barefoot, relaxed, on the speaker phone. Rosa (housekeeper) is playing with the kids because Maria (babysitter) had to leave. My door is shut. My infamous "meeting control switch" is in the ON position and I feel pretty darn good with my fine self. Wonderwoman here, ready to kick some marketing ass.

Oh boy. Oh boy and girl, actually.

Rosa leaves—her daughter is in trouble at school, I think. I don't know. I can't really understand her, plus I'm trying to listen to some account exec droning about market test analysis at the same time. Declan screams. Lily explodes into the office swearing she didn't hit him. Declan screams again—offended beyond reason by his sister's lies. Evidently the words "I'm on a conference call" just don't carry the weight with a 2-year-old the way they do with, say, a trained professional.

I mute and unmute. God knows what they're hearing on the other end. Eva shoots questions with trick answers. Declan shoots Lily with a laser gun. Tom wants my list of industry pundits. Lily wants chocolate-covered potato chips. I can't respond because I'm attempting crowd control with a box of Dots. No can do. Lily wants choc-o-late, Mommmmmmmyyyyy. (Screamed at the top of her lungs.) All I have is my secret stash—a nearly full box of Godiva chocolate-covered raspberry things. (Yes, they are still my weakness.) I shove them at Lily and beg her to watch her brother like a big girl, then hustle them out of the office, which Declan takes as a personal affront. His shriek is so fucking loud, it can be heard through the mute.

The computer screen flashes with an IM. It's Tom. He must

be using a thumbpad PDA under the table. *What's going on?* he asks. *Can you cut the chaos?* Fuck you, I respond politely, with a little smiley face. (He is, technically speaking, my client.) *Any time,* the scumbag writes back with a *winking* smiley face. Declan kicks open my door and fires a laser round at me. Tom sends an IM: *GW just walked into the room.* Declan is covered in creamy raspberry residue. Lady Godiva is right behind him with an empty box. Fraulein R wraps it up, undoubtedly sensing that she's not going to have to work so hard to make me look bad. I can handle it all by myself.

You want to know if there are any action items for Traffic to track? Don't ask me. My head was spinning, my heart was pounding, my pits were dripping. I can just hear Adele when the call mercifully ended: "Are we sure Dale Freidman isn't available?"

Oh fuck fuck fuck. Get out the corkscrew, mama. I am keeping my computer off all night—I don't want to get into it with Tom Markoff. Write to me and let me know if you are really going to the doctor. Are you that sick???

xoxo
Steve

TO: foreveramber@quicklink.com <amber fleece>
FROM: grayscale@connectone.com <gray mcdermott>
SUBJ: all the way back into you
DATE: Thursday 9/02 3:26 AM

---

hi toots. just got in. the band played "back into you" at the gig tonight and it went over really great. i'm not much of a singer, so i generally do backup. Kyle—our lead singer—did a good job and i'm feeling hot about the song. and you. damn, if you didn't just sink your little teeth right under my skin. hell if I don't wanna bite you right back. right in that sweet spot under your ear. you liked that. if i sucked real lightly in that hollow part and then flicked my tongue a little, it made you do all kinds of crazy things. man, you got me goin', toots. now i'm back into you. wish i was.

all the way.

gray

TO: tmarkoff@millenniamarketing.com <tom markoff>
FROM: areinhardt@millenniamarketing.com <adele reinhardt>
SUBJ: Consulting Issue
DATE: Thursday 9/02 7:45 AM

Tom, I stopped by your office to chat with you, but you're not in yet. I'm leaving at 8:00 with GW to visit that new biotech client in Cambridge, but we need to talk! I know you are hot on Stephanie Hilliard's background in travel, but I really am having my doubts that she's the ideal consultant for an account this big and important to the agency. I bet I could pull a few strings and get Dale Freidman to wrap up his other assignment and take this one. Stephanie is a lovely girl and I know she was well-liked at the agency, but let's face it, she's been out of the workforce for so long, I'm just not sure she's even in touch with what's going on in the travel industry anymore! Except for the fact that her husband is in the hotel business, of course. (You knew she married the future CEO of Grand Regent Hotels, didn't you?) We don't have to worry about letting her off this one—Grand Regent is no longer a client of the agency, so it's not like her husband can retaliate! WWA is an account that we've been after a long time, Tom, long before you arrived at MM. We don't want to jeopardize it.

Thanks!

Adele

TO:	jdesmond@millenniamarketing.com <julie desmond>
FROM:	foreveramber@quicklink.com <amber fleece>
SUBJ:	doctor
DATE:	Thursday 9/02 10:26 AM

Hi Jules. All right, all right, all right already! I got your voicemails. I KNOW that I have an appointment with Dr. Franklin at 1:30 today. I'm just checking email and catching up this AM, then I'll be in the office after I go to see him. It's just a cold, for crying out loud. And I know you got all bent out of shape about that little weirdness under my collarbone, but I absolutely know that's a swollen gland. I've had it before. However, I appreciate the concern. Send me all of today's Traffic Reports so I can see what's happening in the world.

Love.

Amber

TO: wonderwoman@usol.com <stephanie hilliard>
FROM: foreveramber@quicklink.com <amber fleece>
SUBJ: You're still mighty in my eyes
DATE: Thursday 9/02 10:33 AM

Don't sweat it, babycakes, it probably sounded worse to you than to everyone else. Listen, I am going to the stupid doctor this afternoon. This is what I get for hiring a *mother* when I really needed a *secretary*. So, I'm not in the office this AM to get the scoop on the conference call. I will let you know what I hear. I stayed off the computer last night, too. You think Tom teases you? Oh, man. Gray actually *scares* me, Stevie. Who knew a man could *write* me into a state of hormonal agitation? And you know what? I haven't even talked to him. He hasn't ever called or suggested that we actually have a conversation. And, yet, I am feeling and thinking things that are stupid and impossible and . . . wild. I don't want to have an online romance with a painter who lives in Dixie with Dixie. I have Chester Cald—what *is* his last name, anyway???

Love.

Amb.

TO: jdesmond@millenniamarketing.com <julie desmond>
FROM: foreveramber@millenniamarketing.com <amber fleece>
SUBJ: Staying Home
DATE: Thursday 9/02 3:18 PM

Jules, the appointment took longer than I thought. It's crazy to come in now. If I still feel a little lousy, I'll stay home tomorrow—nothing will happen on the day before a three-day weekend. (You can go home early, too!) You can shoot any personal calls here—my dad might call about his little Labor Day BBQ or . . . Chet might call about Saturday night. If anyone calls from Dallas named Gray, PLEASE forward that call. Oh, and did you hear anything about yesterday's WWA account meeting? Stevie seems to think it was a bust.

Let me know.

Amber

TO: shilliard@millenniamarketing.com <stephanie hilliard>
FROM: tmarkoff@millenniamarketing.com <tom markoff>
SUBJ: where are you?
DATE: Thursday 9/02 4:25 PM

Haven't heard from my favorite consultant all day. You must be burning up the phone lines with the interviews. Find out anything that would impact the creative process?

Tom

TO: tmarkoff@millenniamarketing.com <tom markoff>
FROM: shilliard@millenniamarketing.com <stephanie hilliard>
SUBJ: RE: where are you?
DATE: Thursday 9/02 5:45 PM

Been busy all day, Tom. Nothing that would impact creative, yet. Did get a raised eyebrow or two from those who think WWA is in no financial position to pull off this concept without a fare hike. I'm laying low . . . after yesterday. Sorry about that. I'll have a sitter next time.

Stephanie

shilliard@millenniamarketing.com: tmarkoff@millennia-marketing.com is sending you an Instant Message at 6:03 PM on Thursday 9/02

tmarkoff: Hey—just got your email—you still there?

shilliard: I'm here.

tmarkoff: Don't apologize, Steph. I told you we'd meet at your convenience. Four in the afternoon is obviously not convenient. I won't let it happen again.

shilliard: You're being too kind. Was there fallout?

tmarkoff: Nothing that I can't handle.

shilliard: That was a nightmare, Tom.

tmarkoff: You probably didn't need my running commentary.

shilliard: Oh yes I did. Thanks for the heads up on GW's grand entrance.

tmarkoff: You got those kids quiet in a hurry.

shilliard: Duct tape. No home office should be without.

tmarkoff: You make me laugh, Stephanie.

shilliard: That was no laughing matter at $150 an hour.

tmarkoff: You're worth every penny. Where was your buddy Amber, by the way?

shilliard: Doctor's appointment. I gave her a complete recap of the meeting.☺

tmarkoff: Did you ask her about opening that research job number?

shilliard: Whoops. I forgot you asked me to do that. Must have been when I was locking Declan in the file cabinet. ;-) I'll do it. Sorry, Tom.

tmarkoff: Quit apologizing. What are you wearing?

shilliard: You're the worst.

tmarkoff: Come on, wondergirl. It's the end of a long hard day. Humor me.

shilliard: Jeans, a black tee shirt . . . nothing underneath.

tmarkoff: Oh, man. I said humor me, not KILL me. Thanks, baby. I'll hold that thought.

shilliard: It's just cause you were so nice about Romper Room at your meeting. Thanks.

tmarkoff: Anytime.

TO: foreveramber@quicklink.com <amber fleece>
FROM: beantownbud@bostonbeerdistribution.com <bud fleece>
SUBJ: BBQ
DATE: Thursday 9/2 7:45 PM

Hi honey. Your secretary told me you were home sick and I called but you didn't answer. Maybe you're sleeping. Just wanted to let you know to come over around noon on Monday. I'm doing my famous beer-bee-que ribs and chicken. George and Doris Borowski are coming and I also invited Alice. I think you'll like her. If you want to invite your new friend Chet, feel free. We each get an opinion that way.

Call me or I'll see you Monday.

Dad

PS. If you want to, I'm in the mood for the jell-o thing you always make.

TO: foreveramber@quicklink.com <amber fleece>
FROM: wonderwoman@usol.com <stephanie hilliard>
SUBJ: I miss you!
DATE: Friday 9/03 3:33 PM

Where have you been??? Haven't heard from you in days and won't for a while—we're all going to Miami for an event at the Grand Regent Resort there and staying to make a weekend of it. It's work for Brent, but at least we'll be together. I was terrified he'd suggest I stay home . . . it's a *resort* property, so that means Heather the Harlot could be on the premises, I suppose. But we're all going as one big happy family. I still haven't told him about the consulting! I will this weekend, I guess. Either that or hide the evidence that WWA has taken over what we always thought was *his* home office. Anyway, have fun on Saturday with Chet—we'll be back Monday night. Email me and let me know how he gets through the first movement. With his mouth shut, we hope.

xoxo

Steve

PS. I finished my first preliminary report on the WWA account, sending to you separately at your MM email address. Let me know if you hear rumblings from Stalag 17.

TO: grayscale@connectone.com <gray mcdermott>
FROM: foreveramber@quicklink.com <amber fleece>
SUBJ: Sweet spots
DATE: Friday 9/03 8:40 PM

Hey Gray. Thanks for that nice email. I always did have a sweet spot for you. <g> It's going on nine on a quiet Friday night and I'm curled up with my laptop and feeling like I sort of need a friend. A couple of my girlfriends are going out tonight, but I just can't face the Boston bar scene tonight. You know what I'm doing? Re-reading your emails. L is for Loser. That's me. I just keep reading your beautiful words—you *are* a poet—unencumbered by capitalization, but a poet. Big sigh, sweetheart. *Why* can't I find someone right here, right now, right away to be my buddy. My partner. My lover. Oh, good God, I won't send this. I'm just blue and if I put the words on paper (screen?) it might make me feel like I've talked to you.

I went to the doctor today. Do you remember that I despise doctors? Oh, I do. I hate them all. With their coats and fake charm and nodding heads and shrugging shoulders. They don't effing know any more now than when witch doctors used leeches. When my mother was dying, they used to gather around my father and pontificate and prognosticate, but they couldn't do a flaming thing to save her. I was only 14, but I knew a blowhard when I saw one.

So I finally go to one. At least I could get George Clooney, right? No, I get Noah Wyle. He couldn't have been old enough to get into medical school, let alone out of it. But he must have, since he knew exactly how to nod and shrug and prod and make casual use of terms like MRI and *chronic*. And then the son of a bitch did the unthinkable. Sends me to an effing specialist. For a cold. He probably gets a kickback.

I hate being sick. I hate doctors. I hate missing work. I hate missing you. I hate having a date tomorrow with a guy who's . . . not you. I wish I could wave a magic wand and have him be you. Oh, Gray. I'll just say what I want 'cause I'm about to delete like hell. I wish I had you tonight. I could hold you and kiss you, warm and long and just the way you described it the other night. I would climb inside your arms and snuggle into your neck. Then I would kiss, kiss, kiss my way down to your sweet spot. You have one, too. Right under your

YOUR MAIL HAS BEEN SENT

UNABLE TO DELETE SENT MAIL

CONFIRMATION OF SENT MAIL TO grayscale@connectone.com 9/03 8:40 PM

UNABLE TO DELETE SENT MAIL

CONFIRMATION OF SENT MAIL TO grayscale@connectone.com 9/03 8:40 PM

UNABLE TO DELETE SENT MAIL

CONFIRMATION OF SENT MAIL TO grayscale@connectone.com 9/03 8:40 PM

UNABLE TO DELETE SENT MAIL

TO:	juliedes@connectone.com <julie desmond>
FROM:	wildthing@usol.com <john rush>
SUBJ:	End of Season
DATE:	Friday 9/03 10:52 PM

Hi, Strawberry. Well, it's official. The Spartanburg Blue Sox suck and we aren't going anywhere near a playoff this year. That's the bad news. The good news is that we've got a few more weeks of meaningless games, then I can start my months off the field. Like I mentioned, I usually spend some time messing around my cabin where I fly-fish. You know, I've been thinking. Now this is just some "food for thought" as they say. But I was just wondering if maybe we could get together in the off-season. I could come to Boston or, if you like, you could visit me here. I don't know. Just kind of fun for old times' sake—no pressure. And I won't leave you sitting on some park bench! You can have your own room. I don't know, Julie. I was just thinking about it. Give it some thought. We always had a good time together and I'd like to see you again sometime.

Talk to ya—

Johnny

foreveramber@quicklink.com: grayscale@connectone.com is sending you an Instant Message on Saturday 9/04 at 2:09 AM:

grayscale: hi toots. just got your message. i know it's 2 in the morning there, but is there any chance in hell you're online?

grayscale: this computer says you are online but you sure aren't answering. i've been waiting ten minutes. come on, amber waves of grain. write to me.

grayscale: i bet you're kicking yourself for sending that email. you musta hit send by accident. i can hear you swearing up a blue streak. i was laughing my ass off, tootsie girl.

grayscale: okay, well you're hearing me even if you're too hot under the collar to answer. i love that i'm the one you want to be going out with tomorrow. ditto on my end. i know just what we'd do, too. get a six pack and go to walden pond. way up in the corner, right where that willow you love is. we'd get a blanket or two and lay down on the soft, damp grass to watch the stars and tell each other everything we've missed over the last ten years. come on, honey. i know you're there. . . .

* * *

grayscale: all right, then. i'll just tell you about our dream date. you're wearing faded old jeans and they curve over your rear like a work of art. you have a yellow sweater on–you look really good in that when your hair is the same rich color as maple leaves when they peak in october. we talk and drink a few beers and snuggle. you tell me all about when the bad doctors made you unhappy and i tell you that it's better to lose a mother who loved you than to live with one who doesn't. you there yet, toots?

grayscale: just when you get all teary-eyed, i make you laugh and while your sweet little head falls back with that giggle i remember so well, i slip right into that spot under your ear for a kiss. mmmm. tastes so good. smells like honey and earth and lemon shampoo. then i find that mouth. you are quiet for one blessed minute. no jokes, just soft lips waiting for my tongue. you kissin' me back?

grayscale: you are kissing in my fantasy. long and hard. deep kisses that make you dizzy and make me so hard it hurts. wanna tell me what you want? don't be shy, amber. we've done this before. when you found <u>my</u> sweet spot. where is it again?

foreveramber: Four fingers to the left of your bellybutton, then down an inch.

grayscale: ah, there's my girl. c'mere, now, angel. squeeze those legs tighter.

foreveramber: I've never had cyber-sex.

grayscale: well, since this is our first date in ten years, we'll just do some heavy petting. you were always real good at that.

foreveramber: I really didn't mean to send that email.

grayscale: i know. but you did. and i'm glad. now let's talk about what we did at walden pond. great memories.

foreveramber: Gray.

grayscale: i love the way you felt, amber. and tasted.

foreveramber: Gray please. I can't do this. I can't.

grayscale: you're crying, aren't you?

foreveramber: No. Oh. How did you know that?

grayscale: i just know you.

foreveramber: I can't believe you know me that well.

grayscale: at one point i knew you better than i knew anyone.

foreveramber: Yep. Me too.

grayscale: i'd like to get back to that point.

foreveramber: Yep. Me too.

grayscale: back into you . . . after all these years of thinkin' how much i changed and grew . . . it's like they never happened cause i'm right back into you. . . .

foreveramber: Did you really write that for me?

grayscale: i did.

foreveramber: Can you call me now so we can talk?

grayscale: i can't right now. small house and i'm not alone. i will though, i promise.

grayscale: you still there?

foreveramber: I'm here. Sorry. I'm just tired. Ready to go to bed.

grayscale: don't go, toots. stay with me. talk to me. tell me all about what the doctor said.

foreveramber: No. Forget it. Tell me about what the agent said. Who's going to record my song?

grayscale: don't know yet. but someone will. i have a feeling.

foreveramber: What kind of a feeling?

grayscale: that feeling i got when i first got to know you. that feeling that everything is going to be okay, everything is going to work out. that the universe is lined up just the way it should be.

foreveramber: I hope to hell you're right, Gray.

grayscale: what do you mean, baby? what's up with you?

foreveramber: Nothing, honestly. I'm just so tired. I want to go to bed.

grayscale: me too. with you.

foreveramber: Not tonight, I'm afraid.

grayscale: sweet dreams . . . of us.

foreveramber: Are there any other kind?

TO: foreveramber@quicklink.com <amber fleece>
FROM: guest@grandregenthotels.com <guest stephanie hilliard>
SUBJ: Miami Vice
DATE: Sunday 9/05 6:50 AM

I'm allegedly doing 3.7 mph on the treadmill right now, but I wormed my way into the business office of the hotel to get online. I have to talk to someone or I'll lose my mind. Someone, you ask? Why couldn't I just turn over on a Sunday morning, in my plush resort hotel bed, and talk to my husband? Because he is not IN my plush resort hotel bed, that's why. And he's been MIA for damn near every moment we've been in MIAmi. Amber, this is not good. I won't go so far as to say BAD, but not good.

Friday night was fine—we got in, the kids were cranky, we got room service, and put them in their room. He had a few calls and we just sort of crashed. A little bit of a letdown, but, hell, we have two more nights. And it's a gorgeous suite—two bedrooms, plenty of privacy, eager staff hungry to do Brent's bidding . . . like provide babysitting so we could go out to dinner.

Saturday morning, we're in the lovely restaurant having as nice a meal as you can have when one person at the table is wearing a bib and another is using a sippy cup, and guess who comes waltzing into to call an "emergency" sales meeting?

Yep. Heather the Harlot. Oh, Amber, she's so fucking pretty I wanted to throw up. But Declan did that for me. And on me. Hurled chocolate-chip pancakes all over my sky blue polyfuckingester tee shirt. Unfortunately, I'm not the person wearing a bib. I'm madly wiping and Lily's doubled over in laughter, trying to get him to spew more and Miss Friggin' Exotic Indonesian Oriental French Polynesian what<u>ever</u> saunters up to the table, with six miles of thick black hair swinging in her wake like a goddamn Vidal Sassoon commercial. She's in white linen Armani head to toe (with nary a wrinkle in sight—how do you wear linen and stay neat??? Forget that I'm in stained polyfuckingester). She also has generous (fake, but well-done) cleavage on display, legs up to her earlobes, and exquisite Chanel shoes. I, of course, am in Target flip-flops, because I, of course, am taking my kids to the beach, because I, of course, am a stay-at-home mom who only wipes chocolate-chip pancake from her breasts . . . not BRENT'S DROOL.

But it wasn't her slightly slanted ebony eyes that worried me, or her perfect, puffy hooters, OR her $428 shoes (they were in the Bergdorf flyer I got in the mail last week). No, it was that itty bit of *nervousness* that got me. You know—the way she *didn't* have extended eye contact with Brent. The way she didn't check me out too long and too hard. Like I might figure out something was going on if she did. And when Lily said how much Heather looked like Pocahontas from the

Disney movie, Brent laughed and said, "See? What did I tell you?" WHAT did he tell her? That she looked like Pocahontas? Or that Lily was precocious???? WHAT DID HE TELL HER? And when? And what the hell did it have to do with Resort Sales??? He shouldn't have inside jokes with co-workers and minions. Just me.

Anyway, she strolled away in her really fine, covet-worthy mules, hair swinging, butt swinging, fake boobs not swinging—but only after she informed Brent that his presence was required at a very, very important meeting that could take a big chunk of the day. Evidently, the convention planners from the Dry Cleaners Association of America are in town, and they want to be sure the two thousand Dry Cleaner owners arriving next month for the great Dry Cleaners of America Annual Convention will be well serviced by the Grand Regent Miami Beach. Brent is needed to ease their fears. I am left to wonder if any of them could get chocolate out of polyfuckingester.

Anyway, he disappeared. Forever. He came back to the room at 6:00, informed me that he had to take the client to dinner, of course . . . I understood, right? Couldn't I come, I ask? I mean, Amber, I know a little about a client dinner. I can talk business. I understand trade shows. I surely have been in a few dry cleaners in my day.

No. Not appropriate, he informed me. No spouses—at least the dry cleaners didn't have theirs, so it would be awkward. WHAT? Like I'm going to put on a Public Display of Affection and make them all wish they had *their* wives at the table?

Then I did it. Oh, yeah. Really sealed the deal on NO SEX FOR THE WEEKEND. "Is Heather going to be there?" I asked. And there was not one molecule of sweetness or even anything vaguely neutral in my tone. In fact, I squirted a good amount of venom into those six words. Okay, honestly? I hissed them. As much as you can hiss a sentence with only one "s" in it.

The resulting argument was not pretty. He stormed out at 7:00 and came home at . . . 2:00. He slept in one of the double beds in the kid's room—they were snuggled up as usual in one bed. I got up at dawn—having slept, oh, five minutes total. When I looked in, Brent opened one eye, which I greeted by giving him the finger (I didn't want to wake the kids, yet needed my message to be exceedingly clear), and left to hit the gym. But some fat guy's on the treadmill and I just had to talk to you, so here I am venting on the Grand Regent computer system. About the future CEO.

You want to know the really scary thing? I almost wrote to Tom. Almost. Then common sense punched its way through my blanket of misery and I emailed you instead.

I don't know what's going to happen today. Brent's not supposed to have any work commitments this afternoon. We're supposed to spend the day poolside, then get a sitter and have dinner. Won't that be fun?

I hope your Saturday date was better than mine. How were Mr. and Mrs. Cald-something? The symphony? The stupid comments? Are you taking him to Bud's BBQ tomorrow? Any word from Painter Boy? Are you feeling better? I don't know when I'll get back on a computer—I don't dare write on Brent's laptop. We'll be home late Mon. afternoon.

xoxox

Stevie the Scorned

TO: beantownbud@bostonbeerdistribution.com <bud fleece>
FROM: foreveramber@quicklink.com <amber fleece>
SUBJ: BBQ
DATE: Sunday 9/05 11:00 AM

I tried calling you at home this morning but someone else answered. *Ahem,* Dad. You'd kill me for that. Anyway, *she* told me you went into work, but I don't want to bug you if you're crunching numbers or something equally scary. I still feel pretty lousy. I went out last night and coughed all over my date and his parents. Ruined the symphony for hundreds of people, including myself. Anyway, I'll let you know if I feel better. But now, I think I'm going to pass on the BBQ.

Love.

Amb.

TO: foreveramber@quicklink.com <amber fleece>
FROM: grayscale@connectone.com <gray mcdermott>
SUBJ: i want your number
DATE: Sunday 9/05 2:30 PM

hi, toots. i tried to im you last night, but you must have been having too much fun on your date. i stayed home all night, just thinking of you. imagining what you wore, how you laughed. he's one lucky son of a bitch, this date of yours. i was alone, sort of. mick was sleeping and dix was out. i wanted to call you, but i don't have your number.

send it to me, okay?

gray

TO: willie542@quicklink.com <william desmond>
FROM: juliedes@connectone.com <julie desmond>
SUBJ: Help me, honey
DATE: Sunday 9/05 3:43 PM

Hi, Willie. Your line has been busy all day—so I guess you are on the computer. This one seems to be working fine, by the way. Thanks for setting it up for me. Are you still going to come over for Labor Day? It's only an hour's drive—and I can cook and you can take home whatever is left over. You can bring your laundry, too—how's that for a bribe? Sorry I missed your call the other night. I've been working late. My job is wonderful, but a bit overwhelming. My boss was sick this week, so I got a little behind.

Anyway, that's not the reason I'm writing. See the subject line above. I've been giving you advice for a long time, sweetheart, and now I need some. Remember how I told you about the baseball player "from my past" that I have been in touch with over the internet? Well, he's invited me to see him. Maybe spend a weekend at his cabin in the mountains of—goodness, I don't even know where! I guess South Carolina. Are there mountains there? Anyway, I know it would be "legitimate"—I'm not about to get involved with anyone. But, I'm really not so sure about this.

What do you think?

Love you, sweetheart.

Mom

TO: foreveramber@quicklink.com <amber fleece>
FROM: beantownbud@bostonbeerdistribution.com <bud fleece>
SUBJ: RE: BBQ
DATE: Sunday 9/05 4:10 PM

Don't give me this keg of BS, Amber. Are you really sick or maybe you just don't want to meet Alice? You better be at the barbeque and bring that jell-o thing. Red—not green. I hate green jell-o. Come on, honey, it just ain't Labor Day without you. Give her a chance. Give ME a chance.

I love you.

Dad

TO: grayscale@connectone.com <gray mcdermott>
FROM: foreveramber@quicklink.com <amber fleece>
SUBJ: my number
DATE: Sunday 9/05 4:58 PM

Oh, hell, Gray, you've had my number since I was 14. My *phone* number is 617-555-8849. But why do you want to call me? Phone sex?

TO: foreveramber@quicklink.com <amber fleece>
FROM: caldingerc@troyhillinvest.com <chet caldinger>
SUBJ: how are you?
DATE: Sunday 9/05 6:04 PM

How are you feeling, Amber? Guess it's fair to say you really "choked" when meeting my parents. Don't worry—Mother and Dad thought you were really nice and they didn't mind that we had to leave the symphony early. Mother said you reminded her of Julia Roberts in that movie where she wants to marry the gay guy. Did you see it? Do you still want to go to the barbeque at your father's house tomorrow? I cleared my calendar for it. Email me at the office—I'm working on a hostile takeover bid we're doing next week and the switchboard is off.

Chet

TO: wonderwoman@usol.com <stephanie hilliard>
FROM: foreveramber@quicklink.com <amber fleece>
SUBJ: Miami (ad)vice
DATE: Sunday 9/05 8:15 PM

I know you're not home yet, but I have to write. Eesh—the whole Heather the Harlot thing sort of reeks—but *was* H the H there for his client dinner? As I recall, Brent has never responded well to—what did he call them when you were in labor—histrionics? My advice: Don't push it. It will blow over.

The Chet date was fine, except I can't get rid of this effing cold and I got one of those dry, sticky, knife-like scratches in my throat as soon as the first violin screeched at Symphony Hall and

I all but had to be escorted out with the cough. His parents are as conservative as he is, but Dad has a (real) sense of humor and Mother (yes, he calls her that) is kind of sweet, which I have to say, since she compared me to Julia Roberts. It must be the curly red hair. Not really red. My hair's more like . . . mahogany, don't you think? Anyway, here's my real problem . . . Gray.

I can't stop thinking about him. I am literally aching to see him, to talk to him, to be with him. He got me online at 3:00 in the morning two nights ago and—oh, sheez, Stevie, he still gets me going—even over the internet. I can't imagine what he could do to me in person. What do I do? Take Chet to my dad's BBQ and act like I like him? I *do* like him. He's nice. He's normal. He has great potential. He could be the husband I've not so secretly yearned for. I just don't want to have sex with him. I'd rather plant myself in front of a computer screen and fantasize about a painter who might live in a trailer park than take the Harvard grad who really wants to go to the BBQ. What is wrong with me???

I'm going to take a ride. I need to get out. You know what? Gray taught me this silly game a long time ago. I close my eyes in the car (not while moving ☺) and hit a radio button. Whatever song comes on, that's going to be the advice I'll heed. The name of the song is telling me what to do, what's going to happen. This scientific method of fortune-telling and decision making is obviously open to a wide range of interpretation, which is why I like it. You should try it with your Heather situation. Consult the Radio Oracle.

Hope today was a day at the beach for you. Literally and figuratively.

Love.

Amber

foreveramber@quicklink.com: grayscale@connectone.com is sending you an Instant Message on Sunday 9/05 at 11:05 PM:

grayscale: tell me you're online and make me happy.

foreveramber: I'm online. Not too happy, Gray. No graphic e-foreplay, please.

grayscale: okay, i promise. how do you feel?

foreveramber: Sick. Scared. Confused.

grayscale: talk to me, toots.

foreveramber: I'm in avoidance mode. Trying to avoid going to my dad's house tomorrow. Trying to avoid going to that stupid doctor next week. Trying to avoid you.

grayscale: don't do that, baby. don't do any of those things. why don't you want to go to your dad's house?

foreveramber: It's complicated.

grayscale: and the doctor?

foreveramber: More complicated.

grayscale: what's going on with your health?

foreveramber: Absolutely nothing. I told you I hate doctors. Guess what I did tonight?

grayscale: read the lhs yearbook?

foreveramber: It's at my dad's house or I would. I did take a long drive down memory lane, however.

grayscale: walden pond?

foreveramber: Of course. Walden Pond. And when I got there, I just sat in my car and tried to shake you out of my system.

grayscale: shake me all you want. but not out.

foreveramber: Well sorry, it worked. You have been exorcised. Gone from my life. Goodbye Gray. Hello—

grayscale: what's his name?

foreveramber: I can never remember! (Just kidding.) It's not about him. It's about you. I played the radio game.

grayscale: i still do that, too.

foreveramber: Cheap therapy, you used to call it.

grayscale: i taught it to mickey—we play it all the time.

foreveramber: It makes driving an adventure. It also always makes me think of you.

grayscale: best part. so . . . what did the radio oracle say?

foreveramber: Honest? First song was "Chasing After Waterfalls."

grayscale: meaningless. did you try another station?

foreveramber: Oldies. I got "Baby Don't Get Hooked on Me." So there.

grayscale: you scanned, i hope.

foreveramber: Yes. "Rock Your Body."

grayscale: the oracle has spoken.

foreveramber: No, it wasn't valid because it took three tries and a commercial. Anyway, I don't need the radio to tell me what to do. I can't do this, Gray.

grayscale: do what? be my bud?

foreveramber: It's frustrating.

grayscale: hang with me, baby. i don't want to make promises that i don't know for sure i can keep. but i'm working on it. does that help?

foreveramber: A little. What are you "working on"?

grayscale: too complicated. you have to trust me.

foreveramber: *You* have to trust *me*. Tell me.

grayscale: not yet.

foreveramber: Gray. I don't want this. I want REAL.

grayscale: i want real, too, baby. go listen to the radio. right now. then tell me what song is on. i will, too. we'll abide by the radio oracle.

foreveramber: You're crazy.

grayscale: for you. go turn on the radio.

foreveramber: Okay. I'll use the clock radio by my bed.

grayscale: is your computer in your bedroom?

foreveramber: Yes–about two feet away from my bed.

grayscale: convenient for cyber-sex.

foreveramber: And for waking up for middle of the night IMs–I hear the ding. Wait a sec.

foreveramber: You lose . . . first song I found: "Who's Sorry Now?" The Oracle has spoken. What did you get?

grayscale: "you take my breath away." so true, toots. so true.

foreveramber: I'm listening to my Radio Oracle, not yours. I don't want to be the one who's sorry now.

grayscale: i don't want you to be either.

foreveramber: Good. Then we agree on that. I have to go–I need to get an email out before it's too late.

grayscale: anybody special?

foreveramber: Could be.

grayscale: tell him hi.

TO: caldingerc@troyhillinvest.com <chet caldinger>
FROM: foreveramber@quicklink.com <amber fleece>
SUBJ: Barbeque Tomorrow
DATE: Sunday 9/05 11:37 PM

Hi there. Anyway, sorry it took so long for me to get back to you—hope you get this email tonight. If not, I'll call you tomorrow. I'm definitely feeling better. Come on over at 11:00 if you still want to get fried at Bud's Annual Labor Day Bash.

Amber

TO: willie542@quicklink.com <william desmond>
FROM: juliedes@connectone.com <julie desmond>
SUBJ: I'm sorry
DATE: Monday 9/06 6:21 PM

Will! I'm sorry you got so upset about this conversation. I had no idea you would look at things like that. But, honey, I have to tell you—you're acting like your father when you run away when you have to talk about something you don't like. Okay, now I understand your feelings about my going to see this man in South Carolina. I don't agree, but I understand. And I know in your heart you think I should still be with Daddy. But, honey I'm not and I'm happier for it. Believe me. And you have to remember—just because I'm your MOTHER doesn't mean I shouldn't have a life. I'm 45 years old, Will, as you like to remind me. I'm not ready to give up and die.

I can see some of the points you made. I don't know anything about him, really. I don't think he's the mad rapist or serial killer you made him out to be. But maybe you're right. Maybe I am a little old to be traipsing around cabins with strange men. And, as you say, what the heck do I know about fly-fishing? I don't even know what it is. Anyway, I just hate that we had a fight. Sweetheart, I've had so many of them in my life and I don't want to fight anymore. But I also don't want a man—any man, even the one I brought into this world and raised—to tell me what I can and can't do. I'm going to think about it, that's all. Call me when you get a chance. And come back and get the rest of this coconut cream pie before I eat it.

Love,

Mom.

PS. Your darks were still in the dryer when you huffed out. I folded them and put them in the laundry room in case you come by while I'm at work.

TO: wonderwoman@usol.com <stephanie hilliard>
FROM: tmark@quicklink.com <tom markoff>
SUBJ: Labor Night
DATE: Monday 9/06 7:30 PM

There's no heart on my computer. ☺ I gave your email address a little heart and it's noticeably absent all weekend from my buddy list. I saw on your cover note that you were headed to Miami for the weekend (always accountable, like a good consultant) and that just left me to imagine you topless on South Beach. So, for sheer distraction, I read the rest of your memo recapping what the aviation experts think of WWA's lofty plans.

Not too much, as you so succinctly put it. We'll have to design a killer ad campaign to change their minds, or make a compelling argument that WWA should drop the whole program and save money and misery. I liked your comments about the trends toward comfort—you've always had a great take on the pulse of America. That's why you're so good at advertising.

Fact is, Stephanie, you're so good at everything. The whole report reminded me of why you were such a high flyer at the agency. You're way too talented to be holed up in Orlando changing diapers. Maybe this taste of real life will lure you back permanently.

Not that agency life is any great shakes these days. GW is still an asshole who thinks "creative" means a unique way to play with numbers so the ink on the P&L statements is black. Therefore, Becker's boneheads in finance are still way too involved in account decisions. And that bitch Reinhardt needs Xanax in her coffee. I've been trying to figure out all weekend what possessed me to move back to Boston and re-enter the halls of Millennia Marketing.

It wasn't <u>just</u> because of you. ;-) Or even the chance of you. I guess I was trying to recapture that feeling we had in the old days. You remember that sense that we could conquer the world (if not each other). I just can't seem to get that anymore. The world just doesn't seem worth conquering anymore—and I hate losing that feeling. If I don't feel like I can get on top of the world, then what the fuck am I doing? My kids are gone. When Casey left for college, it was really a blow. I can't believe he's gone. My wife lives on another planet and I sure as hell am an alien there. My job doesn't get me up anymore. So don't blame me for thinking about how you look in half a bathing suit at the beach. (What color?) Hope you thought of me when you rubbed that sunscreen on your . . . self.

Sorry for the self-indulgent diatribe. Just looking for a pal to talk to tonight. Check in tomorrow when you're back.

T

TO: foreveramber@quicklink.com <amber fleece>
FROM: beantownbud@bostonbeerdistribution.com <bud fleece>
SUBJ: You're a good girl
DATE: Monday 9/06 9:22 PM

Hi honey. I don't want to call and bother you so I thought I'd just turn on my computer here and hope you read your email tonight or tomorrow morning. Everyone left a little after you did and Alice helped me get everything cleaned up before she left, too. (She DOESN'T live here, you know.) I hope you had a good time. Your jell-o thingy was exactly like your mom made it—perfect. Alice says she wants the recipe. I saw you two having a nice little girl chat before dinner. Hope you like her as much as I do. I know this isn't that easy for you, honey. But I like her and I want you to, too.

Chet seems like a real nice guy. Tries a little too hard, but that's not the worst thing in the world. A real Republican, too. Didn't know they grew those at that school. Anyway, I just wanted to tell you I sure am proud of you and that I hope you do something about that cold. Even Doris and George thought you looked kind of pale and I want you to be peachy like you always are.

I love you, honey.

Dad

TO: tmark@quicklink.com <tom markoff>
FROM: wonderwoman@usol.com <stephanie hilliard>
SUBJ: crises—mid-life and others
DATE: Monday 9/06 11:33 PM

Oh my, Tom. I think I sense a massive, classic, straight-out-of-the-movies MLC coming on strong. You have ALL the signs, you know. Dissatisfaction with life. Distance from spouse. Frustration with career. Empty nest. Lust for co-worker. (Well, you've had that one for a while—that's a lifelong, not mid-life, crisis.) Seriously, Tom, about the only thing you haven't done is gone out and bought a bright red sports car. I've heard this passes in a few years, so hang on and don't do anything stupid. I'm happy to be your pal—honored, in fact.

We had a lovely time in Miami. Perfect weather. Children were blissfully well-behaved. Suite was luxurious. Spa treatments were delicious.

Oh, fuck. Why am I lying? WE did not have a lovely time. WE fought and fumed and slept in separate beds. See, Tom? Nobody's life is a rose garden. We all have some thorns.

What is it about you and colors? It's because you're so visual, I guess. Mr. Creative Director wants his model in the right color tankini. It was turquoise. With gold clasps at the hips (for fast and easy removal). And, yes. My thoughts meandered, along with my fingers.

xoxo

Stephanie

PS. Sorry for the tease. You sound like you could use a smile. And a little heart on . . . your computer.

wonderwoman@usol.com: foreveramber@quicklink.com is sending you an Instant Message on Monday 9/06 at 11:52 PM:

foreveramber: Hey, Stevie. You back from Miami yet?

wonderwoman: I'm home, Auntie Em. There's no place like it, even if it is Azure Lakes in Orlando. It is home. I was just writing to Tom.

foreveramber: Oh really? Kind of late for a quick WWA update, isn't it?

wonderwoman: I was responding to his email.

foreveramber: What did he want?

wonderwoman: Oh, any form of intercourse, I think. Social or otherwise.

foreveramber: Steve, ya gotta tell me THE TRUTH. Did you do him?

wonderwoman: No. That's the truth. Almost, damn near, really wanted to, but didn't.

foreveramber: I can believe the really wanted to part. He's a hottie—great shoulders.

wonderwoman: And the cutest ass in advertising, as I recall.

foreveramber: And those really smoldering, come-to-papa eyes.

wonderwoman: And what a mouth! Oh, the places it could go, the things it could do.

foreveramber: You've been reading WAY too much Dr. Seuss.

wonderwoman: Sorry. And we better stop this discussion pronto. He's already yanking my chain without me knowing how good he looks at the other end. We're married. And not to each other.

foreveramber: Speaking of . . . did you manage to dump Heather the Harlot in the pool or at least leave SUV tire tracks on her cool shoes?

wonderwoman: We only fantasize about these things. She effectively wrecked my weekend, though. Which I capped off on the ride home with the announcement that I was working for Tom Markoff as a consultant.

foreveramber: Whoa. What did he say?

wonderwoman: Sadly enough, nothing.

foreveramber: Nothing? He didn't have any thoughts about you working?

wonderwoman: Just that I should be careful not to let it interfere with the kids (let's forget the fact that he spends 200 days a year on the road). No comment on Tom.

foreveramber: Maybe he doesn't remember him.

wonderwoman: Oh, he remembers him. I just think he might have felt it was a case of the pot screaming at the kettle about its coloring.

foreveramber: Want to know about the barbeque?

wonderwoman: Of course! How did we manage to get this far without talking about <u>you?</u>

foreveramber: I was wondering that myself.☺ Anyway, it was okay. I met Alice Ellis. It's her married name. She's divorced.

wonderwoman: What's she like?

foreveramber: She's not my mother, that's for sure. But let's not go there. She's about 50, blond and bland. Nice. Actually, really nice. Let me see . . . I'll go with Florence Henderson–ish.

wonderwoman: ☺

foreveramber: My dad seems happy, the old coot. Made his world famous BBQ sauce with chocolate and beer (of course, beer's free) and he had a little sparkle in his eye. Then again, the sauce was kind of spicy, so who knows?

wonderwoman: He deserves to be happy, too, Amb. How many years has it been?

foreveramber: Fourteen. Well, 13 years, 8 months and 16 days. I'm pathetic, huh?

wonderwoman: You're normal. And not wanting Bud to get remarried is normal. Although, tell him the advice from *this* side of the fence is to just move in together and have fun. Marriage sucks.

foreveramber: No way, woman. You are NOT steering this back to you. I haven't told you about Gray.

wonderwoman: Gray? What about Chet?

foreveramber: Chet who?

wonderwoman: LOL!! You're the one who can't remember his last name.

foreveramber: What can I say? He's forgettable.

wonderwoman: And Gray?

foreveramber: *Un*forgettable. *Un*believable. *Un*imaginable. *Unattainable*.

wonderwoman: Any more info on his living situation?

foreveramber: He says "he's working on it" and then deftly changes the subject and has me teetering on the edge of a whomping orgasm.

wonderwoman: REALLY???

foreveramber: Damn near. It's just that he *knows* me so well. Anything he says goes straight to my heart.

wonderwoman: Sounds further south to me. I might have to try that.

foreveramber: Tommy, can you hear me?

wonderwoman: I was thinking I'd borrow Gray. ☺

foreveramber: Nope. That boy is all mine. And Dixie's. And Mickey's. Oh, what the hell. Have a piece.

wonderwoman: Are you in tomorrow?

foreveramber: Tomorrow, yes. Wednesday, I have a doc's appt.

wonderwoman: Another one? What's the matter?

foreveramber: Nothing. Just routine shit. Making up for years of never going to a doctor. Anyhoo, email me at work tomorrow and I'll tell you what Tommy's wearing.

wonderwoman: Not interested. Well, maybe a little interested. Oh, hell. Take a picture and download it to me.

foreveramber: There you go. All you need is that and . . . your imagination and you are in business.

wonderwoman: In trouble, more like.

foreveramber: You're just flirting with him. (RIGHT???)

wonderwoman: Yes. Flirting with **disaster**.

foreveramber: And Tom would go down faster than the Titanic.

wonderwoman: Very funny. Bye!

TO: wildthing@usol.com <john rush>
FROM: jdesmond@millenniamarketing.com
SUBJ: Your invitation
DATE: Tuesday 9/07 8:45 AM

Good Tuesday morning to you, John. Hope you had a nice Labor Day weekend. Sorry to hear your team is out of the running. I wanted to write to you sooner, but I had a very busy weekend. Well, to be perfectly honest, I took a little time to consider your offer. While it sounds really lovely and I'd like nothing more than to learn to fly-fish (!!), I'm really new on my job and any time off right now would be difficult. There are other reasons, too, but I won't bore you with them. I'll just take a pass for this season. Of course, there's always next year—as they say in baseball!

Take care,

Julie

TO: gwycoming@millenniamarketing.com <gabriel wycoming> jbecker@millenniamarketing.com <jerry becker> tmarkoff@millenniamarketing.com <tom markoff>
FROM: areinhardt@millenniamarketing.com <adele reinhardt>
SUBJ: WWA Initial Aviation Experts Report
DATE: Tuesday 9/07 10:15 AM

Good morning, gentlemen! Hope you all are geared up for our busiest season as things really pick up in the fall. It all kicks into high gear now! I spent the weekend reviewing all of our clients' status reports and P&L statements. Good news, Gabe—profits are up, losses are down!

I also reviewed the report filed by the outside consultant Tom hired, Stephanie Hilliard, for the World Wide Airlines account. I have to admit I was most dismayed by the findings, as well as the presentation. Clearly, it is Stephanie's opinion that World Wide Airlines is making a grave mistake with the new Luxury Line program and she has cleverly supported her position with quotes from aviation experts who agree. I am most concerned that while this is an internal document, should it find its way into the hands of any of our key client contacts at WWA, we could be accused of not playing by "their rules" on "their team." THEY are the client! This program is their strategy and our job is to create the most effective way to communicate and SELL this program to the flying public.

I urge you to reconsider the opinions and quotes put forth in this document. I believe it should be shredded and deleted from our server before someone, somewhere accidentally leaves it on a conference room table at WWA and it costs us the account! That would be tragic! Especially since the views it contains are not those of Millennia Marketing, but an outside consultant.

Looking forward to your feedback.

Adele

TO:	gwycoming@millenniamarketing.com <gabriel wycoming> jbecker@milleniamarketing.com <jerry becker> areinhardt@millenniamarketing.com <adele reinhardt>
FROM:	tmarkoff@millenniamarketing.com <tom markoff>
SUBJ:	RE: WWA Initial Aviation Experts Report
DATE:	Tuesday 9/07 11:01

Sorry, guys, but there is nothing in the *Advertising Handbook From God* that says we have to agree with our clients' marketing strategies. On the contrary, a good ad agency challenges the entire marketing department—and, yes, the Board of Directors—of any client. It's our job to guide them to market EFFECTIVE, PROFITABLE services and programs. This is a business, Adele, not a social function. To that end, I submit that the independent third-party consultant we have hired is doing us and the client a huge favor by saving them millions of dollars before they introduce the next New Coke. Our role is to make sure they understand the impact their ideas and plans will have on their customers.

If the aviation experts who are masters in demystifying the habits of the flying public think that Luxury Line is a big, bad, stupid mistake, then it is incumbent on us to make sure the client knows that. That's our job: Counseling the client from a marketing standpoint. That counsel should be sound and based on intelligence and market information. Information, I might add, that we have BILLED THEM to gather.

Isn't that our job?

Or . . . maybe I'm wrong. Maybe our job is to "YES" the client to death and raise our profits and lower our losses. If it is, we are guilty of short-term thinking and wearing blinders and every other cliché you can dream up. Gabriel, I'd be interested in your take.

Tom

shilliard@millenniamarketing.com: tmark@quicklink.com is sending you an Instant Message on Tuesday 9/07 at 12:15 PM

tmarkoff: Steph?

shilliard: I'm here. Where are you?

tmarkoff: W8ting room–GW's office. Thumbing u on PDA

shilliard: I got your email. Thanks for the heads up. He called you in, huh? Think he'll take Adele's side?

tmarkoff: fuck her

shilliard: Maybe he does.

tmarkoff: GW doesn't think w/ his dick. Becker is staring at my hands–thinx this is a gameboy–call u l8r.

shilliard: Be careful. They already think we're in bed together.

tmarkoff: we shud be.

shilliard: It's just an expression. Good luck. xoxo

TO: afleece@millenniamarketing.com <amber fleece>
FROM: shilliard@millenniamarketing.com <stephanie hilliard>
SUBJ: G-dubs office—NOW
DATE: Tuesday 9/07 12:18 PM

Hey, if you get this message, go run down to GW's office and sniff around.

xoxo
S

TO: shilliard@millenniamarketing.com <stephanie hilliard>
FROM: afleece@millenniamarketing.com <amber fleece>
SUBJ: RE: G-dubs office—NOW
DATE: Tuesday 9/07 1:00 PM

I sniffed and it *stank*! Woowee, baby, what gives? Becker was in there, as was Eva Braun, and, of course, Tommy Boy (wearing jeans—nice—and a scowl). Door was closed; could see through the blinds in the glass. Had to linger at Karen Z's desk for a while (as if she didn't know what I was up to) and OF COURSE, Dwayne Gossipmonger came by, also sniffing for trouble. But, bless his heart, he gave more information than he got. Told me a bit about memos flying between his boss and Tom—evidently der Fraulein is most unhappy with your work. More later.

Love.
Amber

TO: WWA Account Team (All)
FROM: gwycoming@millenniamarketing.com <gabriel wycoming>
SUBJ: WALK THIS WAY, BOYS AND GIRLS
DATE: Tuesday 9/07 2:12 PM

I want to be sure everyone on this account gets this message, straight from me. This is ALL I want anyone at this agency to do EVERY SINGLE DAY:

1) Understand our clients' markets as well as, if not better than, they do.
2) Create advertising that sells their product and services.
3) Make a profit.

After much consideration of the debate that raged in my office earlier, I have come to the conclusion that we are doing all three for WWA. If their decision to launch Luxury Line folds because we have given them wise counsel, then they will be a longER term client than if they launch it, it fails, they file Chapter 11, and they don't pay us the millions they incurred to advertise it. Therefore, I am issuing the following directives to the entire account team:

- Continue to conduct the research.
- Do not sugarcoat any findings.
- Use the information as the underpinnings of our marketing and advertising recommendations.
- Abide by the client's final decision—and if it is to

continue with the LL program, then create the best damn advertising campaign imaginable.

- Ensure our creative, media buy, and supporting services result in a substantial profit for Millennia.
- Play nice with each other.

Got it, gang?
gw

TO: shilliard@millenniamarketing.com <stephanie hilliard>
FROM: afleece@milleniamarketing.com <amber fleece>
SUBJ: gw's missive
DATE: Tuesday 9/07 2:33 PM

Score one for Tommy Boy. Eva is laying low. GW went out to lunch with Becker. Cube walls everywhere are vibrating with gossip. Ha. Ha. Ha. Write.

Love.
Amber

TO: afleece@millenniamarketing.com <amber fleece>
FROM: jdesmond@millenniamarketing.com <julie desmond>
SUBJ: tomorrow's schedule
DATE: Tuesday 9/07 4:20 PM

Just in case your meeting with the Media Director goes late and we miss each other, I wanted to remind you that you have a 9:00 AM appointment with Dr. Salomon, the Ear, Nose and Throat specialist. I will log all Traffic Jobs in a separate email and I will follow up on copy and art deadlines for all. I know that the Berkshire Hills Spring Water magazine ad is very late and I assure you I'll courier that finished art to *Boston Magazine* before the deadline. There are two clients in tomorrow, so I will "pester" (as you would say) the AEs for conference reports and follow up on the open jobs for the week.

Now, all you have to do is see the doctor, get a clean bill of health, and come in when you can. Keep your cell phone on, though, in case an emergency arises.

Good luck—

Julie

PS. I don't need any now, honestly, but I was just curious . . . when am I eligible for a vacation day? I'm just thinking ahead to the holidays. Thank you and feel better.

Julie

TO: tmarkoff@millenniamarketing.com <tom markoff>
FROM: shilliard@millenniamarketing.com <stephanie hilliard>
SUBJ: thank you
DATE: Tuesday 9/07 5:15 PM

I got your voicemail and of course read GW's memo. I was in the car line for kindergarten pickup when you called. (Don't tell anyone.) Thanks for going to bat for me, Tom. I know you feel strongly about the principle of it all, but I also know you would just as soon shrug your shoulders and say, "Who cares." So, I appreciate your support of my work. And guess what? I talked to an aviation consultant today who supports the idea. They are out there, I'm sure. Just let me dig them up. Ooohh—my little natives are getting restless and I'm about to hit the pool to cool them off. Hmmm . . . maybe I shouldn't have said that. Okay, okay. White, but one piece. Dreadfully conservative.

xoxo

Stephanie

TO: wonderwoman@usol.com <stephanie hilliard>
FROM: tmarkoff@millenniamarketing.com <tom markoff>
SUBJ: one piece white conservative . . . mumble, moan ;-)
DATE: Tuesday 9/07 6:00 PM

Why do you do this to me? I know what happens to a white bathing suit when it gets wet.

Yeah, we kicked Reinhardt's skinny ass today, but GW's definitely getting more from her than status reports, so be careful. I love going to bat for you, but I did feel strongly about this one, too. I have to feel strongly about something, right? Otherwise, what is there to live for?

Well, there is the image of you in the pool with your kids. I bet every time you reach up to toss the beach ball in the air, a little more cleavage shows. Then you dunk yourself and your hair gets wet and your suit turns transparent and your nipples pop up like cherries on a sundae.

Great. I finally found something to live for, and it's killing me.

T

TO: wonderwoman@usol.com <stephanie hilliard>
FROM: foreveramber@quicklink.com <amber fleece>
SUBJ: HE CALLED!!!!!!!!!!!!!!!!
DATE: Tuesday 9/07 9:17 PM

OH MY GAAAWWWWWWD. Gray called me. At 9:01:34 PM. Stevie, you would simply collapse in a heap if you could hear his voice. It is so sexy, so low—how can I describe it? Warm and soft, like velvet. Sleek and cool, like satin. A whisper of ice, like silk. Even a little rough, like burlap. And his laugh? Oh, a gentle rumble from his chest that makes me quiver and shake. Here's what he said: (I've listened to it a few times <g>)

> "Hey, toots, where are ya?" [No comment on the toots, okay? He calls me that. Sometimes he calls me "tootsie." Once in a while, "tootsie girl." Cute, huh?] "It's Tuesday night, I think. Must be, 'cause I'm home and I don't have a gig. I'm tryin' to write songs, but there's a wall up between me and the right words. I was hopin' you could help me climb it. [Slight rumbly laughter here. Ooh.] Anyway, I'll call you later. Oh . . ." [Another rumbly laugh, a little deeper, even sexier, if that's humanly possible.] " . . . I like that message. A little off-center. Like you."

I know I am behaving EXACTLY like a 14-year-old. But I can't help it. He does this to me. He does things to me. He makes my heart clutch and my blood sing and my throat ache. I have to go listen to it again.

Love.

Amber

TO: foreveramber@quicklink.com <amber fleece>
FROM: wonderwoman@usol.com <stephanie hilliard>
SUBJ: The Material Man
DATE: Tuesday 9/07 10:15 PM

Silk, burlap, satin, AND velvet? He's a one-man fabric store. And I thought your throat ached cause you're sick. ☺ I'm glad he called. I'm glad he makes you feel like you're about to fall off a ten-story building. Great feeling, isn't it? But I don't get the subterfuge. He's not *married* and neither are you. (Note to self: Married people should not be falling off ten-story buildings with other married people.) Seriously, why can't you just call him or why can't he call you anytime or WHY can't he get on a plane and go up there and see you? There's got to be more to the Dixie thing than he's telling you.

What a day at the asylum, huh? I never talked to Tom, but he left a voicemail and quite the, uh, graphic email. Haven't heard a peep from der Fraulein. But Tom is utterly convinced that she and GW are doing deeds of all sorts. You must get the scoop on this. Ply Dwayne with alcohol, if necessary. Befriend him.

I know you have a dr. appt. tomorrow, which you are handling like the big, brave tootsie roll I know you are. Let me know how it goes.

xoxox
Stevie

wonderwoman@usol.com: tmark@quicklink.com is sending you an Instant Message on Wednesday 9/08 at 12:24 AM

tmark: You there, beautiful?
wonderwoman: Hi. ☺ I'm reading the London *Times*.

tmark: What is it with you and newspapers?

wonderwoman: It's an addiction. Beats drinking and gambling, don't you think?

tmark: Addictions can be dangerous. I know. I've got one.

wonderwoman: What is it?

tmark: More like WHO is it.

wonderwoman: Ah. Yes. I got the cherry sundae email.

tmark: Yep. But you didn't write back.

wonderwoman: Still recovering. Anyway, I'm busy.

tmark: Kids? Hubby?

wonderwoman: Baking.

tmark: <choke of disbelief>

wonderwoman: I bake quite well, thank you very much. I'm taking some cookies into k'garten tomorrow. I'm the Room Mom. So there.

tmark: Why does that thrill me?

wonderwoman: Because you're pathetic.

tmark: Good. Apathetic is what scares me. What's the kindergarten occasion?

wonderwoman: Wednesday. That's enough of an occasion for most 5-year-olds. Has it been that long since you've been around kids?

tmark: Yes. Speaking of that, Casey called from Amherst. Having some trouble.

wonderwoman: With school? Girls?

tmark: Binge drinking.

wonderwoman: Ouch. Has he?

tmark: No. But his roommate went to the ER Saturday night. He's fine, but Casey's smart enough to be scared.

wonderwoman: Jeez. That is horrible. What did you tell him?

tmark: Stop when you're drunk, it doesn't improve after that.

wonderwoman: Good advice. Kind of makes me want to run upstairs and hold Declan while he's small.

tmark: You better do that, sweetheart. They grow fast. One day, Casey was riding a tricycle. The next day he was 10 years old and playing Little League. About a week later he was driving and four minutes after that he went to college.

wonderwoman: Really? It feels like Declan's been two for a decade.

tmark: That's just 'cause you're in the moment and you're there with him. I missed most of Casey's childhood. I was with clients and art directors and media sales reps.

wonderwoman: And account executives.

tmark: That wasn't work. But trust me, being a parent is the biggest job of your life and then, wham, it's over just when you think you might know what the hell you're doing.

wonderwoman: Did you talk to your wife about Casey's problem?

tmark: Oh, Jesus. No. She'd freak out and drive up there every weekend, breathalyzer in hand. Casey and I handle things without getting her too involved. She tends to overreact.

wonderwoman: That's just a mother's love.

tmark: You're sweet to defend her.

wonderwoman: It's the least I can do, considering how badly I flirt with her husband.

tmark: Not badly at all, actually. Is that what this thing between us is–a flirtation?

wonderwoman: There's no *thing* between us.

tmark: If only that were true.

wonderwoman: It's just a game, Tom. We're both married.

tmark: If this is a game, I'm losing.

wonderwoman: How so?

tmark: I can't tell you.

wonderwoman: ????

tmark: Really, I can't.

wonderwoman: You can tell me anything, Tom. I won't judge you. I won't hold you accountable. What do you mean?

tmark: I love you.

tmark: You there, sweetheart?

wonderwoman: I'm here. I'm stunned into finger paralysis and can't type. Better stick with the nipple descriptions, Tom. You don't love me—you have lust for my memory. But you don't really know <u>me</u> anymore.

tmark: You are so wrong. I loved you furiously ten years ago. It was a crush for you, I knew that. But not for me. I loved you then and I love you now.

wonderwoman: Don't do this, Tom. It's wrong.

tmark: Feeling this way isn't wrong. I won't talk you into anything. I won't ask to see you or act on these feelings. But I'm telling you the truth.

wonderwoman: Don't say it again.

tmark: Not saying it doesn't make it go away. I do. I love you.

wonderwoman: I don't know what to say. You haven't seen me in years, Tom. I'm a different woman. Maybe you thought you loved me back then, but you don't now.

tmark: Different, yes. Probably even better. And, honey, I didn't THINK I loved you. I burned for you. I thought about you morning, noon, and night. I made love to you a thousand times. And I will again tonight.

wonderwoman: You definitely have . . . a heart on your computer. You've got to get over this.

tmark: No. It's not a heart on or a hard-on. It's not just about sex, Stephanie. I want you to know that.

wonderwoman: Then, what's it about?

tmark: You are the most beautiful woman I ever met in my whole life. You are alive, alert, and humming with vitality. You make me want to be next to you just for the electrical charge of it.

wonderwoman: Stop.

tmark: I want to kiss you, and taste all that life and force and power that is you.

wonderwoman: Stop!

tmark: I want to be inside of you, Stephanie Walker. I want to feel all that energy wrapped around me.

wonderwoman: STOP. You are making me sad.

tmark: Sad? You're breaking this copywriter's heart. I wasn't going for sad, sweetheart.

wonderwoman: I just want my husband to feel that way, that's all.

tmark: Oh. Well, he does, I'm sure. He's just too stupid to realize it.

wonderwoman: No argument from me. I've got to go now. Don't tell me that again, Tom.

tmark: How 'bout if I just say this . . . ILY. Will you understand?

wonderwoman: I'll never understand. For some reason, it really amazes me. I think we better go back to discussing what I'm wearing. It's more . . . safe.

tmark: I don't want to be safe. I want to be dangerous.

wonderwoman: You are. Bye Tom.

TO: jdesmond@millenniamarketing.com
<julie desmond>
FROM: foreveramber@quicklink.com <amber fleece>
SUBJ: Wednesday stuff
DATE: Wednesday 9/08 8:05 AM

Hey Jules. I'm just about outta here for el doctoro—see? I didn't forget. Thanks for your memo—I know everything is in good hands. PLEASE don't forget about the spring water ad for *Boston Magazine* or else we'll lose the discount and the client will have a cow. One other favor—can you call Dwayne Gallagher, Adele's admin assistant, and set up a lunch or breakfast with me? I'll be in as soon as possible. I hope I don't have to sit for two hours in the waiting room with all the other sick people. Not that I'm sick, mind you.

Vacation? Are you out of your mind? I'd die. ☺ Just kidding. Let me know what you need and you can have it. Got any special plans? We'll talk when I get in today. Thanks.

Love.

Amber

TO: WWA Account Team (All)
FROM: areinhardt@millenniamarketing.com
<adele reinhardt>
SUBJ: Going Forward!
DATE: Wednesday 9/08 9:14 AM

Good morning, gang! Just like our client says, "Let Your Dreams Take Flight!" In fact, that's exactly what I did. I dreamed about the WWA account last night—I hear you all laughing, but it's true! And, as they say, the most creative ideas are born in the night. I think I gave birth to one last night, and I'd like to have a meeting this week to discuss my concept for the ad campaign. I've reserved the conference room for Friday at 3:00—we'll go straight through to the TGIF party that is scheduled in there at 5:00. All account team members are requested to be there—including a traffic representative and the outside consultant. (Phone is okay, Stevie—we know you have the kiddies to watch.)

In addition, I'd like to start the process of scheduling a day-long account meeting. And for that one, no bodies on the phone—everyone should be in the room. Dwayne Gallagher will be calling each of you with optional dates in the next few weeks. In this case, everyone's presence is mandatory.

So be there and let's fly!!

Adele

TO: afleece@millenniamarketing.com <amber fleece>
FROM: caldingerc@troyhillinvest.com <chet caldinger>
SUBJ: Whassssup?
DATE: Wednesday 9/08 9:59 AM

Hey, funny face! Just finished a mega presentation for the hostile takeover and, man, I was . . . hostile. Listen, I'll be down in Back Bay around 11:30 today and I'll stop by and we can go to lunch today.

Chet

TO: tmarkoff@millenniamarketing.com <tom markoff>
FROM: shilliard@millenniamarketing.com <stephanie hilliard>
SUBJ: Is she serious?
DATE: Wednesday 9/08 10:40 AM

Friday at 3:00??? And a mandatory in-person meeting sometime in the next few weeks? Help me, please. I hate her. I think I just lost ALL the notes from that *one* consultant who supported the client's position. :-P

xoxox
Stephanie

TO: afleece@millenniamarketing.com <amber fleece>
FROM: grayscale@connectone.com <gray mcdermott>
SUBJ: which doctor is the witch doctor?
DATE: Wednesday 9/08 10:55 AM

hey tootsie girl. i know you're not there and can't respond. you are somewhere in that mess of doctors offices by brigham and women's, aren't you? i remember taking my brother to the er there once. my dad beat the crap outta him and i really thought he was going to die. wish i could sit with you and make new memories. anyway, just wanted to let you know that i'm thinking about you. i know you hate this, but whatever ails you, they can make it better. and if they can't, baby, i can. i want to call you tonight. will you be home? i need to hear your voice.

gray

jdesmond@millenniamarketing.com: wildthing@usol.com is sending you an Instant Message on Wednesday 9/08 at 11:06 AM :

wildthing: Hi Julie . . . Are you on line?

jdesmond: Oh! John? Is that you?

wildthing: Don't tell me you've never done this before, either. (Hah, hah.)

jdesmond: I'm not an IM virgin, honestly.

wildthing: If we had this thirty years ago, who knows what would have happened to us.

jdesmond: ☺ How are you?

wildthing: Shi . . . lousy. Hah!! Seriously, I was trying to respond to your last email and kept getting stuck, so I decided to try this.

jdesmond: What were you getting stuck on?

wildthing: How to convince you to change your mind.

jdesmond: You've always had trouble there.

wildthing: ROFLMAO.

jdesmond: Now I'm dense. What does that mean?

wildthing: Rolling on the floor laughing my ass off.

jdesmond: Oh. Well, sorry, but you better get up and accept NO for an answer. I'm not coming to South Carolina.

wildthing: No.

jdesmond: Excuse me?

wildthing: I don't like that call, ump.

jdesmond: How about . . . Not now.

wildthing: Getting better. How about . . . when?

jdesmond: I just don't know, John.

wildthing: It's more than vacation time stopping you, I can tell. I'd like to hear about it.

jdesmond: Do you have an hour? A day?

wildthing: I have a weekend and I'm offering it. But let's just start with a few minutes right now. What's up?

jdesmond: I can't get into it now. I have a department to run now. Well, I'm not really running it, but my boss is out and I don't want to mess up.

wildthing: Gotchya. Just gimme the highlights. Are you scared of . . . making the trip? Discovering something new? What your friends would say? Seeing me???

jdesmond: All of the above. ☺ But not my friends, my kid.

wildthing: Since when do kids get an opinion?

jdesmond: Since he could talk.

wildthing: I hate that about kids. Listen—I can't do anything about your son, but I can tell you for sure and certain that you would have fun, fly-fishing is totally relaxing, and I won't do anything to scare you. Any other problems?

jdesmond: I just don't know, John. A lot of time has passed. I don't wear hot pants anymore. I get hot flashes.

wildthing: Hah! I don't match my baseball card anymore. You're worrying about the wrong things, Julie.

jdesmond: Give me some more time to think about it, okay?

wildthing: Whatever you need. Hell, I've waited 25 years. What's another few weeks?

jdesmond: You're sweet. I better go now. Goodbye!

wildthing: So long, Strawberry.

TO: wonderwoman@usol.com <stephanie hilliard>
FROM: hilliardb@grandregenthotels.com <brent hilliard>
SUBJ: FYI
DATE: Wednesday 9/08 1:15 PM

Hi—I tried calling but I can't understand anything that woman who now answers our home phone is saying. Apparently you are on the other line, so maybe you'll get this email. I know I thought I'd be home this week, but the guys from London who are looking at the Colorado Springs property are flying in tonight and I have to go out there. This is a big deal, Stevie, or I wouldn't go. We need to unload that resort property if we're going to make our numbers this year. I'll send a messenger home around 5—can you throw some clothes and my toilet articles kit in my bag for me? I'm flying out tonight with Alex and he wants to go over some other issues in the limo on the way to the airport, or I'd stop home myself. I'll call you late tonight or tomorrow. We'll talk this weekend. Promise.

Love ya,
Brent

TO: shilliard@millenniamarketing.com <stephanie hilliard>
FROM: tmarkoff@millenniamarketing.com <tom markoff>
SUBJ: She is serious . . .
DATE: Wednesday 9/08 2:41 PM

. . . about making our life hell. Starting with a 3:00 meeting and ending with her idea of *creative*. Can't wait for that. You'll have to bring that duct tape out again. Listen, are you around tonight? I want to call you when fire-breathing Account Execs aren't lingering around my office. Lemme know what time is good.

T

TO: jdesmond@millenniamarketing.com
<julie desmond>
FROM: foreveramber@quicklink.com <amber fleece>
SUBJ: today
DATE: Wednesday 9/08 3:23 PM

Guess you figured I'm not coming in by now. Dr. took longer than expected. Email me at above address if the sky is falling down. Otherwise, I'll talk to you tomorrow. I'm tired.

Love.

Amb.

wonderwoman@usol.com: foreveramber@quicklink.com is sending you an Instant Message on Wednesday 9/08 at 3:30 PM

foreveramber: Steve, are you there?

foreveramber: Come on . . . I want to talk to you. You must be on the MM email and I don't want to IM you there. I'm supposed to be home sick. And tired. Which I am, but I wanted to talk to you. Anything new? I don't even want to log on to work. Okay, the truth is . . . if I log onto my work email, then I can't get IMs from my housepainter. Who wouldn't IM me anyway, because he thinks I'm at work. Eesh. Write me later, 'kay? Love. Amber.

beantownbud@bostonbeerdistribution.com: foreveramber@quicklink.com is sending you an Instant Message on Wednesday 9/08 at 3:39 PM

foreveramber: Daddy, are you around?

foreveramber: Are you on your computer, Daddy?

caldingerc@troyhillinvest.com: foreveramber@quicklink.com is sending you an Instant Message on Wednesday 9/08 at 3:47 PM

foreveramber: Hi Chet–are you there?

caldingerc: I stopped by your office but you were out.

foreveramber: I had a dr. appt. I told you on Monday.

caldingerc: That's okay. I ran into some old Harvard buddies in the lobby of your building and grabbed a bite with them. I'm in the middle of something now. Can I call you later? Are you at work?

foreveramber: No. I stayed home.

caldingerc: I'll get back to you. This is time-sensitive.

foreveramber: Okay. Bye.

grayscale@connectone.com: foreveramber@quicklink.com is sending you an Instant Message on Wednesday 9/08 at 3:55 PM

foreveramber: Gray . . . are you home?

grayscale: hi toots–you're back. been thinking about you. how did it go? did you get my email?

foreveramber: Yeah. That was nice. I couldn't wait until tonight. Call me now, okay?

grayscale: oh shit, i just can't. can't i call you later?

grayscale: are you still there?

grayscale: come on, amber.

foreveramber: Yes, I'm here. I just had to take a phone call for a minute from my office.

grayscale: is that the truth?

foreveramber: No, you brat. It's not.

grayscale: i'll call you later, okay? about 9 tonight.

foreveramber: I should be good and drunk by then.

grayscale: what's the matter, baby? please tell me what the doctor said.

foreveramber: Nothing that I effing understood. Nevermind. I'm just being melodramatic about your sporadic attention.

grayscale: nothing sporadic. you're on my mind 24/7. i'm a walking case of blue balls.

foreveramber: ☺ Glad to know I can still tighten you up.

grayscale: woman, you have no idea. i'll call you tonight. be there, okay?

foreveramber: We'll see.

grayscale: you gonna be online for a while? i gotta do soccer practice, but i'll be back in about an hour or so.

foreveramber: Maybe. I want to run some searches on Google. You can check. Bye.

grayscale: don't work too hard, toots. save your energy for my phone call.

foreveramber: ☺

TO: hilliardb@grandregenthotels.com <brent hilliard>
FROM: wonderwoman@usol.com <stephanie hilliard>
SUBJ: traveling plans
DATE: Wednesday 9/08 4:25 PM

Fine.

TO: tmarkoff@millenniamarketing.com <tom markoff>
FROM: shilliard@millenniamarketing.com <stephanie hilliard>
SUBJ: Calling
DATE: Wednesday 9/08 5:37 PM

Don't call tonight. I promised my husband some quality time tonight. Talk to you tomorrow.

Stephanie

TO: foreveramber@quicklink.com <amber fleece>
FROM: jdesmond@millenniamarketing.com <julie desmond>
SUBJ: End of day wrap-up
DATE: Wednesday 9/08 6:00 PM

Hi Amber, I'm sorry the doctor's appointment took so long. Attached as a separate document is a complete status of all open jobs and what happened today. Three notables:

1) Chet Caldinger came by to take you to lunch. I guess he forgot you had a doctor's appointment. Was not happy. ☹

2) I couldn't get lunch with Dwayne Gallagher but he suggested something after work tomorrow at 6:00. Does that work for you?
3) Adele Reinhardt called a meeting for Friday, September 10 at 3:00 to discuss her creative ideas with the WWA account team.

Everything else is in the attached memo. Made the *Boston Magazine* deadline with at least twenty minutes to spare. Oh! One more thing. Someone from the financial department stopped in here looking for some profitability reports you promised Mr. Becker. I found them and printed them out for him—hope that's okay. Get well soon. Do take that wellness herb I gave you. I promise it works. Hope to see you tomorrow.

Take care,

Julie

TO: jdesmond@millenniamarketing.com <julie desmond>
FROM: foreveramber@quicklink.com <amber fleece>
SUBJ: update
DATE: Wednesday 9/08 6:02 PM

Hey Jules, you put the Wellesley grads to shame, you know that? Thanks for everything. I haven't gone over the status report, but I will. I'm sure you did everything right. Good GOD I forgot about that report for Becker. Thank you for covering my a**. I do not mind AT ALL. I can't believe the Nazi Reinhardt (sorry—hope you're not offended by that way politically incorrect reference) called a meeting for 3:00 on Friday. What a jerk. Poor Stevie—her house is a zoo at that time. Anyway, as always, you rule the world. What about that vacation time? I'd love to help you out if you need something special.

Love.

Amb.

TO: foreveramber@quicklink.com <amber fleece>
FROM: jdesmond@millenniamarketing.com
<julie desmond>
SUBJ: vacation time
DATE: Wednesday 9/08 6:10 PM

Thanks for all your kind words about my work. That means the world to me. About the vacation time . . . I'll talk to you about it tomorrow, okay? I could actually use your advice on something.

Thanks,

Julie (or, as you would say, Jules. ☺)

foreveramber@quicklink.com: wonderwoman@usol.com is sending you an Instant Message on Wednesday 9/08 at 8:45 PM:

wonderwoman: Amber, if you're not there, I'll kill you.

foreveramber: ME? Where the hell have you been all day?

wonderwoman: You only sent me one IM. I've been in WWA hell, then spent the afternoon in Lily's class.

foreveramber: Really? How was it?

wonderwoman: No different than a staff meeting. Only the kindergartners are slightly more mature than the copywriters.

foreveramber: How was my Lily-putian?

wonderwoman: Wonderful. Bright. The Queen of the Kindergarten.

foreveramber: The Queen gene—also dominant.

wonderwoman: ☺ She's a lot like me, but she's got a lot of Brent in her, too. His good qualities. (Give me a minute to think of one.)

foreveramber: Where is he tonight?

wonderwoman: Hear me seethe.

foreveramber: Spill.

wonderwoman: Colorado Springs. Oh, God, Amber. I did a bad thing.

foreveramber: What???

wonderwoman: Promise you won't make fun of me and tell me what a loser I am?

foreveramber: Loser? You've never lost anything in your life. Come ON, Stevie. What did you do????

wonderwoman: I called Heather the Harlot's office to find out if she was in town tomorrow.

foreveramber: Well, duh. I'm sorry I didn't think of it myself. And, well . . . ?????

wonderwoman: She's fucking in fucking Colorado fucking Springs.

foreveramber: Hopefully, not fucking.

wonderwoman: I took care of that. I packed his toilet articles kit. Can you believe the condoms fell out? They were only in there for our romantic weekend in Miami, so it doesn't matter that I forgot to repack them . . . *right*????

foreveramber: You be bad. Still, you don't have hard evidence. Just circumstantial. I'm not a lawyer, but that's just not enough to indict and hang the guy. He's always been madly in love with you, Stevie. Remember how he cleaned bird shit off your car one day when he left our office after a meeting? Bird shit!! With his monogrammed hankie, no less. I tell you, the man loves you.

wonderwoman: So does Tom Markoff. At least, he said so.

foreveramber: WHOA! Are you kidding me? Did he say that?

wonderwoman: Yes.

foreveramber: Was he serious?

wonderwoman: Please. You're talking to a page in his textbook mid-life crisis.

foreveramber: I'm just stunned. He said that? "I love you"—that?

wonderwoman: Yes. They're just simple throw-away words.

foreveramber: No one has ever said them to me.

wonderwoman: No one? Ever? I don't believe it. Not one of your boyfriends?

foreveramber: A few have uttered similar sentiments between gasps and grunts of the less emotional kind, but no. No one has ever said they loved me. I'm a love virgin.

wonderwoman: I can't believe that.

foreveramber: You've probably heard it a dozen times.

wonderwoman: A few, but it only mattered when Brent said it in front of 250 people and a priest. That's the one that counts the most, right?

foreveramber: So they say. But can we get back to Tom and how he told you this?

wonderwoman: That's not like you . . . wanting to talk about *me*. What's the matter? How'd the doctor go?

foreveramber: Fine. I'm just fascinated that Tom Markoff is in love with someone a thousand miles away. Not that you're not fabulous, Stevie, cause you're hot and fun and adorable and smart. But in a radius of, oh, six feet around him, you can, at any given time, find a woman who would drop trou at the mere raise of one of his perfectly formed eyebrows.

wonderwoman: Amber, HE'S MARRIED.

foreveramber: Not very happily, it would seem.

wonderwoman: What's going on with our country songwriter?

foreveramber: Smooth subject change. He wants to call me tonight and have phone sex.

wonderwoman: Funny, so does Tom.

foreveramber: He does phone sex?

wonderwoman: Not yet. But the I love you's could start popping up, and then you know what will pop up, too.

foreveramber: It always does. Do you love him?

wonderwoman: Good God, no. I like flirting with him. I like thinking about him. I like the way he makes me feel and, yes, I like playing around in my mind with him. I *love* Brent. And I don't want to cheat on him. Regardless of what he's doing with the Harlot. I don't want to break my vow to him. Phone sex is adultery.

foreveramber: Is computer sex adultery?

wonderwoman: e-dultery.

foreveramber: But I'm not married. So I might do it some time.

wonderwoman: Oh, God—my business line is ringing. I bet it's Tom. I told him I was spending Quality Time with Brent tonight. How's that for a big fat lie? Should I answer?

foreveramber: You're not going to believe this. My computer says I have a call coming in from Dallas. I *am* answering.

wonderwoman: What should I do?

foreveramber: Charge ten dollars for the first minute, $1.50 for every minute after.

wonderwoman: Very funny. Hey Amber, one thing before you go. . . .

foreveramber: What?

wonderwoman: *I* love you.

foreveramber: ☺ You don't count, but I love you, too.

TO: wildthing@usol.com <john rush>
FROM: juliedes@connectone.com <julie desmond>
SUBJ: Why I'm Not Sure
DATE: Wednesday 9/08 10:18 PM

Hi, Johnny. I've been thinking about your IM all day today—and all night. This is the empty nest syndrome, I guess. Thinking about myself too much now that my chicken has flown the coop. I want to throw caution to the wind, and be perfectly honest with you about why I'm not coming to visit you. Yes, my kid would give me a hard time. And, yes, I worry that I'm not the "hot chick" who sat in the bleachers and flirted with you 25 years ago. Remember that game when you relieved in the 12th inning—and won!? I was so proud of you—but I couldn't cheer for the wrong team in the middle of all those Pirate fans. But I remember the way you grinned at me when you came off the mound. You touched your hat, like a little salute. And, honest to God, it felt like the first dip on a wild roller coaster ride.

Sorry . . . took a little sidetrip down memory lane. But, anyway, I'll tell you the truth. Bear with me. I'm not a great writer. Especially about things that are hard to say. My marriage was really . . . bad. Not at first, but as the years went on, it sunk to a really low place. The worst part about it, John, was that I let it go on. I let myself be cheated on. I let myself be verbally—and, one time, physically—abused. I thought I was doing the right thing. I wanted to keep my family together. I wanted my son to have a father. I wanted to appear happy to the world.

Of course, that was a stupid mistake. But leaving my husband was difficult. Very, very difficult. Since you've been through a divorce (or two), you know. One of the things my husband took from me—besides 23 years of my life—was my self-confidence. I'm out here in the world, kind of on my own for the first time, and I'm trying to—believe it or not—figure out who I am. And I'm not the pretty 20-year-old flirting with the relief pitchers in the bullpen anymore. I've seen those guys on TV—they look like my son. ☺ So, I have lots of things "stopping" me from saying yes to your offer of a weekend. My job, my son, myself.

But I don't know if I'll feel that way forever. For instance, when I started my job, I was terrified. I'm still a little scared every day, but I'm starting to really get the hang of it. And with that self-assurance, I can feel little bitty changes starting inside of me. Maybe it will be that way with a man, too. And if it is, then hook me up a line, 'cause I want to learn how to fly-fish.

Thanks for understanding.

Take care,

Julie

TO:	foreveramber@quicklink.com <amber fleece>
FROM:	wonderwoman@usol.com <stephanie hilliard>
SUBJ:	Après my call
DATE:	Thursday 9/09 11:10 AM

Yes, I took the call. No, he did not say the deadly words—I think he knew I wasn't ready to *hear* them. And no erotica was exchanged. He just . . . made me laugh. Told me all these things he remembers about working together. Honestly, I can't believe the details that man has in his head. Said I hung around his thoughts all day like an essence. Warned me that he wasn't going to go away. Made me feel sexy and alive and tingly.

When I got off the phone, I tried to call Brent's room in Colorado Springs, but the operator wouldn't put calls through and his cell is turned off.

So, I wish I felt guiltier, but I don't. Still, I just tiptoed into the kids' rooms and kissed their sweaty little heads. Gotta keep *my* sweaty little head on straight, don't I?

xoxox

Stevie

TO: wonderwoman@usol.com <stephanie hilliard>
FROM: foreveramber@quicklink.com <amber fleece>
SUBJ: Après *my* call
DATE: Thursday 9/09 12:15 AM

Here's my version: Yes, I took the call. No, he did not say the words I'd love to hear. Erotica exchanged? His *voice* is erotic. His choice of words—not as smooth as Tom's, but genuine. And his laugh! Just the sound of it sends sparks through my entire body. What can I say? The guy turns me on. Yes, he's a painter. Yes, he writes country music. Yes, he lives with a woman named Dixie and seems to love a child who's not his. Yes, his dysfunctional family screwed him up and made him bitter. Yes. Yes. Yes.

I swear at this moment, I don't care. The "must haves" on my boyfriend list seem . . . optional. Anyway, Gray's not lifetime material. At least, I wouldn't think so.

Glad you hang all over Tommy Boy like an essence. (Jeez, sorry, but there's something so perfume ad–like about that.) Now, I'm going to bask in the afterglow of a man who makes me forget the things I don't want to think about.

Love.

Amber

TO: foreveramber@quicklink.com <amber fleece>
FROM: grayscale@connectone.com <gray mcdermott>
SUBJ: what she didn't say
DATE: Thursday 9/09 3:33 AM

---

i'm playing every word over in my head . . . she said she wants to see me, i just teased her heart instead . . . i know i made her laugh and i think i made her cry . . . i wish i understood why . . . so i'm rewinding all the words like an instant replay . . . it's not just what she said, it's what she didn't say . . . that's what's got me wondering . . . what she didn't say.

TO: shilliard@millenniamarketing.com <stephanie hilliard>
FROM: dgallagher@millenniamarketing.com <dwayne gallagher>
SUBJ: Onsite WWA Meeting
DATE: Thursday 9/09 9:21 AM

Well hello, Mistress Stevie—how are you? Nice to see your name on MM letterhead again. Remember me? Dwayne Gallagher (previously of the mail room, then flunkie in creative, ended up working for Madame Reinhardt). Here's your morning wake-up call: Schedule me, girlfriend. My boss (who's in Dolce today—eggplant and buttercup yellow—you'd looooovvvvve it) is calling all WWA birds to the nest for La Meeting Extraordinaire. I'm getting your engraved invite early, since you are one of lucky few who have to make travel plans. Pick a day and let me know which one works for you:

- Tuesday, September 21
- Friday, September 24
- Monday, September 27

Those are the ONLY days Adele has open for the next few weeks, so write back ASAP before I alert the rest of the team.

D-Gall (that's my white rapper name ;-))

TO: tmarkoff@millenniamarketing.com <tom markoff>
FROM: shilliard@millenniamarketing.com. <stephanie hilliard>
SUBJ: Conflicts
DATE: Thursday 9/09 9:30 AM

As you know, I have some conflicts. ☺ Conflict du jour involves this all-day WWA meeting. I can't make any of the proposed dates, Tom. For the first two, my husband's out of town and I don't have sleepover help. I assume Lily and Declan are not invited to the meeting. September 27 is a conflict. Plain and simple. You said "no travel"—those were your words. I have it in my contract/letter. NO TRAVEL. I'm not leaving my family for this client or any other one. I'm not leaving my family for any amount of money. And I'm certainly not leaving my family to sit at the well-shod feet of Adele Reinhardt and pay tribute to her. Work this out for me, okay?

xoxo

Stephanie

TO: shilliard@millenniamarketing.com <stephanie hilliard>
FROM: tmarkoff@millenniamarketing.com <tom markoff>
SUBJ: No conflicts, baby
DATE: Thursday 9/09 9:44 AM

Whoa, girl. I'll handle it. But I was kind of looking forward to seeing you.

T

TO: afleece@millenniamarketing.com <amber fleece>
FROM: beantownbud@bostonbeerdistribution.com <bud fleece>
SUBJ: How ARE you?
DATE: Thursday 9/09 11:15 AM

Hi honey! You still haven't called me since you had that doctor's appointment yesterday. Didn't you get my message? I saw that one insta-box or whatever it's called from you on my computer yesterday, then nothing. Is everything okay? What did that doctor say?

Please call me, honey.

Dad

TO: caldingerc@troyhillinvest.com <chet caldinger>
FROM: afleece@millenniamarketing.com <amber fleece>
SUBJ: Missed you yesterday
DATE: Thursday 9/09 12:20 PM

Hi Chet—Hope you got through your time-sensitive issue okay. Sorry again about the mix-up yesterday—I'm around next week.

Lunch?

Amber

TO: beantownbud@bostonbeerdistribution.com <bud fleece>
FROM: afleece@millenniamarketing.com <amber fleece>
SUBJ: Don't *worry*
DATE: Thursday 9/09 1:00 PM

Dad, you are an old worrywart, you know that? I have a cold! This doctor was as stupid as they all are and wants to cover his malpractice butt and send me to someone else. It's NOTHING, I promise. I'm reallllly busy today—I'll call you tonight. How's Alice? ☺

Love.

Me

TO: shilliard@millenniamarketing.com <stephanie hilliard>
FROM: hilliardb@grandregenthotels.com <brent hilliard>
SUBJ: travel schedule
DATE: Thursday 9/09 2:29 PM

Hey Stevie, I got your voicemail. I'm between meetings and I only have a sec. On my calendar, I have meetings on the west coast that whole week of Sept. 20—you've known about them for a while. So you cannot be out of town then. I can be in town on the 27th, if it's drop-dead important. But isn't that Lily's field trip? I thought you mentioned that to me. And I'm not crazy about Rosa staying overnight with the kids and I haven't even met this other woman you use during the day. I can't understand her on the phone, so I sure as hell don't want her sleeping at our house. I thought you said no travel. Anyway, we'll work it out. Promise.

I'll be home tonight around 10.

Brent

TO: afleece@millenniamarketing.com <amber fleece>
FROM: grayscale@connectone.com <gray mcdermott>
SUBJ: amber at work
DATE: Thursday 9/09 4:37 PM

spent the day high on the resonance of our talk last night. i got thinking about you at the office, imagining the people you talked about last night, the way you work. hope you don't mind me invading your desk like this. i like thinking about how you look with your hair pulled back and wearing some hot-for-teacher glasses. wish i could lock you in your office for an hour or two.

i know what you were trying to say about how we said goodbye that summer after high school. you thought it was for good. forever. but i just wanted to come back into your life as a better man. i didn't know if that meant success in music or what, but i wanted to be worthy of you. at that point in my life, i was so beaten—literally and figuratively—that i didn't know the meaning of worthy. i'm just learning it now.

you know, toots, much as i want to, i don't have to see you to absorb your nonverbals. i hear that little drop in your voice when i talk about painting, or raising someone else's kid. you don't quite get it. but that's okay. but sometimes, i hear something else in your voice. and i'm gonna keep calling and calling just to hear it. you know what it is? that little catch in your throat when i say your name or when i surprise you with something. i love that sound. it's the sound of surrender. the sound of a little bombshell exploding in your heart. the sound of how you felt . . . and feel . . . about me.

i love that sound. i'm living for it these days.

gray

TO: shilliard@millennniamarketing.com <stephanie hilliard>
FROM: afleece@millenniamarketing.com <amber fleece>
SUBJ: Heads Up, Hitler
DATE: Thursday 9/09 4:20 PM

Oh, baby, Eva Braun is on a tear. Dwayne just stopped over here to confirm after-work drinks (see, I always do what you ask) and told me that Adele and Tommy Boy are going at it but good over there in account management. Think I need to grab a soda and scope it out. What gives? It's about you—that much I got out of Dwayne. At least your name has been mentioned a few times, from what he was able to hear. Will keep you posted.

Love.

Amber

TO: WWA Account Team
FROM: dgallagher@millenniamarketing.com
<dwayne gallagher>
SUBJ: All Account Status Meeting—MANDATORY
DATE: Thursday 9/09 5:11 PM

The All Account Status Meeting is confirmed for Monday, September 27, starting at 8:30 AM SHARP in the Four South Conference Room. Attendance is mandatory. All account team members are expected to prepare PowerPoint™ presentations on the following:

AGENDA

- Opening and Welcome (Adele Reinhardt)
- Initial Market Analysis (Stephanie Hilliard)
- Customer Segmentation (John Bruchalski)
- Budget Considerations (Bob Jenner)
- Preliminary Creative Concepts (Tom Markoff/Adele Reinhardt)

BREAK

- Media—Broadcast and Print (Gary Mierzwicki and Jeff McGee)
- Supporting Public Relations (Dianne DelVecchio)

- Direct Mail (Clayton Cooper)
- Traffic and Timelines (Amber Fleece)
- Creative Brainstorm (All—Led by Adele Reinhardt)

TO: shilliard@millenniamarketing.com <stephanie hilliard>
FROM: tmarkoff@millenniamarketing.com <tom markoff>
SUBJ: conflicts
DATE: Thursday 9/09 5:15 PM

How the hell did she get that email out in the time it took me to walk back to my office? Honey, I'm sorry. The best I could do was get her to agree that you could leave mid-afternoon, that way you don't have to stay Monday night. I could only fight so far, Stephanie. This is a huge account—and you have no idea what is going on with a couple of others. Not the time to mess with an eight-figure budget like WWA. You can come in late Sunday and be home by dinner Monday night. (Or come in early Sunday and go out and play with me.) You do have to be at the meeting.

Nobody else can fill your stilettos, baby.

T

TO: afleece@millenniamarketing.com <amber fleece>
FROM: shilliard@millenniamarketing.com <stephanie hilliard>
SUBJ: I QUIT
DATE: Thursday 9/09 5:30 PM

Does that woman get EVERYTHING she wants? I am NOT coming to that meeting. Did you see when I'm scheduled? Eight fucking thirty, of course. So I HAVE to fly in the night before. And leave before the brainstorm, of course. She doesn't want my IDEAS. Oh fuck fuck fuck! Amber. That's the day of Lily's FIRST field trip—all the way to Kennedy Space Center. And they are carpooling! I don't want her in a car with some other mother and four other screaming 5-year-olds driving from Orlando to Cape Canaveral!!! I want to be with her! Brent said he could go—but what are the chances?!?! He'll have to be at an emergency meeting somewhere for something! Oh, look at me and my exclamation points. I'm as bad as Adele. Damn Tom Markoff for not getting me out of this. I just don't think he *tried* that hard. I think he wants me there. I think he thinks I'll be all his on Sunday night. He just hasn't fought as hard on this one. Ooh—you're calling me on the other line.

xoxox

Steve

TO: afleece@millenniamarketing.com <amber fleece>
FROM: jdesmond@millenniamarketing.com <julie desmond>
SUBJ: Evening Wrap-up
DATE: Thursday 9/09 5:45 PM

Amber—you're still on the phone, but I have to leave before 6:00 tonight. I'm starting a step aerobics class! Attached is a full Traffic Report for tomorrow's open jobs. I added the WWA meeting on Sept. 27 to your calendar. A couple of open items:

- Don't forget drinks tonight with Dwayne. He's meeting you in the lobby at 6:00 (HURRY UP).
- Mary Beth from Dr. Phillip Grossman's office re-

> garding a referral for consultation. I told her your calendar was really tightly booked for the next few weeks, but she insisted on *now*. They want to see you at 1:30 tomorrow afternoon and she was not taking no for an answer. I know you have a WWA meeting at 3:00. Want me to cover it for you? I don't know if you can be back here if you have a doc appt. at 1:30. They're always running late. Let me know.

That's it—except to say thank you for talking to me today. I feel sort of silly telling you about this baseball player, but you really said a few things that make me think harder about saying no. You're sweet to say I still look good—it's so weird. I don't feel like I'm about to turn 46. I still feel like a young woman. Then I catch myself in the mirror from behind, getting into the shower. Is that MY rear-end? Would I show that to . . . a man? ☺ Anyway, you are such a wonderful, loving girl for listening and, of course, making me laugh. Thanks and I certainly have a lot to think about. Now I better get my sagging butt to my aerobics class—just in case I do go to South Carolina. ☺ Take care, Jules

---

TO: wonderwoman@usol.com <stephanie hilliard>
FROM: foreveramber@quicklink.com <amber fleece>
SUBJ: Don't Quit—It's just getting interesting
DATE: Thursday 9/09 9:40 PM

Sorry I didn't get back to you. Had to barhop with DWAYNE, thank you very much. The man is so GAY. I don't care that he's gay. I like gay. He wears great clothes and actually appreciates the value of a good wax job. (Bikini, not car.) But he wanted to go to all these boy hangouts and I finally ditched him around 9:00 . . . *someone* could be IMing me and I'd miss it!

Listen, Tom *did* fight for you. Dwayne told me everything. Here's Gossipmonger's take on it: She's HOT for Tom. Big time. The thing with GW? Looking like a slowdown. Apparently they have been doing it, but Adele is getting bored. GW is such a scumbag, isn't he? I mean, his wife is like Madame Social Butterfly, running every do-good operation in Back Bay, and he's puttin' it to Adele Effing Reinhardt. I ask you . . . WHAT is wrong with men? Anyway, she and GW are fizzling. At least, they are ever since Tom got back to MM. I would never have picked this up—she's so bossy and bitchy around him. Doesn't she know he goes for sweet and soft, and *wonder*ful? Perhaps she does. And if she can't screw him, she'll screw you. It seems the more he goes to bat for you, the harder she digs in her J-Choos (knock-offs, by the way, according to Dwayne) and refuses to cooperate. That's all I got from Dwayne. He was more interested in the ink job on something named Ginger. I kid you not.

About the WWA meeting on the 27th . . . if you want to blow this whole deal, well, I guess I don't blame you. Who cares about all this garbage anyway? Yes, I work hard and I want to get ahead—but, really, to what end? For a bigger apartment so I can have more room to wander around BY MYSELF? You already have it all, Steverino. House, husband and precious rats on the rug. Count your blessings, not your money. I know I tease you about Tom and how hot he is—but you're better than all that. I hope you're making up with Brent this very minute. Oh! Incoming call . . . Dallas? Damn. No. Chet what's-his-name. ☹ Well, write me later.

Love.

Amber

wonderwoman@usol.com: tmark@quicklink.com is sending you an Instant Message on Thursday 9/09 at 11:01 PM:

tmark: I have a heart on . . . my computer.

wonderwoman: I knew you were going to IM me tonight.

tmark: Still speaking to me?

wonderwoman: No.

tmark: I love it when you play hard to get.

wonderwoman: Not hard. Impossible.

tmark: Listen, I tried.

wonderwoman: You didn't tell me Adele had the hots for you.

tmark: Please.

wonderwoman: Is that denial? Or just cocksure arrogance?

tmark: She's a star fucker–don't you know that? She worked her way up the executive ranks and I'm the flavor of the month. Not interested. Becker can have her next.

wonderwoman: Hah! Becker Has No Pecker. Haven't you heard?

tmark: Oh? So that's a calculator in his pocket every time he looks at her?

wonderwoman: Him, too? Does this woman elicit agency-wide boners or is this phenomenon limited to the executive ranks?

tmark: Not agency-wide, I assure you. Are you jealous?

wonderwoman: Please.

tmark: Is that denial or just cocksure arrogance?

wonderwoman: The ice on which you skate is damn near see-through, Markoff. Don't fuck with me tonight.

tmark: Oh, honey, don't I wish.

wonderwoman: Don't flirt with me, either.

tmark: Okay, you win. What's the matter?

wonderwoman: Besides the meeting conflict?

tmark: Stephanie, I know you well enough to know that's not a conflict for you. You've made your decision about going to or blowing off the meeting, and whatever it is, you'll stick with it. What's <u>really</u> wrong in your perfect life?

wonderwoman: You're right about the meeting, except I haven't decided yet. And you're right about . . . other problems.

tmark: I'd like to help.

wonderwoman: You're *not* helping, Tom. You're making things worse.

tmark: How?

wonderwoman: If I tell you I'm *underappreciated* at home, I think my husband is cheating on me, and I don't feel sexy anymore . . . would I sound like a cliché?

tmark: You don't feel sexy??? You <u>define</u> sexy.

wonderwoman: You didn't answer my question.

tmark: Who cares if it's cliché, your feelings are real. Anyway, you're asking a man you've already diagnosed with a case of mid-life crisis, speaking of clichés.

wonderwoman: ☺ At least you know it has an end point. Don't most men outgrow the MLC by 50 or so?

tmark: Five more years of this? Good Christ, I'll never survive. But, wait . . . back up to earlier comment. I knew Hilliard was an asshole the first time I met him. A company man to the core. He's cheating on YOU?

wonderwoman: I like the emphasis there. You're not shocked he's *cheating*—just on me.

tmark: All guys cheat, baby. Wake up and smell the sheets.

wonderwoman: Do you? Did you? Have you? How many times?

wonderwoman: Tom?

wonderwoman: This is taking too long. Do you need Becker's calculator to add them all up?

tmark: I'm thinking about how to answer this. Define cheating.

wonderwoman: <eye roll> Define evasion.

tmark: Seriously. Is it breaking a promise?

wonderwoman: Having sex outside of marriage.

tmark: What is marriage? A promise?

wonderwoman: Where are you going with this?

tmark: My wife cheated first. Years ago when she broke the promise of marriage.

wonderwoman: She cheated on YOU? (Note emphasis.)

tmark: Noted. ☺ In a sense, yes, she cheated on me. She promised to love, honor, and cherish, right? She stopped having sex with me six months after Casey was born. No love. No honor. No cherishing. No sex.

wonderwoman: But she didn't sleep with anyone.

tmark: Including me.

wonderwoman: For good? For ever?

tmark: Pretty much. Except when I'd beg. For days at a time. Flowers, dinner, sweet talk.

wonderwoman: Hello? We females call that ROMANCE. We sort of like it. Ever since we evolved from the cave man grunt-and-fuck a few million years ago.

tmark: No, this wasn't romance, sweetheart. This was groveling. This was work. This was no fun, and no roll in the marital hay was worth it.

wonderwoman: So, you started cheating on her.

tmark: Not until after . . . you.

wonderwoman: After me? What do you mean?

tmark: Once I left MM and got you out of my system (or tried), after we moved to New York, then I decided no "love"—just occasional lust. A release, pure and simple. There's the truth: a few extramarital relationships. All purely physical and easy.

wonderwoman: How did they leave you feeling?

tmark: Empty. Hungry. Lonely. All the good stuff.

wonderwoman: Why didn't you talk to your wife and go to counseling? Why don't you now?

tmark: It's too far gone, Stephanie. She is not interested in me like that. We're good friends and, oddly enough, we're a good team. She respects me. I respect her. We've never really talked about divorce. But if I pushed it, I bet she'd agree. In the meantime, she sleeps alone. I . . . usually do.

wonderwoman: Oh. This just makes me so depressed.

tmark: Don't be. I've come to terms with it.

wonderwoman: I don't want that to happen in my marriage.

tmark: Then don't cut your husband off.

wonderwoman: He's done that to me.

tmark: He's out of his freaking mind.

wonderwoman: He's working hard. He's gone a lot. And there is this girl.

tmark: Listen, I don't know what to tell you about Brent, babydoll. But I can tell you this. You can't ever doubt your sexiness. It's in your eyes, your walk, your smile, your laugh. Your body is breathtaking, your heart is 24 karat, and your mind is like a titanium trap.

If I were your husband, I'd never go to work. Instead, I would throw you on the bed and consume you for hours, and stay up the rest of the night for the sheer pleasure of talking to you. I would corner you in the kitchen, devour you for dinner, then hand-feed chocolate-covered raspberries into your delicate mouth. I would lay you on the stairs, climb you up to heaven, and keep you there for an entire weekend. You want to know what I'd do in the laundry?

wonderwoman: Wash, fluff, and fold me?

tmark: I'm thinking about lifting you up on top of the hot, vibrating washer.

wonderwoman: ☺ Amber's right about you.

tmark: Amber? What does she say?

wonderwoman: You're *such* a copywriter, Tommy Boy.

tmark: What can I say . . . you inspire me. Is that what she calls me?

wonderwoman: Yep. She's got a name for everybody.

tmark: Could be worse, I suppose. Listen, it's late. Go to bed. Imagine me next to you. Behind you. On top of you. Inside you.

wonderwoman: I'm not going to that meeting, Tom.

tmark: I knew that.

wonderwoman: Listen to me. Take all that delicious sexual energy, all that masculine lust and juicy, erotic thoughts upstairs. Make love to your wife.

tmark: If I did, I'd just think about you.

wonderwoman: She won't know that. You might be surprised at what happens.

tmark: Hey, I thought I was the one dispensing marital advice here.

wonderwoman: You did. You got me all hot and bothered. I'm going to try and put that to good use now. You do the same. Bye.

tmark: Wait!

wonderwoman: What is it?

tmark: What are you wearing?

wonderwoman: Go see what Mary Grace has on. That's what I'm wearing.

tmark: Somehow I doubt that. But I get your sentiment. You're sweet. Bye.

TO: grayscale@connectone.com <gray mcdermott>
FROM: foreveramber@quicklink.com <amber fleece>
SUBJ: Almost midnight
DATE: Thursday 9/09 11:47 PM

You can invade my office anytime, sweetie. Thanks for the note this afternoon. Sorry I didn't write back—did a little barhopping with a wild co-worker tonight and had some fun. I tried IMing you, but your computer's not on. So, I'll have to satisfy myself with one-way communication.

You don't have to worry about being worthy, Gray. About being a better man or good enough or any of that garbage. I hate that I'm so superficial that anything like that matters.

In fact, I hate being so superficial that I just lied to you about what I did tonight. I did go out with a co-worker. Not wild—gay. I tried to have some fun, but I bagged the bars around 9:00 to come home and IM with you. There. The truth. You deserve it. No IM, but I did replay our conversation last night in my head (about six trillion times) and I just have to say—I'm glad you like the catch in my throat. Consider me caught. You know what I like about you?

Everything.

Love.

Amber

TO: foreveramber@quicklink.com <amber fleece>
FROM: grayscale@connectone.com <gray mcdermott>
SUBJ: everything???
DATE: Friday 9/10 1:49 AM

got some unexpected studio time with my band, so i just got in. i'd have given it up in a heartbeat if i ever imagined you sitting at home waiting to im with me, toots. damn, you make me happy. thanks for coming clean. you don't ever have to play stupid games or lie or be coy or any of that shit with me, amber. never lie. neither will i. i'm beat. going to bed to dream of my girl.

gray

TO: jdesmond@millenniamarketing.com
<julie desmond>
FROM: foreveramber@quicklink.com <amber fleece>
SUBJ: doc appt
DATE: Friday 9/10 8:17 AM

Jules. I just opened your email from last night. I didn't look at my MM email box before I went out. Eesh. Pretty obnoxious, those doctors. I don't know what to do, Jules. Let me think a bit, okay? I'll let you know if you need to cover for me at the WWA meeting. I guess it would be okay. I can't imagine why they have to see me NOW. I mean, I can, but I don't want to.

Love.

Amber

TO: jdesmond@millenniamarketing.com <julie desmond>
FROM: foreveramber@quicklink.com <amber fleece>
SUBJ: doc appt
DATE: Friday 9/10 8:34 AM

I guess I better go. Anyway, the WWA thing this afternoon isn't the big mandatory meeting, so if you present the Traffic Report and project timeline, we should be okay. You'll find both in my computer under the WWA files.

I'm going to run an errand this morning, then I'll be in. I'll just slip out quietly at lunch time. You know, I've had so many doctor appts, I don't want to get slammed from HR for overdoing it. Let's just say I had a little family emergency, okay? Don't tell anyone.

Sorry to put you in that position. I'll make it up to you. How 'bout I add that extra vacation day in case you want to go past first base with the ball player? BTW, you don't have to thank me for a heart-to-heart talk, Jules. Who knows when I'll be looking for my own advice one of these days? But I hate to break the bad news to you—your butt doesn't sag. Your confidence sags—and it shouldn't. You are attractive, smart, and more efficient than the rest of the support staff at MM all combined on a good day. 46 is a state of mind. Give the guy in South Carolina a chance . . . more importantly, give the girl that lives in your woman's body a chance. ☺ Thanks.

Love.

Amber

(Although he should be made to suffer a little for the park bench stunt—that was heartless.)

TO: wonderwoman@usol.com <stephanie hilliard>
FROM: hilliardb@grandregenthotels.com <brent hilliard>
SUBJ: last night
DATE: Friday 9/10 9:37 AM

You'd already left to take Lily to school when I woke up this morning, and I had to leave before you got back. Why did you bolt so early and take both of them with you? I wanted to at least see Lily in her little school outfit and give Dec a hug. Anyway, Steve, I feel bad about last night. I had two martinis and the whole trip to Colorado just jet lagged me. It wasn't you, honest. I know what you think. It wasn't you. It was me. You have no idea how much pressure is on me here. I live and die by the numbers and the last quarter of the year is critical. After the year end, everything will go back to normal. Anyway, I'll be home tonight and all weekend. We can take a drive with the kids or something. Gotta run.

Love ya,
Brent

TO: shilliard@millenniamarketing.com
<stephanie hilliard>
FROM: areinhardt@millenniamarketing.com
<adele reinhardt>
SUBJ: Today's Meeting
DATE: Friday 9/10 9:55 AM

Hello, Wonderwoman! Looking forward to today's meeting on WWA. This one is much more casual than what's scheduled for the 27th (can't wait to see you then!). So no PowerPoint™—but I was wondering if you could preview your findings with me. Just email me the docs so I have a heads up on what will be presented. I'm sure it will affect the creative portion of the meeting and I don't want any surprises! I do hope things are a little quieter than last time <ggg>—never know when GW will drop by, huh?

Thanks!

Adele

TO:	tmarkoff@millenniamarketing.com <tom markoff>
FROM:	shilliard@millenniamarketing.com <stephanie hilliard>
SUBJ:	Who's zoomin' who?
DATE:	Friday 9/10 10:01 AM

See attached email from Eva Braun. Impact *creative*???? (I did notice the shared billing on the agenda under "creative"—you have a new art director in your department???)

xoxo

Stephanie

shilliard@millenniamarketing.com: markoff@millennia-marketing.com is sending you an Instant Message on Friday 9/10 at 10:30 AM:

tmarkoff: G'morning gorgeous.

shilliard: Hey. Get my email?

tmarkoff: Blow her off. She clearly doesn't understand that Account Executives "manage" accounts and Creative Directors "create" the advertising.

shilliard: So, I should just ignore the request??

tmarkoff: Yes.

shilliard: Are you sure? I have no problem sending her the prelim report. It's not confidential to the account team and technically she is in charge.

tmarkoff: She isn't in charge of her ass. Just hang on to it. Did you get laid last night?

shilliard: You are disgusting.

tmarkoff: I'm taking that as a no.

shilliard: Did *you*?

tmarkoff: In my dreams. Literally. With you.

shilliard: Stop. This is going through the MM server. I can just imagine that creep Manny Hernandez in MIS reading every word.

tmarkoff: ☺ Expect more from me this afternoon. I'm taking my PDA to the meeting.

shilliard: Good. I need you for my eyes and ears.

tmarkoff: I need you for my hands and mouth.

shilliard: Did you get that, Manny?

tmarkoff: What's up with your buddy Amber? I wanted to give her grief about calling me Tommy Boy today.

shilliard: What do you mean?

tmarkoff: She's not coming to the WWA meeting—her admin is covering. Family problems or something.

shilliard: Really? Haven't heard from her this morning.

tmarkoff: Gotta go. Watch for my IMs during the meeting.

shilliard: Keep it clean, Markoff.

tmarkoff: Keep it real, sweetheart.

TO: jdesmond@millenniamarketing.com
<julie desmond>
FROM: shilliard@millenniamarketing.com
<stephanie hilliard>
SUBJ: Amber
DATE: Friday 9/10 10:15 AM

Hi Jules. I'm getting voicemail for Amber and no response to my IMs. Is she around?

TO: shilliard@millenniamarketing.com
<stephanie hilliard>
FROM: jdesmond@millenniamarketing.com <julie desmond>
SUBJ: Amber
DATE: Friday 9/10 10:25 AM

She's not here yet. I'm doing some checking around. Will keep you posted.

Julie

GOOGLE:

SEARCH FOR: Dr. Phillip Grossman Boston Massachusetts

SEARCH RESULTS:

Leading oncologist joins Brigham and Women's Hospital Staff . . . **Dr. Phillip Grossman** says that treatment options. . . .

One of the aggressive implementers of the Stanford V protocol for five-drug treatment of Hodgkins Lymphoma, **Dr. Phillip Grossman . . .**

The Department of General Medicine at Brigham and Women's Hospital . . . Cancer Institute, and medical oncologist, **Dr. Phillip Grossman** is the author of . . .

SEARCH ENDED

TO: shilliard@millenniamarketing.com
<stephanie hilliard>
FROM: jdesmond@millenniamarketing.com
<julie desmond>
SUBJ: Amber Alert
DATE: Friday 9/10 11:00 AM

Please call me. It's important.

Julie

shilliard@millenniamarketing.com: tmark@quicklink.com is sending you an Instant Message on Friday 9/10 at 3:29 PM:

tmark: r u there?

shilliard: Yep.

tmark: u r very quiet in this mtg

shilliard: Who can get a word in over der Fraulein?

tmark: ☺ i liked ur rpt

shilliard: She didn't.

tmark: w8. im up

* * *

shilliard@millenniamarketing.com: foreveramber@quick-link.com is sending you an Instant Message on Friday 9/10 at 3:37:

foreveramber: Are you on the conference call to the WWA meeting?

shilliard: HEY! How are you? Yes, I'm on the call.

foreveramber: How's it going?

shilliard: Fine. Where have you been? What's going on? Are you all right?

foreveramber: Yeah. Did Julie do the Traffic Report and timeline yet?

shilliard: Are you home? Why didn't you go back to the office?

foreveramber: Taking a long weekend. Did Julie do my report yet?

shilliard: Yes. She was fine. Really good, in fact. She knew her stuff. Tom's up now. He's been IMing me from his handheld. Stay with me, okay? Are you okay?

foreveramber: Will you stop effing asking me that? I'm fine. My dad needed me. No biggie.

shilliard: What's wrong with him? Oh, God. Adele is just cooing now. You should hear her. Dwayne might be right. She wants Tom. What's up with Bud?

foreveramber: Nothing serious. He just had something he needed me to help him on at the beer distributor place.

shilliard: What was it?

foreveramber: Forget about it, okay? Did you do your consultant report already?

shilliard: Yep. First. She tore it up one end and down the other, but I held my own. ☺ Tom's almost done. He'll IM me in another box.

foreveramber: Hell, this is more fun than being at the meeting.

shilliard: Are you going to be around this weekend?

foreveramber: All weekend. Nothing cooking.

shilliard: Want me to call you?

foreveramber: If you want. Isn't Brent around?

shilliard: Yes, but–oh there's my other box.

tmark: u there?

shilliard: Yep. That was great. The whole "your time matters, spend it wisely" works. You're brilliant.

tmark: ☺ did u hear that?

shilliard: Oh my. Adele *doesn't* like Spend It Wisely.

tmark: good

foreveramber: What's going on? Where are you?

shilliard: Cooing has stopped. Adele HATES Tom's tag lines.

foreveramber: Does she want him or does she want his job?

shilliard: Interesting observation. Dwayne may be off base.

foreveramber: You can say that again.

shilliard: ☺ Hey, how's your cold?

foreveramber: Fine. Almost gone.

shilliard: And your swollen glands? Julie told me you had them.

foreveramber: Sheez. I don't need any more mothers, thank you very much.

shilliard: Come on, Amber. I'm you're friend. Please don't forget that. I'm your best friend.

foreveramber: Then back off.

tmark: gw has arrived

shilliard: Interesting timing. He missed creative. Where is he sitting?

tmark: across fr eva

shilliard: What is he doing?

tmark: smiling benevolently

shilliard: Why doesn't she shut up and acknowledge him? She knows I'm not in the room and I can't see what's happening.

tmark: exactly

shilliard: She's waiting for Romper Room to kick in.

tmark: get duct tape ready

shilliard: Not necessary. They are out for the afternoon with a sitter. Now what's he doing?

tmark: staring at eva's pretend cleavage

shilliard: ☺

shilliard: Hey, Amber, too bad you're missing this meeting. Tom says GW has quietly arrived and is ogling der Fraulein.

shilliard: Amber? You still there?

shilliard: Tell me if you're going to leave, all right?

shilliard: You signed off, didn't you?

tmark: are u listening to this? can u believe this crap?

shilliard: I have to go. Cover for me. I have to make a phone call. Sorry.

TO: foreveramber@quicklink.com <amber fleece>
FROM: wonderwoman@usol.com <stephanie hilliard>
SUBJ: Friday night
DATE: Friday 9/10 8:40 PM

You won't pick up, you won't IM, you won't return my six (seven?) phone calls. So I'm resorting to email for this. First of all, don't get mad at Julie. She did the right thing. But, sweetie, why are you hiding this from the people who love you? Amber, please, please, please talk to me and tell me what's going on. I'm just sick. No matter *what* is going on, you are the toughest human I know and will handle it. PLEASE don't cut me off. I know you need someone to talk to. I'm here. I'm going to be here all weekend, unless you want me on a plane to Boston. I can be there in a matter of hours for you, Amber. Please, honey, please call me and tell me why you went to this doctor. Please.

xoxoxoxoxoxoxoxoxoxoxoxoxoxoxox
Stevie

TO: grayscale@connectone.com <gray mcdermott>
FROM: foreveramber@quicklink.com <amber fleece>
SUBJ: What I didn't say
DATE: Friday 9/10 9:03 PM

Did I tell you that I read the lyrics to your new song and liked them? I think I forgot to mention that. Okay . . . here's what I didn't say when we were on the phone the other night. I didn't say that in the last ten years, I've thought about you a million times. That no other boy or man has ever come close to my memory of you.

I didn't say that I'm relieved that you didn't grow up to be my ideal type of guy. Because if you were, the pain of not having you would be too great. As it is, the pain of not having you is becoming slightly unbearable.

I didn't say that for ten years I've been bouncing around, desperate to figure out who I am, anxious to know where I'm going, certain I can find the future I've dreamed of having . . . only to, well, *not* find anything but more of the same.

I didn't say that I still ache for my mom, every day, after all these years. And I think that's why I can't find the right guy—because if I did, I want my mom and dad's perfect relationship and I'll never, ever, ever recreate that, so I don't even try.

I didn't say the three words that are sure to send you running faster than anything. I can't say them yet. I don't know for sure. No, honey, it's not I love you. Those are the three prettiest words in the English language, and I've dreamt that you've said them to me a billion times. No, these are the three scariest words:

I have

ARE YOU SURE YOU WANT TO DELETE THIS MAIL?

MAIL DELETED

TO: beantownbud@bostonbeerdistribution.com <bud fleece>
FROM: foreveramber@quicklink.com <amber fleece>
SUBJ: Hi Daddy
DATE: Friday 9/10 9:39 PM

Hey there. I know I told you I was going out with friends when you called to meet you and Alice for dinner before, but I ended up staying home. Such fun on a Friday night, huh? Hope you guys went anyway, and that it's not too crowded at Quincy Market tonight. Anyway, I just wanted to thank you for thinking of me. That was so sweet. I'm sure you two would rather be lovebirds ☺ than have your obnoxious little daughter around. But it was sweet of you to ask. You always are doing sweet things for me, Daddy. (I'm not too old to call you Daddy, am I?) Anyway, I just want you to know how much I appreciate it. How you've been a dad and mom to me and I really love you, Daddy. I never want to hurt you or make

ARE YOU SURE YOU WANT TO DELETE MAIL?
MAIL DELETED

TO: caldingerc@troyhillinvest.com <chet caldinger>
FROM: foreveramber@quicklink.com <amber fleece>
SUBJ: What's going on?
DATE: Friday 9/10 9:57 PM

Hi Chet! Long time no talk to. How are you? I'm just hanging at home

ARE YOU SURE YOU WANT TO DELETE MAIL?
MAIL DELETED

TO: wonderwoman@usol.com <stephanie hilliard>
FROM: foreveramber@quicklink.com <amber fleece>
SUBJ: All right, you win
DATE: Friday 9/10 10:30 PM

Well, I've tried to email anyone who matters in my life (the list is woefully short) and have ended up hitting delete instead of send. It seems I have a lot to say, but no one whose e-door should be darkened by me. I even thought about writing to myself, just to get my thoughts on paper, but then, how effing lame is that? You win by default, chickie. You're the next best thing to self. I guess that's an underhanded way of saying yes, you're my best friend.

Don't get mad at me for going dark. I just can't talk right now, okay? I'll tell you what's going on, at least as best as I can. Then I will return promptly to my usual witty self who will refuse to discuss this unpleasant business at any length. Yes, Dr. Phillip Grossman is an O. I can't say it, okay? He is some kind of world-renowned expert in the area of C. Can't say that either.

When I went to the ENT (Ear, Nose and Throat specialist—that I can say, it's just so long), he noticed that right under my collarbone on the left side there is a slightly raised area, about the size of, oh, a child's fist. I have to admit I noticed it about a month ago, but really figured it was just a weird imperfection, or maybe swollen glands. Honest. It's not that huge that it would jump out at you like a big, red, deadly flag. It's *slight* but it's there. Anyway, according to Dr. ENT, with a lingering, endless cold like I've had, this could be a symptom of . . . oh. Something worse. Enter Dr. Grossman. (Who, just my luck, is finally the cute doctor I've been hoping for. Very Bruce Willis in a Kevin Costner–ish kind of way.) He's actually kind of funny and sweet and I liked him. Would rather have him as a neighbor or client or dentist doing ten root canals than an effing oncologist (ooh, I said it), but those are my tough *yupkas* as my Polish grandmother used to say.

Anyway, Dr. G did a little test today. Stuck a not-so-little needle in this swollen area under my neck and started telling me about something called Hodgkins. He thinks I might have it. Actually, I might have Hodgkins Lymphoma . . . or non–Hodgkins Lymphoma—an alternate disease Mr. Hodgkins, whoever he is, invented to confuse people. One of them is super curable. The other is a bit trickier. Like impossible.

So, my friend, I won't know until Monday. On Monday, I'll find out if I'm going to have three months of chemotherapy (now there's a word I hate) and a few doses of high-voltage radiation . . . or a packed house at my funeral. Okay. I'm exaggerating. But not really. And I'm a little drunk. More than a little, actually. I'm pretty much toasted. But the best case—yes, you read that right, the BEST effing case is "a little" chemo and "some" radiation. I had a cold. I finally went to the doctor. I expected to get a flu shot. What do I get? Chemofuckingtherapy.

I've never been so scared in my whole life. Well, not since I sat in that stinky hospital room (I *loathe* the smell of antiseptic) and held my mother's pitiful wisp of a hand and said goodbye. I was so terrified, Stevie. Of course, it was a selfish scared. I remember thinking I didn't want my mother to die because she wouldn't be at my wedding. Who knew *I'd* die before I ever managed to snag my prince?

Okay. I'm going to be a big, strong tootsie roll ☺ and send this. I'm not going to hit delete. Just understand—do NOT call me or show up at my door, Stevie. I'll check email. I need to get through this weekend on my own. When I find out what I'm up against, I promise, I'll break your back leaning on your shoulder. But I have to get through this weekend from hell. I have to get through this. I. Cannot. Talk.

Love.

Amber

foreveramber@quicklink.com: grayscale@connectone.com is sending you an Instant Message on Friday 9/10 11:06 PM:

grayscale: you home, toots?

foreveramber: Hi.

grayscale: ah. there's a good girl. gimme a kiss.

foreveramber: ☺ Several of them.

grayscale: how are you?

foreveramber: fine. (I'm going to try this no shift-key stuff. it's cool.)

grayscale: it's easy. i like easy.

foreveramber: no wonder you liked me.

grayscale: i never thought you were easy.

foreveramber: you did on prom night . . . much to steve morgan's dismay.

grayscale: to think i didn't even have to rent a tux.

foreveramber: no, you just showed up at that party, in jeans. in a dark green tee shirt that said sa-something bass guitars.

grayscale: sadowsky. the best. and you were in that thing that looked like a daffodil.

foreveramber: hey. that was cut and sewn by my very own hands.

grayscale: really?? you can make clothes?

foreveramber: i used to. forced by low income and high taste.

grayscale: kewl. you can make your kids halloween costumes instead of buying those stupid things that look like superman pajamas.

foreveramber: i doubt i'll be making any halloween costumes.

grayscale: why not? make your daughter a daffodil. she'll get bunches of snickers and sweet-tarts. and the bad boys will want to pluck her.

foreveramber: i'll never have a daughter, gray.

grayscale: who says?

foreveramber: dr. grossman

grayscale: who's that?

foreveramber: no one. forget it. i'm a little tipsy.

grayscale: oh. i like it when you drink. you get giddy.

foreveramber: i'm not giddy tonight.

grayscale: what's the matter, toots? what's this shit about not having a daughter. do you have problems?

foreveramber: problems-a-plenty, but none down there. i just don't think i'll ever get married, that's all.

grayscale: who is dr. grossman?

foreveramber: nobody.

grayscale: is he one of the doctors you saw? what did he say?

foreveramber: he said i'm doomed. i'm so hard to live with, i'm doomed to be a spinster . . . oh, we call those "career women" now, huh?

grayscale: you're not hard to live with. not at all.

foreveramber: i'm not that neat.

grayscale: who cares? i'm a slob.

foreveramber: i'm always late.

grayscale: i've never been anywhere on time in my life.

foreveramber: i sleep until noon on the weekends.

grayscale: i like to go for 1 or even 2 in the afternoon. now that's a saturday morning to me.

foreveramber: so, what are you saying? we're compatible?

grayscale: we belong together.

foreveramber: oh, gray. don't do this. i'm too weak tonight. i can't go to that place.

grayscale: what place, toots?

foreveramber: dreaming. about you.

grayscale: do you? dream of me?

foreveramber: oh, no, never.

grayscale: what do you dream?

foreveramber: sex dreams only.

grayscale: liar.

foreveramber: did you dream about me—like you said you would?

grayscale: all night long.

foreveramber: sex dreams?

grayscale: i dream about shopping for trash cans with you.

foreveramber: excuse me?

grayscale: the ultimate suburban errand. going to home depot. buying new trash cans.

foreveramber: sorry, but i fail to see the romance in that.

grayscale: the romance is in the mundanity of it. it's life. it's real. it's tradition.

foreveramber: i hate to break it to you, but tradition is like "fish on christmas eve" and snapping the wishbone on thanksgiving. not shopping for trash cans.

grayscale: it's . . . domestic.

foreveramber: i would never have taken you for the domestic type, gray.

grayscale: you would never have taken me at all if i hadn't deflowered your daffodil on prom night.

foreveramber: you're so wrong. i wanted you from ninth grade on.

grayscale: hell. all that sex i missed from you. why didn't you tell me when we were fifteen?

foreveramber: i didn't want to be too easy.

grayscale: easy is good, toots. not distant. what's up with you?

foreveramber: just busy at work.

grayscale: you're not telling me the truth. something's on your mind.

foreveramber: you.

grayscale: right where i want to be.

foreveramber: but you're not where i want you to be. you're there. i'm here.

grayscale: right this very minute, we're connected. a satellite link.

foreveramber: i want real, gray mcdermott. real sex. real kisses. real you. real life. real bad.

grayscale: i know what you want, toots.

foreveramber: what do you want?

grayscale: peace in the world. harmony in my home. you in my . . . life.

foreveramber: how do you make that happen, gray?

grayscale: you are the only person i've ever known who believed i can make things happen.

foreveramber: how?

grayscale: i don't know how you do it, but you do.

foreveramber: i meant how are you going to make all those things happen?

grayscale: i don't know yet.

foreveramber: i'm going to sleep. i'm exhausted. are you around tomorrow?

grayscale: soccer game in the morning; gig tomorrow night. i'll be thinking about you all day and night.

foreveramber: and i'll be imagining the joy of shopping for trash cans. in fact, i think i'll go to home depot and practice.

grayscale: no. wait for me. i want to do it together the first time.

foreveramber: you give me so much to hope for.

grayscale: ah, amber. i don't want to let you down.

foreveramber: me neither.

grayscale: you can't. g'night, toots.

foreveramber: good night, gray.

TO: foreveramber@quicklink.com <amber fleece>
FROM: wonderwoman@usol.com <stephanie hilliard>
SUBJ: research, love
DATE: Saturday 9/11 8:15 AM

Dearest Amber, needless to say, I never slept last night. I resisted the constant urge to call, but only because you asked me not to. However, I did research. I spent the night on the internet, sweetie, and I learned a lot. This thing is beatable, Amb. Honestly. Especially if you don't have the NON one. Does that make sense? We want **no** "non" in front of the diagnosis. Then, you have a lot of options and a 90+% chance of a complete cure!!! (Exclamation marks are merited in this case, Adele.) Especially with your doctor—Grossman is famous for his success in a rapid treatment. I know you don't want me to call you, so I put together this (massive, sorry) attachment of information—attached. Read it, Amber. Knowledge is power and reassurance. Look at all the case studies I've included. There's a site where people tell their stories and hundreds and hundreds of people get through this and are free of anything bad when it's over.

Honey, I don't know much about medicine, but I do know this: Attitude is everything with this disease. And, honestly, things are so different now—they've made huge strides since your mom was sick. You don't have to give up and you won't die.

There I said it. You won't die, Amber. You have to arm yourself with accurate information and a positive attitude, surround yourself with people you love (I'll be there in three hours, say the word), and prepare yourself for a battle you will win. Don't hole up in your apartment and feel sorry for yourself. Talk to me. Talk to Bud. Talk to Gray. Please call me, please let me come up and see you. Please, please, please read what I've attached. So many people in the world love you, Amber. Don't forget that.

xoxoxoxoxoxoxoxoxoxo

Steve

TO: wonderwoman@usol.com <stephanie hilliard>
FROM: foreveramber@quicklink.com <amber fleece>
SUBJ: thanks
DATE: Saturday 9/11 10:44 AM

I'll read it.

Love.

Me

TO: tmark@quicklink.com <tom markoff>
FROM: wonderwoman@usol.com <stephanie hilliard>
SUBJ: call me, please
DATE: Saturday 9/11 11:03 AM

Tom—sorry for the hasty retreat from yesterday's meeting. I need to talk to you. I don't want to bother you at home on a Saturday. If you get this, call me if you can. I'm home alone today—Brent took the kids out . . . just call me, okay? Please.

xoxo
S

TO: foreveramber@quicklink.com <amber fleece>
FROM: beantownbud@bostonbeerdisribution.com <bud fleece>
SUBJ: Missed You Last Night
DATE: Saturday 9/11 12:32 PM

Hi honey. Hope you had fun with your friends last night. I sure understand that you didn't want to hang with me and Alice at Quincy Market. We had fun doing the tourist thing, but ended up coming home pretty early after all. We're not much for late night partying at our age. Anyway, I've been calling your apartment and your cell and even tried your office to see if you were catching up at work, but no answer anywhere. Did you get my messages? Maybe you'll check email. I wondered if you aren't doing anything tonight if you want to come over to Alice's house for dinner? If you're busy, maybe we could do something tomorrow afternoon. I want to talk to you about something, honey. It's kind of important. Let me know. I'm at work for a few hours, then home. Call me.

I love you, honey.

Dad

TO: foreveramber@quicklink.com <amber fleece>
FROM: caldingerc@troyhillinvest.com <chet caldinger>
SUBJ: ???
DATE: Saturday 9/11 1:47 PM

If I didn't know better, I'd think I was getting the kiss off from you. Have you disappeared from the world? I stopped by your apartment this morning, but no answer. I left a message at your office and at home. You know, I like you, Amber. You're a fun, smart, pretty girl and I think we had a good time. You don't have to play hard to get with me—just give me a call. I'm on my cell all day.

Chet

TO: wonderwoman@usol.com <stephanie hilliard>
FROM: tmark@quicklink.com <tom markoff>
SUBJ: our talk
DATE: Saturday 9/11 3:24 PM

Hey gorgeous. Are you doing any better? I'm glad you called my cell phone, I wouldn't have looked at this email for hours. God, you scared me when I first heard your voice. I don't think I've ever heard you cry, Stephanie. You're the strongest woman I know. And from what I can tell, your friend Amber is made of the same stuff. She'll get through this—especially with friends who love her like you do.

Like I told you, I have a good friend who's head of surgery at Brigham. He'll know Grossman. I'll find out what I can for you. In the meantime, don't go crazy with worry. You've already spent too much time on the internet—I know you were trying to get helpful information to Amber, and you did. But all those horrific stories you told me about—they aren't helping you. And, as you know, they won't help her, either. You were smart to only send her the positive ones.

And don't ever apologize for calling me, Steph. I hate that you're going through this and I hate that you have so much on your mind right now, but I definitely like being the one you turn to. You can lean on my shoulder day or night. I'm here all weekend. MG's gone on some road trip with a friend—they're going up to Amherst to see Casey today, then on a leaf-peeping tour. (It's getting real pretty up here this time of year . . . you ought to come see it.) Call me 24/7.

ILY.

T

TO: foreveramber@quicklink.com <amber fleece>
FROM: grayscale@connectone.com <gray mcdermott>
SUBJ: connecting
DATE: Saturday 9/11 3:42 PM

---

i drove by home depot and thought of you.

i thought about what it would be like to hold you every night. to wake up beside you, with my hands on your body, tucked in that sweet, warm spot between your legs. every morning. every goddamn day.

i live my life with a simple rule: no regrets. mistakes? i've made a shitload of 'em. but i despise regret. it's a useless, draining sensation. worse than its first cousin, guilt. i never regretted leaving massachusetts, or my so-called family, or even you. had to go. had to try. but, man, i feel that sucker sneaking up on me, warning me. he's coming. big time regret if i don't color my life amber this time around. big time.

gotta take mickey to a sleepover party—need to go early and check out the parents. no good ever came from any overnight gig i was involved in. then i gotta play your song for a room full of women who . . . aren't amber.

wait up for me.

gray

TO: wonderwoman@usol.com <stephanie hilliard>
FROM: juliedes@connectone.com <julie desmond>
SUBJ: Amber
DATE: Saturday 9/11 3:59 PM

Hi, Stevie. Julie Desmond here. I just got back from Amber's apartment. It took some determination and patience on my part, but she finally answered the buzzer and let me up. We didn't talk much about her health—I could tell she didn't want to. I just sat with her for a while, and made some tea and peanut butter sandwiches because she hadn't eaten all day. You know, even with what she's going through, she's so funny. She told me all about how she met you—how she made you laugh so much in her job interview that you took a chance on her, even though she'd never worked in an office before. I told her what goes around, comes around. She did the same thing for me—only I didn't make her laugh. Ironically, it was my concern about her health that touched her. That got things quiet for a moment, as you might imagine. So, I told her she was an inspiration to me as a professional—and, really, as a woman. We're never too old that we can't learn. She got kind of teary at that, so we changed the subject.

She told me a little bit more about Gray, this songwriter in Dallas. And about her father and his new girlfriend. It was nice to just talk without the phones ringing at work. Well, truth be told, her phone rang a lot, she just ignored it.

Stevie, she's scared. I've been a mom long enough to know when someone's just being tough because they think they're supposed to be. The poor thing is scared out of her wits. You know, she puts on a big show with all her wit and bravado. But, deep inside, she is one hurt little girl who really has never gotten over the death of her mother. She's thrashing around with different boyfriends, trying to find the one that fits some preconceived "list" that she thinks she wants. I told her I married someone who fit that list—and paid for the mistake for 23 years. Anyway, I think she's a little better. And on Monday, she'll know exactly what she has. I think she'll pull it together, then. But you just keep emailing her. She does have her computer on. And although she doesn't really want to see anybody, I think it's good to stay in touch and just keep her mind on other things.

Thought you'd want an update.

Take care,

Jules

TO: beantownbud@bostonbeerdistribution.com <bud fleece>
FROM: foreveramber@quicklink.com <amber fleece>
SUBJ: Saturday afternoon
DATE: Saturday 9/11 4:17 PM

Hi Dad—Sorry I didn't get back to you sooner. My admin came over and we worked on a project. I'm kind of bushed—so I'm going to pass on dinner. And I have plans tomorrow. What's up? What do you have to tell me? Can you just call me? I just am not up for the family dinner scene tonight. Hope you understand. Write or call.

Love.

Amb.

TO: caldingerc@troyhillinvest.com <chet caldinger>
FROM: foreveramber@quicklink.com <amber fleece>
SUBJ: RE: ???
DATE: Saturday 9/11 4:20 PM

Hi Chet—No kiss off! I just really don't feel well. You know I've been fighting . . . something. It might be more serious than just a cold. So, I'm laying low this weekend. We'll catch up next week, I promise.

Amber

TO: juliedes@connectone.com <julie desmond>
FROM: wonderwoman@usol.com <stephanie hilliard>
SUBJ: RE: Amber
DATE: Saturday 9/11 4:40 PM

Jules, thank you, thank you, thank you—for going to see Amber and for writing to me. I feel better just knowing someone was with her today. You are absolutely right, of course, about her brave front. She's so tough and funny on the outside, but, trust me, she's a complete cupcake on the inside. You've been exactly what she's needed the past few weeks—more like a "mom" than I could ever be. She may say she resents the doctor's appointments and coddling, but you know, you may have saved her life by forcing her to go to the doctor. I just don't know how to thank you. I'll be emailing her right away—and a lot. Let's stay in touch so we can both help her.

My husband's just pulling into the garage with the kids—he's had them all day. As soon as I get them settled, I'm going to write to Amber. Thanks again.

xoxox
Stevie

TO: foreveramber@quicklink.com <amber fleece>
FROM: wonderwoman@usol.com <stephanie hilliard>
SUBJ: thinking of you
DATE: Saturday 9/11 5:30 PM

Hey girlie—how's your Saturday going? Okay, stupid question. Well, I want to write and cheer you up and make you laugh and make you forget the hell that is this weekend. So . . . wanna hear about my lying, cheating husband? Hey, that got your mind off things for a second, right? Well, as a matter of fact, the plot thickens. As I told you, I spent the wee hours on the internet (did you read what I sent?) and somehow found the energy to make pancakes and bacon for my crew this morning. I surely didn't look like the Stepford Wife I strive to be, so Brent pitied me and took the kids out—a Disney movie, and then to the Germ Factory. (Really an indoor play place called the Fun Factory, but Declan likes to taste every plastic ball for possible viruses he's yet to contract.)

They came home about an hour ago, all happy and excited and filthy. As I'm stripping them down for a pool bath (hey, there's something good about living in Florida—chlorinated child care), Lily starts telling me how Daddy was on the phone the whoooooole time they were at Germ Factory.

Now, why don't I just accept this as part of being married to the future CEO—a busy man who surely doesn't stop working on the weekends? Why am I so damn suspicious?

Of *course* I redialed the last number called on his cell phone while he was outside swimming with the kids. Yep. You got it, babycakes. He was sending smoke signals to Pocahontas. Do I want to rip him from end to end? Do I want to scream obscenities and accusations? Do I want to stomp my foot and announce that THIS CAN'T HAPPEN TO ME? (See? We're feeling the same thing. I know that's what you want to do right now—I know you want to stand up and scream THIS CAN'T HAPPEN TO ME. I don't mean to make this about me—honestly. ☺)

Anyway, I have no right to scream anything. I was on the phone with Tom for two hours while Brent was gone. I don't know whether to be pissed or cower in my own guilt.

Write to me, okay? Just tell me what you're thinking, feeling, doing. Or better yet, call me. I feel so out of touch, out of control. Not my favorite thing, as you know.

xoxox

Stevie

TO: grayscale@connectone.com <gray mcdermott>
FROM: foreveramber@quicklink.com <amber fleece>
SUBJ: trash cans & life
DATE: Saturday 9/11 8:15 PM

I imagine your band is setting up for your gig now. I keep thinking of your lead singer looking like Colin Farrell (did you have to tell me that?) and how he must sound singing "my" song. Send me a tape, okay? I'd really like to hear it.

You're such a good . . . dad? Guardian? Guy? What are you to Mickey? What does he call you?

No one has *ever* thought of me while passing a Home Depot, I can assure you. But you're sweet and I'd go just about anywhere with you tonight. Not that I didn't have *tons* of other offers. Clubs, dates, parties. You know me, a butterfly in the social stratosphere of life. But, really, I'd rather stay home and wait for my IM to ding. I've always been a bit of a geek. I think that's why I was so scared of you in high school—besides the fact that the sight of you caused exotic and unfamiliar physical reactions in all parts of my body. You were just so . . . cool. And I was so . . . not. Yes, there were hoards of masses around me—but only because I laugh at myself and my uncoolness, and I think that's a relief to people (especially teenagers) who are all stressed out about themselves.

I bet you don't remember this. It goes way back—to early, early tenth grade. A party at someone's house in Lexington—an upscale place. There were about 40 LHS kids in the basement, and the music was really loud—nasty stuff like Pearl Jam or Alice in Chains. I don't even remember who had the party. My mom had died about six months earlier, and it was one of the first times I'd gone out and left my dad at home alone. I knew that when I got home that night, he'd be the only parent there. That was really weird, because even when she was sick, my mom would always be waiting up for me in the family room once I started to go out with friends at night. So, I didn't leave the house for the longest time after she died, because I didn't want my dad to be alone, but more because I didn't want to get home and cry because I couldn't *stand* facing the fact that she was gone and not coming back. Sorry. Big ramble into weepy self-pity.

Anyway, at this party, two boys were sort of hitting on me and I was kind of liking it because I had just realized that even those unimpressive little double As had some kind of mythical power over men. So I was giving it a go in a pretty tight sweater, and the boys were looking. One of them kissed me—he tasted like a cigarette, as I recall, and had the lip finesse of a duck. But I was 15 and flattered—momentarily. And then the other one said something, and the first one sort of pushed me back on a pile of coats and tried to feel me up. It was very, very dark and all I could smell was stale cigarette and wet wool. And all of a sudden, he was yanked off me. And there you were—holding him by the elbow with one strong hand—looking very *Legends of the Fall*–ish cause your hair was kind of long then—just killing this kid with a glare. "Be cool, man."

That's all you said. Three words. "Be cool, man." You didn't even look at me—and I remember how much I appreciated that you didn't make me feel all slutty with one withering glance. You made those guys look like fools, though. And God knows what you saved me from. I doubt this made the lasting imprint on your mind that it made on mine, but please accept my thanks. You know, that was the official start of my lifelong crush on Gray McDermott.

Hey, guess what? I'm not even going to delete this. Normally I would smack that little button but this time I'm going for it. You should know that you were once my knight in shining armor. You rescued me from the bad boys. That's why I let you inside my petals on prom night and why I wait eagerly, years later, for the sound of your ding.

Love.

Amber

foreveramber@quicklink.com: wonderwoman@usol.com is sending you an Instant Message on Saturday, 9/11 at 10:12 PM:

wonderwoman: I have the distinct feeling I'm being avoided.

foreveramber: You are unavoidable, my friend.

wonderwoman: ☺ Oh! A response! How are you?

foreveramber: Fine if you don't ask. Can we just have a nice chat here without talking about anything of substance? Nothing's changed. I haven't keeled over, been taken to the emergency room, had a transplant, or miraculously healed. I have been soul-searching (and -baring) on my computer.

wonderwoman: Gray?

foreveramber: Natch.

wonderwoman: Did you tell him?

foreveramber: No.

wonderwoman: Are you going to?

foreveramber: No.

wonderwoman: Why not?

foreveramber: You are asking too many effing questions, Steverella.

wonderwoman: I've never tiptoed around you, Amb, and I'm not starting now. Like it or not, you're my best friend and I haven't been miraculously cured of *caring* about you, either.

foreveramber: Don't get nasty.

wonderwoman: Don't get weird.

foreveramber: Deal. What's going on in Wonderland?

wonderwoman: Speaking of tiptoeing around one another. We're practically ballet dancing.

foreveramber: What did you talk to Tommy Boy about today?

wonderwoman: Life, love, marriage, you.

foreveramber: I knew you'd tell him.

wonderwoman: Jesus, Amber, you can't act like it's not happening. People love you. They want to do what they can for you. They are worried.

foreveramber: That's what sucks, Stevie. I don't care about dying. I really don't give a rat's ass about living anymore. What am I going to miss? Conference reports? Bad dates? Other people's weddings, baby showers, and housewarmings? I *only* care about hurting the people I leave behind. Trust me, I know all about dying. It's not hard to do. What's hard is to be left behind. You think I want to do that to you? To my dad?

wonderwoman: I just want to do everything humanly possible to make sure that doesn't happen for about sixty years.

foreveramber: You can't control everything, Stevie. You can't change fate with all the information and attitude in the effing world. YOU think you have everything figured out. You think if you just learn and read and work and do things ON TIME and CORRECTLY, you are in the driver's seat. Well, I have bad news, sister. You're not steering this bus and neither am I. Someone Else is and He (She?) says when TIME'S UP.

foreveramber: You still there?

wonderwoman: Yeah. I just don't know what to say.

foreveramber: You don't have to say anything. I'm sorry. Did you send Jules over here or was that her idea?

wonderwoman: Her idea.

foreveramber: It was sweet. I was *not* happy at first, but she was good for me. Sort of comforting—even made me tea. That calmed me down a lot.

wonderwoman: Good. She worships you. Please don't be mad at the people who care about you and want to help you through this.

foreveramber: I'm not mad at them—or you, darla. I'm just feeling way sorry for myself.

wonderwoman: That's normal.

foreveramber: Thanks, Doc. How about being in love with THE WRONG GUY who is 1,200 miles away, un/self/underemployed, and living with another woman? How normal is that?

wonderwoman: You're in love with Gray?

foreveramber: Without proper diagnosis and physical contact, we can't be entirely sure. But it certainly feels like love in various parts of my body, including the one pounding in my chest.

wonderwoman: That's wonderful. That's good. Celebrate that.

foreveramber: Exactly when did you join Up with People?

wonderwoman: I'll let that go, under the circumstances. Are you going to see him? Will he come up to Boston?

foreveramber: I don't know. I just know that I love him. I could die just knowing that, and that would be enough. Might have to be.

wonderwoman: Stop that shit right now. When are you going to tell him?

foreveramber: What? That I have cancer or that I love him?

wonderwoman: Which would be harder?

foreveramber: I'm not sure. I don't think either one will exactly reel him in.

wonderwoman: You're not sure you have cancer.

foreveramber: Yes, I am. I'm just not sure if the cancer gods will look kindly on me and let me be cured. But I'm sure. And I'm sure I love him. Those gods have never been particularly kind to me, either.

wonderwoman: It's your turn.

foreveramber: That's what I'm worried about.

wonderwoman: I mean for LOVE. It's your turn.

foreveramber: What about you?

wonderwoman: Me? I took my turn. Remember—white gown, Ritz-Carlton? Oh, you weren't there. But you've seen the video.

foreveramber: What about Tommy Boy?

wonderwoman: Oh, God, Amber. He's attractive, he's funny, he's sexy, he's tempting, and he's married.

foreveramber: What a package.

wonderwoman: And he's a doll. And since my husband is screwing around. . . .

foreveramber: You don't have any hard evidence against Brent. Are you sure his interaction with Heather the Harlot isn't all work related?

wonderwoman: I don't know. I'm so suspicious–and guilty, too. Ugly, ugly feelings all around.

foreveramber: I know this sounds terribly old-fashioned and obvious, but have you thought about *talking* to Brent about it?

wonderwoman: I assume by "it" you mean about H the H and not Tommy Boy. We have definitely skirted the issue. He hasn't *denied* anything. He turns it around to make it sound like I'm being ridiculous, which I could be, so I shut up.

foreveramber: Why don't you just come right out and ask him?

wonderwoman: Why don't you just come right out and tell Gray what's going on?

foreveramber: tOUCHé. ☺

wonderwoman: I'll give it a little more time. I don't want to cause a train wreck if I don't have to.

foreveramber: Ditto.

wonderwoman: I'm here if you need me, okay?

foreveramber: I know that and I really, really appreciate it.

wonderwoman: xoxox

foreveramber: Same.

TO: foreveramber@quicklink.com <amber fleece>
FROM: grayscale@connectone.com <gray mcdermott>
SUBJ: nirvana
DATE: Sunday 9/12 4:15 AM

---

it was nirvana. they were singing "smells like teen spirit." i think of you every time i hear that crappy song. it was november of 1991, at jason bruchholder's house. you were in a white sweater—yes, very tight with four buttons in the front, but, baby, they weren't double a's even back then. the asshole kissing you was clayton ryberger. and i did look at you. all night long.

it's too late to im you. but i'm thinking about you and all the things i could do to a grown woman dumb enough to have a crush on me.

i can tell you're sad about something. i'm going to call you tomorrow afternoon. sleep in late, then i'll call you.

gray

TO: willie542@quicklink.com <william desmond>
FROM: juliedes@connectone.com <julie desmond>
SUBJ: I miss you
DATE: Sunday 9/12 7:15 AM

Will, I'm about to leave to get Grandma and take her to the 8:00 Mass. I hoped you'd stop by this week. You know something, Will? Life's too short to hold grudges. It's too short to get mad because you don't get your way. And it's too short to miss opportunities for love and laughter. I know this because I'm your mother and mothers are right. And I'm reminded of it because someone I really like a lot is very, very sick, and it made me remember just how short life can be. And how precious.

I love you, Willie. With every fiber in my body. I've loved you since I gave birth to you. I loved you whether you did bad things or good things, whether you made smart or stupid decisions, if you were a joy or a pain in the butt. I will always love you. And you will always love me, even if you're too stubborn and young right now to realize it.

I don't know if I'm going to see John Rush, but if I do or if I don't, it won't be because you or your dad or *anyone* told me what to do. It will be because I want to seize the day before the day is gone. And you will have to accept that because you love me.

I miss you. And you must be pretty darn mad at me to go all week without clean jeans. Come over and get your laundry. No questions asked.

Mom

TO: grayscale@connectone.com <gray mcdermott>
FROM: foreveramber@quicklink.com <amber fleece>
SUBJ: you can crush my teen spirit anytime
DATE: Sunday 9/12 7:30 AM

I can't believe you remember all that. I just can't believe it. You couldn't have given me a better gift. I'm up early today—I know you are crashed, so I won't bother to IM. But I just wanted to start this day off with writing to you. I just can't believe you remember that—or that you picked up that I'm sad. How can you be so in touch with me?

I won't go into gory, boring details about my sadness. Sometimes I feel like life isn't fair, and sometimes, when I think about my mother, I am *sure* life isn't fair. It's been a long time, but once in a while, things happen to make me think about her and how much we missed together. I don't want to dwell on it. I just want you to know I go down that black hole sometimes.

But I usually emerge pretty quickly. Thanks for pulling me out with your sweet note. Don't call me today. I'm really busy, so I won't be around.

Love.

Amber

TO: tmark@quicklink.com <tom markoff>
FROM: wonderwoman@usol.com <stephanie hilliard>
SUBJ: Color me confused
DATE: Sunday 9/12 10:30 AM

I almost wrote to you last night, but felt a little vulnerable doing so. Vulnerable is not a feeling we control freaks relish. So I slept on it. And this morning, I still want to write to you. It wasn't exhaustion, or worry, or even the third glass of wine. It's you. You're on my mind too much, Tom. I'm vividly imagining things I have no right to even think about. Maybe it's Amber's sickness. Maybe it's Brent's distance. Maybe I'm having my own mid-life (well, first-third) crisis. But you are taking over my mind lately and that truly makes me vulnerable. To all sorts of bad deeds.

I'm taking some retail therapy at Saks this afternoon. You can reach me on my cell.

xoxo
Stephanie

TO: foreveramber@quicklink.com <amber fleece>
FROM: grayscale@connectone.com <gray mcdermott>
SUBJ: good morning baby
DATE: Sunday 9/12 10:48 AM

i'm up way too early, but i just had a feeling you'd write back. listen, toots, i'm gonna tell you one more time . . . it's better to have loved and lost—and that means your mama, too. my dad was a whacko, i know you know that. the only person on earth i hate more than him is my mom, 'cause she let him be a whacko. she was so fucking petrified of his temper that she let him shove my brother and me into closets and kick the holy shit out of us just 'cause he ran outta booze. she was no mother. she never hit me, no. but she stepped away when he did and wouldn't walk the fuck out the door when she should have. baby, you only had your mother for 14 years. but i bet in that time, a million different ways, she protected you. she watched out for you. she kept the bad guys away and probably let you sleep in her bed during storms and definitely didn't go in her room and close the door when a telephone came hurling at your head.

don't get mad at life or god or whatever for taking your mother away. just remember what her smile looked like, and how soft her hands felt when she touched you. remember just one dress or shirt she wore. think of the color of her eyes, the smell of something she cooked, the sound of her whispering "amber" when she put you to sleep. no one can take those things away from you, angel. no one. and, don't forget, you got a dad. i remember meeting him, he's a cool dude.

i know you're not really busy, but don't worry, i won't call.

gray

TO: foreveramber@quicklink.com <amber fleece>
FROM: beantownbud@bostonbeerdistribution <bud fleece>
SUBJ: Coming over today
DATE: Sunday 9/12 11:02 AM

Hi honey. Got your message. Hey, I understand how much you have going on—so don't worry about seeing me and Alice today.

We just wanted to talk to you. No biggie. Maybe later this week or next weekend? Call me.

Love,

Dad

beantownbud@bostonbeerdistribution: foreveramber@quick-link.com is sending you an Instant Message on Sunday 9/12 at 11:08 AM:

foreveramber: Daddy, you still there?

beantownbud: Hi! Yep. I'm just reading an email from your cousin Lisa out in California. Remember her?

foreveramber: Don't tell me. She's landed a part in a movie.

beantownbud: No, she's not acting anymore. She's getting married! A lawyer.

foreveramber: Great. I mean, Great! How thrilling for Sleeza. I mean Lisa.

beantownbud: She was always really nice to you.

foreveramber: No threat, that's why. Listen, I changed my mind.

beantownbud: You did?

foreveramber: I'll come over to Alice's today. I need to take the train—can you pick me up at the T station?

beantownbud: Of course! It's just the three of us, is that okay?

foreveramber: What? Sam the Barber's son is unavailable?

beantownbud: You aren't interested in him.

foreveramber: Ya think?

beantownbud: What about Chet?

foreveramber: I just want to be with you. And Alice. Okay?

beantownbud: Wonderful. Call me before you get on the train and I'll meet you. I really do have something to tell you.

foreveramber: Thanks, Daddy. I have something to tell you, too. I love you.

beantownbud: I love you, too, honey. And thanks for changing your plans to see us. ☺

TO: wildthing@usol.com <john rush>
FROM: juliedes@connectone.com <julie desmond>
SUBJ: Still Thinking
DATE: Sunday 9/12 2:56 PM

Hi, Johnny. I haven't heard from you for a few days—are you fly-fishing or just not "speaking" to me? I hope the former. I've been thinking a lot about your offer. The thing is, even though I'm darn near close to saying yes, my boss has gotten very (very) sick and I think the last thing I could do (or would want to do) right now is take even a day off. That's the honest to God truth—I wish it weren't true. She needs me—and that's not something I could ever ignore.

I have such a rush of conflicting emotions right now. On one hand, I'm happier than I've been for as long as I can remember. Part of that is my new job, part of that is rediscovering . . . I was going to say "you" but, in thinking about it, it's "me." But, I'm also scared for Amber (my boss) and all the things in life we'd like to avoid but can't.

I didn't mean to get too deep and philosophical on you. I just wanted to touch base ☺ as they say. Write when you have time.

Take care,

Jules

TO: foreveramber@quicklink.com <amber fleece>
FROM: caldingerc@troyhillinvest.com <chet caldinger>
SUBJ: Laying Low or **Lying** Low??
DATE: Sunday 9/12 3:36 PM

Amber, I can take a lot of things, but not lying. I saw you at the T station this afternoon. You didn't see me. You didn't appear too sick at all. You were on the phone—laughing. Look, if you're not interested, I'm cool with that. But don't lie to me and tell me you're sick. I'm not all about lies. I'm about the truth.

Chet

TO: wonderwoman@usol.com <stephanie hilliard>
FROM: tmarkoff@millenniamarketing.com <tom markoff>
SUBJ: Shopping with you
DATE: Sunday 9/12 5:20 PM

I can't believe you spent that much money and kept me on the phone the whole time. You're amazing. Do you still love the pink shoes? I know, I know, it's fall—they're dusty rose. But I like the suede and the three-inch heel. I can just picture them on you . . . with nothing else.

Jesus, I feel like my head (and more) is going to explode, Stephanie. All I can think about is being with you. I want to make love to you until you can't breathe. Can't walk. Can't think. I could melt you with one touch, one kiss. My God, woman, you have no idea what you do to me. You had me so hot that whole time on the phone—just your voice, the way you laugh, that little rumble in your throat when you tease me. I want you. I want you. I want you. I love you.

Get up here and let me show you.

T

TO: foreveramber@quicklink.com <amber fleece>
FROM: grayscale@connectone.com <gray mcdermott>
SUBJ: change
DATE: Sunday 9/12 6:57 PM

---

i want to talk to you so bad, i can taste it in my mouth. where are you? shit, i've got no right to ask that. i know. but i've had a pretty lousy sunday. wherever you are, baby, hope you're having fun. enjoying life. making everyone around you laugh. giving them the gift of amber. hope they're worthy of it.

toots, i been thinking. hard. wanna know something about me? i hate change. it makes my stomach clench like when you know you're gonna get punched in the gut and all you can do is get ready for the blow. i don't know why—oh, shit, yes i do. so i'll save my money and skip the shrink. it started when i was a kid. change pissed my dad off. and when my dad got pissed off, donovan and gray got black eyes and bloody noses and all manner of crap-kicking. so when everything stays just like it is, and there's no whitewater, then everybody is safe.

the biggest change i ever made in my life was when i left boston. man, that was hard. you'd think it'd be easy to leave that hellhole of a house and get as far away as i could. but my little brother, donovan, he wasn't as tough as i was. my dad called him a fag and really, really went after him. as long as i was around, i could take the worst of the old prick's fury, then donovan might not get it as bad. except once. fuck. nevermind.

anyway, when i was with you, i started to believe i could do anything. (thanks, toots.) and with you leaving, i decided i could go, too. i did it. i got on that bus and blew out of there and in 14 months, i'd saved enough money to get donovan out of there and he booked, too. in one piece, thank god. he went to los angeles and he's doing okay, trying to be an actor. about as successful as i am as a songwriter. (and not gay.)

anyway, sorry. i do have a point. and it is that my stomach is clenching 'cause i'm looking around and it's time for a change. and i hate change. and just like last time, i got someone smaller and weaker to watch out for. and just like last time, amber fleece is spurring me into action.

and just like last time, i want to be worthy of her.

gray

TO:	foreveramber@quicklink.com <amber fleece>
FROM:	wonderwoman@usol.com <stephanie hilliard>
SUBJ:	Phone Saks
DATE:	Sunday 9/12 7:45 PM

Hey—how are you? I know you're not taking calls, but I sure would like to hear your voice. I IM'd you this morning, and left a message. When is the doctor/lab going to call??? What did you do all day? I can tell you what I did—not that I'm proud of it. I really stuck it to my husband today, that's what I did. And it wasn't just the $1,204.56 I put on the Amex. Which doesn't even have the zing it used to because now I'm an earner again. Hell, I make that in a good day consulting for MM. (Which tells you where the $ is in advertising and it ain't Becker's payroll.)

I spent three hours (you read correctly) on the cell phone with TB today. Would have been four, but the battery died. I took him shopping with me (he's exhausted!) and did my damage to the credit card while he did damage to my heart, soul, and nether regions of my anatomy.

Oh, God, Amber. Is that adultery? Write and absolve me. But most of all, let me know how you are doing.

xoxox

Stevie the Harlot. (It just doesn't have the same ring to it.)

TO: juliedes@millenniamarketing.com <julie desmond>
FROM: wildthing@usol.com <john rush>
SUBJ: Touching (Home) Base
DATE: Sunday 9/12 8:39 PM

Hi "Jules"—I like that name. Fits you. You sparkle like jewels. I'm sorry about your boss—what's the matter with her? Didn't you say she was young—in her twenties? Hope it's nothing serious. Of course I understand—but I'm happy that you're still "thinking" about it. We have plenty of time before I hit the road for Spring Training—so don't sweat it. Just keep writing. And you never have to apologize for getting sidetracked with cute memories or being deep or profound. I know I'm just a dumb jock, but I like a good dose of thoughtful philosophy now and then. I indulge when I go up to my cabin and have time alone. When I get thoughtful, I mostly mull on what WASN'T, not what was. I wasn't the ball player I hoped to be. I wasn't ever in a World Series. I wasn't home when EITHER of my kids took their first steps. I wasn't thinking when I left you on that bench.

Anytime you want to get philosophical, I'm your man.

Johnny

TO: foreveramber@quicklink.com <amber fleece>
FROM: beantownbud@bostonbeerdistribution <bud fleece>
SUBJ: Today
DATE: Sunday 9/12 9:18 PM

You should be getting in any minute from the train station. Amber, honey, I'm just sitting here holding my head and wondering what the hell I can say to you. I'm sorry I got so weird when you told me about what the doctor said. Alice is right—that was really hard for you. I hope I came around okay and you're not mad at me for yelling at you when you made a joke. I know that's your way of dealing with stuff. It was just such a shock and I didn't mean to get mad at you for not telling me sooner. I wish you would have stayed and slept here like Alice suggested, but I understand you want to get home and be in your own place. Sweetheart, you're gonna fight this thing and I'm gonna be right with you every single step of the way. I'm coming over tomorrow, just like I said, and I'm gonna be there when the doctor calls. Even if you're at work. I'm going to be there for you. I already called some of the guys at work and warned them that I'm gonna be real busy the next few weeks. Honey, you don't have to go through this alone.

I know what you're thinking. It's all over your pretty face. "It's just like Mom." But, it's not, Amber. She had something different. I know what you said. Cancer is cancer. But you just don't know enough yet. And they've come a long way since then, believe me. Look at Tony Raffelo's wife, she beat it. And that lady who used to give you piano lessons—what was her name? She beat it.

Oh, God, Amber. I love you honey. You are not in this alone. I promise. I'll call you in the morning. Thanks for coming all the way out here on the train. Alice is crazy about you, too.

Love,

Dad

TO: wonderwoman@usol.com <stephanie hilliard>
FROM: foreveramber@quicklink.com <amber fleece>
SUBJ: Back from the Framingham Wars
DATE: Sunday 9/12 10:05 PM

Sex in Saks? That's what I call multitasking for the new millennium. Not adultery unless you have one of those little cameras on your phone and you took it into the dressing room. Then we might be crossing the line. For now, you don't need to go to confession.

Speaking of confession, I did. Confess. My illness. To my Dad and Alice Ellis. Who's really not that bad. At least she didn't YELL at me for getting a disease like my overreacting, overemotional, basket case of a father. Actually, the Budster didn't yell at me for getting sick. He just had to blow up—that's his first response to anything—so he used "my not telling him" as his excuse. He was fine by the time I left. A little shaken by the news, but he sent me a nice email and is going to come over here tomorrow for the sentencing . . . er, call from the lab.

Also see attached crappy email from Chet the Chump. The

only thing I despise more than an asshole with a lousy sense of humor is a PRESUMPTUOUS asshole with a lousy sense of humor. Isn't he going to feel like dog poop when I tell him not only am I sick, I've got . . . you know.

The only good thing in my life is my songwriter. Funny thing, he's struggling with his own shit (his word, believe me) now, and even though I know you think I should tell him, I don't want to. Not yet. Why test this delicate connection so soon? He's admitted to me that he hates change—how well could he respond to cancer? Oh! Oh! Incoming phone call from Dallas. Gotta go. Write. Later.

Love.

Amber

TO: foreveramber@quicklink.com <amber fleece>
FROM: wonderwoman@usol.com <stephanie hilliard>
SUBJ: Sun night
DATE: Sunday 9/12 11:56 PM

I tried IMing you—I can only hope you're still on the phone with Gray—wallowing not in pity, but in the many fabrics of his voice. ☺ I understand not telling him just yet. No indictment from me. Everything will be clearer tomorrow when we know what we're dealing with. I knew Bud would be furious at you for not telling him sooner. But I'm glad he's there for you. You won't be able to do this alone—whatever it is you have to do. Amber, I can be there with an hour's notice. I may bring rugrats along, but I can get help for them if you need me to take you anywhere or do anything.

Two words for Chet: Good fucking bye. Okay. That's three.

Here's my happy life: I had sex with my husband. Sounds good, right? Well, it was nice not to be turned away because he's tired, or *bored*, or busy, or preoccupied, or whatever. He didn't call me "Heather" (whew) and he seemed to have a good time. A really good time, as a matter of fact. But, Amber, all I could think about was Tom. I kept hearing his voice, thinking of the words he whispered to me all afternoon, of the things he said he'd do to me.

God help me, Amber, I was thinking about him when I came. It was his face I saw, his mouth I kissed, his hands on me. I feel unfaithful and disloyal, but . . . should I? Maybe Brent was having sex with Heather while I was having sex with Tom. And, really (I know you are sick of this question), is that cheating? Or is that using outside stimulus to heighten the excitement of an otherwise dull seven-year-old marriage? I just don't know. IM me if you get this. I'll be on the computer for a while.

xoxo

Stevie

TO: wonderwoman@usol.com <stephanie hilliard>
FROM: foreveramber@quicklink.com <amber fleece>
SUBJ: Better than "I love you"
DATE: Monday 9/13 1:15 AM

Sorry I didn't IM you. I was on the phone with Gray. I almost told him, really, Stevie. I came so damn close. He wants the truth out of me and I know I'm lying by omission, but I'm so scared to screw this up. I'm so scared of adding this to his world. Listen to what he did—he told Mickey about me. I don't know exactly what that means, but he told me he took him for a long ride and they talked about girls (cute, huh?). In the process of explaining about girls (he said quantum physics would have been easier to explain), he told Mickey that he had a girlfriend in Massachusetts. A girlfriend? Did I miss something? Anyway, I let it slide. In no mood to argue with a Brad Pitt look-alike who calls me his girlfriend. THEN get this—he told me that tomorrow, he's going to tell Dixie that he wants to move out. He says he doesn't like change of any kind—and he has some pretty compelling psychological reasons—but I get the impression he's also worried she'd "do something stupid" if he left her. Those were his words. I guess he means take Mickey, and never let Gray see him again? I don't know. Before I could ask any questions, he sang me songs . . . that he wrote for me! Beats "I love you" (almost). So, that just basically erased a weekend's worth of pain and misery and fear and worry and bad memories and horrible imaginings about what might happen to me. How could I bring it up after that?

Hmmm. It just occurred to me. We both spent three hours on the phone with our long distance boyfriends (who are living with other women) today. P is for the Pathetic Pair of us. Anyway, I'm tired beyond description. But for the first time in 48 hours, I forgot about . . . it. And you got laid. So, are we cheating our way into temporary happiness? I don't know. But tomorrow . . .

Well, tomorrow is another day, Scarlett. Without knowing it, Gray made me feel strong and I'm ready for tomorrow and whatever it holds.

Love.

Amber

TO: shilliard@millenniamarketing.com <stephanie hilliard>
FROM: areinhardt@millenniamarketing.com <adele reinhardt>
SUBJ: WWA issues
DATE: Monday 9/13 8:14 AM

Good Monday Morning, Stevie! Hope you had a great weekend. At our meeting on Friday afternoon, Gabriel Wycoming had a question regarding the aviation industry experts we (you) have been interviewing and evidently, you decided to sign off from the call on without telling anyone. Other than Tom, who seemed to have his own connection with you that he held in his lap. I know that meeting was internal and fairly casual, but I would really appreciate if you would plan to be on the call for the duration of the meeting—especially when the President comes into the room.

Gabe wants a breakdown of the industry experts we are interviewing regarding the WWA Luxury Line concept; specifically, he wanted to know if you've talked to anyone at Avion Associates or the travel expert at National Data Gathering, Inc. Since you were unable to forward me the latest report as I asked, I was unable to answer these questions. I'd appreciate a copy of that updated document, ASAP. I need it for a 10:00 meeting. Working with an outside consultant on a major aspect of a marketing campaign is difficult enough when they are local, but I'd appreciate if we'd all try to "go the extra mile" to eliminate the confusion caused by the fact that you are in Florida, not Boston. I know you are truly a team player and Tom has nothing but stars in his eyes for your work, so I know this won't be a problem in the future!

Thanks!

Adele

TO: afleece@milleniamarketing.com <amber fleece>
FROM: shilliard@millenniamarketing.com <stephanie hilliard>
SUBJ: Forward from Eva
DATE: Monday 9/13 8:48 AM

Had to share the attached. Are you there? Jules said you're definitely coming in today. I'm here—online and next to my phone.

xoxox
Stevie

TO: shilliard@millenniamarketing.com <stephanie hilliard>
FROM: afleece@millenniamarketing.com <amber fleece>
SUBJ: Mrs. Hitler
DATE: Monday 9/13 9:15 AM

Thanks for forwarding the bitch-o-gram. She really needs a valium cocktail with a chaser of estrogen. Yes, I'm here. What could I do at home? Wait??? Jules brought me a bagel the size of Fenway Park, and she's wearing her really bright smile o' optimism. Dad has blown off BeerLand for the day and is lurking around the building downstairs, even though he thinks I don't know it. I think he's called Jules ten times in the last ten minutes. The lab only opened at 9:00, so no call yet. Sit tight, all ye who profess to adore me.

Oh—just saw the object of your lust in the fourth floor kitchen. He gave me a pity smile (I better get used to that) so I asked him if he'd done any shopping this weekend. Hah! He said he never could resist a Stuart Weitzman slingback in suede. Dwayne (one of the few individuals at MM who'd appreciate such a purchase) caught the whole thing. More. Later. I *promise* you'll be my second call.

Dad's first.

Amber

TO: shilliard@millenniamarketing.com <stephanie hilliard>
FROM: hilliardb@grandregenthotels.com <brent hilliard>
SUBJ: my schedule this week
DATE: Monday 9/13 9:33 AM

I'm at the airport. Stevie, why did you disappear last night . . . after? And this morning, when I got out of the shower, you were gone again. You're the one accusing me of being distant, but, honestly, it's like I can't pin you down for five minutes anymore. (Not counting the 25 before I fell asleep last night.) Listen, this is going to be a really hard week. Alex is testing me and I'll be goddamned if I'm going to fail. To fail isn't in my vocabulary, any more than it's in yours. Remember our pact, Stevie? And I don't mean our marriage. We agreed—long before we got married—that we would always respect each other's need to succeed. Remember "us"—a couple of overachievers? The whole Ayn Rand concept? I still buy into that. When this fiscal year is over and Alex announces his retirement and makes my promotion official, everything will be back to normal. Or as normal as life can be for a CEO of a major corporation. There will always be meetings and travel. But I want the center of my life to be our home. That's why I'm doing all this. Okay? I'll call you when I can and I'll be checking my email a couple times a day, so let me know how the kids are. And you. And Amber. I know you're worried about her and I am, too.

Love ya,

Brent

TO: shilliard@millenniamarketing.com
<stephanie hilliard>
FROM: jdesmond@millenniamarketing.com
<julie desmond>
SUBJ: Amber
DATE: Monday 9/13 9:42 AM

Hi Stevie—no word yet. I was just wondering about something, though, and thought I'd get your opinion. When I talked to Amber this weekend, and again this morning, she's talked a lot about Gray, her friend in Dallas. She told me she doesn't want him to know anything about what she's going through. Even if the prognosis is the "lesser of two evils"—as she puts it. I don't want to butt in where I don't belong, but I'm just thinking—maybe he should know. Maybe he'd come up here to see her. There's something in her eyes when she talks about him . . . I don't know. I'm just a little crazed today, as you might imagine. Every time her line rings, my whole body turns to ice, then melts. Which it's doing right now.

Gotta go—

Jules

TO: shilliard@millenniamarketing.com
<stephanie hilliard>
FROM: tmarkoff@millenniamarketing.com <tom markoff>
SUBJ: Rumblings
DATE: Monday 9/13 9:51 AM

Hey gorgeous. I know you're hangin' on by a thread today, so I don't want to make it worse. You will call me as soon as you hear from Amber, right? I'm here—just in and out of meetings and on the phone. Listen, the natives are getting restless up in account management. You know that latest report you sent me before the meeting on Friday? Don't send it to anyone else yet. We need to talk about it. I can't call you now—I have a 10:00 meeting. I'll call you when it's over. Thanks. I still can't stop thinking about you . . .

T

PS. My buddy, Davis Gilmore, at Brigham, says Grossman is one of the best oncologists in the world—bar none. She's in good hands.

TO: areinhardt@millenniamarketing.com
<adele reinhardt>
FROM: shilliard@millenniamarketing.com
<stephanie hilliard>
SUBJ: Report
DATE: Monday 9/13 9:55 AM

Adele, I'm just putting the finishing touches on a new report, so I'll send it as soon as I've completed it.

Stevie

TO: tmarkoff@millenniamarketing.com <tom markoff>
FROM: shilliard@millenniamarketing.com
<stephanie hilliard>
SUBJ: Report
DATE: Monday 9/13 10:01

I stalled her. I didn't like it—in fact, I hated it. I have a report—it's perfectly legit and she wanted it by 10:00. (Same meeting?) The woman doesn't need *ammunition* against me, you know. What gives? Let me know.

xoxox
Stephanie
PS. Thanks for the word on Amber's doctor.

TO: hilliardb@grandregenthotels.com <brent hilliard>
FROM: shilliard@millenniamarketing.com
<stephanie hilliard>
SUBJ: Overachievers Anonymous
DATE: Monday 9/13 10:30 AM

This doesn't have a thing to do with *objectivism*, Brent, but a wall that sometimes comes up and sometimes comes down. I appreciate you're trying to push it down. I know what's going on at work—at least I think I do—and how difficult it is. I'll keep you posted on Amber. Oh—I have to go.

xoxo
S

shilliard@millenniamarketing.com: jdesmond@millennia-marketing.com is sending you an Instant Message on Monday 9/13 at 10:45 AM:

jdesmond: Stevie, are you there?

shilliard: Yes–any word?

jdesmond: She's on the phone with the doctor right now.

shilliard: The doctor called–not the lab?

jdesmond: Yes. Dr. Grossman.

shilliard: Oh. I hope that's not bad. Can you hear the conversation?

jdesmond: Her door's closed.

shilliard: How did he sound?

jdesmond: Very serious. Brian Williams-ish, as Amber would say.

shilliard: ☺ Stay right here with me until she's off, okay?

jdesmond: Okay. We'll hold hands and wait. Did you get my email?

shilliard: Yes–about Gray? I don't think you should contact him, Jules. She's very nervous about that relationship.

jdesmond: I knew you'd say that. I agree. I just want to do something, anything, to help her.

shilliard: You are helping her. Believe me. Is she still on the phone?

jdesmond: Yes. Oh, God, I'm shaking.

shilliard: Me too. Just keep talking to me. It helps.

jdesmond: I saw pictures of your beautiful kids in Amber's office. And your husband's good looking, too!

shilliard: Thanks. My kids are amazing. Yes, my husband is cute . . . he travels a lot. ☺

jdesmond: You should go with him.

shilliard: Can't leave the kids.

jdesmond: Bring the kids!

shilliard: Makes for a long trip.

jdesmond: I'm sure, but, still, if you have a good marriage, you should nurture it. Trust me, the kids grow up fast and then there's nothing's left to talk about.

shilliard: Voice of experience?

jdesmond: Voice of a divorcee. ☺ Oh–she just hung up. WAIT.

shilliard: I'm waiting.

shilliard: I'm still waiting.

shilliard: JULES! I'm going CRAZY here!

jdesmond: NOT JULES, ME. Your best effing friend who ISN'T GOING TO DIE! AAAAAH! Stevie! Call me–good news. Not fabulous, but not "non"–I'm going to be okay. Call me–Jules and I are dancing in the Traffic Department!!!

tmarkoff@millenniamarketing.com: shilliard@millennia-marketing.com is sending you an Instant Message on Monday 9/13 at 11:07 AM:

shilliard: TOM! I just left you a voicemail. Are you there???

tmarkoff: Here. I just walked in. What's up?

shilliard: Amber. It's Hodgkins, not "non" Hodgkins. It's good news. Well, better.

tmarkoff: Awesome.

shilliard: She just called me. She's crying, she's so relieved, but scared, too. And so am I. Oh, God, so am I.

tmarkoff: What's the treatment?

shilliard: She has to have tests this week to determine what "stage" she's in, then chemotherapy for a few weeks—how much depends on the stage—then a blast of radiation and she's done. It's cancer, but Grossman said, "If you're going to get it, this is the one you want." Well over 90% curable. She'll be completely better by Christmas.

tmarkoff: Is she still here? I want to go over and see her.

shilliard: Oh, you're so sweet. You can try. She's leaving for an appointment with Grossman in a little while, and then taking a few days off for tests. CAT scans, and MRI and I can't remember what all she has to do. I'm just so happy, Tom. I'm so relieved. I had to share it with you.

tmarkoff: ☺ I'm going over to Traffic now. She won't mind, will she?

shilliard: No. Give her a kiss from me.

tmarkoff: I will. ILY.

shilliard: Wait!

tmarkoff: What?

shilliard: What's going on with Fraulein Reinhardt?

tmarkoff: I'll call you.

shilliard: Use my cell. I won't be here. I'm taking the rest of the day off.

tmarkoff: More shopping?

shilliard: No. I just got a big, bad bout of mommy-itis. I'm taking Declan out to a park for a while—just the two of us—and then we're going to pick up Lily from school and just hang out together.

tmarkoff: Your priorities are shifting.

shilliard: My priorities are solid: Declan and Lily.

tmarkoff: Good for you. I won't bother you. Tonight, maybe. Can I call?

shilliard: Late–after they're in bed.
tmarkoff: Sounds good. Wear something . . . black.
shilliard: You're bad.
tmarkoff: You bet.

TO:	shilliard@millenniamarketing.com <stephanie hilliard>
FROM:	dgallagher@millenniamarketing.com <dwayne gallagher>
SUBJ:	You got what I need ;-)
DATE:	Monday 9/13 12:20 PM

Hello, little Miss Stevie Wonderwoman. Greetings from sunny Boston. (Actually, it *is* sunny for once.) I still can't conjure up a lasting image of you in Orlando, of all places. Well, maybe Cinderella's castle. Yes. That would fit you. There is something adorable about all that Disney faux-kitsch. And I hear through the grapevine that the shopping's decent enough for a true thread hound like you. Score any great shoes lately? (wink, wink)

Anyway, on to business matters at hand. My boss has left for the day—GW is being profiled in the *Herald* (so down-market, I know, but any publicity is good publicity—at least that's what the flacks in PR tell me). Adele is doing the official hand-holding and spin control. She's asked me to call you (which I did, but you're not returning messages today, are you???) and remind you to please send the WWA report—she said you'd know which one she wants. She also asked that you cross file everything into the MM computer server, as all the other account service people do, so we can reference docs even when you're out. So if you could just download all of your files on WWA to date, I'll start a handy little file folder that we can all access.

Have you heard about our darling Amber? Scary shit, if you ask me. Her admin is very tightlipped about it all, but I got the gist of it. Do you think she'll be able to work? Perhaps I could lend some assistance—it would be an excellent use of my masterful meddling/organizational skills in the Traffic Department, don't you think? ☺

Gotta run . . . do send that doc ASAP. Oh! I still don't know your arrival/departure time for El Meeting Grande on the 27th. You *are* going to be here, correctomundo?

Lots of love,

Big D-wayne

TO: jdesmond@millenniamarketing.com <julie desmond>
FROM: wildthing@usol.com <john rush>
SUBJ: Tempting You with Pictures
DATE: Monday 9/13 3:12 PM

Hi Jewels—hope you don't mind me writing to you at work. I wasn't sure if your home computer could handle a picture, but I figured since you work in an ad agency, you'd have no problem downloading at the office. This is a shot from the back porch of my cabin—that's the stream I fish in. And, yeah, that big lug with the shit-eatin' grin is me. I just wanted you to see how pretty it is (the lake, not me—Hah!). The cabin is big (two bedrooms!) and there's lots more to do than just fish. We can hike in those hills. It's real beautiful. I'd really like to share it with you sometime. Drop me a note and let me know how your boss is feeling.

Johnny

TO: hilliardb@grandregenthotels.com <brent hilliard>
FROM: wonderwoman@usol.com <stephanie hilliard>
SUBJ: Thanks
DATE: Monday 9/13 4:58 PM

Hi. I took the kids to the Cherry Hill Park after Lily got out of school—so I wasn't here when your package arrived. Unfortunately, the delivery person didn't see the "perishable" on the side, so the raspberry and chocolate were kind of melted together. Don't worry, I stuck it in the fridge, so it should chill back to an edible state. That was very nice of you, honey. I didn't even know you heard me when I mentioned that Lily had depleted my Godiva stash. I liked your note, too. But I haven't been too sweet lately. Hey—I have really good news about Amber. I'll tell you when you call, but honestly, I've just been on a cloud all day, appreciating life and how short it can be. Anyway, thanks for my favorite treat.

xoxo

Steve

PS. Lily finally mastered the monkey bars! She's so proud of herself. I think it was killing her that the kids in her class could do it and she couldn't. Hmmm. The competitive gene. She comes by that honestly.

PPS. Declan "held" it until we got home. Yes! A dry Huggie! Progress all around the Hilliard Home today. ☺

TO: foreveramber@quicklink.com <amber fleece>
FROM: jdesmond@millenniamarketing.com <julie desmond>
SUBJ: Report and update and . . . a Wild Thing
DATE: Monday 9/13 5:46 PM

Hi Amber. I know you had a hellish day (that was so kind of you to call after your last test this afternoon—you sounded really tired), so I'm not going to call you at home. I'll just send you emails and updates and you can read them throughout the week as you feel like it. I've attached a couple of docs you may want to see (Traffic Daily Status, etc.), but for the most part, there are no crises and I can handle what's going on. Some highlights:

- Dwayne Gallagher has been looking for several WWA files, specifically a report by Stevie Hilliard that we don't have. He said he hasn't been able to reach her. Are you aware of this? Is there anything I can do? I haven't called her, since you said she was taking the afternoon off to celebrate. Dwayne, by the way, has been over here about six times today.
- I've left your calendar untouched for the next few weeks. Won't add anything, but won't cancel until you have more specifics about what's going to happen. Big highlights to consider: 1) photo shoot on Wed., 9/15 at the Back Bay Studio for Beacon Hill Financial Group print ads—the AE says the client really likes you to be there because of the huge quantity of shots that need to be tracked; 2) WWA

Mandatory Team Meeting, Monday, 9/27—all day, here. I can cover both for you, if you like.

- Couldn't resist forwarding you the attached photo. Here's the Wild Thing, number 45 . . . I wasn't expecting him to still be so good-looking! I mean he's darn near fifty, but boy oh boy! He looks better than I do, don't you think??? No "retired baseball player" gut! Now I'm really intimidated. I better not quit that step aerobics class.

Most important—I know we "celebrated" good news this morning—and it was. But remember, Amber, the next few weeks and months are going to be very tough on you physically and emotionally. I want you to always know you can count on me for anything—whether it is work-related or not. I'll do everything I can to keep things moving along—not as well as you do, but I'll do my best. And if you need anything at all, let me know. For instance . . . can I stop by this week and grab your laundry? I can have it done and back in one day. It's my specialty—ask my son! I don't want to impose, I just want you to know you don't have to do everything yourself.

Love,
Jules

TO:	grayscale@connectone.com <gray mcdermott>
FROM:	foreveramber@quicklink.com <amber fleece>
SUBJ:	some news
DATE:	Monday 9/13 8:03 PM

I can't think of a clever subject line for this email. I can't think of a clever anything, frankly. I can't think. I have just finished one of the most exhausting days of my life and the sad and scary thing is, it's the easiest one I have in front of me for several months.

My news. Well. The good news is I'm not going to die. The bad news is that I would if I don't have some serious medical attention, which began today. Actually it began a few weeks ago, I just haven't told you. It appears I have something called Hodgkins. Which is lymphoma. Which is cancer.

But I don't have just any ordinary, common man's cancer. No. I got the best form of cancer in the world, they tell me: "The cancer you want." (How's that for medical spin?) Damn near 100% curable. (Eesh—with my luck, I'll fall into the "damn near" percent.) Anyway, here was my day, honey. After a roller coaster ride of a morning waiting to hear if I would live or die, I found out that I am, indeed, going to live. To do so, I must be fixed. Before they can fix me, I must be tested. So, for four hours today, I was stabbed with needles, drained of blood, scanned for tissue masses, x-rayed, radared, touched, probed, studied and magnetized, until every cell I have is preserved on a reverse negative hanging on a laboratory wall in Newton, Massachusetts. I tried to look at the bright side. I look bone skinny in x-ray vision. (Miserable attempt at humor, I know. I'm desperate.)

No, I'm not. I'm scared. I'm so tired and scared. I don't want to do this. I can't. I mean—I know I will, I have to. But I don't want to. My dad just left—he's been with me all day. I have to thank you for that email you sent—it really made me stop and consider how my dad has been both parents to me for so many years. I shouldn't begrudge him his new girlfriend. He's given me all his love and deserves some happiness. But, now that he's gone home and I'm alone, I just want to cry. And I can't even *drink*! I guess I could, but what about tomorrow's blood test? I'd hate for my blood alcohol level to outweigh my white cell count or something.

I know what you're thinking. I should have told you this sooner. Especially after we talked for so long last night and you shared so much. But, honey, I just couldn't. It's been hard to tell anyone. I just hate what I'm facing. The chemo made my mother so tired and nauseous and . . . her hair fell out.

That's going to happen to me, Gray. All my beautiful hair you love, all my gorgeous, song-inspiring mahoga

ARE YOU SURE YOU WANT TO DELETE?

MESSAGE DELETED

TO:	jdesmond@millenniamarketing.com <julie desmond>
FROM:	foreveramber@quicklink.com <amber fleece>
SUBJ:	Monday night
DATE:	Monday 9/13 8:40 PM

Jules. I'm trying so hard to tell Gray the truth. I wrote him a long, honest email and then I started thinking about my hair and, oh, shit. I just can't.

I just can't stop crying. Why did this happen to me? What did I do to deserve this? All I ever wanted to do was be happy and have a safe, comfortable life and a good marriage with the right guy and a couple of kids. And now I have cancer and am in love with someone who is all wrong and I'm all alone. And feeling really, really sorry for myself.

Thanks, once again, for being there, Jules. You are a godsend to me. Oh! And thanks for sending me the Wild Thing. Ooh baby. Love the little goatee—verrrry Russell Crowe–ish. Yum. You are so completely wonderful to worry about the Traffic Department—just do what you can, but not at the expense of a weekend in the mountains with the Gladiator. Puhleeze. Also, watch Dwayne. He's not Tinkerbell. He'd love your job—or mine.

I know it's early and that I may be missing out on some prime IM time with the man I love, but I'm done in. Okay . . . I'll leave the computer on in case I hear an IM come in. I know. I know. Desperate, thy name is Amber. Call. Tomorrow.

Love.

Amber

foreveramber@quicklink.com: wonderwoman@usol.com is sending you an Instant Message on Monday 9/13 at 10:53 PM:

wonderwoman: Amb? Are you there? I don't want to call and wake you if you're sleeping.

wonderwoman: You must have crashed. We can talk tomorrow. I just wanted to say I'm thinking about you. I hope you're doing okay. I love you. (I know, worthless from me, but still . . . ☺)

foreveramber: I'm here, princess. I was half asleep, waiting for the ding.

wonderwoman: The ding?

foreveramber: Of IM. Of Gray.

wonderwoman: Oh, sorry to be the wrong ding.

foreveramber: That's okay. I'm really tired, but I can't sleep. You know the feeling?

wonderwoman: Of course. You're stressed to the max. Can you talk about it?

foreveramber: Not the tests. They sucked. I don't want to relive them.

wonderwoman: I'm so sorry, sweetie. I wish I could be there. Want me to come up?

foreveramber: Not just for me. Of course, there's always Tom. ☺

wonderwoman: Don't go there. I just got off the phone with him.

foreveramber: We've moved into daily phone calls, I see.

wonderwoman: I guess we have. I'm alone. Lonely.

foreveramber: Now you *are* starting to sound like a suburban cliché.

wonderwoman: Complete with the cheating husband.

foreveramber: Any news on the Harlot?

wonderwoman: No. Brent's in . . . oh, I don't even remember where the hell he is. Hilton Head! Yes. He's in Hilton Head.

foreveramber: God, I'm too tired to even make Head jokes. But is she there?

wonderwoman: I don't know or care. I don't want to talk about my brush with infidelity—or his. Have you talked to Gray? Have you told him yet?

foreveramber: About my near-death experience?

wonderwoman: Near being the operative word. Yes.

foreveramber: Almost. I deleted it through my tears.

wonderwoman: Oh, Amber. Tell me.

foreveramber: No. I hate pity. I already emailed Julie with a pity party and she called me in six seconds flat. I had to beg her not to come over and rock me to sleep.

wonderwoman: She's the best. Listen, Amber, you got good news. I know it's going to suck for a few months, but you'll be alive.

foreveramber: Bald.

wonderwoman: ?

foreveramber: Don't ? me. You know what I mean. I'm going to go B.A.L.D. I hate to be as shallow as a rain puddle here, but you know how I am about my hair. I *am* my hair. Like you are your shoes.

wonderwoman: I am NOT my shoes.

foreveramber: No, but they make you feel pretty. Feminine. Powerful. Confident.

wonderwoman: That's a bit of a stretch, but okay. I get your point. We have our superficial crutches to help us be women.

foreveramber: Not just to help us. In a sense they define us, these feminine attributes. My hair is like my security blanket, my badge of honor, my . . . pride. That's it. I'm proud of my gorgeous hair. Pride goeth before the bald spot, I suppose. Better bald than dead. Be bold . . . be bald.

wonderwoman: You are *not* your hair. You are a woman with an incredibly loving heart, a deep soul, and a quick, brilliant mind.

foreveramber: You've definitely been spending too much time with a copywriter.

wonderwoman: You're the one creating the bald tag lines. Listen, you are so much more than a great head of hair. You're selling yourself short.

foreveramber: But I don't want Gray to even *think* of me cue-ball style.

wonderwoman: You know this isn't all about being bald. This is about having the disease you dread most in the whole world. I know that–and, Amber, I respect your fear. And so will Gray. Do you think he's that superficial that he'd stop writing, calling or caring because you have a temporary hair loss as a result of treatment that *saved your life*? If he is, I hate him.

foreveramber: It doesn't matter what I'm scared of or how he'll handle it. I've made my decision. I'm not telling him until it's all over. I'll be all better by Christmas, and in a year or so, my hair will be . . . to my ears.

wonderwoman: First of all, you'll be adorable with a spiky red 'do. I can just see it. A whole new excuse to buy awesome earrings. Second, hats are cool. And THIRD (and most important) . . . HOW will you know what this guy's made of if you don't tell him?

foreveramber: Maybe I don't want to know.

wonderwoman: Fine. Just keep him as your fantasy Mr. Perfect and don't ever test his love.

foreveramber: Love? We're never—Aaahhh!

wonderwoman: What?

foreveramber: He's IMing me in another session.

wonderwoman: See? Go. Bye!

foreveramber: No! No, Stevie, wait. I'm not going to talk to him. Don't sign off yet.

wonderwoman: I'll stay here all night if you want me to. But why don't you want to talk to him?

foreveramber: I'm too weak right now. I thought I could handle an IM, but I can't. I'll tell him. Then it'll all be over.

wonderwoman: I bet it won't.

foreveramber: No. I'm just not ready yet, okay? I'm not ready.

wonderwoman: All right. Fine. What's he saying?

foreveramber: Just "are you there?" (Okay, he says, "are you waitin' for me, toots?" Big sigh.) He can tell when I'm online. I want to think about something else for a while. What did you and Tom talk about?

wonderwoman: My shoes.

foreveramber: *Ahem,* Madame I-Am-Not-My-Shoes.

wonderwoman: ☺ We discussed other things.

foreveramber: Such as?

wonderwoman: My legs *in* my shoes.

foreveramber: Did you have phone sex?

wonderwoman: Not technically. I don't think I could do that. But it gets kind of hot. Is that cheating?

foreveramber: You keep asking me that. What do you think?

wonderwoman: I think Brent is screwing Heather the Harlot. He sent guilt candy today.

foreveramber: Maybe he sent "make up" candy. Maybe you want to think Brent is screwing Heather the Harlot so you can forgive yourself for screwing Tom the Troublemaker.

wonderwoman: I'm not going to have sex with him.

foreveramber: Then what are all the hot calls leading up to? The final client report—then the kiss off?

wonderwoman: I don't know, Amb. I don't know if it's leading up to anything. He just makes me feel so attractive and charming and . . . young and flirtatious again. Brent makes me feel dull and drab and motherly.

foreveramber: Maternal can be beautiful. You were the prettiest pregnant woman I'd ever met.

wonderwoman: Thanks. There is one thing about Tom, though.

foreveramber: Hard to pick one. Shoulders? Face? Hair? Jean bulge?

wonderwoman: He's very vague about stuff at work. I think this professional rivalry with Adele is part of his whole mid-life meltdown. Plus, I don't think she has the hots for him, even if Dwayne does (think that, not have the hots for him—although he probably does). All I know is that I'm starting to feel like the rope in their tug of war.

foreveramber: I wish I could be there to investigate. Want me to get Jules on it?

wonderwoman: Nah–I'll manage.

foreveramber: Oh boy oh boy. I thought he gave up, but now there's an incoming call from Dallas, Texas. The cowboy/song-writer/painter/ poet/stud *wants* me.

wonderwoman: Saddle up, tootsie pop. You need him more than you need me.

foreveramber: I need you both, but I'm not answering. Let him wonder if I'm out with Chester the Jester. I'm tired and really want to go to bed. Tomorrow's another CAT scan and blood test. Oh joy.

wonderwoman: ☹ Chet's real name is *Chester*? Ooh. Strike two. Amber: Tell Gray.

foreveramber: Steve, he writes *songs* about my hair. What rhymes with mahogany, he asks?

wonderwoman: Tobogganу? Lobotomy?

foreveramber: Monogamy, I told him.

wonderwoman: Never thought of that.

foreveramber: Really? And it's *always* on your mind.

wonderwoman: Glad to see you're still a smartass.

foreveramber: They can't radiate that outta me. See ya, girlie.

wonderwoman: Night, Amb.

TO: foreveramber@quicklink.com <amber fleece>
FROM: grayscale@connectone.com <gray mcdermott>
SUBJ: g'nite sweet girl
DATE: Monday 9/13 11:25 PM

where are you, baby? did you fall asleep and leave your computer on? i've been trying to reach you . . . but you're out of reach. too bad. had a long day—with some serious hassles that i won't bore you with. i got a woman pissed at me and a boy disappointed in me and more work than i want or can handle. and no amber waves of grain to get lost in tonight.

so, you in bed? i can just see you. your eyes closed, your lips parted with slow, steady breaths. your hair floating across the pillow. the sheets are pulled up over your chest and i can't tell if you're wearing anything or not. gotta know. gotta see. i tiptoe over and slooooooowly slide the sheet over your shoulders, inch by sweet, luscious inch. lookin' good in there. lookin' . . . naked. yeah. i tug a little more, to be sure. the sheet slips down your breasts, and i blow softly, to tease your nipples into precious pink points. my mouth waters for a taste, but . . . not . . . yet. slide some more. down goes the sheet, over your . . . oh?—what's that? a bellybutton diamond. nice. might like to taste that, too. later, later. you stir under my breath, your hips rise up a little as i reveal more. oh. my. where are your underpants, young lady? tsk tsk. i'll have to just take a peek, let's slide those precious thighs apart. oh, baby. you are so beautiful. i'll be back for some of that. let's just continue with this sheet slide. over your sexy legs, those adorable knees, along each perfect calf, pause at that cute little ankle bracelet. we're just about there. over the perfect arch in that little foot . . . oh. there. delicate, delicious, delectable . . . toes. and what have we here? a silver toe ring. your body was made for jewelry. and for me. i'll just slide my tongue over that ring and start right here on this little baby toe at the end. shhhh. go back to sleep. it's gonna take all night to work my way back up.

gray

TO: grayscale@connectone.com <gray mcdermott>
FROM: foreveramber@quicklink.com <amber fleece>
SUBJ: good morning
DATE: Tuesday 9/14 7:19 AM

I had the strangest, sweetest dream last night. I felt this little chill as my sheet slipped off, but then I got very, very warm. All over. And my toe ring was missing! I hope you didn't swallow it.

Love.
Me

TO: wildthing@usol.com <john rush>
FROM: jdesmond@millenniamarketing.com <julie desmond>
SUBJ: Tempted!
DATE: Tuesday 9/14 11:15 AM

Hi John. Thanks for sending the picture—wow! You're right. It's really tempting. The mountains are nice, too. ☺ Seriously, it's going to get a bit hectic here—my boss is going to have treatment for Hodgkins over the next few weeks—she's going to be okay, the doctors say, but I want to really hold things together here for her. Since fair's fair, I've attached a picture from my son's graduation last year that a friend of mine took with her digital camera. Will's the one on the left—isn't he handsome? The other boy is his friend, Jared . . . and that's me, in the middle.

Take care,

Jules

TO: tmarkoff@millenniamarketing.com <tom markoff>
FROM: areinhardt@millenniamarketing.com <adele reinhardt>
SUBJ: WWA Aviation Experts Report
DATE: Tuesday 9/14 2:45 PM
CC: gwycoming@millenniamarketing.com <gabriel wycoming>

In an effort to "play nice" (as our President has instructed), I am formally requesting a copy of the latest report from Stephanie Hilliard for the account files of WWA. I am required to do a mid-month status for the client, so they are not astounded by the hours we bill them for at the end of the month. (This was part of a lengthy contract negotiation that took place before you arrived at MM, Tom. Trust me. Our behinds are on the line if the hours exceed the agreed-upon amount!) Frankly, Stephanie has been completely uncooperative on this issue, refusing to return messages, and ignoring requests from my administrative assistant! Since you seem to have an excellent personal relationship with her, please instruct her to forward this and all WWA work to the group server so that we might all share in the information she is obtaining.

Thank you.

Adele

TO:	shilliard@millenniamarketing.com <stephanie hilliard>
FROM:	jdesmond@millenniamarketing.com <julie desmond>
SUBJ:	Amber
DATE:	Tuesday 9/14 4:31 PM

Hi Stevie. Just thought you'd like to know that Amber is home from her tests, and resting. I think the whole thing is starting to really get to her—I could hear her voice crack when she talked to me. I wouldn't call her, though. She said she wanted to unplug her phone and sleep, but I think she's worried about missing a call from Gray.

She did get some information, and I wondered if you wanted to think about it. She said her first chemo treatment will be on September 28. And I remembered that you're coming up for a meeting on the 27th. You know how she is—she won't ask for help under any circumstances. But I thought you might want to alter your travel plans to stay here an extra day or two and be with her. The first treatment is really hard, I've read. At least until they find the right drugs to keep her from getting too nauseous. I've been working with HR to figure out all the vacation, sick, and personal time she has left for the year, so she can take three days off that week (and this week) and other days after the treatments. Anyway, she loves you so much, I thought since you're going to be here already, you might want to stay. I mentioned it briefly to her and she said no, no, no, you have something to do with your daughter, and might not come at all. What do you think? Let me know.

Take care,

Jules

TO: tmarkoff@millenniamarketing.com <tom markoff>
FROM: shilliard@millenniamarketing.com <stephanie hilliard>
SUBJ: WWA
DATE: Tuesday 9/14 5:16 PM

Hey Tom. I got your voicemail. I am not crazy about this . . . but okay. I made the changes you want, and sent all the reports. You're not really changing the findings, but there's a definite shift in the emphasis. Not at all how I would write it up. Anyway, we can discuss in detail later. Yes, I'm home tonight and you can call. Signing off MM email for tonight—duty calls from the playroom.

xoxo
Stephanie

TO: hilliardb@grandregenthotels.com <brent hilliard>
FROM: wonderwoman@usol.com <stephanie hilliard>
SUBJ: schedule
DATE: Tuesday 9/14 8:45 PM

Hi Brent. I know I told you on the phone this morning that I'd definitely decided *not* to go up to Boston for that meeting, but there's been a change. Amber's chemo starts the next day and I want to be there for her. I know you're on the West Coast all next week, but you did say you'd be in town on the 27th, right? And for a few days after that? You'll have to take Lily on the school field trip and be sure to be home those nights. Between Rosa and Maria, we can be covered all day. Trust me, I don't like this any more than you do. But everything's different, now. This isn't just business. This is for Amber. I know you're at that awards banquet tonight (hope your speech goes well), so I guess we'll talk tomorrow. Kids send their love. Me too.

xoxo

Stevie

grayscale@connectone.com: foreveramber@quicklink.com is sending you an Instant Message on Tuesday 9/14 at 9:45 PM:

foreveramber: hi there.

grayscale: hey! you're there. why aren't you answering your phone?

foreveramber: Call me coy.

grayscale: can i call you now?

foreveramber: No. I lost my voice.

grayscale: why don't you want to talk to me?

foreveramber: Long story. Can we just e-chat?

grayscale: whatever you want, toots. i'm yours.

foreveramber: If only.

grayscale: if i could be, i would be.

foreveramber: That's okay. It's better this way. You're my dream lover.

grayscale: does your company have an office in dallas?

foreveramber: No. <gulp> Where are you going with that question?

grayscale: just wondering.

foreveramber: Millennia Marketing is only in Boston.

grayscale: there are other ad agencies in the world, you know.

foreveramber: So I've heard. There are garage doors to be painted in Massachusetts, you know.

grayscale: no can do, toots. i will never breathe the air in the same state as my alleged parents.

foreveramber: That's sort of drastic and draconian, don't you think?

grayscale: that's my parents: drastic and draconian mcdermott.

foreveramber: ☹ No word from Nashville?

grayscale: actually . . . yeah. it seems tim mcgraw heard "back into you" and kinda likes it.

foreveramber: OMG! That's huge! Even *I've* heard of him.

grayscale: a million hoops to jump through. i'll let you know if anything happens.

foreveramber: Would you go to Nashville?

grayscale: would you?

foreveramber: To Nashville? Why?

grayscale: to see me.

foreveramber: Maybe someday.

grayscale: i can't wait that long.

foreveramber: You've waited ten years.

grayscale: i'm gonna get really rich and buy you a mansion overlooking a lake in tennessee. we can have six kids and sex all day.

foreveramber: Not with six kids.

grayscale: they'll go to school eventually. and we can go to bed and make a seventh.

foreveramber: You want kids?

grayscale: i didn't think so. but mickey has changed my mind. you?

foreveramber: I don't know.

grayscale: dr. grossman again?

foreveramber: Don't go there.

grayscale: okay. then what's going on with your new boyfriend?

foreveramber: Let's see . . . he lives in Dallas with some woman and her son.

grayscale: your <u>other</u> boyfriend.

foreveramber: Not much, to be honest.

grayscale: did you sleep with him yet?

foreveramber: No.

grayscale: you gonna?

foreveramber: When I can have cyber-sex with you? Are you nuts?

grayscale: evidently, i am. about you. i have to figure out my life.

foreveramber: It's like we talked about the other night. Start with your priorities, Gray. What's number-one to you?

grayscale: mickey's my number-one priority.

foreveramber: I understand that. But he's not your son. If you move out, what will happen?

grayscale: baby, i'm up to my ass in worrying about it. we talked enough. kiss me instead.

foreveramber: What are you going to do?

grayscale: nibble under your ear.

foreveramber: Seriously, Gray. What are you going to do?

grayscale: lick you until you shudder.

foreveramber: Not in the mood. Sorry. I'm going to bed.

grayscale: i need some time, amber. don't be mad at me.

foreveramber: I'm not mad at you. I'm mad at the world. I'm mad at my bad luck. Bye.

TO: foreveramber@quicklink.com <amber fleece>
FROM: wonderwoman@usol.com <stephanie hilliard>
SUBJ: Guess who's coming to dinner?
DATE: Wednesday 9/15 8:10 AM

Hey Amb . . . how are you? I heard it sucked yesterday. Hang in there, honey. Guess what? I've decided to come up the week of the 27th. I know you're going to get mad and tell me not to come and that you don't need me and that I was planning to stay for Lily's field trip—but Brent's going to handle things here and I'm coming up no matter how hard you work to convince me not to. Please don't try to talk me out of it.

xoxox
Stevie

TO: wonderwoman@usol.com <stephanie hilliard>
FROM: foreveramber@quicklink.com <amber fleece>
SUBJ: RE: Guess who's coming to dinner?
DATE: Wednesday 9/15 8:25 AM

You're kidding, right? I'm not talking you out of anything except staying at a hotel. Excuse the bad play on words, but I'd *die* if you weren't here. Thank you.

Love.
Amber

TO: dgallagher@millenniamarketing.com <dwayne gallagher>
FROM: shilliard@millenniamarketing.com <stephanie hilliard>
SUBJ: WWA Meeting Logistics
DATE: Wednesday 9/15 9:06 AM

Hi Dwayne. Hope you received all the information I sent and filed it in the appropriate server to be accessed by one and all. Thanks for your patience while I updated the docs. FYI, I'll be arriving on Sunday, September 26 and will attend the entire meeting (including the afternoon brainstorming session) on Monday, September 27. I don't need a hotel and will handle the flight arrangements on my own.

Thanks—
Stevie

TO: shilliard@millenniamarketing.com <stephanie hilliard>
FROM: tmarkoff@millenniamarketing.com <tom markoff>
SUBJ: Heard in the Halls
DATE: Wednesday 9/15 9:54 AM

Just picked up the most bizarre water cooler gossip. Is it possible you changed your mind about the meeting, and told Adele's administrative assistant *before* you told me? Is that because you're planning to surprise me by showing up at my office late at night in a mink, pink shoes, and . . . a smile? I certainly hope so . . .

T

TO: beantownbud@bostonbeerdistribution.com <bud fleece>
FROM: foreveramber@quicklink.com <amber fleece>
SUBJ: What were you going to tell me???
DATE: Wednesday 9/15 9:59 AM

Hi Daddy. Just wanted to let you know I decided not to go in today—you're right. I need a day to veg with no tests and no work. My super-capable assistant is dying to do the photo shoot that I had scheduled. Anyway, I don't feel like dealing with all those well-meaning idiots who are scared to ask what they are thinking, "Are you going to make it, Amber?" I think I'll have a button made: "Bad, bald, and bound to stick around." See why I'm in advertising??? You know, I woke up in the middle of the night and remembered that on Sunday you said you had something to tell me, but I stole the show at Alice's house and you never told me anything. What was it? Write or call when you have time.

I love you.

Amber

TO: tmarkoff@millenniamarketing.com <tom markoff>
FROM: wonderwoman@usol.com <stephanie hilliard>
SUBJ: The servers have ears
DATE: Wednesday 9/15 10:06 AM

Perhaps you are unaware that int**RA**company emails delivered via the MM server—such as the one you sent about ten minutes ago—are easily intercepted, read, and even occasionally slipped into personnel files by the powers that be at Millennia Marketing. If you feel the need to spend billable hours fantasizing about my clothes, or the removal of them, would you be kind enough to send that email to my personal address? Better yet, use your *own* personal email service? I'd appreciate it.

Yes, I told Dwayne first. I hope you're not mad. The real reason I'm going to Boston has nothing to do with WWA (or the not-so-subtle beggings from certain account team members). I'm going because Amber's treatment starts on the 28th and I want to be there for her. I just made the decision sort of impulsively, so I hadn't had a chance to tell you. Also, just for your edification, I do not wear mink—ever—and under the circumstances, I may not be wearing a smile. Pink shoes? Now there's a safe bet.

xoxo

Stephanie

TO: afleece@millenniamarketing.com <amber fleece>
FROM: jdesmond@millenniamarketing.com <julie desmond>
SUBJ: Morning update
DATE: Wednesday 9/15 11:43 AM

Good morning, Amber! I hope you're resting and taking advantage of this one day you don't have any tests. I got your voicemail and I'm really excited about the photo shoot. Thanks for giving me a chance. Don't bother to check your work email—I'm keeping an eye on it. I did see a note from Chet, which I'm forwarding. Everything is running fine here. I'll be out from 2–4 for the shoot—but then I'll be back to check on things. Do me a favor and pile all your laundry in one basket and put it outside your door. (It's safe in that building, don't you think?) I'm stopping by tonight and I don't want to bother you.

Take care—extra, extra care,

Jules

TO: afleece@millenniamarketing.com <amber fleece>
FROM: caldingerc@troyhillinvest.com <chet caldinger>
SUBJ: let's try again
DATE: Wednesday 9/15 11:16 AM

Amber—I feel kind of bad about coming down so hard on you after I saw you in the train station. I suppose you do have a life—and even had one before I showed up. I'd like to take you to lunch today. Any chance? I'll be near your office around 1:00.

Call me or email me.

Chet

TO: jdesmond@millenniamarketing.com <julie desmond>
FROM: foreveramber@quicklink.com <amber fleece>
SUBJ: Update
DATE: Wednesday 9/15 12:06 PM

Have I told you lately that I love you? You're awesome, Jules. The photo shoots are usually a lot of fun. The most important thing to remember is to log the shots and make sure the "must haves" that the client ordered are taken. The models are occasionally a handful, but I know who they are using for this shoot and you should be fine. About the laundry . . . you are a living doll, you know that? I'm going to take you up on that world-class offer. None of the old bubkas in this place would steal my undies, but I won't put the basket out. Just ring the bell. I would love to see you. Don't worry about Chet. I just left him a message on voice-mail magnanimously offering to make him lunch if he wants to come over here. I guess it's time Chet and I have a little heart to heart. Speaking of heart to heart . . . how are things with Russell Crowe-magnon man? Any word from him? Thanks again. You are really good to me.

Love.

Amber

TO: wonderwoman@usol.com <stephanie hilliard>
FROM: tmarkoff@millenniamarketing.com <tom markoff>
SUBJ: your serve(r) . . . your serv(ant) . . . your serve
DATE: Wednesday 9/15 12:36 PM

Stephanie, my love. I was only trying to make your life easier with one email. Don't worry about the powers that be—I am (one of) the powers that be and employee emails are the last thing we discuss at Exec Committee meetings. If only it were that interesting.

You didn't answer my indirect question. Will I see you when you're up here? Can I pick you up at the airport? Where are you staying? I can arrange to spend Sunday evening with you. Let me put it this way . . . I want to be with you every minute that I can.

T

TO: foreveramber@quicklink.com <amber fleece>
FROM: grayscale@connectone.com <gray mcdermott>
SUBJ: [none]
DATE: Wednesday 9/15 1:50 PM

some shit—some really, really bad shit—is going on. i may not be around today, tonight. tomorrow. i don't know. i'll try to call or write later.

i'm not disappearing, honest.

gray

TO: wonderwoman@usol.com <stephanie hilliard>
FROM: hilliardb@grandregenthotels.com <brent hilliard>
SUBJ: Week of 27th
DATE: Wednesday 9/15 3:11 PM

Got your message. I'm sorry I didn't get back to you sooner—I've been in meetings since the crack of dawn. The banquet went late and, of course, moved into the bar where I had to schmooze a little more with Alex. He all but called me "the next CEO"—he's really happy that the Resort numbers are up 14% over last year, and said so to the entire Resort management team. Listen, I understand about Amber. I cleared my calendar for the 27th to do the field trip and will move heaven and earth not to have to leave town until you're back.

Love ya,

Brent

TO: jdesmond@millenniamarketing.com <julie desmond>
FROM: wildthing@usol.com <john rush>
SUBJ: A picture I like
DATE: Wednesday 9/15 3:36 PM

Well, I've wasted the whole afternoon looking at the same damn picture on my computer. And what a picture it is! Jules, I forgot how damn pretty you are. And I'm not surprised that your son is a good-looking kid—and sizable, too. Bet he could handle himself on the diamond. Your hair is a longer than I remember it—but still that sunny blonde. And your eyes twinkle just like they always did. And I forgot you have that really sweet tilt to your head when you laugh. Thanks for sending that excellent distraction—I was supposed to be watching videos of games and strategizing new plays. Instead, I imagined what you'd look like sitting out by my stream, wearing a vest pack and carrying my new Sage fly rod. Now there's a picture I'd like to take. Hope you're doing okay—not working or worrying too much.

Thinking about you . . .

Johnny

TO: wonderwoman@usol.com <stephanie hilliard>
FROM: foreveramber@quicklink.com <amber fleece>
SUBJ: Men and Why We Hate Them
DATE: Wednesday 9/15 4:02 PM

There's no answer on your home phone and you're not online. You are probably doing something fun with the kids, so I'm not going to drag you down with a cell phone call. I'll just drag you down with an email.

What men do we hate? you ask when you read the subject line.

These men, the men we think meet our criteria for love and affection and relatively happy ever afters. The ones that have *po*. The ones that seem financially and emotionally and spiritually and psychologically secure. The ones that look good, drive the right car, hold the right degrees, carry the right business cards, and visit their sick aunts.

That list would NOT include Chester Marshall Caldinger III.

Great. I finally nail his name, just in time to forget him. He's NOT one of those above mentioned criteria-meeting guys. Nope. He *doesn't* look *that* good, the car is leased, they let damn near anybody into Harvard now, he's only a JUNIOR investment banker, and his aunt has a fortune and a failing heart, so of course he's nice to her.

And worst of all, he turned tail at the first mention of the "C" word. He didn't even have the social grace to offer *faux* support. He came over for lunch, made a joke (not funny, what a surprise) about me not wearing any makeup, looked askance at the food *I* bought for him at DeLuca's (what did he expect—a hot lunch???), and demanded an explanation of why I was on a train on Sunday when I told him I was sick.

So I told him. I AM sick, Chet. I said those three words that make grown men cringe and cower: **I have cancer**. Guaranteed to provide a good view of a man's backside . . . heading out the door.

I didn't cry or act like I needed sympathy. I didn't crack one joke, thank you very much. I copped the "I am woman, I am strong, and this is just a challenge that I'm going to meet and beat" attitude (that I don't feel in the least, but am trying desperately to project). And he . . . well, he seemed . . . how do I sum up his response?

Inconvenienced. That's it. Somehow I got the distinct impression he viewed chemo and radiation as a *scheduling* problem. Just in case you fail to believe me, here are some highlights of his response:

- "I guess you won't have time for a relationship." (Yep, that's a real, Honest To God quote.) My internal comeback: Wouldn't that depend on what *kind* of a relationship???
- "You need to get through this with your family and friends." (Another HTG quote.) A group that clearly doesn't include him.
- "I was thinking we'd go skiing this winter, but probably not." (Could be my favorite effing quote.) Not this year, I quietly agreed.

Then he left. He made a few attempts at cheek kisses and wimpy words of encouragement, but basically, he left with the speed that would make one believe that Hodgkins is contagious.

I know it's really a good thing that I've seen his true colors before I did anything stupid, like sleep with him. Or actually grow to like him. But, damn, Stevie. This is PRECISELY WHY I haven't told Gray. Write.

Love.

Amber

PS. I'm going out for a while to destinations unknown. Let's catch up later on office dirt. I'll need to be fully briefed before I go in tomorrow.

TO: foreveramber@quicklink.com <amber fleece>
FROM: beantownbud@bostonbeerdistribution.com <bud fleece>
SUBJ: RE: What were you going to tell me???
DATE: Wednesday 9/15 4:45 PM

Hey honey—I hate that you wake up in the middle of the night and worry about stuff like that. I did have something to tell you, but it wasn't important. Let's just get you all better before we think about anything else. I'm leaving work now, going to make one stop, then I'll be home. Call me later and let me know how your day went.

Love you,
Dad

TO: foreveramber@quicklink.com <amber fleece>
FROM: wonderwoman@usol.com <stephanie hilliard>
SUBJ: Strike THREE for Fester
DATE: Wednesday 9/15 7:15 PM

Just had a chance to read your email. Exactly *what* did you see in this guy in the first place? Good riddance. But, Amb, you're crazy to think every man you care about is going to act that way. If you think you have something *real* with Gray, then you need to tell him. If he isn't what you want him to be, then you shouldn't be wasting your time with him.

You know, you've always held back where men are concerned. Why exactly do you think that is? You are pretty and funny and easy to love. But you put that wall around you. You quip, you hold back, you don't give in to the possibility. I've seen it happen over and over with you. What are you looking for? I know what you *think* you are looking for—stability, good family, movie star looks. But what are you really looking for?

I remember when I asked myself that question, and found myself staring into the eyes of Brent Hilliard. And it wasn't his blind ambition or steely determination to climb to the top of the ladder that attracted me. Maybe at first. Maybe I sensed a kindred spirit. He seems to think so. But that's not why I floated down the aisle with him. That's not what made me joyous with both pregnancies (or roll into a ball and weep after that miscarriage). And ambition is certainly not why the thought of him with someone else feels like an acrylic fingernail stabbing my heart.

What I was looking for . . . and what I found . . . was a grounded man. A man with inner fortitude that matched his outer strength. A man who never flinched at my success, but cheered it. A man who viewed me from the beginning as an equal. A man who wanted me as a woman, but also as a partner. That man, my man, used to make me laugh. We used to talk about everything and nothing at all. We used to be so comfortable in a room together, we didn't even know how *not* to feel that way. And now. Now . . .

Oh . . . now I'm all teary-eyed. What went wrong, Amb? Did Brent stop seeing me as a partner? Does my work as a mother fail to impress him as much as my highly paid prowess in business? Does he need a professional equal to bring out his strengths? When did we stop being partners, and start being sniping, snapping husband and wife?

Sorry, Amb. This was supposed to be about *you*—and you made me see my own problems more clearly.

xoxoxo

Stevie

TO: wildthing@usol.com <john rush>
FROM: juliedes@connectone.com <julie desmond>
SUBJ: Life!
DATE: Wednesday 9/15 7:41 PM

Hi, John. You wanted deep? Profound? What was your word . . . philosophical? Well, here goes. It occurred to me today that it took a life-threatening situation to give me the opportunity to discover my own life. Amber, my boss, handed over the reins for a photo shoot today. A fairly simple assignment—it's not like she asked me to write and execute a marketing plan. But this was my first professional task outside of the office. It was great, John! I had so much fun—making decisions with the Account Exec about shots, keeping a formal log of every shot we'd taken, watching the lighting and sets be changed, dealing with the models. I felt a little guilty—poor little Amber is home facing the realities of what she's about to face, and here I am like a starry-eyed kid out of college on her first day of work.

It felt so good to have that confidence that I belonged there, that I was an integral part of a company with goals, clients, revenues, and purpose. Not that raising Will and all that entailed (sports and projects and chauffeuring and friends and worry) wasn't an important job with a purpose. God knows, it was. But I always watched the women who showed up at the school functions in suits and dresses and wondered, "What it's *like* out there?" And today, I experienced "out there" firsthand. And I really, really enjoyed it. But, of course, this little groundswell of pride and excitement comes with so much guilt. Why didn't I get this kind of "high" from being a mom? And I wish it hadn't taken Amber's illness to kick me out of the office. I can't answer those questions, but I can tell you this—I'll be doing more and more of it, even when she's back.

I just wanted to share my excitement with someone . . . and you seemed to be the perfect someone.

Now, I'm going to doing something I *know* I do well . . . Amber's laundry. Thanks for sharing a little bit of my life.

Jules

TO: tmark@quicklink.com <tom markoff>
FROM: wonderwoman@usol.com <stephanie hilliard>
SUBJ: next week
DATE: Wednesday 9/15 8:36 PM

Kids are in bed, house is quiet. Bliss. I've been sitting here for a few minutes trying to think of what to say to you. How to respond to your last note. I guess honestly—right? Tom, I'm just not sure about seeing you next Sunday night when I get into Boston. I could give you a shitload of excuses about Amber and my time, but the truth is, I'm horrified to imagine what might happen. I have to give this some more thought—so don't pressure me. I'll just let you know, okay? Thanks.

xoxo

Stephanie

TO:	wonderwoman@usol.com <stephanie hilliard>
FROM:	foreveramber@quicklink.com <amber fleece>
SUBJ:	Telling Gray
DATE:	Wednesday 9/15 10:13 PM

I'm going to tell him.

You're right, of course, about finding out what kind of man he is. But that's not why I'm going to tell him. It's more about what kind of woman I am.

Something happened today to change my mind—and it wasn't Chet's inelegant kiss off. I left this afternoon and took the T out to Framingham. Not to see Dad . . . to see Mom. I went to her grave, something I do about once a year, to collect my thoughts and talk to her. I know: How clichéd is *that*? Clichéd with a capital "Clee," because guess who showed up? The Budster. Yep. There I was, sitting on the grass, bundled up in that dude ranch suede jacket that you hate. I was plucking the fringe, staring at her headstone, wondering, of course, what my own gravesite will look like. I'm thinking . . . do I get Dad's plot if I go first?? I know, I know. It's 90% curable and all that drivel. But once it's in you, once those cells have made their nasty little selves at home inside you . . . Stevie, I wouldn't be human if I didn't imagine how it would feel to waste away (bald, no less) and shrivel up and die. Because I watched it happen to Marilyn Walsh Fleece, and it could happen to me.

Anyway, there I was deciding if I wanted a flat stone, a raised one, or just a statue of Brad Pitt (nude) above my grave, and who walks up but my Dad. He looked old out there—the wind lifted his little tuft of hair and his eyes looked watery, like mine felt.

Neither one of us said anything stupid like "imagine finding you here at a time like this." He just sat down next to me. And the three of us talked.

I'm sorry to be so maudlin, but this is what happened. We pretended she was there, answering us. (Dad probably heard different things than I did, but that happened in real life, too, as I recall.) We talked about my having . . . cancer. I told him a little bit about Gray—he didn't remember him from high school (bet Mom did!!)—and what happened today with Chet. He told me about what he felt like the day he found out Mom had cancer. He said it was like two steel hands clamping on his throat and slowly, horribly squeezing the passage until he couldn't take a single breath. Mom was his air, he said. His lifeline.

And he told me that he and Alice have decided to live together. He was going to tell me over the weekend, but . . . well, I took center stage. He says it's the first time he felt like he could take a deep breath of air in 14 years. You know, I'm glad, and I told him that. I want him to be happy. (Mom was quiet, but she came around. ☺)

We stayed until it got dark and then went to that Italian dive in Waltham and overdosed on comfort food. Dad is so funny sometimes. You know, he really has no doubt that I'm going to be fine—he says he feels it in his bones. He knew Mom was going to die from day one. He just *knew* it. But he doesn't have that feeling about me. He says I'm going to dance at his wedding. (Nice thought, but shouldn't it be the other way around??) Anyway, I decided it's time to tell Gray. Next time he calls, I will.

I tried IMing you, but you are off-line. On the phone with Tommy Boy? I'm in the office tomorrow; Friday I get my port installed—it's the hole in my chest that takes the chemo. More fun. Write. Soon.

Love.

Amber

PS. I think Gray could turn my evening into a hit song. Sounds country, don't you think? "Talkin' to Ma" by Willie Nelson. But I haven't heard from him since his weird note today.

TO: dgallagher@millenniamarketing <dwayne gallagher>
FROM: areinhardt@millenniamarketing <adele reinhardt>
SUBJ: Employee Files and Records
DATE: Thursday 9/16 8:56 AM

Dwayne—I'll be in at 11 today. I'm working with Gabriel on a new Employee Recognition Program and I need your help in obtaining some files. Can you please speak directly with Jerry Becker and tell him I've requested a copy of the employee files for the individuals listed below. Gabe and I want this to be a big announcement at the Christmas Party, so don't breathe a word of it. We really want to surprise people! By the way, some of these employees have left the agency and then returned. For those who have, please be sure to include their files from their first period of employment, regardless of how long ago it is. Thanks!!

Here it is . . . in alpha for you!

- Alper, Lydia
- Fitzgerald, Dan
- Hickey, Diane
- Markoff, Tom
- Sunter, Frank

- Vanderton, Paul
- Walker-Hilliard, Stephanie

In addition, please contact Manny Hernandez in MIS and set up an appointment at his earliest convenience.

Adele

TO: afleece@millenniamarketing.com <amber fleece>
FROM: grayscale@connectone.com <gray mcdermott>
SUBJ: checking in
DATE: Thursday 9/16 10:05 AM

---

sorry to be so abrupt, babe. i can't talk to you now, but i hate to disappear without an explanation, which you can't have now because it's long and it's ugly. dix is in trouble. she's in the hospital. i can't go into it all now, but i just have to handle this and take care of mickey and work some things through. i'll call or write when i can.

won't be too long.

gray

shilliard@millenniamarketing.com: afleece@millenia-marketing.com is sending you an Instant Message on Thursday 9/16 at 10:17 AM:

afleece: Are you there?

shilliard: Right here. Where are you?

afleece: At work. I just got an email from Gray. Dixie is in the hospital and he told me he'd be "gone" for a while.

shilliard: What's wrong with her?

afleece: He didn't say. Just that she's "in trouble." There goes my big plan to tell him my own sob story. I can't, now. I can't demand he show his loyalty.

shilliard: I understand, but you're not asking him to come up and see you or anything.

afleece: But that's what I want him to do. While I still have hair ☺. Can you spell s-u-p-e-r-f-i-c-i-a-l?

shilliard: Do you think he would come up?

afleece: I was secretly hoping he would—but not now. Now I'm not telling him.

shilliard: This sucks.

afleece: Story of my week, year, life.

shilliard: I'm sorry—try not to be depressed. How are things at the office?

afleece: A thrill a minute. The cubes are emptying out in a rush to get to my office, offer condolences and see if I can still make them laugh. (My funny bone is cancer-free, I assure them.) Julie is fussing over me, Dwayne flitted by and implied he was in on some big management secret. Becker sent flowers.

shilliard: Becker did? Really?

afleece: Remember the reorg? Traffic reports to Finance, so he's my boss now. "Get well soon, Jerry," says the personal card signed by his secretary.

shilliard: Roses?

afleece: This is Becker we're talking about. Mums.

shilliard: ☺ Still, that was nice.

afleece: Ooh—Tommy Boy's outside my office talking to Jules. He wants to see me.

shilliard: Okay—I have a phone interview scheduled for 10:30 anyway.

afleece: Want me to say "hi" for you or just show him that picture I took of you in your bra and my shower cap the time you slept over at my apartment?

shilliard: You do that and I'll email Gray for you.

afleece: Gotcha.

TO: shilliard@millenniamarketing.com <stephanie hilliard>
FROM: afleece@millenniamarketing.com <amber fleece>
SUBJ: Boy-o-boy-o-Tommy Boy
DATE: Thursday 9/16 10:49 AM

I called, but got your voicemail—you must still be on the interview. I have to go into an 11:00 account meeting, but this can't wait. T- Boy's got it *bad*, Stevie. Are you aware of how gonzo he is over you??? I guess I didn't quite realize the extent this thing had moved. He spilled his proverbial guts to me—all in an effort to have me persuade you to see him on Sunday night when you get in. This is more than casual lust, my friend.

Love.
Amber

TO: jdesmond@millenniamarketing.com <julie desmond>
FROM: wildthing@usol.com <john rush>
SUBJ: RE: Life!
DATE: Thursday 9/16 1:43 PM

Hi, Jules. I just came in from a long morning of fishing and hiking. I've been out since about five, thinking about your note and

"Life" as you call it. Been a long time since anybody called me "a perfect someone." I like it—hah! It's a funny thing about finding your true calling. It's a mixed blessing, in a way. You know how you feel this new part of your life is so exciting and "right"—but then you wonder why the hell didn't you feel that way about what you were doing before? I really understand that.

When I was so badly injured that I had to quit pro ball, I thought it was the end of the world. At least, the end of my world. And it wasn't just the money or the "fame" or any of that. It was that I thought playing ball was all I could do. I didn't think it was all that great shakes while I was doing it, it just was *what I did*—like you were a mother. When I didn't play anymore, I was lost for a while, I really was. Then I got offered the pitching coach job and at first I thought it was a really shitty thing—to coach Triple A ball—and not even manage a team, just the pitchers. But the funniest thing happened after the first season—I realized I liked it better than actually playing. And I realized that sometimes, when life throws you a curve, you hit it out of the park. That's what I think you're doing.

See that? The questions of the world can be answered while standing in a foot-and-a-half of icy water. If that don't do it, then you can climb a steep hill and see sixty different colors of green. You ought to try it sometime.

Johnny

TO: hilliardb@grandregenthotels.com <brent hilliard>
FROM: wonderwoman@usol.com <stephanie hilliard>
SUBJ: Need to talk
DATE: Thursday 9/16 3:45 PM

Hi Brent—I can't get through on your cell phone, and your secretary says you're in meetings today. I just wanted to let you know that I got a sitter for Saturday night so we can go out. Please don't tell me you have a client dinner or you're tired or golfing late with Alex or ANYTHING, okay?

xoxo

me

wonderwoman@usol.com: foreveramber@quicklink.com is sending you an Instant Message on Thursday 9/16 at 9:04 PM:

foreveramber: Hey, wonderwoman. You're not answering your phone.

wonderwoman: I'm here. I left the phone with caller ID downstairs and I'm scared it's going to be Tom. So I'm not picking up.

foreveramber: Did I upset you with that email about him?

wonderwoman: No. I suspected that he is elevating this from flirtation to finish line. And I'm a little unhinged by my response to it—and to him. I thought I'd try to focus on work, family, marriage. You know, the things I can control.

foreveramber: Sorry, darla. Knowledge is power. You need to know that that man is in love with you.

wonderwoman: He *thinks* he is. He's really having a midlife crisis, Amb.

foreverambber: Call it what you want, but know that it's going on.

wonderwoman: What did he say?

foreveramber: It wasn't really what he said, more like how he said it.

wonderwoman: Which was?

foreveramber: He's so damn sure of himself. I never met a human with more confidence in my life. He's a little cocky about loving you, and you reciprocating the feeling. I doubt if he'd be that open with anyone else, but he sure didn't mince words with me.

wonderwoman: He knows we're close and that I trust you. What should I do?

foreveramber: What do you want to do?

wonderwoman: Oh, Amber. The truth?

foreveramber: I'm thinking you want to screw his brains right out of his gorgeous head.

wonderwoman: The thought has occurred to me. But what I really want is for Brent to feel that way about me (NOT some raven-haired witch named Heather). And I want to feel that way about him.

foreveramber: Yeah, that would simplify things, since you already married him. ☺ Okay, we know what you *want* to do . . . but what are you going to do?

wonderwoman: Hold Tom off—but I'm not quite ready to give up the thrill of it yet. Is that wrong?

foreveramber: Would you QUIT asking me that? Just be prepared, Tom is a force to be reckoned with. He doesn't want to be held off. He wants to be held *on*—on top of you. And, the man is just hot enough to talk the habit off a nun.

wonderwoman: If I am physically satisfied, if I'm emotionally enriched, if I'm psychologically secure, and if I'm happily married, he can't talk me into or out of anything.

foreveramber: What *if* you're not???

wonderwoman: You don't give Brent enough credit.

forevereamber: You haven't seen Tom. ☺ Just kidding, Brent's a great guy and I'm not convinced he's doing anything with Heather except what's legal among married co-workers. But you need to kick start him back into romance with YOU so he forgets her.

wonderwoman: Exactly!! I've planned a great night for Saturday—we're going to our favorite restaurant and I'm wearing my favorite shoes and his favorite lace underwear. We're going to *talk* and reconnect and then have wild car sex on the way home from dinner.

foreveramber: In his Corvette? Be sure it's Brent and not the gear shift.

wonderwoman: ☺ You sound like your old self. How are you?

foreveramber: Oddly calm about getting the port tomorrow. Incredibly ticked off that Dixie decided to be hospitalized just when I was ready to bare my soul to her live-in lover. God, do you think she tried to kill herself? Is that what he meant when he said she might do something stupid???

wonderwoman: Good Lord, I hope not. Nothing from him yet?

foreveramber: Nope. Not a word.

wonderwoman: Would you call him?

foreveramber: I almost did. But Jules said, "Don't Call Boys." She's *such* a mom.

wonderwoman: A good one. But you might have to be the one to call him.

foreveramber: With Dixie in the hospital, I'm just going to wait.

wonderwoman: I'm sure he'll check in soon. And you should tell him right away. I bet he comes to Boston in a flash.

foreveramber: We can dream, huh?

wonderwoman: We sure can. Oh–Declan's crying. Gotta go.

foreveramber: Kiss him for me!

wonderwoman: Good luck tomorrow–will Bud go with you?

foreveramber: Natch. He's my new best friend.

wonderwoman: Kiss him for me, too!

TO: wonderwoman@usol.com <stephanie hilliard>
FROM: tmark@quicklink.com <tom markoff>
SUBJ: Where are you?
DATE: Friday 9/17 12:17 AM

I don't want to call you this late, so I'm emailing. I tried a few times this evening, but was relegated to your electronic voice, which is beautiful, but not satisfying. I had a long talk with your buddy Amber today (she looks good, actually—still has a sparkle in her eye and a killer smile). Is that why you're avoiding me?

Babe, you've got to do whatever you want to do. Whatever feels right. If you want to shake my hand in a meeting, skip the electric eye contact, and keep it all business, that's fine. If you want me to pick you up at the airport, take you somewhere, and satisfy myself with an air kiss goodbye, it works for me. If you want to sit in a dark corner of a restaurant and share a bottle of wine and relive old times, I'm there for you. If you want to drive around town and let me French kiss your mouth and run my fingers up and down your sexy thighs before I drop you off—count me in. If you want to let me take you somewhere private, lay you down, and climb inside your body until you shudder and scream in ecstasy, I'm definitely your man.

It's your call, Stephanie. I want to do what makes you feel good and happy. I love you. I don't love the *idea* of you, or the possibility of having you, or the challenge of *not* having you. I love *you*. So making you happy will make me happy.

Tom

TO: hilliardb@grandregenthotels.com <brent hilliard>
FROM: wonderwoman@usol.com <stephanie hilliard>
SUBJ: Where are you?
DATE: Friday 9/17 12:43 AM

Brent—why aren't you answering your cell phone? Did you get my email? It's almost one in the morning and I haven't heard from you. I miss you, honey. I love you. Can't wait until you come home.

xoxo
Stevie

TO: shilliard@millenniamarketing.com <stephanie hilliard>
FROM: jdesmond@millenniamarketing.com <julie desmond>
SUBJ: Amber
DATE: Friday 9/17 11:45 AM

Hi Stevie. I just got a call from Amber's dad that the port implant operation went really well, she's in recovery and he'll be taking her home this afternoon. He's staying with her until evening, then I'm going to pop over. She refuses to leave her apartment, the stubborn little thing. So, write or call her when you can.

Take care,

Jules

TO: wonderwoman@usol.com <stephanie hilliard>
FROM: hilliardb@grandregenthotels.com <brent hilliard>
SUBJ: your message
DATE: Friday 9/17 11:59 AM

Hey Steve. Sorry you couldn't reach me last night. I crashed and my phone was charging. I can't wait to get home this weekend. Yes to the Saturday night sitter. Sounds like fun. I have a lot to tell you about Alex—things are looking good. Kiss the kids—and get one for yourself.

Love ya,

Brent

TO: tmarkoff@millenniamarketing.com <tom markoff>
FROM: shilliard@millenniamarketing.com <stephanie hilliard>
SUBJ: Latest report
DATE: Friday 9/17 2:03 PM

Hi Tom. Sorry I didn't return your call yet—or your email. I've been hard at work on the latest report—with lots of new information that will most certainly impact creative. It's attached. Let me know if you're going to distribute it to the WWA team or if you want me to do it.

Well, if you intended to confuse the hell out of me with that last email (and your creative list of multiple choices), you succeeded. Still, I remain determined to control my life and my reactions, however visceral they may be. In other words, I'm giving 110% to my marriage over the next 48 hours, so I'll talk to you Monday. I trust you understand. (And recommend similar therapy for you.)

xoxo

Stevie

TO: foreveramber@quicklink.com <amber fleece>
FROM: grayscale@connectone.com <gray mcdermott>
SUBJ: thinking of you
DATE: Friday 9/17 5:40 PM

---

i've had a hell of a few days here—but things are looking a little better. dix came home from the hospital and i got a friend of hers over here to watch her tonight, 'cause i have a gig to play. i'll fill you in sometime—like i said, it ain't pretty.

i miss you. i miss foreveramber on my computer. i miss you so much it actually hurts my heart. i'll be home late tonight.

i'll im you, if you're still up.

gray

TO: wonderwoman@usol.com <stephanie hilliard>
FROM: foreveramber@quicklink.com <amber fleece>
SUBJ: Self PORTrait
DATE: Friday 9/17 7:40 PM

Hey, Steverella. I'm up, eating soup, and feeling just fine with my new port. You can't see anything, but a little hole in my breastbone (lovely) and I didn't puke after the anesthesia, thank God. Dr. G was very sweet—I really like that guy. I've heard women fall in love with their oncologists—kind of like the gyno. They just know you so intimately and are still so kind and comforting. I feel okay. Ready to start the hard stuff, and even a little frustrated that I have to wait a week to do it.

Anyway, I got a miserably short email from Gray promising the possibility of IM tonight. Now I have to leave my computer on, wait for the ding, and find out all about Dixie Cups. I might have to hate that woman if she went and got cancer before I did. You know what I've been thinking? About uncomplicating my life. Instead of telling Gray I have the big C, why don't I just tell him we should break this off. That's actually funny, considering there's *nothing* to break off. But, seriously, this isn't good for either one of us right now and we'd be better off apart. Or more apart. Oh, I am soooo confused.

Jules came by, delivered my folded and pressed laundry, brought me this soup, and showered me with love and attention. (Give that woman a raise.) I do love her. And you, for worrying about me. Write.

Love.

Amber

TO: wildthing@usol.com <john rush>
FROM: juliedes@connectone.com <julie desmond>
SUBJ: *deep* fly-fishing
DATE: Friday 9/17 9:35 PM

Hi Johnny. I just got back from visiting Amber—she's doing pretty well—and I realized I never had a chance to respond to your thoughtful email today. It's been a long day, even longer week. But thank you for thinking of me while you are out there catching . . . trout? Salmon? (I confess . . . I looked up "fly-fishing" on Google and now I have just a little knowledge—enough to be dangerous. Also enough to be impressed by a Sage fly rod. They're expensive!)

I wish my son Will could hear you explain all that—about moving on and how it feels to leave behind what you thought you were meant to do, only to find out you were meant to do something else. It would mean more coming from a man than a mom. I don't think he wants me to move on, or make progress. Of course, he still harbors hope that his father and I will reunite—but, trust me, that will never happen. And I guess there's part of him that doesn't want me to be anything but his mom. And another part of him that absolutely doesn't want to think about me "with" anyone else. (Even if I'm only fishing!) You're kind to give it so much thought on my behalf.

I did something else today . . . I looked at the calendar for the next few months. Just thinking about weekends when I might be able to get away. So, I'm still thinking.

Take care,

Jules

TO: grayscale@connectone.com <gray mcdermott>
FROM: foreveramber@quicklink.com <amber fleece>
SUBJ: Maybe someday . . . but. . . .
DATE: Friday 9/17 10:48 PM

Hi there. I'm so sorry about Dixie. I hope she's okay. I know that any trip to the hospital—for whatever reason—is nightmarish. So I hope it's all over and that she's better and that Mickey survived the trauma of seeing his mom sick. I know that's no fun.

You've got a gig tonight, right? I can just picture you standing in front of a throng of screaming women right now. Playing bass (always the sexiest guy in any band, the bass player), being cool. Being Gray. Wish I could see you for real. Maybe someday.

But . . . I've been thinking about this for a while now, and the whole thing with your girlfriend going to the hospital has really spurred me into action. I love emailing you, talking to you for hours, thinking about you. I love it just a little too much, as a matter of fact. Your situation is . . . well, it is what it is and I understand that. But I really think we should just let this little internet romance run its natural course to completion. Don't you think that would be easier on both of us? A little less pressure at home for you. And to be perfectly honest with you, I have some very serious personal issues I'm dealing with, too. Not anything that has to do with you—they are personal. And serious. And that's all I'm going to say. Please don't ask me. Please.

I have enjoyed every minute of our reunion, but I really think we need to stop and focus on what's going on in our lives. Don't you agree?

Love.

Amber

foreveramber@quicklink.com: grayscale@connectone.com is sending you an Instant Message on Saturday, 9/18 at 2:03 AM:

grayscale: tell me you're there.

grayscale: amber, your computer is online. answer me.

grayscale: you want to know what i think of your idea, don't you?

grayscale: i think it's about the stupidest thing i've ever heard.

grayscale: come on, baby. talk to me.

grayscale: i know why you wrote what you wrote, but you just don't understand. i mean, you can go dark on me and not answer and not take my calls, i can't do a damn thing to stop you. but do it for the right reasons. let me be sure you understand something: this is not "a little internet romance" that needs to run its course or whatever the hell you said. amber, i don't want to complicate your life. no. no. i DO want to complicate your life. i just don't want to do it this way. i know i've been really elusive about what's going on here. and i have a good reason for that.

foreveramber: So tell me.

grayscale: hey. hi.

foreveramber: You woke me up.

grayscale: you woke <u>me</u> up. about two months ago. i was in a deep sleep, a fog. oblivious to the world around me, the feelings inside me. and then, wham. i got fleeced.

foreveramber: ☺

grayscale: don't leave me baby.

foreveramber: Tell me the good reasons—tell me what's going on.

grayscale: okay. now? you want to go back to bed?

foreveramber: Nope. Let's talk. Now.

foreveramber: Are you there—what's taking so long?

grayscale: i'm just thinking how to tell you this.

foreveramber: Just tell me.

grayscale: okay. dix is an ex-heroin addict. she's been clean for a long time, because of me. but i tried to tell her that i wanted to leave and she wound up in the hospital. overdose.

foreveramber: Oh.

grayscale: yeah, oh. you know what, amber? i don't care if she wants to poison her body. i don't do drugs, never really have, beyond the basics, and i don't understand why anyone would choose to do it. but, hell, it's her body.

foreveramber: And?

grayscale: it's mickey. i love that kid, i really do. and i don't want to leave him. i've told him that. i even hired a lawyer to see if i could get custody of him.

foreveramber: What happened?

grayscale: as long as she's employed and can get people to attest to her sobriety, i can't touch him. he's not mine biologically. she'd have to agree and she's in no state to do that.

foreveramber: What about his real father?

grayscale: essentially disappeared when he was conceived.

foreveramber: Eesh. Poor kid.

grayscale: yeah. and he's a good kid, too. if he gets the right influence, he'll be a great man. he's smart and funny and has a good, true heart. but if he doesn't have someone to guide him and love him, if i'm not around—all right, i know what you're thinking. this kid isn't my problem and why the hell can't i get my life together and stop picking up stray heroin addicts and their kids.

foreveramber: That's not what I'm thinking at all.

grayscale: what are you thinking?

forevamber: That he's lucky to have you. That you are smart and funny and have a good, true heart, and he probably learned all those things from you. That your parents—horrible as they were—did teach you something after all.

grayscale: yeah—what not to be.

foreveramber: Maybe.

grayscale: amber?

foreveramber: Yes?

grayscale: i don't want to even think about a day without you in my life.

foreveramber: Gray, don't talk like that. It's futile.

grayscale: why not? listen, in the middle of all this bullshit, i got some really good news.

foreveramber: What is it?

grayscale: remember the agent shopping "back into you"? he's got a real interested party. real interested.

foreveramber: Great! What does that mean?

grayscale: they want a couple more songs from me. i have two that would work. i need to write one more. then they want to meet me.

foreveramber: Who's "they"?

grayscale: tim mcgraw's people.

foreveramber: Wow! That is awesome!

grayscale: they're talking about a meeting in like 10 days. september 28 or 29. i don't know if i'll have a song done that fast.

foreveramber: You can do it. You write them in one night. I know you can do it. Will you meet Tim?

grayscale: i don't care. will i meet you?

foreveramber: ???

grayscale: meet me there.

foreveramber: In Nashville? On September 28?

grayscale: meet me there, toots. i want to see you.

foreveramber: I'm busy.

grayscale: come on. get a vacation. call in sick. get on a plane and fly to me.

foreveramber: I can't do it, Gray. Sorry.

grayscale: can't do it or don't want to do it?

foreveramber: I'm not playing games. I can't.

grayscale: why not?

foreveramber: I have too much going on at work. Really important meetings.

grayscale: come on.

foreveramber: Honestly, Gray, if I could, I would.

grayscale: it's time, amber. it's time to be together.

foreveramber: No. It's not.

grayscale: you're doing it again.

foreveramber: ???

grayscale: one of the songs i'm submitting is "what she didn't say."

foreveramber: What's the other one?

grayscale: no title yet–i'm writing it this minute. it's a heartbreaker.

foreveramber: Gray, if I could, I would. I can't.

grayscale: if you really wanted to, you would.

foreveramber: I cannot come to Nashville that week.

grayscale: the next?

foreveramber: No.

grayscale: the next?

foreveramber: No.

grayscale: ever?

foreveramber: Maybe someday.

grayscale: you say that a lot. i think it's my song title. thanks. i gotta write. night, toots.

foreveramber: Bye.

TO: foreveramber@quicklink.com <amber fleece>
FROM: wonderwoman@usol.com <stephanie hilliard>
SUBJ: After our call
DATE: Saturday 9/18 2:45 PM

Hey Amber. God, it was nice to hear your voice. I'm sorry you can't sleep on your stomach. Better for your skin, though, you know? ☺ Seriously, I've been thinking about you nonstop since you called this morning. I wish I had the answers for you, I really do. I can't believe of all days, he wants to meet you on September 28. You know my advice, obvious as it may be. Tell him the truth. Now he thinks you're playing games with him. He's going to understand that you have your first round of chemo scheduled that day, for crying out loud. It's not about "scaring him away" with those three words anymore, Amb.

You're so worried about him losing interest. But the more I think about it, the more I think this is about how interested *you* really are—or aren't. He's not your "type." He doesn't fit this old "list" you have in your head for the perfect guy. In fact, he's the polar opposite of everything you've ever wanted. So, you're using your illness as an excuse to implode this whole relationship.

I'm sorry. I'm not helping, I bet. I just want you to be happy and I think you ought to tell him the truth and see what happens.

You know, this is such a classic case of the blind leading the blind. I have NO right to give lectures about telling the truth and seeing what happens. After I got off the phone with you this morning, I sat down with Brent. We were interrupted sixty times by the kids—who are just so happy to have him home, they can't leave him alone—but I managed to tell him that I'm really concerned about how things are between us and I want to go out tonight and spend some real quality time.

In his defense, he listened. But he thinks I'm jealous of his job. He thinks I'm feeling worthless (that was his word and I really didn't like it) because I don't work anymore, and that I'm jealous of his success. I told him: It's not your JOB I'm jealous of. It's the people you work with. But we couldn't have a halfway decent conversation because of the kids. Plus I could feel it escalating into an argument, and I didn't want to be fighting during the only two days he's home in two weeks. So we'll see what happens at our lovely dinner tonight.

So maybe you should ignore advice given by me. But my gut says you're doing yourself—and Gray—a huge disservice by not just telling him why you can't go to Nashville. He's *asking* you to meet him. He said it's *time.* And all you say is "maybe someday"??? What are you waiting for, Amb? What did you say to him? Maybe someday. Maybe someday's here already. Obviously you can't meet him on the 28th. Maybe he could fly up here after the meeting. I know, I know, he won't cross the Massachusetts state line. Well, he might change . . . if he knew the truth.

There *are* ad agencies in Nashville, you know. And it's

closer to me! You could bring all six of your kids to see Aunt Stevie—you know, the divorced one. ☹

xoxox

Stevie . . . who "maybe someday" will have her own act together.

TO: foreveramber@quicklink.com <amber fleece>
FROM: grayscale@connectone.com <gray mcdermott>
SUBJ: calling you
DATE: Saturday 9/18 3:15 PM

---

i'm calling and calling and calling. cell phone. home phone. office phone. hey—you gave me the numbers. but you are not answering. all i wanted to do was play you my new song. it's almost the best thing i've ever written . . . but i can't quite get the hook down. wanna help? it's kind of an uptempo ballad, if there is such an animal. . . .

it seems like i've been waiting forever and a day . . . to have my time with you, girl, with nothin' in the way . . . maybe someday, maybe someday soon. maybe one day. . . .

i just can't get the next line.

gray

TO: juliedes@connectone.com <julie desmond>
FROM: wildthing@usol.com <john rush>
SUBJ: an idea!
DATE: Saturday 9/18 4:44 PM

Hi Jules—how are you on this fine Saturday afternoon? I'm still up at my cabin, planning to have a few friends over in a little while—grilling fish (what else?), and enjoying the incredible scenery. You should see the leaves! The most unbelievable colors of red and gold and orange, all mixed in with the deep, deep green of the pines. The sky is so clear and blue, and the air is just crystal clean. There's a bit of a chill—definitely sweater weather up here—and I used the pine cones to start an amazing fire in the kitchen woodstove. Next up . . . a good bottle of wine.

Where are you, Strawberry?

Listen, I had an idea. (Scary, huh?) Seriously, just think about it—no pressure. What if you brought your son along when you come down here? He'd love it here—no boy is immune to the call of the wild. Even a 20-year-old. Especially a 20-year-old. I'd make him comfortable, I promise, and he (and you) might feel a little less like it's a weekend "date" and a little more like you just had a chance to get away. He's more than welcome, so consider it. I'll be happy to email him a personal invitation, if you like.

Anyway, gotta go. Just wanted to let you know I'm thinking about you. Johnny

---

TO:	foreveramber@quicklink.com <amber fleece>
FROM:	beantownbud@bostonbeerdistribution. com <bud fleece>
SUBJ:	tonight
DATE:	Saturday 9/18 5:43 PM

Hi honey. Alice just called me at work and told me you're coming over. Hooray! I'll be at the station to pick you up at 6:30. I'm just finishing up some Saturday stuff here and going to stop at Star Market and get some really nice steaks for dinner. We'll just take it easy and you can sleep in your room—I won't even make you get up before noon. It's okay if Alice stays, right? See you later, honey.

Love,

Dad

TO: wonderwoman@usol.com <stephanie hilliard>
FROM: foreveramber@quicklink.com <amber fleece>
SUBJ: Wild Saturday Nights
DATE: Saturday 9/18 5:34 PM

Hey, Steve. Gray keeps calling and IMing and sending song lyrics. So . . . I'm going to bury myself at the Budster's tonight (or should I say at "Dad and Alice's house"). Okay. I'm hiding. I'm scared. Maybe I'm *not* ready for what he has to offer. Or I'm just terrified that when he sees me again, it won't be the same. But, what if it is? What then? I'm in love with someone who couldn't be further from my "perfect man" and yet, he *is* my "perfect man." I'm rocked with fear and confusion and worry—so, I'm going home to my daddy for tea and sympathy. Well, beer and sympathy. Hope you have more moonlight than madness tonight. Good luck. I do appreciate your advice, regardless of the train wreck that is your own marriage ;-). I value your opinion. Maybe someday <g>, I won't ignore it.

Love,

Amber

TO: tmark@quicklink.com <tom markoff>
FROM: wonderwoman@usol.com <stephanie hilliard>
SUBJ: It's late . . .
DATE: Sunday 9/19 1:06 AM

. . . and I'm lonely. This is probably the dumbest thing I've done (to date), but I'm kind of looking for someone to talk to—you don't appear to be online, so I just thought I'd write to you. Amber has gone underground to her Dad's house, my husband is . . . well, he's a little too involved in my problems to be objective, and any other friend or casual acquaintance would be truly scandalized if they had an inkling of what a mess Miss Perfection has made out of her life.

I had a pretty shitty night, all around. I went out with Brent for what was supposed to be a quiet, romantic one-on-one and it turned into a silent, bitter one-against-one. And, damn it all, *I* picked the fight. I just pushed him and prodded him and irked him until he responded. Why did I do that?

Try as I might, I'm screwing up my marriage. I don't want this to happen, Tom. I don't want to lose what I've built with Brent. I don't want to offer my children a life of two homes and multiple parents. I don't want to fail.

And maybe that's at the root of all of this. My fear of failure. It drives me; sometimes it overtakes me and makes me do superhuman things. I can't imagine where it came from. I had a pretty normal childhood with nice, loving parents, a couple of great older brothers, nothing remarkable. I always wanted to *stand out* somehow. I needed to be the prettiest, smartest, fastest, richest, best dressed, most popular, most successful. As I got older, that's toned down a bit. But the fear of failure is still strong. And the idea of my marriage failing is sickening to me.

Giving in to what you're asking me to do—regardless of how much my body and soul aches for that kind of passion—that would be failure. A ride I'd never forget, yes. But failure.

I couldn't even let this evening "fail." Regardless of our fight, I was determined to make love to my husband. I smoothed things over as well as possible, donned the appropriate lovemaking clothes, and, yes, we did have sex. To completion. Just not to my emotional satisfaction. He tried, he really did. I have to face something: This is my problem, not Brent's. I put up this wall and I've let myself get emotionally involved with you and I am fucking up my marriage and I hate to admit that.

Oh—your name just came up on my screen. You're up. Think I'll send this and see what happens. I'll get another glass of wine while you read it.

xoxox

Stephanie

wonderwoman@usol.com: tmark@quicklink.com is sending you an Instant Message on Sunday 9/19 at 1:32 AM:

tmark: Chardonnay or cab, gorgeous?

wonderwoman: Cab. So, you're up.

tmark: Oh, yeah. ☺ You might say so. I like that you need me tonight.

wonderwoman: Did I say that? I have to go back and look at that email. I never said I need you. I don't like that. It makes me feel helpless.

tmark: Give in to it. Helpless looks good on you. Out of control looks better. Still wearing the lovemaking clothes?

wonderwoman: Under a robe.

tmark: Can you change?

wonderwoman: Why?

tmark: I don't want to talk sexy to you while you're wearing clothes another man touched.

wonderwoman: Forget it. Don't talk sexy. Talk sweet.

tmark: Okay. But sweet can get sexy when I'm in this mood.

wonderwoman: What mood are you in?

tmark: Hard. Hot. Hungry for you.

wonderwoman: Do you ever *not* write copy?

tmark: You're funny, sweetheart.

wonderwoman: Admit it, you have a smooth way with the keyboard.

tmark: I have a smooth way with everything. Give me a chance to show you what my fingers can do on flesh. The keyboard will be history.

wonderwoman: I don't want to give you that chance. Didn't you read my email?

tmark: Yes. But you're wrong. It won't be failure. It will be unbelievable, unparalleled success. You will quake in my arms, shiver under my tongue, whimper as I slide into you.

wonderwoman: Stop it.

tmark: All right. I just re-read your email. You're taking too much blame for the problems in your marriage. What about the other woman?

wonderwoman: Heather the Harlot.

tmark: ☺ That name has Amber Fleece's fingerprints all over it. What's her deal?

wonderwoman: She's on Brent's executive team–director of Grand Regent Resort Sales. Imagine Lucy Liu meets Demi Moore.

tmark: Not in your league.

wonderwoman: Thanks, but, she's very much in my league and in my husband's . . . heart.

tmark: But not his bed?

wonderwoman: I don't know.

tmark: Did you confront him?

wonderwoman: I don't like confrontation. I implied that I suspected.

tmark: And?

wonderwoman: He thinks that Heather has become the embodiment of Grand Regent Hotels in my mind. I am merely taking out my frustration on how much Brent is investing in the company on Heather, who is merely an innocent, if admittedly gorgeous, bystander.

tmark: Are you frustrated by how much he works?

wonderwoman: No, not really. It's part of the deal and I accept it. I wish he were home more often, but I wouldn't complain if I thought he was sleeping alone on the road.

tmark: Infidelity is part of the deal, too.

wonderwoman: WHO says???

tmark: Most men in business. Look at Gabriel Wycoming. Is the pleasure of owning the most successful ad agency in Boston enough for him? No. He has to get the goods from Reinhardt.

wonderwoman: Well . . . what about you?

tmark: Me? I told you my gig.

wonderwoman: Why don't you get divorced so that you can have a relationship that is not vow-breaking in nature?

tmark: With you?

wonderwoman: With anyone.

tmark: I'm not interested in anyone. I'm interested in you.

wonderwoman: I'm not available.

tmark: If you were, I would be.

wonderwoman: You don't mean that.

tmark: Why do you always doubt me? Yes, I mean it. If you were free, I would free myself for you.

wonderwoman: Sheez. This is getting out of control.

tmark: I told you—out of control suits you. You should try it more often.

wonderwoman: Never. I live for control. Anyway, I'm not free.

tmark: Then, I will take whatever crumbs of your affection or attention you drop. Although I'd like a five-course meal. Starting with your mouth. And ending with your . . . ☺

wonderwoman: Don't talk dirty.

tmark: There's <u>nothing</u> dirty about what I want to do to you, Stephanie. I love you. I would like nothing more than to demonstrate that to you in every imaginable position and place.

wonderwoman: Ah. You're good, Tom. You do get me going.

tmark: I could, baby. I could get you gone.

wonderwoman: I have no doubt.

tmark: Can I call you in a few minutes?

wonderwoman: No. Why?

tmark: I could take a drive and call you on my cell phone. I will tell you exactly what I'm going to do to you when I see you next week.

wonderwoman: No phone sex. No computer sex. No sex sex.

tmark: You sure?

wonderwoman: Yes. No. God, I'm shaking. You have me shaking.

tmark: That's lust. That's love.

wonderwoman: That's lunacy. This is a two-dimensional screen, for crying out loud.

tmark: You know what's at the other end. And so do I. Want to shake some more, Stephanie?

wonderwoman: No. I'm going to bed.

tmark: I can't sleep. Take your phone off the hook if you don't want to hear from me.

wonderwoman: Don't call me, Tom. Don't do it.

tmark: Okay. I won't. But I'll be thinking about you. I'm going to have a hard-on all night.

wonderwoman: You *know* my solution for that.

tmark: She's sound asleep.

wonderwoman: Wake her up.

tmark: Stephanie, I love you.

wonderwoman: Good night, Tom.

TO:	wonderwoman@usol.com <stephanie hilliard>
FROM:	afleece@millenniamarketing.com <amber fleece>
SUBJ:	Monday Morning at the Zoo
DATE:	Monday 9/20 9:15 AM

It's not even 10:00 and the animals are all rattling their cages. Did you *know* that Tom called an off-site meeting for the WWA creative team to do something he calls a CIAW? Campaign In A Week. An entire collection of creatives has disappeared to some remote, unknown site for four solid days of brainstorming and ad development. According to the memo left in our boxes (dated YESTERDAY—that is SUNDAY, when no one is in the office), they'll be back on Friday with a complete print, broadcast, billboard, and web campaign ready for presentation on Monday at the WWA powwow.

Meanwhile, his Dwayneness already pirouetted through the

Traffic Department, mostly to show off his new red hair tips (not horrible, to be honest), dropping hints that Fraulein Reinhardt is MOST unhappy about the Creative Department being MIA for a week . . . and wanting to know if you filed a final report. Why ask me, I reply, go right to the source. But you're so close to Stevie, he says, surely you know everything about what she's working on. Not everything, I respond, here's her number, call her. He gives me a heavy sigh, laden with secrets and lies, then asks . . . Is Stevie at the creative meeting with Tom? Hell no, I tell him; Stevie's a research consultant—not on the creative team. He raises a knowing (and shapely) eyebrow and smirks a "yeah, right" expression. What are you implying, I demand. Oh, come *on*, girlfriend. Everyone knows what's going on between Tom and Stevie. Everyone? No! They can't! It's secret. (That's what I *thought*—not what I said.) I *said,* NOTHING's going on between Tom and Stevie. He gave me a big eye roll.

I told him the dye had sunk into his brain, and adjusted your family pic to a jaunty angle at the corner of my desk. You're quite happily married, and anyone who doesn't think so is high. Right? You better watch your size four butt, my friend.

BTW, I stayed at Dad's until almost 8 last night—that's why you never heard from me. I crashed as soon as I got home and didn't turn on the computer or return phone calls. (Someone else is after me, too.) So, call and give me the scoop on your dream date. That is, if you're not at some remote site writing ad copy.

Love.

Amber

TO: afleece@millenniamarketing.com <amber fleece>
FROM: wonderwoman@usol.com <stephanie hilliard>
SUBJ: Butt watching
DATE: Monday 9/20 9:45 AM

I *hate* that people are gossiping about me and I'm not there to defend myself. They can all go directly to hell. I am NOT at a remote site with Tom. I didn't know a thing about the CIAW business—he never mentioned it. I sent him my last report on Friday (first, before anyone else got it, like he wanted) and he never even talked about it over the weekend. Not that we were in constant contact. We IM'd—once—that's all. (Late Saturday night after my dismal (not dream) date . . . don't ask.) Except for my one message to you yesterday, I spent the day with Brent and the kids and tried to stay FOCUSED on them. Screw Tom (not literally), I'm sending the report up to the WWA files right now. She can have it—there's no reason Tom should be keeping it out of the hands of anyone on the WWA team.

All right. All right. Saturday was a bust, leaving me to pick up a lot of broken pieces of my marriage and life on Sunday. We're back to tiptoeing around each other—but the kids don't notice and we just showered them with attention all day. But Brent left for L.A. this morning for a week in California. At least he's only going to hotel properites, not any resorts—so the Resort Sales Staff won't (or shouldn't) be around. The sad thing is, I check that now.

xoxox
Steve

TO: tmark@quicklink.com <tom markoff>
FROM: wonderwoman@usol.com <stephanie hilliard>
SUBJ: Disappearing Act
DATE: Monday 9/20 10:08 AM

Where are you? What is this CIAW? Forgive me, but I didn't get the memo. I don't know if you're checking your personal email, but if you get this, call or write. You can call me any time this week—I'm flying solo.

xoxo
Stephanie

TO: afleece@millenniamarketing.com <amber fleece>
FROM: grayscale@connectone.com <gray mcdermott>
SUBJ: maybe someday
DATE: Monday 9/20 11:56 AM

this song is killing me. the words are just eluding me. like you are. i don't like it. i don't like it at all.

gray

TO: willie542@quicklink.com <william desmond>
FROM: jdesmond@millenniamarketing.com <julie desmond>
SUBJ: need to talk
DATE: Monday 9/20 2:33 PM

Hi honey. I hope you check your email before you go to work tonight. How's school? I know, it's the first day. Did you get into the biology class you wanted? I know you're really busy, but I need to talk to you when you get a minute. Call me when you can. I'm home most nights this week after work or my aerobics class. Don't forget it's your father's birthday today. You should call him.

I love you,

Mom

TO: foreveramber@quicklink.com <amber fleece>
FROM: wonderwoman@usol.com <stephanie hilliard>
SUBJ: How are you?
DATE: Monday 9/20 9:15 PM

What's going on, Amb? Haven't heard from you since this morning. Lily came down with a fever at school and I had to pick her up and take her to the pediatrician. She tested negative for strep, but has a brutal sore throat and is running a low-grade fever. I got a prescription for an antibiotic which the doctor strongly recommended, but when I talked to Brent he went ballistic and said she didn't need it. Can't we agree on anything? She's sleeping now, but I suppose it'll run its course and then Declan will get it, too. I spent most of the day with her in my arms. Beats calling blowhard aviation experts, I tell you true.

I have my flights for next week. I'm coming in Sunday around 5—still trying to decide if I should see Tom or not. I haven't heard a word from him today. I still don't know where the hell he is or whether he's even reachable. Any word on the whereabouts of the creative team? You're probably crashing early tonight, so I'll talk to you tomorrow.

xoxo

Stevie

TO: afleece@millenniamarketing.com <amber fleece>
FROM: grayscale@connectone.com <gray mcdermott>
SUBJ: maybe someday, maybe not
DATE: Tuesday 9/21 2:45 AM

i'm sending this to work because i know you keep your computer on all night and i don't want you to wake up if it makes a noise. plus, i want to be the first email you read when you get in to your office later this morning.

the agent called today. things are moving fast. i cut a demo of "what she didn't say" with the band tonight in a studio and we all screwed around with "someday" but the general consensus is to bag it. i don't want to bag it. i want to write that song. i want to nail it. i want you to have it.

things are looking (slightly) up around here. at least reasonable conversations are taking place and mick seems to be holding his own. tonight we were working on his homework (u.s. history—i'm finally getting all the shit i missed as a kid) and he told me he wanted to be a musician. i said screw that, you just don't want to study the constitution. he said he just wanted to be like me. there's a little pressure, huh? he could do so much better than to be like me. but you know that, don't you?

i miss you, toots.

i miss you so damn bad.

gray

TO: wonderwoman@usol.com <stephanie hilliard>
FROM: afleece@millenniamarketing.com <amber fleece>
SUBJ: CIAW!!!
DATE: Tuesday 9/21 8:23 AM

I've been summoned to the CIAW meeting. It's taking place out in the Berkshires—how he pulled this off with no one knowing, I can't imagine. Anyway, they need me (and that dingbat Mierzwicki from the Media Department) for a few days to review the creative schedule they are proposing and develop a mock traffic and media plan. Tom's going full out for this meeting next Monday. Anyhoo, I could use the distraction and don't mind a trip to the B'shires this time of year. Doc said I could go. So . . . I'll have my laptop and assuming I can get online, I'll be in touch. Cell phones are spotty up there, I've been told. Jules might have # of where I'm going—but Tom is being so effing *secretive*. I'll be back on Thursday night and will see you Sunday!!

Love.
Amber

TO: afleece@millenniamarketing.com <amber fleece>
FROM: shilliard@millenniamarketing.com <stephanie hilliard>
SUBJ: RE: CIAW!!!
DATE: Tuesday 9/21 9:45 AM

Jules says you're on the phone, but that you're leaving in a few minutes. I'm glad you see all the positives about getting away, going to the Berkshires, and escaping all that's going on. I don't blame you. Just be sure you're going for all the right reasons. You're not *running away* from Gray, are you? Will he be able to email you? IM you? Call you? I'm just curious. Try to stay in touch—with the people who love you.

xoxo

Steve

TO: shilliard@millenniamarketing.com <stephanie hilliard>
FROM: areinhardt@millenniamarketing.com <adele reinhardt>
SUBJ: WWA Final Report
DATE: Tuesday 9/21 12:15 PM

Hi, Stevie! Just finished reading your final report on the Aviation Industry Experts for WWA. Since this came in yesterday, I'm going to assume you hadn't sent it to the Creative Department before they took their little sabbatical this week. Unless you somehow were able to get a copy to Tom before he left. I want to be sure we're all singing from the same hymnal, as they say! Please confirm. Thanks! Looking forward to seeing you next week—so glad to hear you can stay for the afternoon session!

Adele

TO: tmark@quicklink.com <tom markoff>
FROM: wonderwoman@usol.com <stephanie hilliard>
SUBJ: help me
DATE: Tuesday 9/21 3:55 PM

I'm getting all kinds of mixed messages and innuendoes from friend and foe. If you would be kind enough to call and let me know what the hell is going on, I'd so appreciate it.

xoxox
Stephanie

TO: wonderwoman@usol.com <stephanie hilliard>
FROM: hilliardb@grandregenthotels.com <brent hilliard>
SUBJ: FORWARDING ARTICLE FYI
DATE: Tuesday 9/21 6:18 PM

Hi. Someone sent me this article about the dangers of antibiotics and some suggestions for more holistic treatment. Thought you'd like to see it. Busy day. Have a client dinner tonight. Will check in later. Kiss Lily for me. Dec, too.

Love ya,
Brent

Click here: http//:www.medcenter.com/septemberupdate/pediatrics/antibiotics

Hey there—I heard you were masterful with Dash Communications today. Word is all over GRH that they all but signed on the dotted line to have their sales meeting in San Juan. I wish I could have been there, but you were right about my staying here. I was worried after we talked about your little girl. I dug around the web for medical sites and found this article. You are so right about the possible harm from giving too many antibiotics. Lily's lucky to have you. ☺♥☺

TTFN,

H

TO: foreveramber@quicklink.com <amber fleece>
FROM: wonderwoman@usol.com <stephanie hilliard>
SUBJ: Hell hath no fury. . . .
DATE: Tuesday 9/21 8:35 PM

FUCK FUCK FUCK! Read the attached. The WHOLE thing. Skip the stupid article, go below the link to the email that Brent accidentally (oh God, I hope) left attached to what he sent me. Who the FUCK is she to research and discuss the health and well-being of MY DAUGHTER? And advise MY HUSBAND! She's **my** daughter! Should I tell him? Should I forward it back to him? Should I just write to H and tell her to please get the god-damn hell out of my personal business and sign it TA TA FOR NOW? (Who *says* that anyway?) How about TA TA FOR EVER???? Should I just ignore it? Amber, what should I do??? HELP.

xoxo

me

wonderwoman@usol.com: foreveramber@quicklink.com is sending you and Instant Message on Tuesday 9/21 at 9:58 PM:

foreveramber: Have you calmed down yet?

wonderwoman: It's been a Kendall-Jackson kind of night.

foreveramber: Did you get in touch with Brent?

wonderwoman: No. Didn't do anything yet. Well, yes, I did something.

foreveramber: Called Tom.

wonderwoman: No, worse. I called the all-night pharmacy.

foreveramber: For the antibiotic, of course.

wonderwoman: Natch. I'm the *mother*—remember? Lily's on Zithromax and her fever has dropped to 99. So there :-P Heather you Harlot. How's the mountain retreat?

foreveramber: Back to me, already? We've dissed the Harlot enough? ☺ It's very cool. We're in a lodge—we have the whole place to ourselves—an amazing feat in the middle of leaf-gazing season. He has spared NO expense and taken over everything—brought in Macs to do design and layout, printers, everything. He's essentially set up a little agency here and everyone's working 18-hour days on the Luxury Line launch.

wonderwoman: What got into him? Why didn't he tell anyone he was doing this?

foreveramber: I don't know, but I suspect Eva Braun is part of it.

wonderwoman: What do you think is going on?

foreveramber: The underground rumblings are that they are being pitted against each other by GW—possibly for a newly created position of General Manager. They both want it. I guess the WWA launch is sort of their test.

wonderwoman: He never mentioned any of this to me. I bet he went off-site so the work is *his*—she can't possibly take a bit of credit.

foreveramber: Bingo.

wonderwoman: Sheez. Who needs this? And I'm the human Gumby doll between them. Do me a favor and email me a copy of what you are using for my report, okay? I want to see if it's been doctored.

foreveramber: Sure—no problem.

wonderwoman: How are you feeling?

foreveramber: Oddly enough, great. My chest is sore from the effing funnel they put in me, but being away from home is the best possible thing. It's keeping my mind occupied.

wonderwoman: Have you heard from Gray?

foreveramber: Yes, but I haven't answered him.

wonderwoman: Aren't you going to tell him where you are?

foreveramber: Why? It doesn't make any difference to him. What are you going to do about Heather the Harlot?

wonderwoman: Don't you dare volley that back at me. Are you hiding from him?

foreveramber: Yes. (Hah! You didn't expect that, did you?)

wonderwoman: Why? Why are you cutting him out of your life when you need him the most?

foreveramber: I don't need him. Dixie needs him. Mickey needs him. I need stability and security and lifelong happiness. Not an internet lover.

wonderwoman: He's more than that.

foreveramber: Not at this moment in time, he's not.

wonderwoman: You have to give him a chance.

foreveramber: Stevie, I DO NOT want to discuss him anymore. Okay? He's not the one. What are you going to do about that email?

wonderwoman: What do you think I should do? Did you think that email sounded like a woman he's having an affair with? I really hated the "you were right about me staying here" line.

foreveramber: The message did have a tone of intimacy, but not overtly sexual. (Nothing like I imagine passes between wonderwoman and tmark, *ahem*.) I did notice a lot of "you're right"s and "Lily's lucky." Could be some major sucking up to (as opposed to just sucking) the boss. I think you should follow your own advice to me.

wonderwoman: ???

foreveramber: Quit hiding in the computer with some quasi-affair with Tom Markoff, tell your husband that your marriage is SICK, and see how he responds to make it better.

wonderwoman: Hmmm. Good advice. Do you think he sent it on purpose?

foreveramber: Maybe he wanted to force the issue, but I doubt it.

wonderwoman: I'm not hiding with some quasi-affair with Tom.

foreveramber: You know what his first words to me were when I walked into the lobby of this lodge?

wonderwoman: ?

foreveramber: He hugged me and whispered, "Wouldn't Stephanie love this place?"

wonderwoman: ☺

foreveramber: He always calls you Stephanie, doesn't he?

wonderwoman: Yeah, he never called me Stevie. Told me years ago it wasn't feminine enough for me.

foreveramber: The creative looks awesome. The client's going to flip.

wonderwoman: So's der Fraulein.

foreverамber: She's going to be chewing nails at that meeting on Monday. But be careful, chiquita. She's looking for a way to bring him down and I wouldn't put *anything* past her.

wonderwoman: I haven't done anything wrong.

foreveramber: Yet. ☺ or should I say ♥?

wonderwoman: TTFN!

TO: hilliardb@grandregenthotels.com <brent hilliard>
FROM: wonderwoman@usol.com <stephanie hilliard>
SUBJ: Antibiotic poison
DATE: Tuesday 9/21 11:11 PM

Please thank Heather for her concern.

TO: wonderwoman@usol.com <stephanie hilliard>
FROM: tmark@quicklink.com <tom markoff>
SUBJ: Where I am and where do we go from here
DATE: Wednesday 9/22 1:17 AM

I wish you were here. I'm tucked into a corner of a wooden balcony, overlooking the dark hills of the Berkshires in the wee hours, studying the sky. I have my laptop. A beer. A cigarette bummed from a jr. copywriter. But no Stephanie. There are a million stars. A billion. It's breathtaking. I would love to hold you in my arms, count them. And rename each constellation after a part of you I love. The tender earlobe . . . the alluring cleavage . . . the inny navel . . . the secret passageway. We could reinvent astronomy.

I'm sorry I didn't tell you about the CIAW trip. I'd been cooking it up for a while, but wasn't sure I could pull it off until the weekend. It's a trick I learned when I was in NY. The juices flow when you yank these guys out of their normal environment. The work they're doing is phenomenal already. This campaign will kick major ass. My blood is running hot again and for the first time in years, I'm enjoying the art of advertising. It's been a while.

Sweetheart, if I had you in my life, it would be perfect. I don't know how to figure this out; I don't want to make you unhappy or put you into a place you don't want to be. If you are in the right place, with the right man, doing the right thing—then stay there safe in the knowledge that somewhere, a thousand miles away, another man loves you. But if you have any doubt, Stephanie, any doubt at all . . . I want a shot. I want a chance to watch you bloom in the light of my love. This is not just about sex, Stephanie. That's part of it. I know what our chemistry is, I know how I can make your body come apart. But that's only one aspect of how I feel about you. I need your fire. I need your brilliance. I need to hear you laugh and watch you sleep and bask in the glow of your insights and imagination. You are a magnet, drawing me to your power.

But let's start slow. <g> Let me pick you up on Sunday night, take you somewhere you've never been before (literally and figuratively) and give me a chance to show you the power of us together. Just give me one chance. Then, we'll decide where to go from there. One chance, Stephanie. One night. One time.

ILY . . .

T

TO: willie542@quicklink.com <william desmond>
FROM: jdesmond@millenniamarketing.com
<julie desmond>
SUBJ: Our talk last night
DATE: Wednesday 9/22 8:54 AM

Hi, honey. I just had to write to you this morning—I know you're in class already. Will, honey, I'm sorry Dad was so nasty when you called for his birthday. I could tell in your voice that really hurt your feelings. I'm sorry, but nothing he does surprises me anymore. Maybe this will help you let go of this notion that your father and I are ever going to patch things up. Haven't I taught you empathy? Put yourself in my shoes. Imagine how I might like a chance to be the woman I never got to be.

You can't stop me, honey—I've already started. I'm involved in my work (excited by it, in fact) and I'm making friends and using talents I didn't even know I had. Letting the right man into my life (even in the most casual, platonic way) is a huge step for me, Will. It's scary enough in principle. It would be just petrifying if I had to pick a man vs. my son. Because there is no choice, of course—I love you above all things.

Don't hold me back, honey. I'm only 45. I know that seems like 450 to you at 19, but believe me, I still have a lot of good years ahead of me. I'm not ready to jump back into marriage with ANYONE, nor do I plan to jump into bed with ANYONE. I might just want to dip my toes in the water of life, though.

So, let me ask you again. You coming fly-fishing with me or not?

I love you.

Mom

TO: afleece@millenniamarketing.com <amber fleece>
FROM: grayscale@connectone.com <gray mcdermott>
SUBJ: one word
DATE: Wednesday 9/22 10:04 AM

one word, toots. just one word. write and say "okay" and i'll know you are. i'm starting to worry. no answer on any of your phones, no email and you haven't been online. you've been holding something back from me lately and i just want to know if you're okay.

gray

TO: wonderwoman@usol.com <stephanie hilliard>
FROM: hilliardb@grandregenthotels.com <brent hilliard>
SUBJ: email forward
DATE: Wednesday 9/22 11:19 AM

Sorry, I bet that upset you. It was about the article, not the sender. Don't get hysterical, Steve, okay? Heather is a friend—nothing more, nothing less. But especially nothing more. I talk to her about work, life, kids, everything. She reminds me a lot of you, to be honest. The way you used to attack work and mix charm with guts and brains to get the business. Listen, just write and tell me how Lily is, okay? I'm worried about her. I'm worried about you.

Love ya,
Brent

TO: shilliard@millenniamarketing.com
<stephanie hilliard>
FROM: areinhardt@millenniamarketing.com
<adele reinhardt>
SUBJ: Monday's meeting
DATE: Wednesday 9/22 1:40 PM

Hi, Stevie! I'm just organizing my calendar for next week and it occurred to me that you must be coming in on Sunday evening. Wouldn't it be fun to catch up and go over your presentation before the meeting starts the next day? Why don't we have dinner on Sunday? Where are you staying? Dwayne said you didn't need hotel reservations. Let's meet and have a late bite. Let me know where you'll be. Looking forward to it!

Adele

TO: foreveramber@quicklink.com <amber fleece>
FROM: jdesmond@millenniamarketing.com
<julie desmond>
SUBJ: Update
DATE: Wednesday 9/22 5:05 PM

Hi Amber. Hope you're having fun in the Berkshires. I've attached a quick Traffic Report so you can see how things are progressing here. All the open jobs are listed with status reports. Things are under control.

You'll be so proud of me. I made the decision. You've been so encouraging whenever we talk about this—and I believe you when you say the place won't crumble if I take a few days off. In

November, how's that? I want you to get through most of your treatment. I left a formal Vacation Request slip in your inbox, but I wanted to let you know that I'm going for sure. I'm trying to talk Will into coming with me . . . but he hasn't committed yet. Either way, I'm going.

Other than that, not much is new. Dwayne Gallagher has made it his business to poke around Traffic enough to actually bother me. He never shuts up. He yaks about his boss. He yaks about his boyfriend. He yaks about the good-looking guy working on Tom Markoff's computer. (Actually, he had me so curious, I went and looked!! That's what YOU would have done, right???) I didn't see the guy; he'd finished his work and was in Adele's office.

Anyway, sorry to drag on. But I MISS YOU! Write if there's anything you want me to worry about. I hope you're enjoying the break from real life and being happy. I know this is a tough time, but you're going to be fine.

Talk to you soon—

Jules

tmark@quicklink.com: wonderwoman@usol.com is sending you an Instant Message on Wednesday, 9/22 at 9:16 PM:

wonderwoman: Are you there, Tom?

tmark: Hey. Just going through my emails before I go back into the War Room. How are you?

wonderwoman: Fine—just a little confused.

tmark: Still?

wonderwoman: Why is the report you're using for creative different from the one I sent?

tmark: It's not fundamentally different. I just adjusted the emphasis to really align with the campaign.

wonderwoman: You changed the findings to suit your creative strategy?

tmark: Trust me, when you see this campaign, you'll agree with what I've done. It rocks. I didn't change the findings. I reworded them so we can mitigate the inevitable trashing from Mrs. Hitler.

wonderwoman: She *has* the original.

tmark: Then you'll back me up that this is the latest.

wonderwoman: Only if the campaign supports the real findings, Tom. I still have a professional reputation to maintain.

tmark: You will love this work, baby. It's the best thing I've done in years. Don't put a shadow on it.

wonderwoman: You do sound happy.

tmark: I'm happy with the work. It's solid, smart and sexy. Reminds me of a woman I love. Make me even happier and tell me when to pick you up on Sunday night.

wonderwoman: American Airlines 618; arrives at 5:03 PM, from Orlando.

tmark: Really?

wonderwoman: Really.

tmark: Drive, drinks, dinner . . . the works?

wonderwoman: The works? ☺☺☺ We'll see about the works, Markoff. But pick me up and take me somewhere you can show me your . . . campaign.

tmark: You won't be sorry.

wonderwoman: Yes I will, but I want to see you anyway.

tmark: I love you, Stephanie Walker.

wonderwoman: Hilliard.

tmark: Her, too. ☺ Gotta go, sweetheart. See you Sunday. I'll call you when I'm back tomorrow night.

wonderwoman: No, don't call tomorrow night. Just email me.

tmark: Got it.

wonderwoman: Wait! How's Amber?

tmark: She seems cool. Maybe a little distracted, but she's into the show here and we're glad to have her. She's funny as hell.

wonderwoman: Keep an eye on her. She uses humor to cover all sorts of pain. Just make sure she's okay, please.

tmark: She's fine. Don't worry. I'll keep an eye on her. I can't wait to see you.

wonderwoman: Yep. Me, too.

TO: hilliardb@grandregenthotels.com <brent hilliard>
FROM: wonderwoman@usol.com <stephanie hilliard>
SUBJ:
DATE: Wednesday 9/22 10:30 PM

Once again, I can't reach you. And you know what, Brent. I want to talk to you. Desperately. You're never *there*—you're always in a meeting, on a plane, somewhere other than here. So, I'm resorting to email. You're coming home tomorrow night—I THINK. We have three days until you leave again. I have to make a huge decision about the future. We need to—*I* need to find that woman you fell in love with. She's gotten lost in Orlando, or somewhere, and I need to get her back. I'm open to suggestions.

xoxo

Steve

TO: areinhardt@millenniamarketing.com <adele reinhardt>
FROM: shilliard@millenniamarketing.com <stephanie hilliard>
SUBJ: Meeting Sunday
DATE: Wednesday 9/22 10:42 PM

Hi Adele—I appreciate your offer to have dinner on Sunday night, but I'm getting in too late to get together. I'd be happy to come in an hour early to go over the reports with you—want to meet at the office at 7:00 AM on Monday morning? Or downstairs at the Starbucks for coffee? Let me know.

Thanks.

Stevie

TO: jdesmond@millenniamarketing.com <julie desmond>
FROM: grayscale@connectone.com <gray mcdermott>
SUBJ: friend of ambers
DATE: Wednesday 9/22 11:02 PM

---

hi—i'm not completely sure if this is the right email—i'm taking a guess that all of the company emails are the same and that i have the spelling of your name right. i'm a friend of amber's. i usually talk to her (or email) every day or so. but i haven't heard from her in a while, and she's not replying to my messages. she may be real busy, or just giving me some frost—which i completely understand—but she's mentioned you and i thought it might be okay to write. would you do me a mega favor and write and let me know if she's okay? it would mean a lot to me. or you can call me tomorrow morning at 214-555-9902.

thanks,

gray mcdermott

TO: jdesmond@millenniamarketing.com
<julie desmond>
FROM: shilliard@millenniamarketing.com
<stephanie hilliard>
SUBJ: Next week
DATE: Wednesday 9/22 11:45 PM

Hi Jules. I haven't heard from Amber since the night she got in, I'm not sure if she's logging on. So, I'm sending you this info: I'm getting in on Sunday at 5:03, American Airlines. I have a ride from the airport and a dinner meeting so I'll get to Amber's apt. late that night. I'm planning to stay until Thursday afternoon, so I can be with her after the treatment and spend two nights with her. If anybody asks, I'm *only* planning to be in the office on Monday—the rest of the time is for Amber. Thanks—looking forward to finally meeting you in person!

xoxo

Stevie

TO:	wonderwoman@usol.com <stephanie hilliard>
FROM:	hilliardb@grandregenthotels.com <brent hilliard>
SUBJ:	your email
DATE:	Thursday 9/23 1:11 AM

Stevie, I want to call you right now, but I don't want to wake you and the kids. I just read your email. I know you've been unhappy with how much I'm working—and I have been grossly self-absorbed in this quest for numbers and the CEO's office. I can't promise that quest will change, but I'll be damned if work will come before you. First of all, I swear on our marriage vows that I have not had an affair with Heather Vitale. Honey, she's young and ambitious and climbing the corporate ladder the only way she knows how. Believe me, she'd leave Grand Regent in a heartbeat if she got a better offer. But, Stevie, I would never leave you for a better offer. Not now, not ever. Don't you know that? I love you. I married you for better or worse (and all those other things we said, like richer and poorer, sickness and health). We are a unit. You, me, Lily and Dec.

Call me when you get this.

Brent

hilliardb@grandregenthotels.com: wonderwoman@usol.com is sending you an Instant Message on Thursday 9/22 at 1:16 PM:

wonderwoman: Are you still online?
hilliardb: Yes! Are you up?
wonderwoman: Are you alone?
hilliardb: Come on, Stevie. Yes.

* * *

hilliardb: Are you there? What's taking so long?

wonderwoman: I'm trying to think of what to say.

hilliardb: How 'bout "hi honey"?

wonderwoman: ☺ I'm still pissed about the antibiotic thing.

hilliardb: I'm sorry. Thoughtless.

wonderwoman: I refuse to apologize for overreacting.

hilliardb: You didn't overreact. Is her fever still down?

wonderwoman: Yes. She's going to be fine.

hilliardb: What about her mom?

wonderwoman: TBD

hilliardb: Why do you think you're lost, Stevie?

wonderwoman: Am I boring?

hilliardb: NO. Who told you you're boring?

wonderwoman: You did.

hilliardb: ??? When? What?

wonderwoman: Before I took the consulting job.

hilliardb: YOU thought you were boring. I think you are the best wife in the world.

wonderwoman: Come on, admit it. When I'm in mommy mode I am not the glam girl you married.

hilliardb: When you are in mommy mode, you are—I don't know the right words, honey. You make it look so damn easy, Stevie, I forget how hard it is. And you're so good at it, at being their mother. Shit, I'm so sorry. I'm really, really sorry.

wonderwoman: How come you never want to make love?

hilliardb: How come you leave in the middle of the night and go on your computer?

wonderwoman: How come you spend so much time with Heather?

hilliardb: We sound like kids on a schoolyard.

wonderwoman: Are you mad that I'm working again?

hilliardb: No, no, no. I think it makes you happy and excited. Doesn't it?

wonderwoman: One of the aviation gurus offered me another consulting gig today—I couldn't believe it. No agency work, just writing reports on changes in the travel industry for investment bankers.

hilliardb: Is that the big decision on your future that you mentioned?

wonderwoman: No.

hilliardb: What is, then?

wonderwoman: We'll talk when you get home. Which will be . . . ?

hilliardb: Dinner time. I'm taking Friday off, too.

wonderwoman: ??? Really? When did you decide that?

hilliardb: Five minutes ago. No calls, no meetings. Just you. Can Maria take Declan out for a few hours in the afternoon?

wonderwoman: Yes. Why?

hilliardb: If you have to ask, it HAS been too long.

wonderwoman: I mean why now, why are you doing this? Guilt?

hilliardb: Stevie, bottom line: I don't want to lose you. I love you.

wonderwoman: You and your bottom lines. Here's mine: I don't feel so loved lately.

hilliardb: I can fix that. I'll see you tomorrow night. I miss you and the kids.

wonderwoman: Declan told me you said it was okay to pick his nose. He said you said all boys do it.

hilliardb: That little traitor. I better get home fast and fix everybody.

wonderwoman: You can try.

hilliardb: You bet I can. Goodnight, schnooks.
wonderwoman: ☺

TO:	shilliard@millenniamarketing.com <stephanie hilliard>
FROM:	jdesmond@millenniamarketing.com <julie desmond>
SUBJ:	What I did
DATE:	Thursday 9/23 12:33 PM

Hi, Stevie. I tried to call you, but got voicemail. I think we better talk. I called Amber's friend Gray—he wrote to me to see if she was okay, and from his email I thought he must know about her illness. It was kind of vague. It seems she'd mentioned Dr. Grossman to him once, too, and he did the same searching that I did. But he didn't know the first name and wasn't absolutely sure it was the oncologist. Anyway, he knows now. And he said he suspected something was wrong ever since she'd mentioned Dr. Grossman to him. Stevie, he was so NICE—he's really sweet and concerned and really, really worried about her. God, I hope I didn't blow it. Do you want to call him? (I'll forward his email, so you can see how I made the mistake.) Do you want to tell Amber? Should I try and find her at the meeting and tell her? Oh, God! I'm just sick about this. I think I've meddled one time too many.

What should I do?

Jules

PS. I got your email and just in time, too. Dwayne Gallagher came by to see if I had your flight information (I gave it to him) and if you had any dietary considerations for the meeting on

Monday. I told him none, but if you're a vegetarian, you better let him know.

TO: wonderwoman@usol.com <stephanie hilliard>
FROM: foreveramber@quicklink.com <amber fleece>
SUBJ: From deep under cover
DATE: Thursday 9/23 1:51 PM

Hey—I'm taking a break in my room and just wanted to drop you a note. Tom told me not to expect you to arrive at my apartment until "late" on Sunday night . . . if at all. A**HEM**. What is this about??? Doing the deed, are you? You better talk to me first. The creative team is very *loquacious* after midnight and a few pitchers of beer. Tom's underlings tell of some serious competition and subterfuge between the members of the Exec Committee . . . there are already rumblings about an affair. And they aren't talking Eva Braun and GW. They mean between the Consultant and the Creative Director. I hate to see you ruin your stellar reputation—but you're a big girl. Do what you need to do. Just do it carefully. Of course, I'll cover for you. Write. Soon.

Love.

Amber

PS. *Why* was someone working on Tom's computer . . . and then going up to Adele's office? I don't like this, Steve. I don't like it at all.

TO: wonderwoman@usol.com <stephanie hilliard>
FROM: grayscale@connectone.com <gray mcdermott>
SUBJ:
DATE: Thursday 9/23 3:00 PM

thanks for the call, stevie. amber is lucky to have a friend like you. i respect what you're telling me and what's going on in her head. please don't tell her we talked. i don't want her to have any expectations about how i should react. please. i trust you because we both care about her. thanks again.

gray

TO: shilliard@millenniamarketing.com <stephanie hilliard>
FROM: areinhardt@millenniamarketing.com <adele reinhardt>
SUBJ: Miscommunication
DATE: Thursday 9/23 4:05 PM

Stevie, evidently we had a breakdown in communication. There seems to be a lot of that lately! I was able to obtain the report that you had forwarded first to Tom Markoff last Friday; it is the document that they are using as the foundation for the creative campaign. There are some serious discrepancies, Stevie, with what you filed with the rest of the Account Team on Monday morning. I doubt that the findings changed over the weekend. I would appreciate if you could clear this up for me. Today. Now!

In addition, I understand you've changed your flight on Sunday afternoon, not Sunday night as you told me. I would really appreciate if you could find some time in the evening to preview your presentation with me; I will be unable to make it into the office at 7:00 AM on Monday morning.

Thank you.

Adele

TO: tmark@quicklink.com <tom markoff>
FROM: wonderwoman@usol.com <stephanie hilliard>
SUBJ: RE: Miscommunication (see attached memo)
DATE: Thursday 9/23 4:34 PM

I can't reach you on your cell phone and your room just rings at the Lodge. I'm going to cover for you, just because. But you owe me, pal. You owe me big.

xoxo

Steph

TO: foreveramber@quicklink.com <amber fleece>
FROM: wonderwoman@usol.com <stephanie hilliard>
SUBJ: gettin' ugly
DATE: Thursday 9/23 7:44 PM

You're not home yet and I really need to talk to you. Was Tom going back to Boston tonight or tomorrow? I haven't heard from him. Did you see that crap I forwarded from Adele? I had to go on record with a lie and I HATE that.

I don't know why a computer guy would be on Tom's PC, then up in Adele's office. I don't know why he thinks it's necessary to doctor up my report to fit his creative genius. I don't know why Adele is so hellbent on having a meeting with me. But nothing *feels* right, that's for sure.

Actually, one thing feels very right. I haven't even told you this.

I took your advice. (Aren't you proud of me?) I sent up a warning flare to Brent. And guess what? He responded—quickly and thoroughly. He swears he's been faithful, and tonight he walked into the kitchen, kissed me full on the mouth, and his first words were "I love you, Stevie." He announced to the kids over dinner that his only goal in life is for our family to be safe, secure, and happy. And together. They thought he'd gone nuts, and I had to swallow a lump in my throat.

Now who's the Harlot? I'm just sick with guilt and worry. Totally confused. Scared to end my marriage. He's upstairs giving the kids baths right now, planning to spend the day in bed with me tomorrow, and I'm—oh, God, Amber, I'm trying to decide which underwear to pack for Boston. (Hint: Not what my mom sent.)

Wait—I'll be right back—it's too quiet up there.

Oh, Amber, I wish I could take a picture of what I just saw. I'd download it to Tom Markoff and say LEAVE ME ALONE. Brent was on Dec's bed, holding our worn copy of *Bark, George* (a perennial fave book in the Hilliard house), Dec was cuddled under one arm, thumb in mouth, moose in arm (don't ask). Lily (my genius overachiever) was reading, periodically glancing at Brent to make sure he's suitably impressed by her skills—he was. The room was bathed in the soft glow of twilight, the kids were all clean and jammie-clad—Norman Rockwell couldn't have painted it better. When he heard me, Brent looked up with that really sweet sparkle in his eye, that incredible half-smile.

God, I love my little family. This is crazy, but there I was, looking at him—at them—and all I wanted to do was have just one more baby. Wouldn't that be the stupidest thing, considering what's been going on?

What am I doing, Amb? What the hell am I doing????

xoxo

Stevie

PS. Have you talked to Gray lately?

TO: wonderwoman@usol.com <stephanie hilliard>
FROM: foreveramber@quicklink.com <amber fleece>
SUBJ: The Hilliard Antibiotic
DATE: Thursday 9/23 11:06 PM

What are you doing? Making a big, fat, stupid mistake.

As far as the falsification of expert testimony for the purposes of creating an ad campaign—creepy and underhanded, yes. But I will tell you this. The campaign is effing brilliant. If WWA doesn't want to launch the Luxury Line, we should take it to another airline that will. Tom knows it, too. He's struttin' his stuff like the cock of the walk. Doesn't hurt that you agreed to see him on Sunday—he told me with something that could only be described as a gleam of victory in his eye. Of course, that was before George Barked. (A moose? The child sleeps with a moose?)

Speaking of mistakes, let's talk about me. ☺ To answer your question, I haven't talked to Gray. I've been avoiding him bigtime and I think I know why. I've been thinking about this a lot—thinking of my mortality and all that lovely philosophical baggage that gets dropped on you in the cancer ward.

I need every ounce of personal and mental strength to get

through this, Stevie. I'm really serious about this—no jokes. My life is on the line. My body has to respond to treatment if I'm going to live. I can't be mooning over some guy in Texas who lives with a psychopath and dreams of moving to Nashville, but has no map for how to get there. I have to give everything I've got to getting better. Then, we'll see about Gray. Does that make sense?

Now, I have a huge favor to ask you. When you come up on Sunday night—AFTER you ditch Tom <evil grin>—will you cut my hair? I've read it's a smart thing to do before you start chemo. But I can't bear to go to a salon and have all that attention and fuss that the long-hair people get when they go short. I'd ask Jules, but I know you're really good with hair. And you've seen me cry before. Will you do that for me?

Love.

Amber

TO: tmarkoff@millenniamarketing.com <tom markoff>
FROM: areinhardt@millenniamarketing.com
<adele reinhardt>
SUBJ: For your consideration
DATE: Friday 9/24 7:49 AM

I understand your unexpected sabbatical is coming to a close today and that you'll be making an appearance in the office later on. I'll be out most of the day at client meetings with Gabriel. I want to give you the weekend to consider something.

Tom, as we both know, there is an important pending promotion available when Gabriel creates the position of General Manager. I will not hide the fact that I would relish the opportunity to run the day-to-day operations of this agency, and have made my desire to obtain that role clear to the entire Executive Committee. Becker is strictly a manager of money, not people, so the only other internal candidate for the management job is you. If, however, Gabriel senses that we cannot work together or that either one of us would refuse to report to the other, he will undoubtedly look outside the agency for a person to fill the GM slot. I don't think either one of us wants that—another seat on the Executive Committee could further dilute all of our authority.

In the process of trying to obtain complete copies of documents and reports filed by all members of the WWA team, I have, quite by accident, uncovered some information of an extremely personal nature. This information highlights what Gabriel might very well consider reprehensible behavior on the part of members of his Executive Committee and outside consultants acting as employees of Millennia Marketing. In addition to a breach of ethics in the form of discussions about the most intimate of human behavior, I have, unfortunately, discovered references to employees that include offensive and politically incorrect terminology and name calling. Should this documentation find its way to clients or, God forbid, the media, it would irrevocably ruin the reputation of this fine agency and negatively impinge on our long-term success.

Under the circumstances, I am willing to disregard this information, file it under immature and indiscreet behavior, and opt not to take disciplinary actions against any of the individuals involved. That would, of course, be my first choice. In fact, deleting all of the MIS records from the individuals involved would be my first executive mandate in my role as General Manager of the agency.

I hope we'll be able to get past our differences, Tom, and agree that my background in management, my experience as a long-term team player for MM, and my leadership capabilities make me the wisest choice for the GM position. With your blessing, Gabriel's decision will be all but made.

Have a great weekend. Looking forward to seeing your creative presentation on Monday. I heard it's wonderful! I tried to get together with Stevie on Sunday night to preview her presentation, but she's made other plans and doesn't seem to be staying under her own name at any hotel.

Adele

TO: areinhardt@millenniamarketing.com <adele reinhardt>
FROM: tmarkoff@millenniamarketing.com <tom markoff>
SUBJ: Consider this
DATE: Friday 9/24 8:15 AM

Last time I checked, blackmail was illegal.

Fuck you, Fraulein.

Tom

TO: foreveramber@quicklink.com <amber fleece>
FROM: wonderwoman@usol.com <stephanie hilliard>
SUBJ: About last night
DATE: Friday 9/24 9:06 AM

Jules said you'd be home until 10 or so this morning, but I got your machine when I called. Hopefully, you'll check this email before you go in. Picture me, catlike, purring with satisfaction and happiness. ☺ Things went very nicely last night. We stopped fighting like kids on a playground (his words) and . . . played. I was definitely *not* boring, or bored.

And I made a decision. When I see Tom on Sunday, I'm going to tell him that I can't do this. I can't flirt and play with him and be in love with my husband at the same time. It's cheating. And I'm not a cheater.

And speaking of ending things, I totally understand what you're saying about concentrating on your health and recovery. And you think Gray is a distraction. But, Amber, you haven't given him a chance. Maybe he could help you be even stronger. Think about that, okay?

xoxo

Stevie

TO: dgallagher@millenniamarketing.com
<dwayne gallagher>
FROM: areinhardt@millenniamarketing.com
<adele reinhardt>
SUBJ: Confidential directive—as discussed
DATE: Friday 9/24 11:38 AM

Please release the documentation.

Adele

TO: foreveramber@quicklink.com <amber fleece>
FROM: gallboy@connectone.com <dwayne gallagher>
SUBJ: Heads will roll
DATE: Friday 9/24 11:52 AM

Girlfriend, you owe me so big. I hope you're checking personal email. I've been instructed to send the attached records of emails and IMs to a long list of people, including clients, husbands, journalists, aviation experts and, of course, our own illustrious Executive Committee. Call me a wussy (you've certainly called me worse), but I just don't want the blood of people I really like on my hands.

But, sister! Der Fraulein? Eva Braun? And the sex talk! Oh, my. Don't you people know that anything that is sent **from** MM and **to** MM is forever recorded in the annals of Manny Hernandez? (As opposed to the anals of Manny—don't go there, honey.) Since I happen to love you and think you are all things delightful, witty and genuine, and since my little heart is breaking that you are under the worst imaginable personal burden right now, I'm giving you a heads up before heads roll. Better tell Stevie Wonderwoman. Better tell her boyfriend. Better have a story ready for calling the next GM of the agency a Nazi. Better look into unemployment.

I'm going to make my own executive decision and hold on to this for one hour. Then, bombs away.

Hugs,

Dwayne

PS. DELETE THIS IMMEDIATELY OR ELSE.

TO: wonderwoman@usol.com <stephanie hilliard>
FROM: foreveramber@quicklink.com <amber fleece>
SUBJ: E-effing-MERGENCY
DATE: Friday 9/24 11:56 AM

GET OFF YOUR PHONE AND CALL ME! WE HAVE A SITUATION ON OUR HANDS.

TO: foreveramber@quicklink.com <amber fleece>
FROM: wonderwoman@usol.com <stephanie hilliard>
SUBJ: speechless
DATE: Friday 9/24 12:30 PM

Okay, okay. I finally got through to Tom on his cell phone; he's driving back from the Berkshires. I'm just speechless, Amb. Listen to this—she tried to blackmail him! She offered to keep all those emails and IMs quiet if Tom would back off and let her get the GM job (that GW is creating so that he can back out of the day-to-day operations and—GET THIS—spend more time with his wife.) Tom not so diplomatically told her to stick it. That must be when she gave the green light to Dwayne (who deserves a medal for going way above and beyond the call of duty).

Tom's trying to call her now. But, damn it, he won't back down. He's gone noble and REFUSES to be blackmailed. While that is so very honorable, what about us? I TOLD him not to write sexy notes in interoffice email, and while you and I are pretty careful, we let a few nasties slide. Can you believe she has all those notes about the field trip and why I didn't want to come to the meeting? And the bitch-o-gram and estrogen chaser? And the note about my stalling her and changing the report to suit him? Taken out of context (even in context) it makes us look so *unethical.* Not to mention the legions of people we have offended with careless IMs and emails.

Oh, God, I can't imagine how hard this is on you. Please remember your own speech to me about using your energy for getting better. Brent is home today—being totally wonderful and oblivious to the ruination that is about to blindside him. And here I am practically buying new underwear for a *liaison* with Tom and he is . . . what? Utterly cavalier about having our "relationship" exposed and selling me down the river for his fucking PRINCIPLES.

xoxo

Stephanie the STUPID. Yeah. That has a nice ring of truth to it.

PS. Have you talked to Gray yet?

wonderwoman@usol.com: tmark@quicklink.com is sending you an Instant Message on Friday 9/24 at 1:45 PM:

tmark: I'm back in the office, baby. Are you at your computer?

wonderwoman: Yes. Did you reach her?

tmark: Yes.

wonderwoman: And???

tmark: She's going through with it. This afternoon.

wonderwoman: TOM!!!! She can't do that?

tmark: Who cares, Steph? It's no biggie. She can't blackmail me with gossip. She knows the campaign alone will get me the promotion.

wonderwoman: For crying out loud, Tom. This isn't about

your fucking promotion. This is about your reputation. And mine. Did you read those excerpts? Telling you what bathing suit I'm wearing–comments about GW staring at Adele's pretend cleavage!

tmark: It *is* pretend. Hey, this is nothing, sweetheart. It'll blow over by Monday night, trust me.

wonderwoman: Dwayne told Amber that she instructed him to BCC the *client*.

tmark: I talked her out of that.

wonderwoman: You NEGOTIATED with her?

tmark: She's not a terrorist, Steph. She's actually being a shrewd businesswoman. We worked out an arrangement.

wonderwoman: I can't believe this.

tmark: Don't worry. She won't go to the client or the media; the gossip fest will be internal.

wonderwoman: And you don't think this just might get to someone who knows my husband or your wife?

tmark: I doubt it. But, sweetheart, does that matter?

wonderwoman: Excuse me?

tmark: I love you, Stephanie. We can weather this and still be together. Stronger, even.

wonderwoman: What are you talking about "be together"??? I'm married. You're married.

tmark: I told you I'd leave Mary Grace in a New York minute to be with you.

wonderwoman: I'm not leaving my husband, Tom.

tmark: We'll talk on Sunday. Right now, some shit is going down and GW just paged me.

wonderwoman: I'm not leaving my husband, Tom. I'm not hurting my children or breaking my vows or thinking with any other body part except my brain.

tmark: Steph–let's talk on Sunday. I gotta go. Listen, babe, I will not force you to think, act, talk or otherwise perform with any other body part except your brain. I promise. I told you–if you're happy, then you have to stay where you are. If you're not–and it hasn't sounded lately like you were the picture of marital bliss–then I'm here ready to love you for the rest of your life.

wonderwoman: My life has already been committed to someone.

tmark: People change their minds, Stephanie.

wonderwoman: Yes, Tom. Yes they do.

tmark: Stay off your computer and don't answer the phone this afternoon. By the time you log back on, this will all be over. ILY

wonderwoman: I plan on it. Bye.

TO: grayscale@connectone.com <gray mcdermott>
FROM: wonderwoman@usol.com <stephanie hilliard>
SUBJ: Amber?
DATE: Friday 9/24 2:00 PM

Gray—This is Stevie Hilliard again. I just talked to Amber and she said you two hadn't talked in a while. I haven't told her we spoke—only because you asked me not to. I am really uncomfortable with this—she's my dearest friend and I owe her the truth. Please call her or write like you said you would. Please.

Thanks—

Stevie

TO: wonderwoman@usol.com <stephanie hilliard>
FROM: foreveramber@quicklink.com <amber fleece>
SUBJ: What happened???
DATE: Friday 9/24 7:04 PM

Well, file that under much ado about nothing. I know you went "dark" after we talked. But if you log back on, let me put your mind at ease. NOTHING was released. Nothing was said. Dwayne had a great big shrug for me when I pestered him at the end of the day. Adele and Gabriel have been gone most of the day—they came back around 2:00 and were behind closed doors. (Tommy B, too.) And some unknown suits were here. Lawyers??? Don't know. So—at least for now, our demise is on hold. I do owe Dwayne a big, fat favor. He risked his own job with that warning. And Tom, apparently, didn't let on that he was the security leak.

Listen, I've been thinking. Are you *sure* you want to come up here at all? I know I said I'd die without you, but Jules and Dad and Alice are there for me—Jules even offered to stay in my apartment if I need her. This doesn't seem like a particularly good time to leave Brent—just as things are getting back on track—especially to put yourself in harm's (Tom's) way. I loved your verbal snapshot of the Happy Hilliard Home. You have a lot to be thankful for, Steve. Don't screw it up with one trip to Boston. Trust me, there's lots more chemo ahead—what a thrill!—and you don't have to be here just 'cause it's the first. Jeez, all this drama at the office practically made me forget about it.

And Jules is on a cloud—making plans to go down to South Carolina in November to see her baseball boyfriend. And her son is going with her! Maybe you could come up that weekend, so she won't feel like she's abandoning me.

And to answer your question for the 20th (and last effing) time, I haven't talked to Gray. He must have gotten the message, because he quit sending me pleading little emails. Write. Soon.

Love.

Amber

TO: tmarkoff@millenniamarketing.com <tom markoff>
FROM: wonderwoman@usol.com <stephanie hilliard>
SUBJ: What's going on?
DATE: Saturday 9/25 2:10 PM

Hey—I finally decided it was safe to go online. Nothing. Amber said it was all quiet on the western front yesterday. What gives? Did she change her mind? Did you negotiate a better deal? I heard there were some suits in the office on Friday afternoon. Lawyers?

Anyway—more important—I need to talk to you about tomorrow. But don't call me at home. I'll try your cell later.

xoxo

Stephanie

TO: juliedes@connectone.com <julie desmond>
FROM: wildthing@usol.com <john rush>
SUBJ: Sweet November
DATE: Saturday 9/25 4:49 PM

Hey Jules. Great to talk to you last night. I'm so glad you caught me before I left for the cabin. November 12 it is! We'll have a blast. Maybe a tad too cold to fish, but we'll find plenty to do.

And Will won't be disappointed in the mountains, I promise. I'm really looking forward to it. And if everything goes well, maybe you'll come back. The dead of winter is so beautiful up here—especially if you get snowed in. But I don't want to push it—I'm just really happy you guys are coming.

Have a great weekend, Strawberry.

Johnny

foreveramber@quicklink.com: wonderwoman@usol.com is sending you an Instant Message on Sunday 9/26 at 1:55 AM:

wonderwoman: Why is your computer on at 2:00 AM?

foreveramber: Why are you at your desk at 2:00 AM?

wonderwoman: I can't sleep.

foreveramber: Everything okay?

wonderwoman: Yeah. Really okay. Very okay.

foreveramber: ???

wonderwoman: Brent and I went out tonight.

foreveramber: And?

wonderwoman: It's just good, Amber. It's flowing. The ebb is over. I know this is such a cliché, but it really does take a lot of work to hold a marriage and family together. And that's the work I want to do. He admitted that there was a lusty flirtation with Heather. And I admitted to him that I'd been going through a little bit of the same thing myself.

foreveramber: Queen of Understatement that you are. What did he say?

wonderwoman: That the only thing that matters is that neither one of us gave into it. Only lusted in our hearts, as they say. Okay, I also lusted a little on email and cell phones, but I think

Brent had a few too many "client" dinners. Anyway, we were totally honest with each other and both ended up crying. And making love. And remembering what's important. He said he'd marry me again tomorrow, and I know he was telling the truth. I'm so lucky to have him. He's my grounded man.

foreveramber: Oh, I have tears in my eyes. I'm so happy for you. Don't lose it. Don't come to Boston. Don't even give Tom the satisfaction.

wonderwoman: I'm not going to give Tom any satisfaction. I've ignored 3 IMs from him; I don't want him to breach my happiness right now. I'm quitting my role as consultant on Monday—but I'm going to take the offer from Avionics for the trend write-up job I told you about.

foreveramber: I'm not surprised.

wonderwoman: You're not?

foreveramber: You like consulting at home, I can tell. It's the client who's killing you on this one.

wonderwoman: That's true. I can manage the work from home, and not take away anything from my family. I want to do both. As long as I can do them both well.

foreveramber: Hey, they don't call you Wonderwoman for nothing, darla.

wonderwoman: ☺ I'm emailing my PowerPoint™ presentation to six different people (including you) so no one can *alter* it. But I am coming up to Boston. I have to be with you.

foreveramber: Don't. Really, Stevie. Don't come. I have Julie and Dad and Alice, and I might need you later. Really. I mean it.

wonderwoman: You're just being a tough chick.

foreveramber: No, I'm really serious. I'd rather you stayed home. I'll need you in November when Julie goes away. You can come then, okay? Please???

wonderwoman: Are you sure?

foreveramber: Completely. I promise, promise, promise. In fact, I'd prefer if you came up in November. You could still go on Lily's field trip.

wonderwoman: That would be nice. Brent and Declan are both going. We could make it a family outing.

foreveramber: Please. Please do.

wonderwoman: Are you absolutely sure?

foreveramber: Yes! I swear on the solemn vow of our friendship.

wonderwoman: Okay. Have you heard from Gray?

foreveramber: Good GOD you are relentless. He hasn't written or called. It's *over*.

wonderwoman: You don't know that for sure.

foreveramber: I do. I feel it in my bones, as the Budster would say.

wonderwoman: You're full of it. Why don't you call him?

foreveramber: I told you, Jules told me, "Don't Call Boys." Or sleep with them, for that matter. She's my surrogate mother. I'm listening to her.

wonderwoman: Julie told you not to call Gray? Recently??

foreveramber: No, we haven't talked about it. We were too busy going over old emails to see how many human beings I can insult in, say, one week.

wonderwoman: Boy, did we learn a lesson, huh?

foreveramber: Yep. No more name-calling in email.

wonderwoman: Will Jules be with you FOR SURE on Tuesday?

foreveramber: Yes. Don't worry. Dad and Alice are taking me and staying with me the whole time (I heard it's brutally boring) and Julie told me if you didn't come, she wanted to spend the night. I'm well taken care of, believe me.

wonderwoman: What will you do if Adele releases those emails?

foreveramber: None of them make her look too good, you know. She might not.

wonderwoman: I still can't believe Tom negotiated with her.

foreveramber: When are you going to tell Tom you're not coming?

wonderwoman: I guess tonight. Or tomorrow morning. I'd rather not think about him.

foreveramber: Wish I could get there with Gray. I can't *stop* thinking about him.

wonderwoman: Amber! Please call him!

foreveramber: When this is all over. Oh! Now I'm going to have to ask Jules to cut my hair.

wonderwoman: Don't cut it yet, Amb. See what happens. Not everyone loses their hair.

foreveramber: We'll see. I gotta go to bed. I'll talk to you later–definitely after the meeting on Monday to give you the scoop.

wonderwoman: You know what? I really don't care what happens at that meeting.

foreveramber: ☺ I don't blame you.

wonderwoman: Thanks for understanding, Amber.

foreveramber: No problem. I love you, darla.

wonderwoman: I love you more. xoxo

TO: grayscale@connectone.com <gray mcdermott>
FROM: foreveramber@quicklink.com <amber fleece>
SUBJ: maybe someday . . . but not today
DATE: Sunday 9/26 6:45 AM

I'm watching the sunrise over Beacon Street. I haven't slept all night. This is a big week coming up for me. A big one. Hang on tight, honey. I'm going to shock you.

On Tuesday, I start chemotherapy. I'll have it every other week for eight weeks, followed by a few blasts of radiation. Then, God willing, a cancer that has invaded my body will be gone. There will be some side effects. But I'm going to live.

And this is how I plan to live, Gray. I will never again take a busy day, a sleepless night, a familiar scent, a good friend, a great hairstyle, an easy joke, a lost love, or a good mother for granted. I will continue to laugh at my own expense, but not others. I will tell my Dad I love him every day, I will visit my mother's grave every month, I will welcome a stepmother into our family, and I will not feel incomplete because I am single.

In fact, I will stop looking for Mr. Right. I am no longer on a hunt for a man who meets a list of superficial criteria so impossible that they might as well include Royal Birth and Flawless Genes. Even if I found such an unlikely and unlikable guy, he probably wouldn't be into my buzz cut.

But I'm not going to start my new life without some closure on my old. Here's what I need to tell you. Gray, I love you. I've loved you from the minute you pulled that guy off me in tenth grade, through the whole summer that you brought me to my knees (and on my back), and every moment in between. I've measured every man against you. And no one has measured up. You'll always be my dream man.

But dreams don't always come true. And I don't want to live one minute of the precious life I have remaining *waiting* and *wanting* something I can't have. And I can't have you. Maybe someday. But not today.

Love.

Amber

TO: wonderwoman@usol.com <stephanie hilliard>

FROM: foreveramber@quicklink.com <amber fleece>

SUBJ: Attached copy of my confession

DATE: Sunday 9/26 7:00 AM

Tootsie Girl has grown up, taken best friend's advice, and moved on. I told him—my way. Here's proof. Don't write me a missive about dreams coming true. The only dream I have right now is to live—and live well.

Love.

Amber

TO: tmark@quicklink.com <tom markoff>

FROM: wonderwoman@usol.com <stephanie hilliard>

SUBJ: Change in plans

DATE: Sunday 9/26 9:56 AM

Hi Tom—I hope you get this before you go to the airport this afternoon. I won't be there. I've decided not to go to Boston. I'm sending my presentation to the entire WWA team, along with a formal termination of my consulting agreement.

I hope you understand why I'm doing this. It has nothing to

do with Adele's threats and your unwillingness to capitulate. In an odd way, I understand and respect that. But I don't respect myself. For a while, I really liked the way you made me feel. I enjoyed being the woman you believe I am. But I've looked long and hard at her, and I don't want to be that woman.

Tom, I don't want to risk the happiness and stability of my two beautiful children for the thrill of requiting my lust. And I don't want to tarnish a lifelong reputation as an intelligent, capable, ethical woman. I don't want to jeopardize my real, dynamic, vital, rewarding marriage for a fleeting few hours of passion. That would be the ultimate failure. And for someone who is terrified of failure, I damn near embraced it for the last two months.

As for your current state of mid-life crisis, and your future, here's some really smart advice I got from the most unexpected source: Your family lasts long after any job. They should be the most important part of your life. I'm heeding that advice and I recommend you do the same. I hope you get your priorities straight, Tom, and take care of what matters.

xoxox

Stevie

wonderwoman@usol.com: tmark@quicklink.com is sending you an Instant Message on Sunday, 9/26 at 5:29 PM:

tmark: well, hell. i'm at Logan. and you're not. just checked email on pda. u there?

wonderwoman: Ooops.

tmark: hear my heart break?

wonderwoman: All the way to Orlando. Sorry, Tom.

tmark: ok i understand

wonderwoman: I knew you would. Why didn't you check email sooner?

tmark: at office. emergency meeting–all weekend.

wonderwoman: Really? Blackmail?

tmark: that's dead. other news. can't say.

wonderwoman: You can't tell me???

tmark: i would if u were here

wonderwoman: That's blackmail. ☺

tmark: can i change your mind

wonderwoman: No.

tmark: i still love u

wonderwoman: Don't, Tom. Let it go.

tmark: we were so close

wonderwoman: Too close. It would have been a deadly mistake.

tmark: but what a way to go

wonderwoman: ☺ Thanks for being my friend.

tmark: gotcha, sweetheart. 1 last ? what r u wearing?

wonderwoman: A smile.

tmark: good 4 u. it's ur best look

wonderwoman: Bye, Tommy Boy.

tmark: bye, wondergirl

TO: wonderwoman@usol.com <stephanie hilliard>
FROM: foreveramber@quicklink.com <amber fleece>
SUBJ: British Invasion
DATE: Monday 9/27 5:16 PM

I know you're on your field trip, Mother Stevie, but I am busting in with news. (See, I even remembered to use personal emails, in case I drop a politically incorrect joke or two.) Guess what was announced this morning???????

GW has SOLD the agency to megaconglom Brand-Aid. You know the British firm that has sucked up half the ad agencies in America? Well, WE are going to be their Boston office. He announced at an All-Staff meeting this morning (they barged right into Adele's WWA party and took over the conference room!). GW is LEAVING—not even going to consult. He and Mrs. W are going to sail the Caribbean for the next few years and he's writing a book about managing the next generation of workers. (What's he going to call it? *Play Nice, Kids*???) Anyway, they are paying him GAJILLIONS to go away. And guess who's going to be General Manager—BECKER. Which tells you where their heart i$.

Evidently Adele and Tom were briefed all weekend on the details of the merger. But still, her smile was as fake as her diamond studs. Dwayne told me she's planning to bail and open a shop with Dale Freidman before they boot out her shapeless ass. Auf Wiedersehen. (Did I say that???) She's already asked Dwayne to go with her, but he said NO. Wants to work in Traffic, of all places!!!

Oh—but the best part—the guy who's going to be our "liaison" with the London office! Be still my fluttering heart. His name is Quentin Hargrave. Does that not BEAT ALL? Verrrry Hugh Jackman–ish. (Note to self: Big issues in Traffic. Must schedule long meetings with QH. Use Bridget Jones's quippy style.)

Tommy Boy was oddly subdued, until the Brits (including hunky Quentin) stayed for the creative presentation of the WWA campaign and just about stood on their heads when they saw it. Jolly-good, spot-on, Markoff, and all that rot. I'd say his job is safe for the moment.

And no one has breathed a word about the Great Email Disaster. No surprise there—she wouldn't want the new owners to be dragged into our mudslinging. Dwayne thinks we're in the clear all around . . . and he brought me a romance novel to read during my treatment. He's a doll.

I hope you got your rockets off at the space center. I'm spending the night at Dad's, then we file into the lovely House o' Chemo at Brigham and Women's. Expect updates whenever possible.

Love.

Amber

TO: foreveramber@quicklink.com <amber fleece>
FROM: wonderwoman@usol.com <stephanie hilliard>
SUBJ: Brigham and Women's House of Chemo ☺
DATE: Tuesday 9/28 9:13 AM

You're there now. I did a little research so I could picture the room. I wish I were there with you, Amb. I will be, I promise. I know where you are, though, so I'm with you in spirit. I found a picture of the facility (not quite the jail cell you expected) and I can imagine you with Bud and Alice, making jokes all the way. Every cell in my body is sending you love and goodwill.

We had a wonderful field trip—Declan got his picture taken with an astronaut! We ate space ice cream balls (don't ask) and saw a shuttle, and Brent and I held hands all day like we were on our first date. I'm so happy NOT to be in Boston. Every time I think of how close I came to completely blowing this, I just cringe inside. It really makes me a little sick.

Interesting news about the agency. Tom will be fine, of

course—he always is. Adele will get hers—at least we can always hope. Maybe GW finally had his own personal awakening. And you're right about Dwayne. Good as gold.

Honey, I have to tell you something. This is killing me, Amber, but I just have to tell you. Please don't be mad at me and please, please, please don't be mad at Julie. Please understand why we did what we did.

Gray knows about your illness. He contacted Julie and it seemed like he knew, so she called him—he'd asked her to. As soon as she talked to him, she realized he didn't know. But it was too late. She was beside herself after telling him, so I called him, too, to see if I had to smooth things over, but things seemed very smooth. ☺ I wanted to tell you for a few days—I HATE having secrets from you, but he really didn't want me to. He was adamant that I not tell you and I decided to honor that request.

He was very nice, Amber—unbelievably concerned about you (he does have a delicious voice). He asked a lot of questions and I told him the truth. He wanted to know when you were getting treatment, what to expect. We talked a little about your mom—of course, he knew all that history. He said he'd handle this his way. I don't really know what that meant—but if you haven't heard from him, you might want to call him when you feel up to it.

Amber, I didn't mean to overstep the bounds of friendship and Jules honestly thought she was doing the right thing. We all love you. No matter how Gray handles this, I can tell that he cares very, very deeply for you. I got a very good vibe from him.

I hope you're well into Dwayne's romance novel, falling in love all over again, and getting through this difficult time like the brave tootsie roll you are. I love you so very much and treasure our friendship.

xoxoxo

Stevie

TO: wonderwoman@usol.com <stephanie hilliard>
FROM: foreveramber@quicklink.com <amber fleece>
SUBJ: tootsie's in bed
DATE: Tuesday 9/28 5:20 PM

---

don't be fooled by the header, stevie, this isn't amber. it's gray. i'm sitting at amber's desk, which is perilously close to her bed, where she is currently residing. propped on pillows, sipping tea, and smiling benevolently at me. damn but she's pretty.

i want her to rest, but she wants to talk to you. we came up with a compromise (i think we'll be doing a lot of that for a long time). she'll dictate and i'll write. if i am unable to resist the urge to stop and kiss her, i will. if i have to editorialize something, i will do that in bold. just so you know who's talking to you.

hi steverella. (this is amber.) i'm fine. **(she's way more than fine. she's exquisite)** oh, sit tight now. she wants to get out of bed and get on this computer. wait. we're fighting.

that was fun. i won. did ya ever notice how her eyes get all gold when she wants something really bad? (like me.) okay. she's getting impatient with me. i am going to write this exactly as she says it.

hang on. i have to kiss her.

okay. i'm back. she's giggling. nice sound. better than puking, which she hasn't done yet. she is a brave tootsie roll (i read your email—and so did she. she's not mad that we talked). she's insisting that i type exactly what she says. here goes, her words ahead:

hi stevie. **(didn't we do that already?)** you're not going to believe the day i had.

it started like any other day—wake up, get dressed, see a woman come out of dad's bedroom, go to chemotherapy. but that's where everything normal ended. i was so shaky when we parked near the hospital—i don't know why this whole business terrified me so much, but it did. anyway, i was using every brain cell to stay calm. i didn't want to get dad upset. i didn't even make a single joke because he hates when i make light of something serious. plus, i felt like i was going to hurl for sure, even though the whole chemo thing hadn't even started.

anyway, it looked like rain, which really suited the mood. all i could think about were those dark winter mornings when i'd say goodbye to my mom, and i knew she had chemo that day. it was a horrible, icky sense of déjà vu, and mostly i felt bad for inflicting it on dad. the whole scene was mega depressing and somber to the point of a bad movie cliché.

i tried not to think about mom. i just locked arms with alice and dad and the three of us walked like the mod squad about to detonate chemoworld.

wait a second. she has to pee. while she's in there, i'll give you the scene from my perspective. mick and me were hanging at the front door looking like a couple of homeless people. i didn't really want to surprise her like that, but i had to do some serious last-minute rescheduling and figured she'd try to talk me out of coming up. i couldn't leave dallas till late saturday cause i had to bring mickey—long story. anyway, the two of us made the whole drive together. he's good company, but couldn't help with the driving. we crashed at rest

stops and ate in the car and i basically drove like a maniac (within reason—i had a kid in the car) to get here by this morning.

so, there we were—lurking like muggers and i'm starting to wonder if maybe this wasn't the dumbest thing i'd ever done. then i looked over at the parking lot and saw these three coming at me. there she was. sandwiched between dad and dad's chick, staring at her feet. she was wearing this giant fringy coat with jeans and little white tennis shoes. all i could see was the part in her hair. but i knew. i knew without the whisper of a doubt. this was definitely not the dumbest thing i'd ever done. in fact, this was actually pretty smart. except i had no idea what to say to her.

Okay. Jules just took Mickey out to dinner (those two are meant for each other!) and Gray is getting some food but he left this email up. I'll finish the story. You know, I feel really fine. Just tired, not anything worse than that. So I'm going to write this myself while Gray is in the kitchen. Wait a second . . . Can you believe I said that? Can you re-read those words? Gray is in MY kitchen, singing "Back Into You" and making a BLT. Stevie, I've never been so happy in my whole life. Chemo? Who cares? I've got Gray. I've got Gray right here with me. Right now.

Okay, imagine this, I was clinging to Alice and Dad, staring at my shoes (sorry, yes, I did wear sneakers and that lovely jacket—I didn't see this as a high-fashion moment) and for the one millisecond of my life for the past ten years that I was NOT thinking about Gray McDermott, I looked up toward the door of the building and I saw a guy. Okay, a god. Scruffy, yes. Honey blond hair going in six different directions, unshaven, circles under his eyes, and the most incredible cornflower blue eyes you have ever seen locked on me. The world literally stopped revolving. My heart did a triple-flip and landed in the vicinity of my throat. I opened my mouth to speak, but no sound would come out. I tried to process the image in front of me, but I couldn't. How can this be??? Gray. Gray. Gray has come to be with me.

Again, I tried to speak, but some horribly unattractive croaking sound came out. All I was capable of doing was staring at him. Slowly, I realized someone was standing next to him. Someone small, with dark hair and penetrating brown eyes.

Dad pulled me closer. I almost laughed. Forget it, Daddy, you can't protect me from this man. My gaze drifted back to Gray, feasting on the sight of him. His smile slid into a grin. And he said, "Hey, toots. Mickey and I want to keep you company."

Suddenly I had a horrible thought. Could nausea prevention pills have made me hallucinate? No, I heard him say "toots." I managed a witty comeback. Something like: "Gray? Is that you?" He nodded. Then I asked him, "Why are you here?" And guess what he said???

Oh, shoot, I better send this. He's coming back, he

i said i'm here because i love you. why would that be so hard for her to understand? hey, stevie. be our witness. commit this to paper and forward it to the world:

I LOVE AMBER FLEECE.

I WANT TO SPEND THE REST OF MY LIFE WITH HER.

clear enough? sorry, we gotta go. amber's going to let me cut her hair. we're taking the ponytail to locks of love tomorrow, then, if she feels like it, a little shopping at home depot. but, most important, i gotta take care of my girl.

we'll be in touch.

gray

TO: foreveramber@quicklink.com <amber fleece>
FROM: wonderwoman@usol.com <stephanie hilliard>
SUBJ: Maybe Someday
DATE: Monday 2/14 10:43 PM

Hi Amb—we're home! Happy Valentine's Day!! Just got the kids down and unpacked most of our stuff. Whose idea was it to make that trip by car? Julie's, I think. Oh, sure, she drives to South Carolina every other weekend to see her hunky baseball stud, but she doesn't have a 3-year-old with her.

That was a *great* wedding, Amb. Alice looked so happy and Bud was positively glowing. They are going to be very happy together. (I'm sorry Declan sat on the ring bearer's pillow. At least he didn't wipe his nose with it—well, not after Mickey snagged him and held him for the whole ceremony.) Of course, the maid of honor was gorgeous, too. ☺ Dwayne was absolutely right about the blond tips in your little spiky 'do. (Okay, it's a buzz. But it's growing fast.) I know you want to grow it longer for your own walk down the aisle next year (we're *flying* to that wedding, trust me), but I think you've never looked more beautiful. No wonder they love you at that record company! It had (almost) nothing to do with my letter of recommendation or your successful songwriting fiance—you have the whole hip music look going on. Helps to be madly in love, healthy and happy as hell, too.

Oh, bless my husband. He just brought me a much-needed glass of merlot and told me to tell you he said hi. Wait a second. There's more.

A box of Godiva raspberry chocolates—tucked inside a TO DIE FOR Fendi chef's bag. Well, Happy Valentine's Day to me! You know something? I *love* that man.

So, I better make this quick—I need to give him his present and it can't be done in this office. Well, it *has* been, but since it's Valentine's Day, we'll go traditional. You and I can do a formal post-wedding debrief when you guys get back to Nashville. The adoption hearing is tomorrow, right? So you'll be home by Thursday. I have some conference calls with Avionics scheduled on Thursday, but we'll catch up. I just have to tell you something before I forget. . . .

On the way back from Boston, we were on I-95, somewhere between here and nowhere, and Declan was actually asleep for the first time in, oh, 847 miles. We were talking about our future and the kids and our jobs and life, and I told Brent about the Radio Oracle game you play. So we decided to give it a try. Of course, the only station we could get out there was country and when the DJ promo'd the upcoming songs, he mentioned Tim McGraw's newest hit. I think: Perfect! "Back Into You"! ☺ The absolutely ideal message from the Radio Oracle.

But guess what? It wasn't "Back Into You." It was his *new* newest. I've never heard it before, Amber! I love it! What will you wear to the Country Music Awards for the Best Songwriting Award???? (Don't even think about that jacket.) Seriously, I loved every word. In fact, I've been singing it all day. . . .

It seems like I've been waiting forever and a day
To have my time with you, girl, with nothing in the way.
And when I ask you, baby, how long it's gonna take
I hear the heartbreak in your voice every time you say
Maybe someday, maybe someday soon.
Maybe one day, you'll know that I love you.
Maybe someday, maybe someday soon
Maybe one day, dreams can come true.

Then guess what happened??? The very moment that I heard that song, I felt the baby kick for the first time. Just a little tickle down the middle of my tummy, but it was definitely a little baby flutter. S/he liked the song, too!!!

So, I guess the Radio Oracle has spoken. Dreams can come true.

xoxoxoxoxoxox

Stevie

UP CLOSE AND PERSONAL WITH THE AUTHOR

WHAT INSPIRED YOU TO WRITE *HIT REPLY?*

I'd love to tell you it was the mountains of emails from ex-boyfriends admitting that losing me was their greatest regret . . . but the inspiration came from several sources, not my email inbox. I have a friend who reconnected with an ex through a random Google search, but that reunion turned into a heartbreak as deep as anything that happened in "real" life. Her experience stayed with me and made me consider the profound impact that the internet, email, and instant messaging now has on relationships at every level. Are these two-dimensional love affairs *real?* They seem to be—especially when they involve two people with a passionate history. The concept fascinated me and dovetailed perfectly into my longing to explore the power of friendship between women.

WHO DO YOU THINK IS THE MAIN CHARACTER OF THE BOOK?

When I started writing, *Hit Reply* was Amber's book. Without a doubt, her story is the most emotionally draining, but her character was a blast to write. By the time I'd finished, I realized that the story was as much about Amber and Stevie's rock-solid friendship as it was about Amber and Gray's reunion. Stevie's conflict became a central focus as the story evolved, and had potential to be as troubling as the life-threatening illness Amber faced. I also think Julie's journey from stay-at-home mom to career woman is one that resonates with millions of women. I enjoyed watching her change—thanks to the discovery of her skills, and the hunk who had broken her heart decades earlier.

DO YOU THINK STEVIE COMMITS ADULTERY (OR "E-ADULTERY") WITH TOM?

That's the question at the heart of the book. Is *online* flirting less of a transgression than when you are at a party and your husband is in the next room? Is a renewed love affair over cyberspace really a reunion? I do think a powerful e-relationship is capable of releasing the same endorphins, of generating the same longing, and of causing the same heartache as one that takes place in person. And that's what makes the all email and IM format so potent in this story. The reader actually experiences the emotions with the characters in real time. I also love the feeling of "reading someone's private journal" that *Hit Reply* evokes—it appeals to the voyeur in all of us.

WHO'S JOURNEY IN THE BOOK WAS THE MOST DIFFICULT TO WRITE? THE EASIEST?

Amber's is certainly the most gut-wrenching story in *Hit Reply* and her character and her emails were never difficult to write. She's the embodiment of my favorite kind of girlfriend—funny, self-deprecating, loyal, honest, and just insecure enough to be endearing. Tom was probably the hardest because I had to blend both hero and villain qualities in one man (which makes him the most real character in the book!). I wanted the reader to go up that roller coaster with Stevie and then come crashing down with her as she realizes how close she's getting to making a huge mistake. Tom's a user, but he's the one guy who has the power to undo the controlled and disciplined Stevie. No matter how tempting that is, he's a vice that she has to overcome or risk losing everything.

HOW DID YOU MANAGE TO CAPTURE ALL THE DIFFERENT VOICES AND MAKE THE EMAILS DISTINCT?

Years ago, I was an actress, so I called upon many acting techniques I learned to write this book. Before long, I knew each character intimately. I knew their patterns of speech, their punctuation (or, in Gray's case, lack of), their favorite expressions, their distinct sign-offs, their written "voices." I take it as a huge compliment when readers tell me they didn't have to read the "to and froms"—it was obvious in the first line who had written the email.

ARE ANY OF THE CHARACTERS AUTOBIOGRAPHICAL?

They are an amalgamation of people I know and some who live in my imagination. Stevie is the closest to autobiographical because I used to work at a large PR agency in Boston and moved to Florida because of my husband's transfer. I remember the "I used to be somebody somewhere and now I'm nobody nowhere" sense that accompanied my early days as kindergarten mom. I also started a marketing consulting business from home and have had many experiences with a crying baby in the background and a client on the phone. I once overheard my son tell a friend, "We only have one rule at our house. No screaming when mommy's on a client." I've always wondered how that might have been translated to that child's mother.

IS THERE ANYTHING ELSE IN THE STORY RIPPED FROM YOUR REAL LIFE?

The Radio Oracle! I was reluctant to share this with the world, but I have played that game since I had a driver's license and never told anyone about it. When I put the key in the ignition, I ask a question and imagine the first song I hear tells me the answer. Now I find out that millions of people play a similar game with themselves. No wonder the Eight Ball is a hit.

HOW WOULD YOU CATEGORIZE THE THEME OF *HIT REPLY*?

At the heart of the story, *Hit Reply* is about friendship. Even if we are only connected through the computer—and in this day and age, that is it for many of us—humans seek out relationships to help them through the most trying times. The book is also about those lovers whose memory haunts us, the ones that got away but we've never completely forgotten. Most women I know have at least one in their past. But now, with the internet and search engines, the fantasy of reconnecting with them is very real, and could happen to anyone. With disastrous—or amazing—results.

HOW HARD WAS IT TO TELL A STORY WITHOUT NARRATIVE, DESCRIPTION, OR DIALOGUE?

It was exhausting. I can usually write for up to six or seven hours a day, but I stopped at ten pages regardless of how quickly I wrote. I found that assuming the mindset of each character to be physically draining—very much like acting—and nearly impossible to plot. When I write my complicated, multi-plot romantic suspense books, I use a massive white board to visually plan chapters and scenes and track pacing. With *Hit Reply*, I used a yellow notepad. Every morning I wrote a vague list of about three things that I hoped to accomplish to move the story forward. Then I opened the document and literally waited for the right person to start writing the next email. Wacko, but it worked.

WILL YOU DO ANOTHER ALL EMAIL BOOK?

If *Hit Reply* resonates with readers, I will certainly consider writing another book in a similar style. Right now, I'm back at work on the romantic suspense novels I write under my "grown-up" real name of Roxanne St. Claire for Pocket Books. There is another girl/buddy story brewing in my heart, but I haven't started to write it yet. I will be anxious to hear what readers think of *Hit Reply*.

WHEN DID YOU START WRITING AND WHAT ADVICE DO YOU HAVE FOR WOULD-BE WRITERS?

I've written stories for pleasure since I got a typewriter as a tenth birthday present, but I didn't attempt publication until 2000. Then, I completed a full romantic suspense manuscript and decided to close my marketing consulting business and write fiction full time. My advice for writers is always the same: persistence and tenacity is as important as talent in the business of publishing. If you think too hard about what is involved, you'll quit. Don't think—keep writing, reading, and submitting. Try Googling ex-lovers when you hit a creative wall. That oughta get your juices flowing. ☺

Like what you just read?

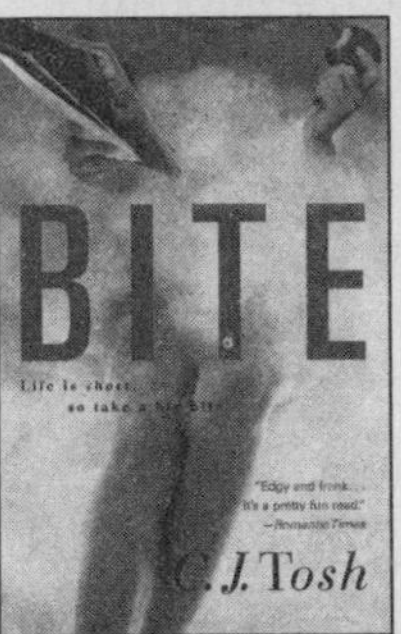

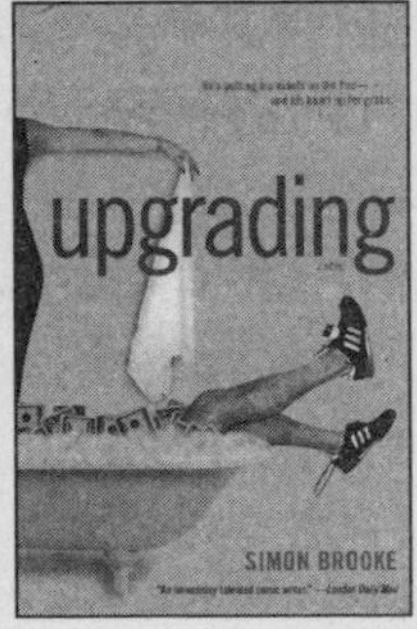

Going Topless
Megan McAndrew
Is it possible to reveal too much under the Mediterranean sun?

Dinner for Two
Mike Gayle
A one-night stand with lifelong consequences....

Bite
C.J. Tosh
Life is short. Take a big bite.

The Dead Father's Guide to Sex & Marriage
John Scott Shepherd
Just when life can't get any better, it usually gets a whole lot worse.

Babes in Captivity
Pamela Redmond Satran
Love. Marriage. Baby carriage.... Now what?

Upgrading
Simon Brooke
He's putting his assets on the line—and his heart up for grabs

My Favorite Mistake
Beth Kendrick
How do you un-do "I do

The Hazards of Sleeping Alone
Elise Juska
A king-size bed all to yourself isn't al it's cracked up to be.

Great storytelling just got a new address.

PUBLISHED BY POCKET BOOKS

Then don't miss these other great books from Downtown Press!

Scottish Girls About Town
Jenny Colgan, Isla Dewar, Muriel Gray, et al.

Calling Romeo
Alexandra Potter

Game Over
Adele Parks

Pink Slip Party
Cara Lockwood

Shout Down

Liner Notes
Emily Franklin

My Lurid Past
Lauren Henderson

Dress You Up in My Love
Diane Stingley

He's Got to Go
Sheila O'Flanagan

Irish Girls About Town
Binchy, Marian Keyes, athy Kelly, et al.

he Man I Should Have Married
ela Redmond Satran

Getting Over Jack Wagner
Elise Juska

The Song Reader
Lisa Tucker

The Heat Seekers
Zane

I Do (But I Don't)
Cara Lockwood

Why Girls Are Weird
Pamela Ribon

Larger Than Life
Adele Parks

Eliot's Banana
Heather Swain

How to Pee Standing Up
Anna Skinner

sold or visit us online at www.downtownpress.com.

Great storytelling just got a new address.

PUBLISHED BY POCKET BOOKS

10403